William Joseph Roberts
Presents:

Magic
And
Mischief

Three Ravens Publishing
Chickamauga, GA USA

William Joseph Roberts Presents Magic and Mischief
Is a collective work of contributing authors and Published by Three Ravens Publishing
Published by Three Ravens Publishing
threeravenspublishing@gmail.com
P O Box 851, Chickamauga, GA 30707
https://www.threeravenspublishing.com

Table of Contents

On Fantasy Literature and the Writing Thereof

By: D.J. Butler

We're lucky to be readers and writers of fantasy literature. Fantasy is the oldest literature we have left, and one of the best.

No one's writing mythology anymore, because mythology has been bottled and dissected and exists now as fossils and specimens in formaldehyde, leeched of most of its meaning and all of its power. No one's writing epics, either, despite the fact that the twentieth century savagely served up a true *Volkswanderung*, shuttling Poles in one direction and Ukrainians in the other while an entire continent's worth of Jews emulated Father Abraham and got going. There are people writing scripture, but very few, and no one whom the world takes at all seriously.

But we still have fantasy. Fantasy exists in the same family as those great old genres of yesteryear. Threaded with the idea of magic and populated by elves, ghosts, and demons, fantasy is a metaphysical genre, a genre of spiritual imagination and the unconscious mind. Fantasy is the what-if literature of the human spirit, and since we humans still have spirits (at least, as of this writing), we had better have someone asking the important what-if questions about them. We need writers who will look into their hearts, see there the same images that fascinated and terrified the Lascaux painters, and bring them to the tribe in story form to be battled, understood, and assimilated.

We need you.

You are lucky to be called to write fantasy. And we are lucky to have you.

But I should warn you, there are false roads to take in writing fantasy fiction. One such path is grimdark. I understand well that the self-licensing to transgress boundaries of genre, convention, and taste is thrilling, but the problem is that it's a race to pointless nihilism. "Nothing matters, no one is good, and we're all just food for worms" is the mindless slogan of a swaggering college sophomore. It's a metaphysical statement, but it's cheap, impoverished, and enervating to your audience, with the additional disadvantage that the statement is utterly false. The boys of *Lord of the Flies* are a sordid lie; the six shipwrecked boys of Nuku'alofa are the much more interesting and important truth.

Another false road to be wary of is so-called "hard magic," which, echoing the old joke, is neither hard nor magic. Its hardness is only apparent, the result of focusing on an imagined mechanism with game-like quantified "rules," rather than on the wonder of the not-fully-comprehended and the underlying invisible connections that bind the universe together. But a writer whose description of a battle focused on how many calories the heroine had consumed in the preceding twenty-hours, the rise and fall of her caloric burn rate over the course of the scene, and her necessary pauses to excrete, rather than on the clash of arms and the adrenal waves across the ebb and flow of battle, would rightly be seen, not as an innovative artist, but as a tedious pervert. And while counting arcane caloric units might be necessary in a tabletop roleplaying game, it bears no resemblance to what magicians in the real world have thought or claimed they were doing.

A third false road is to ignore or sleight the muse. Of all genres, fantasy is the one with which the muse is most concerned. It is the genre of the spirit, and demands that you seek revelation. Mere craft will not get you through, and nor will rifling through the *Players Handbook* for ideas; powerful fantasy requires you to tap powers greater than yourself, and those powers are fickle. Treat them with respect, or lose them. You can make money writing fantasy, but if you write fantasy only to make money, your product will be flawed, inferior, and false.

I know, some of you are upset with me now. I had better hurry up and give you some positive, constructive advice about working in the genre, before you tear these pages from the book out of sheer rage. The following may sound like a grab bag of overlapping suggestions, rather than a comprehensive schematic. That's because this advice comes from experience with reality (as real magic does), and is not someone's artificial concept, to be imposed on reality ("hard magic").

Stay connected with the real world. The more connected you are with the real world, the stronger your fantasy will be, and the stronger the real world will be for the fact that your fantasy is contained within it. Read history, anthropology, and scripture. Study science and language. Pore over maps. Observe the people you know in your real life as closely as you observe the people you invent.

Pace yourself. Consistency is much more important than speed for most of us, and a page a day will produce a novel in a year. Giant efforts will burn you out and leave you adrift and demoralized.

Try not to set goals. I know, I just talked about the result of writing a page a day, which sounds like I think you should set a page-number or a word-count goal. I don't mind goals, they can work. But better than setting a goal is committing to a process. Have a process of sitting down every morning and writing for an hour, and stick to it; you'll have a book in a year, and probably less. Even better than committing to a process is developing a habit. When you get up every morning and write for an hour not because it's on your checklist, but because *that's just how you live…* books will flow from your fingertips.

Find friends engaged in the same quest. Your family loves you, but they probably can't help you figure out why the middle part of your book feels boring, or connect you with an editor or agent, or pass on a convention appearance opportunity. Give all the help you can to your friends on the road. Some of them will feel perfectly entitled to your help and will not reciprocate; others will pay you back, tit for tat, as if watching a moral balance sheet; others still will pay you back more than you ever did for them, and then keep giving. What you give might come back to you from different directions than you expect, but it will come back.

Kick envy in the teeth. You will likely have to do it again and again, because envy is a bitch, and will keep coming back, and the moments when someone other than you seems to be having the big success will be legion. But envy will destroy your soul and undercut everything you're trying to do as an artist, so fight it. When you realize you're feeling envious of another writer, identify the feeling. Say it out loud. "I feel envious of Marie because she got picked up by an agent, and I'm still looking." Then laugh at the little demon of envy and move on.

Have an abundance mentality. I am echoing what I've already written in the two preceding paragraphs, but, in almost all things, there's enough room for everyone to win. That's really true. Believe it. Behave accordingly.

Plan for down time. In my experience, the muse often speaks while I am writing. But she also speaks when I'm idle, looking at the rain through the window, or waking up slowly without the annoyance of an alarm.

Don't worship at the altar of the big franchises. You know what I'm talking about; the giant movie series, the massive television shows, the marquee authors. The mega-corporations in their glass and steel sheathes and the bloated mega-writers in their muumuus and feather boas do not love you, so don't waste your love on them. Watch the movie or read the book if you like it, but pour your enthusiasm, especially your public enthusiasm, into your own work, and into the work of your friends and allies. Build up your peers and small creators, not the shareholders of Superheromoviecorp.

Think consciously about what success means. Every writer thinks she's going to be J.K. Rowling, aspiring zero to planetary hero with the first book. Then we all discover that we're not. Except J.K. Rowling, of course, the lucky cow. Ask yourself often, *What do I want out of this? What does winning look like for me in this enterprise? What makes writing fantasy worth it?* Your answers may change over time, so keep asking the questions. Remind yourself why you're doing what you're doing, and be prepared to change paths if you're not getting what you want out of the journey.

Finally, don't quit. The means to publish have come down radically in cost and have become universally available. If you are listening to the muse and have a vision of monsters or angels that you are called upon to share, you live in an age in which no one can stop you. You might not get rich off your vision, you might not get the movie deal or the action figures. You might drive an eighteen-year-old minivan and live under a roof that leaks, but you can still tell the truths you were called and sent to tell.

You're so lucky.

And so are we.

God Blood

By: Lee Ellis

"For nothing is evil in the beginning."
-J.R.R Tolkien

The King From Before

"Men are strong," he told the boy. "Steel is stronger."

Rogot lowered himself onto the stoop of a ruined cottage. What was left of the building smoldered behind him, the smell of soot mingling with the rot of a dozen naked corpses piled nearby. The boy sat crouched in the shadow of the dead, an unnatural golden hue illuminating his frail body. Rogot laid the double-edged axe across his lap, half-moon blades shimmering in the darkness. He gazed across the dilapidated village, stroked his grey-black beard, then carefully dragged his whetstone across one of the huge blades.

"What about magic?" the boy asked, peering out from behind the piled bodies, golden haze reflecting on dead flesh.

"Stronger yet than steel," Rogot grunted, then turned his weathered face to the boy, "but more dangerous to he who wields it. Tainted steel. Steel that corrupts."

"Aye," said the boy. "Tainted steel. Because it's given to us from the Outer Things?"

A twig snapped in a leafless forest beyond the village. Black clouds parted, and dull grey light fell between knotted branches and swirling smoke.

"Shh," Rogot hissed. "Be quiet, my son. Men approaching."

The boy cowered, shrinking away behind the rotting mound.

Seven men emerged from the shadows, all of them big and burly, wearing tattered rags and mean faces. Rogot worked his stone, sharpened his axe, paid them little mind.

The foremost man cleared his throat. "Old timer," he said, then nodded to the pile of bodies. "You do all this fuckery?"

"No," said Rogot, whetstone scraping. His eyes rolled up to the group. "Did you?"

"No," the man answered, though he didn't seem certain. "Spare some coin, would you?"

"No," Rogot said softly.

"Come on now, don't be a cunt. Spare some coin. We've been wandering seven days out here in the rot."

Rogot hummed, then tucked the whetstone away in his furs and stood. The bearskin cloak fell around his broad shoulders, tumbling down his bulky arms and around his muddy boots. The men gazed up as he shouldered his axe, standing two heads higher than their biggest man. His weapon alone was nearly as long as they were tall. They inched back all at once.

"Seven days?" Rogot asked. "Or seven years?"

The other licked his lips and shuddered. "What?"

"How long have you really been wandering? Perhaps… seven *hundred* years? Do you really know?"

Rogot saw a rising fear in the man's eyes. A panic. A realization of something terrible just then remembered, like waking from a dream only to find himself lost in a nightmare.

"We… we… we…"

"You'll be on your way," Rogot suggested.

The man swallowed. "We'll be on our way." He turned to lead his men off, then paused. "Where are *you* going?"

Rogot sat again, retrieved his whetstone, and dragged it over the blade once more. "Me? I'm going to kill Sour Foot."

"*Sour Foot?*" the man balked.

"Aye."

"Sour Foot can't be killed."

"Aye," Rogot repeated, eyes trained where his stone met steel. "Not by men."

The man looked Rogot up and down, eyes narrowing, fear replaced by wonder. "You're Rogot the God Blood, King From Before."

"I was for a long time, a long time ago." The stone *scraped scraped scraped* along the blade. "But who really knows? Who can really remember?"

"Aye," the man agreed. His face fell slack, cracked teeth showing in the moonlight. "We've been wandering for seven days."

"Wander on then, my friend."

"Right," said the man, then he and the others turned before disappearing into the lifeless thickets.

Rogot stood and pulled a burlap sack from his coat. He loosened the drawstring and held it open towards the pile of bodies. "Come, Arigot. It will be morning soon."

The boy came slowly from hiding, dropped to his knees and crawled into the bag. Rogot pulled the string tight, extinguishing the golden glow from within. He slung it onto his back, shouldered the axe, and moved away from the smoldering village.

Wraiths in the Valley

With morning came the brown sun, a dirty light and its futile effort to pierce black clouds. Once out of the forest and on the road, Rogot released the boy from his satchel to let him walk on his own. The path was mostly mud, though compacted enough to make walking easy, and skinny grey-green trees lined the way. The boy's golden aura shone brighter than the rust-colored sky, and he walked knee-high beside Rogot, a stark contrast against the dark and dusty man.

They hiked along the path all morning until the forest gave way to open pastures. The field on their left was spotted for miles with the black and bloated bodies of cattle, air thick with gnats, and squawking vultures whirled in the sky above. To their right were fields of grain, all of it crawling with locust. Another twenty paces and they came to an overturned carriage. Three bodies lay face down in puddles of black blood, trousers pulled down around their knees, rumps cleaved off and hauled away.

"Look away, my son," Rogot said, covering the boy's eyes as they passed the carnage.

"Can we bring them back?" the boy asked, leaning against his father's leg as he walked blindly. "Once it's finished?"

"No," said Rogot. "But we can save whoever's left."

Then Rogot saw a fourth body farther ahead, a woman lying face up, arms and legs spread wide, belly sliced open and scooped out like a gourd.

"Why don't you ride on my back for a bit?" he said, retrieving the burlap sack. Arigot agreed, climbed inside, and Rogot swung him up and over his shoulder.

He hiked up and out of the farmland, stopping atop a colorless ridge. Grey hills rolled ahead, disappearing behind a foggy horizon. In the valley below was a deep crater rimmed with the broken remains of a forgotten castle, once home to a forgotten lord, the ruler of lands now diseased by rot and the residual spirits of angry men. Scattered all around the ruins were old weapons, a carpet of rusty blades and broken pikes littering the valley and hillside beyond. Torn banners boasting faded sigils whipped in the acrid breeze, and the skeleton of some titanic beast topped the distant ridge like the crowned jewel of Death's masterpiece.

The boy's small and muffled voice came from the burlap sack. "Where are we, Father?"

"Larin Fol," said Rogot. "Or Chesterian's Folly, depending on who you ask, who remembers and how. A great battle was fought here long ago when the Invaders came. Not the last battle, but one of the last."

"Is it safe?" the boy asked from within the bag.

"Nowhere is safe," Rogot said simply. "Many spirits linger here, some still searching for a healer, some for a companion separated in combat, some simply waiting for orders that will never come."

"Should we go around?"

Rogot looked to his left at the far-off wilderness, a forest such a dark green it was nearly black. "To the west is the Mushroom King." He grimaced and gazed off to his right, to steep mountains and needle-sharp spires. "Troll Eaters rule in the east, locked in constant warfare with Mad Gorman's undead militia."

"Hmm," said the boy. "Who's worse?"

Rogot grunted, then gazed back at the forest to his left. "I'd say the Mushroom King is worth avoiding." He nodded straight ahead to the ancient battleground below. "Sour Foot is north, and so too the Bubbling Crone."

"And we need her?"

"Yes, my son. Now, keep quiet, lest the spirits catch scent of your words."

Rogot gripped his axe in both hands, then moved slowly into the valley. After twenty paces his boots crunched down on overlapping sprawls of weaponry. Dry shafts splintered, and brittle metal cracked like shards of ice. He descended, the smell of festering wounds filling his nose, whispered pleas wafting in his ears, and a meaningless dread pressed dully at his ribs. Shadows shaped and reshaped on the edge of his vision, movement flashing just beyond sight. All the while, stained and rusted weapons crumbled beneath him. With each gust of wind came the sound of a distant battle, of scraping steel and dying men accompanied by feelings of terror and hopelessness.

Rogot came to the crater where a stone tower leaned dangerously over empty air, gutted earth beneath all scarred and scorched black. Mist rolled into the valley, dipping into the hollow before whisking up and over Rogot.

"God Blood," the mist whispered, a voice like crumpling paper. "Send reinforcements. Hold the Eastern Front." As clouds drifted overhead, dirty brown sunlight writhed in the crater. Mist spun, and the voice grew louder. "God Blood. God King. Failure of Amon Rul."

Rogot closed his eyes and ground his teeth, fists clenching the haft of his axe. He waited, screaming in his mind for the moment to pass, for the spirits to lose his scent and sleep again.

"Father?" the boy asked, voice quivering.

"Shhh!" Rogot spat.

A sudden gale of wind nearly knocked him off his feet, and a scream as shrill as a whistle cried out. "Rogot! God Blood!"

A figure took shape in the mist, something like a man with bat ears and a serpent's tail. With a roar that loosed stones from the ancient tower, Rogot spun, swung his axe, and the blade sang hard against solidified mist.

"I'm sorry!" the boy screamed.

"Quiet!" Rogot ordered, spun, struck again.

This time the blade cleaved straight through, emerging from the mist wet with green phlegm. The creature disfigured, became shapeless again, and when Rogot roared, it curled up into a smoky spear aimed for his mouth. A foot of white mist made it down his throat before he bit off the stream, rolled away and spun the axe round and round over his head.

Rogot's mouth opened, and a voice not his own spoke from deep in his belly. "Rogot! God Blood! Where are the reinforcements?!"

Rogot spoke again, only now with his own tongue. "Don't speak to it, my son! No matter what it says, don't speak to me nor the creature! Tap once if you understand!"

Rogot felt light pressure against his shoulder as the boy pressed from within the sack.

"They're coming over the walls!" Rogot screamed in that other voice. "Left flank! Left flank! Push-" Rogot dropped to his knees, clawed up a handful of grey dirt, and shoved it into his mouth, stalling the onslaught of words. "Vanguard!" he screamed, dirt spewing from his lips, though he replaced it with another handful, chewing vigorously. He tore a strip from the front of his shirt, then went to work wrapping it around his mouth, knotting it tight around the back of his head. He grabbed one of the nearby spears and snapped off the end, hands moving frantically, breath rushing in and out of flared nostrils. The length of rotten wood crumbled easily in his big hands, and he pushed the splinters into a pile between his knees. All the while, the voice in his throat fought to break free, causing Rogot to groan and grumble behind clamped teeth.

He pulled a square of flint from his furs and slapped it against one of the axe blades, dusting the kindling with sparks. He did this three more times until the pile caught fire, then he drew a curved dagger from his thigh and placed it against his forearm. *Fire*, he told himself. *Living flesh*. He flayed a thin piece of skin from his arm. A stream of blood ran down his wrist, across his hand, and dribbled from the tip of his middle finger.

At last, Rogot tore the strip of cloth from his face. Instantly, the spirit within caused him to spew dirt from his mouth, followed by mad ramblings. "God Blood! God King! False King! King Killer! Wife Killer! Son Killer! World Killer!" Rogot grabbed a fistful of flaming kindling and shoved it into his mouth, grimacing and groaning as he chewed. Smoke curled from his nostrils. He then pinched up the strip of bloody flesh still stuck to his knife. He tossed that into his mouth and chewed on.

Rogot swallowed. "I command you to vacate!" He boomed, at last with his own voice. "Hear me, spirit!" he yelled, fists balled, face turned to the sky. "You trespass on holy kin, and I forbid you entry! Be gone, or be banished!"

Rogot roared, blood and dirt and ash smearing his lips and beard. He arched his back, spread his arms and howled as the white mist finally raced from his mouth, hissing and squealing as it sped back into the crater. Rogot doubled over, gasping for air. "Stay silent, my son," he huffed. "Good boy."

"Listen," the boy whispered, so soft, so fearful.

"Hush!" Rogot hissed, but then he heard it too, a sound like rattling bones, like an army of skeletons stomping into battle formations.

All the thousands of ancient weapons strewn about the valley were vibrating, clattering against one another, and they began to hover, waving side to side like stalks of grain.

Rogot grabbed his axe in one hand, then used it like a cane as he climbed to his feet. "They know we're here," he grumbled, then tightened the burlap sack across his shoulder.

"How many?" the boy asked.

"All of them."

He twisted the haft in both fists and ran. Broken spears and rusted swords rushed up at him without wielders, spinning through the air like living creatures. Rogot swung, hammered, stabbed and slashed, clearing a path through the rogue melee as he charged from the valley. Despite his efforts, the dirty blades nipped at his skin, clipped his beard, and dull arrows thumped against his arms and legs. He ran hard, boots digging into grey dirt as he ascended the valley, now shielding his face against the storm of weapons. He glanced up, and what he saw there froze him mid stride.

The skeletal beast was now lumbering across the hilltop, bones held together by strips of dry tendons. With each step, it swung its elongated skull side to side, giant tusks sweeping inches over the dusty ridge. It dropped its head to one side, empty eye socket training on Rogot.

Rogot growled, then screamed, "Come on then, you big dead fucker!"

He swung the axe side to side, swatting away the rogue weapons still attacking as the skeletal monster charged down for him. The hillside rumbled. Wood, metal and bones clattered. Rogot rolled into the beast, up and under its fossilized snout, and he smashed his axe into its clavicle. The bone exploded against his steel, showering Rogot with powder and splintered bits. The beast spun round, tail swinging, and Rogot's world was suddenly pain and weightlessness. He crashed to the ground rolling, grey mud flying, earth trembling. Blood and dirt in his mouth, bone all around, axe whirling.

Rogot clawed his way into the monster's empty rib cage, then onto its spine. Now straddling the undead thing, he took his axe in both hands, using it like a hammer as he pounded away at the vertebrae. The monster was on the hilltop again, running along the ridge, bucking and thrashing as it galloped away from the obliterated castle. One, two and then three of the vertebrae burst into powder under Rogot's heavy blade, and the spine buckled inwards. The monster collapsed snout first, flipped forward, tore up earth and dead grass before bursting into countless individual bones.

Rogot went flying, slammed against a steep embankment and continued on. Down he went, tumbling head over heels, slipping on soggy leaves and slick rocks. He came to a violent stop, chest first against the base of a tree. He sucked for air, sat up and tore the burlap sack from his back. He opened it, face washing over with golden light, and the boy came crawling out unscathed.

"Was that magic you used?" asked the boy. "When you defeated the spirit?"

"Yes," said Rogot, still catching his breath. "A little. But I didn't defeat it, only scared it away for a time."

The boy looked to his left and right, then above his head. "Where are we now?"

Rogot stood with a groan, then turned to the tree that had broken his fall. His eyes followed the trunk upwards, and he realized it wasn't a tree at all. It was a huge mushroom, cap so big it shaded him, the boy and another twenty feet of circular space.

Rogot sneered and ground his teeth. "The beast took us west."

"To the Mushroom King?"

Rogot looked back the way they had come, to the steep embankment they had tumbled down, covered in rotten leaves, wet rocks and loose dirt. His eyes traced the top of the hill where dead yellow grass swayed in the breeze, and a stream of mischievous whispering came following down. He didn't much like the idea of climbing back into that valley with all those lost spirits waiting for him and his son. Instead, he set his jaw and turned back to the forest.

"Aye," he said at last. "The Mushroom King."

Garigot, King of Mushrooms

For every five or six trees there was a mushroom equal in size. The trees themselves were covered in mushroom caps, leaves replaced by thin webs of fungus, all of it sucking water from the roots of the very trees they clung to until the bark had become as dry and brittle as discarded snake skin.

"Why all the mushrooms?" Arigot asked as they traversed the forest.

Rogot's keen eyes scanned the distance, axe resting over his shoulder. "After Sour Foot killed the Invaders and broke the world, mushrooms were the only thing that grew here. People ate them, not knowing they carried dark magic."

"Wow," the boy said. "And the king ate them too?"

"He wasn't a king then," Rogot explained. "He was a lord."

"And Garigot was his name?"

"Aye."

"It's kind of like your name," said the boy. "And mine. Why is that?"

Rogot stopped walking, eyes narrow. "Be silent."

What he thought to have been a tall mushroom suddenly moved, stepped into a pool of dusty light, and appeared to be something like a woman. She had soft grey-yellow skin and green hair matted like moss. One of her eyes was swollen shut, crusted over by a plate of porous fungus, and the other was yellow and dewy. A small mushroom sprouted from one cheek, and another grew directly from her ear canal. She was naked, and where her genitals should have been, there was a bulk of grey mushrooms, caps growing into one another, stalks knotted together, all of it squishy and moist.

Rogot lowered the axe from his shoulder, glaring at the thing that had once been a woman. "Another step, and you'll be feeding shrooms on every point of the compass."

She smiled, teeth as big and round as a cow's, and she licked her mouth, smearing her lips with yellow grit. Rogot glanced to his side, relieved to see that Arigot had already disappeared into hiding. When he turned back, another creature had joined the first. This one was a man, or had been long ago, though he was just as disfigured as the woman, covered in moss and fungus, engorged mushroom stalk dangling between his legs. The two were wielding spears, and more circled in from behind to corner Rogot, each as grotesque as the next. Rogot lowered his axe.

"Take me then," he sighed. "I'll go peacefully."

Garigot was seated in a wooden chair turned green by algae, placed atop a mound of moss in a circle of pale sunlight falling through overhead mushrooms, illuminating the king in the otherwise dark forest. All around him stood his subjects, deformed and buckled humans in a myriad of nightmarish shapes. Rogot stood before him, half a dozen spears trained on his back. Garigot himself was a big man, as big as Rogot, skin crusted with overlapping disks of hardened fungus. His beard was a matt of ivy, and his eyes glistened yellow like infected mucus. His crusted fingers rested on the hilt of a tall sword, upside down, with the point stuck in the moss beside the chair. The blade wasn't metal rather some sort of grey carapace, pocked with barnacles and patches of green fuzz. He smiled, teeth like a mouthful of gravel.

"Brother," he said.

"My brother is dead," said Rogot.

Garigot chuckled. "Oh, I am very much alive, only now I'm diseased and disfigured due to your folly." The Mushroom King examined one bulbous arm, clenching and unclenching his fist. "Though perhaps I should thank you, Rogot. It seems I may very well be invincible now that I'm infused with this magical forest."

"*Magic*," Rogot grumbled with contempt.

Garigot looked to him again, grinning. "You always preferred steel over magic."

"And for good reason." Rogot gestured to the forest and its mutated inhabitants. "Look what it's done to you and your people."

The Mushroom King leaned forward in his mossy chair. "And whose fault is that?"

"He was trying to save us from the Invaders," Rogot growled.

"And such a good job he did," Garigot said, voice sour with sarcasm. "Now we're all trapped here together, us and them, all of us destined for eons of insanity."

Rogot breathed deeply, big shoulders rising and falling. "I'm going to kill Sour Foot," he said seriously. "I'm going to fix this. That's where I was headed when your people stopped me."

"Bah!" Garigot laughed, ooze splattering his lips and beard. "You can't kill a man with no soul, a man who's already dead!"

"I have a way."

The Mushroom King stood at last, fist balling around the pommel of his huge sword. The fungus crusting his joints crackled and popped as he climbed to his feet, then he pulled the weapon from the mound with a grumble. He held it in both hands, carapace blade swaying before his face. "Maybe you have a way to fix things, but maybe I don't want things fixed."

Garigot nodded, and two of his subjects hobbled forward, Rogot's giant axe held between them. They tossed it at Rogot's feet before scurrying back into the crowd. Rogot thought of protesting, thought of speaking reason, but in the end he simply sighed and heaved up the weapon.

The Mushroom King leapt, soared high, up to the treetops, teeth bared as he snarled and swung the sword. Rogot spread his legs and raised the axe. Carapace and steel collided, Rogot's boots raked into the dirt, brothers face to face, snarling and scraping blades. Rogot kneed the king in his mutated groin, shouldered him back and swung his axe. Garigot ducked, and the axe blade bounced off the top of his head, mushroom slivers spinning high. The sword blade came up for Rogot's belly. He parried, elbowed Garigot in the teeth, then slammed him into a tree, through the tree, out the other side and into the dirt. Splinters fell all around, and the severed tree came falling, crushing a giant mushroom to the earth.

Garigot kicked Rogot and he went soaring, flipped backward and crashed down twenty paces away. The Mushroom King was up and after him. Rogot grabbed his axe, pulling up a handful of leaves with it, and leapt to his feet. Their weapons collided and they were at it again, snarling, hacking, shoving and punching, god blood thumping in their veins. Garigot thrusted the flat side of his blade hard against Rogot's axe, pressed him back, then shoved a crust-covered finger deep into Rogot's ear, just like he used to do when they were boys. Rogot screamed, hating the sensation as much as he had all those years ago.

"Die!" Garigot growled. "Die, fucker! Die!"

Rogot ground his teeth so hard one cracked, then crammed his thumb knuckle-deep into Garigot's eye. Garigot roared, but he kept his footing, kept shoving his brother back with the big blade. With Rogot's thumb filling most of the socket, Garigot's eyeball bunched up to one side, then popped, spewing them both with yellow gelatin. Ticks with bellies as big as corn kernels came rolling out in the puss. The Mushroom King howled and stumbled back, then rebounded with a jab. Rogot parried the blade but not enough, carapace point puncturing his shoulder.

"Agh!" Rogot snarled, grabbing the blade with a bare hand and wrenching it free.

He kicked Garigot's knee, buckling his leg with a wet pop, yellow mist wafting out from the broken flesh. Rogot spun, axe whirling, and the huge blade sank into Garigot's side, splitting him wide open from hip to groin. Rogot pulled the weapon free, spun the opposite direction, and like a lumberjack felling a tree, he put the axe in Garigot's other hip. Both wounds met in the middle, cleaving the Mushroom King through the waist. His upper body went reeling one direction, legs and groin the other. Black blood and purple guts filled the space between.

Rogot dropped the head of his axe, leaning on the haft as he caught his breath. He stared down at his brother, feeling little more than exhaustion and something dull and distant that might have been remorse. Garigot sucked for air, face twisted with confusion. His shoulders rocked and he tried to sit up, tried to climb to one elbow, then finally fell back, hands fumbling in the gore around his waist.

"Bastard," he croaked. "I knew you'd be the death of me. Ever since I can remember, I knew you'd kill me."

Rogot said nothing, simply sucked for air.

Garigot spat, blood splashing his face, mixing with the ooze from his ruined eye. He seemed to realize something, seemed to calm as if easing into a tub of warm water. He exhaled slowly, whispering, "Your boy, Rogot. Your only boy. I'm so sorry." He sucked in another breath, gargled it back out, then ceased to move.

Rogot finally looked up, just then noticing all the deformed faces looking at him. They were all pointing, all beginning to chant. "Rogot, King of Mushrooms. Rogot, King of Mushrooms. Rogot, King of Mushrooms."

Rogot looked to where they were pointing, to the tear in his shirt and the wound in his shoulder. The puncture from Garigot's sword had turned black, was no longer bleeding, and from the open flesh small tendrils were beginning to sprout.

"No!" he cried, grabbing a fistful of the tendrils. When he yanked them free, he felt a tugging sensation run through his arm, across his chest and deep into his back. "No!" He crammed his fingers into the wound, rummaged around and pinched more fungal growths from deep within the tissue.

"Rogot!" they chanted. "King of Mushrooms!"

"No!" Rogot protested. "Enough!"

He picked up the axe and lunged, one swipe cleaving four of them in half. He turned, swung his fist, and another's misshapen head exploded against his knuckles, blood and grey pulp spewing. The others scurried back, cowering away from the axe as he spun it round and round. He slowed, gathered his balance, then bound off into the dark forest.

Sour Foot Wants His Soul Back

When Rogot burst from the forest into a clearing, the sun had fully set. The world was full of dark days and darker nights, overcast all hours with rains and fog that hindered the already weakened sun and moon.

"Arigot!" he screamed, one hand dragging the axe behind him, other hand clasping his wounded shoulder. "My son! My boy!"

"Father?" came a small voice.

Rogot spun and nearly fell, muscles weak from the spreading infection. He could see a soft golden light radiating behind the trees, and a moment later, his son scampered out towards him.

"Arigot," Rogot sighed, then coughed, gritty phlegm clotting in his beard.

The boy's smile fell away. "Father, what's wrong?"

"We need a tinker," Rogot groaned.

"A tinker?" the boy asked fearfully, looking around at the black and empty landscape. "There's no one out here."

"One will come," Rogot assured him before breaking into another spasm of coughs. "They always come. Enough speaking. Follow closely."

They made their way across the field, the boy's aura the only source of light from horizon to horizon. Rogot was slowing, breath growing heavy, axe like the weight of a mountain in his hands. "Come on, you bastard," he cursed through clenched teeth.

"What's a tinker?" the boy asked, having to slow his pace for Rogot.

"They're merchants from other worlds," Rogot said breathlessly.

"Outer Things?"

"No, not from that far," Rogot explained. "They're like us, but they use wizardry to project into our world, to sell us overpriced provisions in moments of desperation."

"Why come here if they have a world of their own, a world that's not sick?"

"Greed," said Rogot. "There are few of us left here, but plenty of gold and plenty of suffering. Easy profits for an opportunistic tinker."

They came to the bottom of a steep incline slick with mud. To their right was a vertical cliff crisscrossed by a winding track. Rogot dropped his axe, doubled over and vomited. It was a green-yellow muck, and something like tadpoles flickered and flopped along the surface.

"We must hurry," Rogot croaked, wiping bile from his mouth and beard. He found a thin noodle hanging from his lips, pulled it, felt it tugging at the back of his throat and gagged as it slipped free.

"There!" said the boy, pointing to the top of the cliff.

Rogot peered up and saw light flickering from atop the cliff. "Come," he said, and they started up the track.

Rogot collapsed near the summit, black and green foam spewing from his mouth. He wrenched the bear furs from his shoulder, finding a small grove of juvenile mushrooms growing from the wound.

"Father!" the boy cried. "Come on! We're almost there!" Arigot tried valiantly to lift the axe, but only managed to raise the haft a few inches.

Rogot said nothing, only rolled to his belly, dug his fingers in the gravel, and pulled himself forward. He was so tired, so thirsty, yet he crawled until his fingers bled, until his nails cracked and ground to the quicks. All the while, the boy encouraged him on, cheering and crying all the same. At last, he could see the fire, a small tent, and the silhouette of a man behind the flames. Rogot climbed to one knee, then another, then waddled forward like a crippled dog until finally collapsing by the fire.

"Hello, traveler," the tinker said conversationally. He leaned to one side, peering around the flames to lock eyes with Rogot. He was a slender man, healthy nonetheless, with dark black hair and maroon robes. He pulled the cork from a leather flask and drank. "Seems you're in some trouble."

"Help my father!" the boy begged, but the tinker kept expectant eyes on Rogot.

Rogot reached into his furs, drew out a heavy purse, and dropped it clinking to the ground. It was a sound exclusive to precious metals.

"Ah!" the tinker exclaimed. "There we are." He reached out a long and skinny arm, scooped up the purse and inspected its contents. He drew from it a handful of golden coins, tucked them away, then tossed the bag back across the fire. "That should do it," he said with finality.

Rogot lay still, arm outstretched by the purse, ribs digging into the gravel beneath him. He stared straight ahead, past the fire, past the tinker, past the cliff, and out into the darkness. His breath was very shallow, eyes blinking slowly, mouth full of sour spit and tiny squirming things. The firelight dimmed as the tinker came over, knelt beside him and inspected the wound. A bottle was placed to his lips, bitter fluid drenching his throat, and then something furry came next. The tinker rolled him onto his back and started cutting away at his shoulder. Rogot felt pain, a whole world of anguish, but there was nothing he could do. No strength left to even grimace. The tinker smiled down at him, angular face orange in the firelight.

"There you go, big guy," he said.

Rogot blinked, and the world was a little darker. He blinked again, darker yet, and then he faded into sleep.

\#

Rogot's eyes peeled open, lids crusty with mucus. The sky was black above him, campfire hot on his cheek. He sat up with a start, then reached around frantically for his axe.

"It's just there," said the tinker. He was sitting close by, eating from a wooden bowl. He used his spoon to point out the axe leaning against a splintered tree stump. "I went down and got it for you. Heavy thing."

Rogot looked away from the tinker, saw his son snoozing on a bedroll in the shadows and felt his heart ease. Lastly, he checked his shoulder and found it wrapped with fresh bandages, no sign of infection in the surrounding flesh. "Thank you," he said gruffly.

The tinker smiled, then bowed as much as one can bow while seated on a rock. "My services aren't cheap, but no man can say I'm not thorough."

"Thank you," Rogot repeated. "I guess you'll be on your way now?"

"Soon," the tinker confirmed, then handed Rogot a bowl of stew.

In Rogot's hand, the bowl looked no bigger than a tea cup. The savory smell of beef, vegetables and salted broth hit his nose instantly, filling his mouth with drool. He spooned a bite, and although he refused to admit it aloud, it was the most delicious thing he had eaten since the world broke somewhere between seven days and seven hundred years ago.

"A god blood, huh?" said the tinker. "Been a while since I worked on your kind. Descendants of the Creator himself!"

Rogot said nothing, only spooned another bite of stew into his mouth.

"Not many of you left," the tinker added, then looked around the camp as if he could see the entire realm. "Not here, at least."

"One less than there was yesterday," Rogot grumbled.

"Ah," the tinker sighed. "Family drama, I see." He took a bite of stew. "So which one are you? Marrigot? Togot? Shemigot?"

Rogot said nothing, chewed, didn't look up from his bowl.

"I found something curious in your belongings."

Rogot was suddenly very interested in the conversation. His eyes darted to the tinker's, jaw clenched, spoon gripped tight in his fist. "You went through my things?"

"Easy," the tinker said diplomatically. "I left it all right where I found it."

"If you were here right now, *really here*, I'd take your fingers."

The tinker chuckled. "I'm sure you would." He smiled and licked his perfectly white teeth. "So what is it you're planning, god blood?"

Rogot's eyes were back on the soup. He swallowed a bite and said, "What's it matter to you?"

"You could say we have a mutual interest."

Rogot eyed the man for a moment. "I'm going to kill Sour Foot."

"Are you?" he asked doubtfully. "You know, Sour Foot wants his soul back. What do you think might happen if he gets it?"

"He'll die."

"Maybe," the tinker agreed. "Maybe not. He can't die without his soul, but he also can't leave his castle without it."

"He won't leave," Rogot said matter-of-factly.

"I hope you're right, because if he does leave, it might be my world he visits next."

"He won't leave," Rogot repeated.

The tinker took a final bite of stew and sat his bowl aside. He leaned forward, elbows resting on his knees, eyes narrowing. "Will you really kill him… *Can* you really kill him?"

"Enough," Rogot warned.

"Or will you bargain with ole Sour Foot?" The tinker flashed a sarcastic smile, white teeth reflecting the firelight. "Perhaps, you'll bargain for your wife… Rogot."

Rogot threw out his hands, bowl and spoon soaring, and he leapt for the tinker's throat. "I said enough!" he bellowed, but when his hands clasped down on the man there was a flash of white light. Rogot went flipping backwards, crashed into the gravel groaning and spitting, then looked up to see the tinker gone, flames guttering in the wind.

"Fucking tinkers," he grumbled as he climbed to his feet.

"Father?"

Rogot turned to see his son rubbing sleep from his eyes. "Rest, my son," he told him. "I'll stoke the fire."

"Okay," Arigot said softly, then snuggled back into the bedding.

Rogot kept his gaze on the boy for some time, wrinkles in his face picked black by the campfire. His throat grew tight, accompanied by that pressure behind his nose that came just before crying. His vision was soon blurry with tears that tumbled down his old face, wetting his grey-black beard. "My son," he whispered while Arigot slept, "my sweet and perfect boy, forgive me for what I must do."

The Binding of Three

Rogot stood on the edge of a lake, boots ankle-deep in brown sludge. Morning sunlight pierced a greenish haze, causing the water's surface to glow fluorescent green. Water bubbled at the lake's center, sending ripples across the floating ivy before clapping the muddy shore. He had fashioned a rope from a length of rusty chain, another several yards of rawhide, and three feet of steel braiding for good measure. He tied the steel end to his axe before sitting it down in the muck. A dying fish flapped on the ground next to his boot, belly swollen with roe. The hook was still in its mouth, line and stick just beside it. Not far away, Arigot was tossing rocks into a puddle, laughing as if he was the first boy to discover throwing rocks and splashing water.

Rogot worked his arm and rubbed his shoulder. He had been injured there, but when and by whom? Ah, his brother, the Mushroom King. And he had killed Garigot, but when had that been? Yesterday, or the day before? Perhaps a decade even.

"Arigot, my son, come to me."

The boy dropped a handful of rocks and rushed for his father, glowing like a firefly bobbing across the barren landscape.

Rogot took up the axe in one hand, slack rope in his other. "Stay behind me. She may try to curse us."

"But you will curse her first?"

"I will *charm* her, yes."

He reared back, groaned from deep in his gut, then sent the axe flying. It flipped end over end high above the lake, makeshift rope whizzing out behind it, until finally it splashed down some distance beyond the constant bubbling. Rogot let the axe sink, waiting for the line to grow firm. Afterward, he began reeling it in, pulling the chain fist over fist. The line snapped taught as if swallowed up by a monster.

Rogot grinned. "I got you, you bubbling bitch."

He pulled hard, and the line was moving again, only this time much heavier. He ground his teeth and worked, one fistful after another, a few feet at a time. At last, a shape emerged under the water, then broke the surface near the shore. It was an iron chair, half-moon axe blade hooked around one leg. A woman was strapped to the chair, arms and legs clamped with iron restraints. She was wearing a white gown, soaked through and transparent, black hair plastered to her face. She was thin, middle-aged, and might have been attractive if not for the pruned and waxy look of her skin, like a fresh corpse left to dissolve in water.

She gasped, sucked for air and howled, screamed, shrill terror shattering the otherwise quiet morning. Rogot pulled her ashore and made quick work to silence her. He had a rag ready in his pocket, and he crammed it into her gaping mouth. Although silent, she continued writhing, bucking and fighting against her restraints.

"Good work, my son," he said, moving back to the hooked fish that had finally died on the bank.

"I didn't do anything," said Arigot.

"Nonetheless," said Rogot, "good work."

Rogot drew his knife and sliced open his own palm. Then, he cut open the fish's belly and squeezed the pink roe into his bleeding hand. He spat on the eggs, then smashed them with his thumb, mixing the spit, blood and roe into a handful of orange goop. He returned to the woman and knelt over her, ignoring her bright and hateful eyes. Using his thumb, he took some of the mixture and marked her forehead, sketching three geometric symbols as best he could while she thrashed and snapped side to side. Once finished, he pulled the rag from her mouth and stepped aside.

"Rogot!" she screamed, voice full of hate and terror. Water flowed from her mouth with every word. "Coward King! Witch Killer! You charm me with elementary runes?!"

"Aye," he said calmly, wiping his hands on his trousers. "Elementary, yes, but effective. Try lying to me, and they'll burn right through your soggy skull."

She bit her purple lips. "You don't trust me, Rogot?"

"No witch can be trusted."

She grinned. "Clever. What is it you want? Be out with it and toss me back!"

"I've come to trade."

"Ha!" she laughed, eyes rolling to meet his. "Suck my bloated cunt! What could you possibly offer me?!"

"Freedom," he said simply.

Something changed in her face. The mingle of fear and contempt gave way to silent curiosity. "Freedom?" she asked softly.

"Aye."

She bunched up her soggy lips, eyes squinting and suspicious. "What do you need?"

"To kill Sour Foot."

"Ha!" she laughed again. "Sour Foot can't be killed without his soul!"

"Aye," said Rogot.

Her eyes narrowed again. "Oh, what have you done, god blood?"

"I did what I had to do to save my kingdom."

"Little good it's done." Her eyes rolled as she strained to look around. "So it was you who took his foot, you who bound his soul to it. It's been you all along."

Rogot squatted by the overturned chair, resting his forearms on his thighs. "How do I make him whole again?"

"The Binding of Three," she purred. "His essence is bound to the Outer Thing, body bound to the woman, to your wife. Though, of course, I'm sure you are aware."

Rogot ground his teeth. "How do I break the binding?"

"Sour Foot must release himself on his own accord, at his own time."

"I imagine he wants that."

She gave Rogot a nasty smile, yellow teeth set into black gums, all of it circled by purple lips and porcelain skin. "The unbinding will require a still-beating heart. Not just any heart, but the heart of an innocent."

"An innocent?"

"Yes, you fucking fool! An untainted youth! An unflowered girl or a boy without seed! A virgin!"

Rogot glanced to Arigot standing nervously behind him. He turned back to the witch. "Is there no other way?"

"Stupid imbecile! You charmed me, didn't you? I'm incapable of lying!"

Rogot grunted. "The still-beating heart of a virgin. Then what?"

"The heart will give him what he needs to reform his flesh, to become independent from your wife. When this is done, he can carry his own soul once more. Then you can cleave that big axe of yours right through his fucking skull."

"A still-beating heart," he pondered aloud, gazing around the empty valley stained with mud, sprouting nothing but dead trees.

"There is a homestead northwest of here," she said. "If you leave now you can be there well before nightfall."

"That's it?" Rogot asked doubtfully.

She smiled and cocked her head. "That's it. Easy peasy. Now, you'll release me?"

Rogot grabbed his axe, then unlaced the steel braiding. "Aye, but if you try sorcery, if you utter one syllable of witchcraft, I'll slice you from scalp to snatch."

She smacked her purple lips. "Deal."

He unlatched her wrist restraints, then her ankles. The witch rolled from the chair into the mud, facedown, breath bubbling in the sludge. She pushed herself onto her knees, pulled her shoulders back, and turned her filthy face to the sky, purple nipples standing out against the thin gown. She breathed deeply, cackled, and finally stood.

"You're welcome," Rogot murmured, axe tight in both fists.

She wiped the mud from her face, runes along with it, then threw out her hands and shrieked like a hungry vulture. Purple shards of lightning exploded from her fingers. Rogot started, lifted his axe and blocked the attack. The force of it caused him to slide backward, boot heels tearing up mounds of brown slime. They remained locked this way for several seconds, her throwing lightning, him pressing against it as he muttered counter spells of his own. When the attack finally ended, Rogot leapt forward and cleaved her from left armpit to right shoulder. Her head, part of her chest and right arm went spinning upwards as the rest of her body collapsed. She landed headfirst, teeth clicking until she died a moment later.

Arigot clapped his hands to his head. "Why did she do that?!" he shrieked.

Rogot shouldered his axe, eyes trained on the severed corpse. "It's what she wanted," he said morosely.

"To die?"

"Yes, my boy. Some things are worse than death. I pray that you never understand."

Little Slice of Heaven

Rogot and the boy strolled through rolling fields of dead grass, brown landscape almost indistinguishable from the brown sky. Somewhere far to the north, left of the father and son, a geyser spewed yellow steam.

"Father," Arigot asked, "what was it like before? Before the world broke? Can you remember?"

Rogot allowed himself a small smile. "Certainly, my son. I might not remember things between then and now – time broke the same as everything else – but I remember each day from before, as if each and every one of them was yesterday."

"Which one was your favorite?"

Rogot ruffled the boy's hair. "The day you were born, of course."

Arigot smiled up at his father. "Really?"

"Yes. Your mother, the queen, wanted nothing more than a child. She didn't long for gold, power, not glory or songs, but a child. And I, as a king, thought I needed an heir, a legacy. But then you came, and you were so much more than that. You *are* so much more than that. People traveled from all over the realm to see you. Nobles and commoners alike. Lords, ladies, farmers and milkmaids. I held you over the western ramparts so that all could see." Rogot let out a deep chuckle. "And you pissed right there over all those people." He threw his head back, chuckle becoming full-fledged laughter. "Your mother and I laughed until we cried."

Arigot giggled along, both of them stopping to wipe their eyes and hug their guts.

"What a time that was," Rogot said, joy turning somber. "The sun shone everyday, fields were green and ripe. You could eat right off the trees and drink straight from the rivers. There were no wars to worry about, no usurpers, no political scandals. I remember that summer like a dream come true, like I had finally united our people."

"And then the Invaders came?"

"Aye," Rogot said darkly. "The Invaders came, and we did what we could, but in the end, they were simply too many. Sour Foot tried to stop them, and he did, I suppose. But in his ignorance, in his lust for glory and power, he communed directly with an Outer Thing, the only one who would listen, the worst of them all. The Invaders were all but destroyed, oh yes, but with them we lost everything. Stolen from the Creator, tucked away where he can't see, shrouded in darkness. We can't even die here, robbed of our own mortality, cursed to roam these lands in life and after." He glanced to his son, saw a fearful look on his face. "Forgive me, my boy. I've said too much."

"It's okay," Arigot said softly. "You really think you can change things back to the way they were?"

"With you, I know we can."

"With magic?" the boy asked gleefully.

"Yes," Rogot said with regret.

"I know you hate magic, Father, but I love it. I think we can use it for good."

Rogot frowned. "I know you do, boy. I know. And it *can be* used for good, but it also has a tendency to corrupt. I've told you this. It's like the elixirs tinkers and healers use. A measured amount in the hands of a trained individual is healing, lifesaving even. But too much in the wrong hands can be lethal."

"I know," the boy said reluctantly. "All I have to do is look around to see that, but still…" his words trailed off, and he said no more for a long time.

The homestead was at the top of a hill surrounded by a thicket of dead trees. There was mostly grey dirt, save a few spots of brown grass and something like a small garden, though it was mostly weeds and wilting sprouts. A goat with one horn munched on a grassy patch, and two mostly bald chickens clucked and pecked around its ankles. The house itself was a small cabin that looked like it might tumble over with one gust of strong wind.

"I want you to wait here," Rogot told the boy as they viewed the homestead from hiding.

"But I want to meet people too," Arigot pleaded.

"Obey me," Rogot said. "It might be dangerous."

"Yes, Father," the boy pouted.

Rogot sat his axe by the boy before leaving the forest. He strolled across the open hilltop, bear furs collecting dirt around his boots. He passed the small garden, the goat and chickens, then came to a stop at the front door of the cabin. He took a deep breath, attempted his best smile, and knocked. He was so tall that his eyes leveled with the crossbeam above the entrance, forcing him to lower his fist for the awkward knock.

There was a rustle of movement inside and some frantic whispering. Rogot simply sighed and waited. After a moment, the door creaked open, and a heavyset older woman peered through the crack.

"We're poor!" she exclaimed, fear and anger mixing in her eyes. "We ain't got nothin' worth stealin'! Take the goat if you need, the chickens too. Just leave us be, would you?"

Rogot's smile widened, and he leaned down to see beneath the door frame. "I've not come to steal. Don't you worry." He pulled the coin purse from his furs, holding it out in his palm as he jingled the metal inside, pleased when he saw the woman smile. "I was only hoping for a little food, and I'm willing to pay. I'll double it if it's warm."

She broke a small smile, opening the door a little wider. Rogot could see a sliver of the inside, an open room, rickety table and chairs, a hearth, some cookware on the wall, all bathed in the orange glow of a fire.

"You can put that weapon down," he said, still smiling.

She chuckled shyly, then revealed the hatchet she had been hiding behind her back. She wiggled it between them like nothing more than a child's toy. "Can't be too safe these days."

"You can say that again," Rogot laughed, then he gestured inside. "May I?"

"Yes," she said, moving away from the threshold, "please."

"Thank you," said Rogot, and he slipped inside, having to duck low to fit through the entrance.

"Come on out, Agnes," the woman said.

A moment later, a preteen girl with blonde hair and big eyes emerged from behind some hanging linens. "Hello," she said sheepishly.

Rogot nodded. "M'lady."

"You're a big ole man," Agnes said.

"Agnes!" the older woman balked.

Rogot chuckled. "It's okay. I am bigger than most. It's a compliment, as being big here and now comes in handy.

The woman flattened her thinning hair. "My name's Gemma. This here's my daughter Agnes."

"Good to meet you both. You're all alone out here?"

Gemma frowned. "Not 'till Shamus died last month." She turned to her daughter Agnes. "Or was it last year?"

Agnes only shrugged, sad look on her pretty face.

"I understand," said Rogot. "Time doesn't move like it used to." Last month very well could have been last year, but then again last year might have been a decade ago. "Anyways, you seem to have a nice place here. No problems?"

"Well, it seems we found us a perfect little haven. Too close to the castle for anyone to come lookin', yet too far to be bothered by Sour Foot's magic."

Rogot flashed his yellowing teeth. "A little slice of heaven right in the middle of hell."

"Just about, yes," Gemma agreed. She turned to her daughter. "Agnes, some milk and egg chowder for the man, please. Warm it in the hearth."

"Delicious," said Rogot. "Any luck with the garden out front?"

"Nothin' but roots. Carrots, potatoes, yams, you know. But we aren't picky. Just happy to eat." A thought fluttered in her eyes. "And your name?"

"Ah, my apologies. Serenhelm is what they called me before. Seren for short. My father called me Helm."

Gemma nodded. "Nice to meet you, Seren. Please, have a seat."

Rogot did so with a nod, big legs spilling over the thin piece of furniture, wood creaking like it might explode beneath him.

"What brings you out this way?" Gemma asked while her daughter stirred the kettle.

"If I'm truthful, and I believe you've earned it, I'm a grave robber."

Gemma sat across from him. "Well, compared to most everyone else these days, that's honest work. The dead got no need for coin."

"At least not the ones I borrow from," Rogot added. "And that's what it is. *Borrowing*. It all goes back to the dirt someday."

"Truth be told," Gemma agreed.

The young girl Agnes sat a steaming bowl before Rogot. It was a creamy soup made from goats milk with chunks of boiled eggs, carrots and potatoes. Rogot took a bite and moaned. It was nowhere near the quality of the tinker's stew and lacked a good deal of salt, but it was warm and hearty nonetheless.

He took a second bite, grinning as he fingered a stack of gold coins from his purse. "Well worth it," he said, placing the coins on the table.

Gemma was clearly holding back her delight, then after a moment she snatched up the coins and they disappeared into the folds of her clothing. "Thank you, fine man. Kindness is few and far between these days."

He nodded as he chewed, then gave Agnes a sidelong glance. She was standing in the corner of the small cabin, hands clasped before her, eyes on the floor.

"Any prospects for the girl?"

"Pardon?" Gemma asked.

"A man," Rogot clarified. "She's pretty enough. Looks fertile too."

"Oh no," Gemma said. "Nothing's out there but the dead, dying and utterly insane."

"That's a fact," Rogot agreed. He then pulled another pile of gold from his purse and stacked those where the first had been.

When he didn't explain, only continued eating, the woman asked, "And what's that for?"

"For the trouble," Rogot said, all politeness gone from his voice.

"It's no trouble?" Gemma chuckled.

"Not yet," Rogot said simply, then took the last bite of soup, chewed, swallowed.

"Pardon?" she asked at last, voice quivering.

Without a word, Rogot was up and out of his seat, head clocking the ceiling. He grabbed Agnes by the wrist, spun her up, around and onto his shoulder. Agnes shrieked, and Gemma was up dashing around the table, arms flailing at Rogot. Rogot grabbed the woman's pudgy face, lifted her into the air, then slammed her down on the table. The table broke in half, and the woman hit the floor with such force the boards buckled.

"Ooooh!" she howled. "My ribs!"

"I'm sorry," Rogot said calmly, voice completely void of sympathy. "You'll be grateful come morning."

He opened the door and stepped outside, girl still screaming and thrashing over his shoulder. As he made his way across the clearing, Gemma scrambled outside, falling to her knees in front of the cabin.

"Please!" she cried. "She's my only daughter! My baby!"

He glanced back. "There's more at stake," he said. "More things to lose than this girl."

He looked away, then turned again, pausing this time. The goat and chickens were gone. The garden too.

"She lied to you," a man said.

Rogot spun towards the dead thickets. Leaning against the colorless trunk of a knobby tree, leather flask in hand, was the tinker. He was wearing the same maroon robes, shiny leather boots as black as his hair.

"You," Rogot said.

The tinker smiled, white teeth glistening. "She lied to you," he repeated.

"Who?"

"The witch."

"She can't have lied," Rogot retorted. "She was charmed."

The tinker came off the tree and put away his flask. "Forgive me. She didn't lie, only withheld the truth."

Rogot was partially aware that Gemma had stopped screaming, and Agnes was now limp and silent over his shoulder. "If you have something to say, then fucking say it."

"Sour Foot needs a still-beating heart, yes. One from a virgin, yes. This is a homestead northwest of the lake, yes. Except, she never specified who actually lives here."

There was suddenly laughter coming from behind Rogot. Shrill, inhuman cackling. Rogot turned. Gemma was still on her knees in the dirt, only now she was smiling, teeth sharp as daggers. If she had looked old before, now she looked ancient. Someone else was laughing, this one right in his ear. It was Agnes, only now she too was as old as her mother, as withered and bruised as an apple left in the sun.

Rogot slung her to the ground. She reached out a clawed hand and he slapped it away. She then rolled to her belly, arms and legs bending inwards like a spider's, and she began scuttling back to the cabin. Rogot grabbed her ankle, wrenched her back, then stomped hard on the back of her head. Her skull crunched under his boot, black brains bursting out in every direction.

Gemma leapt to her feet. "You fucker!" she screeched. "I'll eat your cock for dinner!" She jumped into the air. Five feet, ten feet, fifteen feet. As she soared over Rogot, purple tentacles uncoiled from her back, slapping down at him like whips. He latched onto one and bit it, black ichor spewing into his beard. The woman howled and flopped down into the dirt, tentacles writhing.

Rogot drew his knife with one hand while he tore the shirt from Agnes's corpse with the other. He cut a symbol into her back, pulseless blood oozing, then smacked his hand down on the carving. "I exile you both!" he screamed. "With the power of god blood, I banish you from my kingdom!"

Gemma squealed like a dying coyote. "Not your kingdom anymore!"

Rogot ground his teeth. "As long as I draw breath, this land is mine!"

He balled his fist, then hammered it down on the dead witch's back. The ground beneath the corpse split open with a sound like lightning. The opening was only a half foot wide and three feet long, but it was black and bottomless. A rush of air burst upwards, carrying with it the insane wailing of countless tortured souls. A dozen sets of bony fingers reached up from the darkness, pinching, grabbing at empty air, grabbing at each other. Agnes was pulled through, spine snapping as her body folded in half.

Gemma was next, wrenched backward, bones crunching as she too was folded in half, then folded a second time, a third time and a fourth time. Her crumpled body bounced across the field like a tumbleweed before disappearing into the screaming void. Rogot fell back, the ground slammed shut and thunder rolled out for miles before all was silent again.

His shoulders rose and fell, chest heaving. "Fucking witches," he grumbled.

"Some useful tricks you have there," the tinker commented as he waited nearby.

Rogot climbed to his feet. "Doesn't always work." He slapped his hands on his trousers and gazed around the dusty clearing. "Why would she trick me?"

The tinker sighed and smiled. "Rogot, god blood, King From Before, don't overthink this. Why *wouldn't* she trick you? What other motive does she need besides causing you trouble?"

Rogot grunted, then asked, "Why are you here? Expecting me to pick up a few more wounds?"

"Quite the opposite," said the tinker. "And I have this for you." He reached into his robes and pulled out a spherical glass jar, exterior wrapped tightly in metal netting. Inside was a pinkish liquid, something pulsing deep within.

Rogot squinted and took a step forward.

"A still-beating heart," explained the tinker. Then, as an afterthought. "Oh, a virgin, too."

Rogot grimaced. "From where? Whom?"

"From my world. A young male."

Rogot took another step. "Why?"

"As I said, mutual interest."

Rogot closed the gap between them and snatched the jar away, then glared down at the heart pumping in the liquid. "It looks… *small.*"

"Oh, yes. It's from a hog."

Rogot's eyes flashed up to the tinker's. "A hog?"

"Exactly. There's no need for it to be a human heart. Another detail the witch failed to mention."

Rogot bunched up his lips. "This better work."

"If it doesn't, you'll be dead." He sipped from his flask and shrugged. "Besides, what other choice do you have?"

Rogot simply grunted, then dug for his purse. When he looked back, the tinker was gone.

"Wow!" Arigot cheered as he ran from the forest. "How did you do that?"

Rogot ignored the boy, eying the tree line for signs of the tinker.

"Will you teach me?" the boy begged. "Please!"

"Hush, boy," said Rogot. "You shout as if all danger has been extinguished from the world. Far from it."

The boy rolled out his bottom lip. "Sorry," he said softly. "But, how did you do it? Will you kill Sour Foot like that?"

"No," Rogot answered as he tucked the jar into his furs. "He's too powerful, and one must break certain rules to be banished. Besides, it wouldn't do us much good. They're not truly gone from this world, just imprisoned."

"Oh," the boy said, eyes full of wonder.

"Now come on. Follow me."

The Chamberlain

The rolling land gave way to a flat expanse of barren earth. A light breeze whipped up loose dirt, clouding the air and turning the sky dirty brown.

"I am Rogot!" the boy screamed, slamming his stick into the ground. "God blood! I banish you out!" Then he pointed the stick at the shit-colored sky and roared, forcing something deep and unnatural into his voice.

Rogot chuckled. "What are you doing?"

"I'm being you, Father. I'm banishing Sour Foot."

Rogot shook his head with a smile. "I told you it won't work like that."

The boy tossed his stick away and rushed to catch up with his father. "It's still fun to pretend."

"That it is," Rogot agreed. "Pretend all you can, my son." He clapped Arigot on the shoulder. "But there's no need pretending to be me. You are a great prince, a protector, and one day you will rule these lands."

"Yes!" Arigot cheered. "I will save the realm, and all will sing my name!"

Rogot gave the boy a sad look, then turned to the dusty horizon and set his jaw.

"It's okay, Father. They will sing your name too."

Rogot snorted. "I have enough songs. Perhaps they'll name an ale after me instead. That would be nice."

They walked on for what seemed like days. It *could* have been days, *could* have been years, *could* have been five minutes. The sky lay hidden behind a veil of swirling dust, no sunrise or sunset, and the light never changed, air always charged with an ugly brown glow.

A town emerged in the haze. Just a hut at first, taking shape in the dirty gloom, and then five huts. They found the first two homes abandoned, wooden furniture coated with an inch of dust. In the third hut they found a smear of black blood dried to the wall above a circle of bowls. The dishes were crusty with chunks of grey meat, dead flies spotting the rot, and the bowls themselves had been cut from the crowns of human skulls. Eight partially decomposed corpses lay in the fourth hut. Six adults, two children. The children had black yawning gouges across their throats, and the others had similar wounds up their forearms.

"Should we bury them?" the boy asked.

"No," said Rogot, and they moved on.

Some miles later, the wind eased and the dirt became a rippled floor of green glass. Oily black clouds choked the sky, thick as coal smoke, and blue lightning pulsed silently on the horizon.

"We're getting close," Rogot said dreadfully.

"Father?" the boy asked, voice quivering with fear.

Rogot looked to Arigot, finding him kneeling there on the glass. The boy was examining his ankle. A dark scab had formed in a perfect circle around the base of his leg, just above the ankle bone.

"It itches," the boy said.

"Leave it be," Rogot ordered. He pulled the burlap sack from his coat and lowered it to Arigot. "Ride for a while; rest your legs."

"Okay," the boy agreed softly, then crawled inside.

Rogot pulled the bag shut, and once again, Arigot's golden glow was snuffed from the world. He slung it over his shoulder and marched. Crows cawed overhead, crickets chirped and toads bellowed around his feet, yet there was no sign of life anywhere he could see. It was as if the air itself was mocking him, full of dead things laughing. He hunkered away into his mind, consciousness drifting as his body marched on without command. He reminisced on the day he was brought into the world. Not born. No, created, then given dominion over the Creator's most recent iteration. He was then given his wife, a piece of his very own soul, and together they had made his son, a piece of them both.

Life had never been easy, but it was happy. Eras came and went, generations drifted on like clouds, and always Rogot served. There were wars and there was peacetime, famine and droughts, a plague once every hundred years or so, but his kingdom endured it all… all until the invasion. The end was a blur, like the final moments before sleep, but the emotions remained. Fear, strange things from far-off lands, war, fire, death and then Sour Foot's attempt to save it all. Afterwards, only this. This never-ending nightmare, this hell, this stretching and shrinking of time, insanity now some contagious thing, everyone lost to wander in a place where life and death are no longer opposites but a spectrum of cruelties.

The boy's soft moaning pulled Rogot from his thoughts. He knelt on the glass, swung the sack down and gently opened it, releasing the golden light from inside. "Arigot?" he asked. "My boy, what is it?"

Arigot slowly crawled forth, rolled onto his back and pulled his knee to his chest. Rogot saw that the circular scab around his ankle was now an open wound, leaking blood that dribbled from his heel.

"It hurts," the boy groaned.

"Don't touch it," Rogot ordered. "It's okay. Be still." He tore a strip from his already torn shirt, then used it to wrap the boy's ankle. "We're almost there."

The boy looked around, clutching his ankle with a grimace. The ground was solid green glass as far as he could see in every direction, rippled like an ocean frozen still in the midst of a storm. Above was no sky, rather a high ceiling of clumpy black clouds. "What is this place?"

"This was our home," Rogot said, voice tight with sadness. "The outer borders, at least. When Sour Foot communed with the Outer Thing, when he swung his final blow against the Invaders, the energy incinerated everything within ten miles of the castle. It vaporized all living things, reduced dirt to ash and sand, turning the ground itself into liquid fire. When it finally cooled, nothing remained but this lifeless glass."

"It's awful," said Arigot.

"Yes, it is. Now, come. Back inside."

Rogot held the sack open and the boy climbed in once more. Rogot shouldered it, situated his axe and hiked again. After another mile, he noticed the clouds beginning to move, drifting from left to right like the current of a black ocean. Another mile and the motion was faster, clouds curving ever so slightly as if circling something in the distance. Blue light crackled ahead, and Rogot saw something out there on the edge of the world, something hulking and black, alone on the horizon like the last remaining tooth in an empty mouth.

"I'm coming," he growled.

An hour or so later and he was coughing, black tar speckling his lips and beard. He spat a big black glob onto the glass between his boots, wiped his mouth and raised his chin. The motion above was faster now, clouds wheeling over a dark castle, circling a pillar of blue light erecting from the structure's center. No, not light. Energy. Raw, quivering, unstable power.

The ground began to slope upwards, glass folding over and over like molten steel overflowed from a crucible. They made fine enough steps, and Rogot climbed, brow furrowed at the castle above. Blue lightning crackled around the blue pillar, black clouds pulsing as they circled, monstrous wings backlit with each flash. *Wings of what?* It didn't matter. Almost finished. Death and salvation now neck and neck.

Rogue gales of wind hammered against him, grain and soot stung his skin, beard whipping, furs snapping, god blood pumping. Black froth gathered in the corners of his mouth, and he gritted his teeth, grumbling as he climbed the ever-steepening slope. His boots slipped and his knees thumped hard on the uneven glass. He tried to catch himself but sliced open his hand. "Fuck!"

His hair whipped in his face, beard flapping wildly. The castle was just ahead, staring down at him like a living thing. The blue pillar was so bright now Rogot had to squint, and the oily clouds continued round and round like a maelstrom.

"We should turn back!" Arigot cried from within the bag. "I think we're dying!"

"No, boy!" Rogot boomed over the howling winds. "Be strong!"

Rogot reached the base of the castle and fell against it with a groan. He let his axe clatter to the ground, then lowered the burlap sack from his shoulder. Arigot slithered weakly out, golden aura dim and flickering like a fire in rain. The boy rolled onto his back, twisted face turning to the hateful sky. Rogot's makeshift bandage had fallen loose, and the boy's foot was covered in blood, wound around the ankle now deep as bone. Rogot stared down at it with parted lips as he blinked against the wind.

"Look at me, my son," he said sternly, and Arigot peeled open his eyes. "Whatever happens in there, know that I love you."

The boy nodded silently.

"And you love me?"

The boy nodded again.

"Say it," Rogot demanded.

"I love you, Father."

Rogot smiled, black slime coating his teeth. "Good. Now, let's finish it."

He scooped the boy into his arms, then easily placed him into the bag. He shouldered the bag, shouldered his axe, then made his way along the castle perimeter. The portcullis was halfway up, one of the two inner doors standing wide open, just the way Rogot had left them all that time ago. The wind eased once he was under the archway, yet still it roared through the empty halls as if the castle itself was screaming. A courtyard lay beyond, grey grass over a field of grey dirt. A score or more corpses littered the area in every stage of decomposition. In the center was a large fountain encircled by statues of female angels. Water had once flowed from the stone carafes they held, though now most were dry, except for one dropping globs of black sludge and another whose carafe simply bellowed yellow steam.

Rogot walked into the yard, eyes instantly pained by the vertical beam of blue light piercing the clouds above. He could hear it. Warbling, throbbing, beating. Despite the discomfort, Rogot was tempted to look at it, to turn up his face and bask in its power. He wanted to cook in it, to *die* in it. He fought the urge, lowered his gaze and jogged across to a second archway beyond the clearing, zigzagging and skipping over corpses. Finally across, a dark hall stretched out before him lined with statues, some of them toppled over and broken on the cobbles.

From the gloom came a menacing voice. "Who dare trespass this holy temple?"

Rogot gripped the axe as he peered into the darkness. A figure was coming down the hall, not walking but gliding, feet hidden beneath tattered robes. Maybe it had no feet at all; maybe under all that soiled cloth were eight spider legs ushering it forward ever so smoothly. It could have been either or anything in between.

"I am Rogot the God Blood, King From Before."

"Rrrooooogot," the creature drawled.

He saw its face then, shadowed in a deep hood, slack and ashen skin, black lips and empty sockets where eyes should have been. Black tar rimmed the sockets and ran down its cheeks like poisoned tears. The only color was a gold chain hanging over the robes, a huge red stone swaying over its chest.

Rogot swallowed. "Mathilen?" He gazed with horror into those empty eyes, thought of the blue beam and his own suicidal desire to stare upon it, and he thought perhaps he might look similar after enough time in this place. "Mathilen, is that you?"

The creature's head shifted, eyeless face revealing nothing. "I was called that once, yes. Before the great Salvation."

"Mathilen, you were my chamberlain. We were friends. I trusted you."

"A dream within a dream," the creature mused. Then, casually changing the topic, it said, "None pass the threshold without my permission, and none are permitted without Sour Foot's approval."

"I have that which Sour Foot seeks."

The thing's head cocked again, so subtle it was hardly noticeable. It blinked its empty eyes, leathery lids smacking down over empty sockets. Then, it hovered backward and spun around as smoothly as a compass needle. "Come, god blood," it said as it glided back down the hall.

Rogot followed.

This place had been his home for many lifetimes, but now it was something almost entirely unrecognizable. A tomb? No, a corpse, for it had once been full of life. But like all living things in this ruined world, it wasn't quite dead either. There was power here, dark and twisted, hungry and merciless. Whispers leaked from empty rooms, shadows moved on their own accord, and someone or something seemed always just beyond the edge of his vision.

The chamberlain led Rogot through corridors stained black with mold, up a wide stairway littered with rat carcasses and across a dining hall where three headless corpses lay stacked within an enormous hearth. The bodies were naked and partially burnt, as if someone had attempted to set them on fire before losing interest. A brief yet horrified scream shot from the back corner of the room. Rogot spun, clutching his axe, but there was no one there, just some scattered chairs and an overturned table. Not entirely surprised, Rogot grunted and turned back to follow the chamberlain. At some point, the chamberlain had stopped, turned without a sound and was now waiting for

Rogot, empty eye sockets staring. That tar-streaked and lifeless face chilled Rogot all over again.

"They do that sometimes," it said, lips like the spasming sphincter of a dying monster.

Rogot had many questions, but said nothing.

Sour Foot

They wound down a narrow stairwell. Rogot remembered it being used by the castle staff, though Arigot liked to sneak off and use it himself, pretending it was his own secret passageway. They exited the stairs into a narrow hall, through another wide corridor, then at last they traversed a side entrance into the throne room.

The sound of the wind rose again, and Rogot saw that most of the ceiling was gone. A tight cluster of black clouds whirled above the opening, and the awful beam of blue light came directly inside. Except the pillar didn't simply stop when it touched the floor; it turned at an angle and slithered across the stones like an irradiated serpent, the entire length crackling and popping all the while. After several feet of slack it arched upwards, finally coming to an end between the shoulder blades of a giant man, currently hunched over with his back to Rogot.

Rogot was huge, all of eight feet tall and nearly half as wide. This other thing connected to the beam was twice Rogot's size. As the chamberlain drifted off into the darkness, Rogot wandered forward, making a wide semicircle around the giant. Sour Foot, enormous and swollen, back charred and discolored from constant contact with the blue light feeding him like the umbilical of an unborn child. His hair was white and unkempt, and shredded cloth hung around his waist and groin. He was sitting on his haunches with a corpse over one knee. One big hand was wrapped around the dead man's head, and the other was wielding a knife. Sour Foot was scalping the corpse one thin strip at a time. Rogot could hear the awful sound of tearing flesh mingled with the blade scraping along smooth skull. The corpse convulsed, wide eyes flashing between two of the fingers gripping its face, and Rogot realized with horror that it wasn't a corpse at all. The man was still alive, now screaming, voice muffled in Sour Foot's hand, but Rogot could see the eyes clearly. Glassy, huge and full of terror. There was no sentience there, not anymore. Just pain and insanity.

Sour Foot ripped what was left of the scalp from the man's bleeding head, then tossed him spinning across the room. The man shrieked for only a moment before he collided with a wall, bones crunching, blood bursting, and he crumpled to the floor.

Sour Foot waved his hand lazily. It glistened red with blood. "Mathilen brings me these things," he said with disgust, voice rumbling across the floor and up the walls, "these people, to help ease my pain. But it never does."

Not far from the giant was a huge pile of severed feet. The lowest and widest section was all bones, the ones at the top looked fresh and bloody, and every manner of decay formed the center bulk.

Sour Foot stood, shoulders hunched, and he turned to face Rogot, glowing umbilical trailing behind him. He had sunken eyes, bulbous features and a long, sharp chin. He wore no shoes, and his left foot remained in a constant state of change, always forming and rotting one after another. It was whole one moment, then would turn black, green, flesh rotting away to muscle and bone, then the flesh would reappear, fresh and moist, toenails would sprout, and again it would all decay, reform, decay, reform. He hobbled forward, left foot leaving behind sticky puss with every step.

His foot wasn't the only thing in constant transition. Random parts of his body were resizing and reshaping, as if none of it knew exactly what to be. His right pectoral muscle swelled, dropped and became a woman's breast. One arm lost all of its muscle, the hairs fell away and it shortened to something slender and feminine. The right side of his face became that of a beautiful woman for half a second before snapping back to the brutish appearance. It wasn't just any face, not some random wraith, but one Rogot recognized. It was his wife.

"I've been waiting for you," Sour Foot grumbled. "Waiting for my soul. It was you who took it, wasn't it?"

"You'll give her back to me?" Rogot asked though it sounded more like an order.

Sour Foot shrugged his massive shoulders. "I'll have no need for her."

Rogot pulled the glass jar from his furs and tossed it over. Sour Foot caught it, and the thing looked like a marble in his huge hand. "A still-beating heart. You've done well." His cold eyes met Rogot's. "And the other?"

Rogot lowered the burlap sack from his shoulder, opened it hesitantly, then slowly upended it before him. It wasn't Arigot who came forth, but a severed foot. It was partially decayed, skin brown and tightly dried to the bone beneath. It thumped to the floor, sending up a plume of golden dust.

Sour Foot hobbled forward, eyes gleaming.

Rogot drew back his shoulders and gripped his axe. "You'll give her back?" he repeated.

"Aye," Sour Foot said, voice flat as he gazed down at the rotting appendage. He moseyed closer like a man entranced, slack face shifting from monster to muse, foot rotting and healing over and over. He paused. "You'll try to kill me when it's done?"

Rogot nodded. "Aye."

"Very well," and he took the foot in his hand, gasping when it touched his fingers.

"Father?" the boy asked, and Rogot turned to see Arigot standing beside him. "What are you doing?" The boy's golden shimmer was fading, losing brightness and turning grey.

"It's okay, my son," Rogot said, voice quivering. "You'll be alright."

Sour Foot cocked his big head. "Who do you speak with? You have only one son, and-" He gasped again, body spasming, and he began to shrink. He doubled over and shriveled like a wilting flower. As he did so, something else was protruding from his side, swelling and writhing beneath the skin like a burrowing maggot. The more Sour Foot shrank, the larger the growth became, until finally the flesh there was so tight it burst. A naked woman came flopping from inside his body like a newborn baby, floundering to the floor in a puddle of red gelatin. Sour Foot let out an orgasmic moan, body shuddering. At last, his transformation ended, and he stood equal with Rogot. The severed foot he had been holding was gone, and at some point during the process the glass jar had shattered, leaving blood and shards scattered all around. The woman lay still, dark hair plastered to her face.

"I don't feel so well," Arigot whined. His skin was waxy and pale, aura now completely extinguished.

"It's okay," said Rogot, eyes wet with tears. "You're saving us. You're saving everyone. It's what you wanted. It's magic."

Sour Foot began to laugh. "Oh, how deserving! The madness has taken hold of even our great king! Rogot the God Blood, as crazed as the rest!"

Sour Foot drew back his shoulders and the glowing umbilical fell free, along with a black scab as big around as a serving dish. Beneath the wound was a glistening circle of pink flesh. The blue cord slithered back across the cathedral before reeling up into the sky and disappearing. The spinning clouds slowed, then began drifting apart to reveal a grey sky. Sour Foot shrugged and rolled his shoulders, grinning with relief as if finally free from a great weight. He stepped forward, rotten foot healing one final time.

He spread his arms and smiled. "Have you forgotten your only son?"

Rogot's eyes darted from the naked woman to Sour Foot to Arigot, then back to Sour Foot.

Sour Foot chuckled. "Or have you simply replaced me, Father?"

Rogot pounced, roaring as he swung the giant axe. Sour Foot ducked, catching the haft with his forearm. He shot up, throwing Rogot off balance, then kicked him square in the chest. The old king went flipping back across the cathedral, smashed through a stone column, then slid to a stop some fifty paces from Sour Foot. He had managed to retain his axe the entire time, and he stood, shrugged off the bear furs and bolstered his stance. His huge arms, now exposed, bulged under the weight of his weapon, knobby veins and sinew standing out against tight skin.

"Let me help you!" Arigot pleaded, suddenly appearing at Rogot's side.

"You already have, my son. You've done your part."

Across the room, Sour Foot leapt. He soared in a high arch, wailing as he came down over Rogot. Rogot swung upwards, but Sour Foot grabbed the blade with bare hands. The force of his landing sent Rogot skidding back on the cobbles.

"Focus, old man!" Sour Foot demanded. "You speak to wraiths and illusions while your enemy stands before you!"

"He is not a wraith!" Rogot snapped. "Nor an illusion!"

Arigot circled around them, wringing his hands nervously. "What is he saying, Father? What's happening?"

Rogot pushed Sour Foot back, then jabbed his axe like a spear. The upper point of each blade stabbed into Sour Foot's chest. Sour Foot slapped the axe away and two lines of dark blood came dripping down his torso.

Sour Foot gazed around, eyes narrow. He looked over the boy but didn't seem to notice him. "Not a wraith," he muttered, "not an illusion, and if I'm to believe you aren't mad…" His words trailed off, but his eyes came to lock on Rogot's. He dropped his brow and smiled. "Oh! You don't say? Could that really be possible?" He spun, greasy hair whipping. "Boy? Can you hear me? Did your father tell you what he did? Did he tell you what you are?"

"Don't listen to him!" Rogot countered.

"Father?" Arigot wept as he hunkered nearby.

Rogot charged. Sour Foot spun, caught the axe in one hand, Rogot's throat in the other, then slammed him to the floor so hard the cobbles shattered.

He wrenched the axe free, spun it around his head, then chopped Rogot's hand off at the wrist. The old king howled, grabbed his spewing nub and rolled away.

Sour Foot followed, shoulders hunched like a gorilla's. "A limb for a limb, dear Father."

Rogot rolled onto his feet and jumped, came over Sour Foot's head and grabbed a fistful of his hair. He pulled Sour Foot off his feet and onto to his back, then stomped on his face. Rogot stomped again, and again and again. Teeth and blood splattered, Sour Foot's nose collapsed and his lips tore to ribbons. Alas, he managed to grab Rogot's foot and toss him aside.

"Tell him!" Sour Foot roared through a mouthful of blood and devastated meat. "Tell *me!*"

Rogot grabbed his axe in one hand, then climbed to his feet. He stood ten paces from Sour Foot, the two warriors standing ready to pounce.

"I loved you," Rogot declared, shoulders heaving.

"And what happened?" Sour Foot asked, blood oozing from his ruined mouth and nose.

"Father?" Arigot whimpered.

Rogot looked to the boy. He was crouched off to the side, skin colorless and slightly translucent. "You were my greatest achievement, my greatest love. I remember you like this. Small, frail, perfectly innocent. But you grew, my son. You became a man, a soldier, and a leader of men. You were my equal, and I was proud to admit it. But you were ambitious, dangerously so, and you longed to control magic." Rogot breathed deeply, tears rolling from his eyes. "I warned you, my son. But when the Invaders came, you're desire to save us outweighed your reason. You sought greater power, and you communed directly with the source, with an Outer Thing, the worst of them all."

Arigot whimpered. "What are you saying, Father? I don't remember!"

"I'm so sorry, my boy."

"Look at me!" Sour Foot demanded. "And say my name!"

Rogot did so. "Arigot, my son. I am sorry."

Sour Foot, *Arigot,* stepped closer. "You mutilated me, took my soul, and *what,* befriended it? Used it to mend your guilt?"

Rogot's eyes found the boy again. He was thinning and fading away, almost completely invisible now. "I protected him."

The boy stood and reached out. "Father, wait!" He then dissolved into a thin mist, curled upwards, drifted across the room and into Sour Foot's body. Sour Foot sucked in a breath, rolled his neck, and smiled.

"Oh," he moaned, "to be whole again." His eyes trained on Rogot's. "I tried to save us, and you made me a cripple, stole my soul and fused me to my own mother." His face grew slack, and he turned to the naked woman lying lifeless on the floor. "She was there all the while, yet I couldn't speak to her. I could feel her sorrow like it was my own, though she was impossible to console. I had all the power in the universe, and still I couldn't set her free."

"There was more at stake!" Rogot said desperately. "The entire realm was twisted beyond recognition! Arigot, there was more to consider than our own family! And I didn't know… I didn't know taking your flesh would bind you to hers! I didn't know taking your soul would bind you to *that thing!* I thought I could spare you!" He curled the fingers of his remaining hand, groping the air as if he could hold that ancient moment and watch it all play out again. "I thought I could spare you, that maybe I could keep your spirit safe and hidden while I found a way to free you from the Outer Thing! I didn't know, Arigot! I thought it would save you, not imprison you! I-"

Sour Foot leapt like a baboon, cutting Rogot short. They collided, snarling, biting, punching and shoving, exchanging the axe like children fighting over a toy. Handfuls of Rogot's beard and Sour Foot's hair drifted to the ground around their contest. Growling, pinching, hacking. Gouts of blood streaked the air and slapped the stone. They tumbled and wrestled, teeth bared, twisting arms and breaking fingers. Sour Foot came up on top, axe between them, and he pressed it down against Rogot's face. Rogot fought back, only elongating the pain as the steel slowly cleaved away his cheek muscle. Blood oozed from Sour Foot's mouth onto Rogot's face, blurring his vision and filling his mouth with the taste of iron.

Motion caught Rogot's eye. Someone was hunched over his wife. Someone in maroon robes, treating her, feeding her elixirs as he rubbed balm over her bare skin. Rogot growled, straining to press against the axe as it flayed his cheekbone, though still he watched. The woman began to move. She sat up, fingered hair from her face and covered her breasts.

"Rogot?" she said, voice full of confusion. "Arigot, my son?"

Sour Foot's eyes widened. He released his grip on the axe and spun around to face his mother. Rogot grabbed the weapon, swung wide and sank the huge blade into Sour Foot's neck. Sour Foot's head drooped to one side, neck yawning open like a red mouth. The axe slipped free, and Rogot heaved it up into Sour Foot's forehead. The blade cracked open his skull and stuck there, pressurized blood and brain gargling from the narrow crevice where bone met steel. Red mist hissed out with the gore, and fleshy sludge came rolling down Sour Foot's face. He stood, axe still in his head, haft sticking out like a horn. He pawed the air before him, fingers grazing the wooden handle, then at last, he collapsed.

Rogot rolled to his side, sucking air through a mouthful of blood. He coughed, rose to his knees, then staggered to his feet. He groped the bloody nub where his hand had been, blood leaking through his fingers. His cheek muscle was a sliver of meat hanging from his jaw, wet bone glistening beneath. His eyes were swelling and turning black, nose crooked and bloody, and great red patches of flesh showed through his tattered beard. "Fuck," he grumbled.

He tried wiping blood and tears from his face, though only made it worse. Looking through the ruined ceiling he could see hues of orange in the grey sky. *A sunrise? A real sunrise?* A white cloud drifted by, the first white cloud he had seen since the world broke.

His gaze turned down to the corpse at his feet, to his son, to the boy who had become a man, a hero, and then a villain. He was nearly decapitated, and the weight of the axe had turned his head at an unnatural angle, neck twisted open and gushing.

"A dirty business," a man said over Rogot's shoulder. "Unfair all around."

Rogot turned to see the tinker draped in maroon robes with a flask in his hand. "I did what was necessary," said Rogot, "and now it's finished."

The tinker sipped from his flask. "A good king, after all."

Rogot sneered. "I assume you'll want something in return?"

The tinker shrugged. "Mutual interest, remember? Now, every world is safe from Sour Foot, same as yours. You've served the Creator well."

Rogot's shoulders rose and fell. "It is my purpose."

"Easier said than done. If everyone served their purpose, all the worlds would be balanced, coexisting in perfect harmony, and you and I both know that isn't the case."

Rogot simply grunted, eyes locked with the eyes of his dead son.

"Perhaps you'll be rewarded."

"I'm not seeking-" but when Rogot looked over his shoulder, the tinker was gone.

Farther back was his wife, now standing with an old curtain draped around her shoulders. Her face was pale, expression like that of a confused child. "Rogot?" she asked nervously. Her eyes flashed to the severed cheek hanging from his face, to his missing hand, to the battered corpse on the cobbles.

"Sweet Love," said Rogot, closing the space between them. "Everything is alright."

"What… What happened?"

"Don't worry now. You should rest. I'll explain everything."

He placed his arm around her, but when he moved to usher her forward, she stopped him.

"Wait," she said. "Who was that man?"

"Just a tinker, Sweet Love. Nothing more."

"But." She blinked and licked her lips. "He gave me something. A gift."

Rogot's eyes narrowed. "A *gift?*"

She pulled the linen back to reveal her stomach. It was swollen slightly, protruding with the first signs of pregnancy.

Rogot blinked. "How?" he breathed. "Another baby?"

"No," she said. "Not another. *Arigot*, made new again." She rubbed her belly. "Our baby boy."

He placed his hand over hers, and together they grazed her swollen stomach. "My son," said Rogot. "My boy."

He gazed around the empty cathedral now glowing with rays of yellow sunlight. A bright blue sky shone overhead, scattered with clumps of white mist. He grumbled deep in his throat, then muttered, *"Mutual interest."*

END

The Sacrifice

By: Richard Cartwright

A neirin took a sip of tea. *Perfect. Hamish was right. This was an excellent blend.* He reminded himself to get a couple more chests from the tea merchant the next time he flew to the capital. As he reached for his new book, a gonging sound echoed down the tunnel from the cave entrance.

High pitched wailing joined the metallic beat. He sighed.

Another one. He stood up and removed his warm robe and willed the shift, bronze skin and brown hair morphing into blue scales.

He stopped at the enormous door, breaking up the walls of floor-to-ceiling bookcases that dominated the room. Grabbing the large iron ring set some fifteen feet from the floor with his blue scaled arm. The door opened on noiseless hinges.

Aneirin's presence triggered the spell to light the first of the torches spaced down the passage, illuminating the dressed stone walls. The sound wasn't wailing, as he first thought, but cursing. *Interesting.*

Torches lit as he lumbered down the path, wings closed tightly to his sides. The stonework gave way to rough rock. What had started as a bright dot in the darkness had grown into an opening centered by the setting sun streaming through the cave entrance.

The cursing had slowed considerably over the half-hour journey. The peculiarity of the tunnel to pass sounds down the two-mile length from one side of the mountain range to the other allowed him to be aware of anything trying to poke around. Occasional roaring usually sufficed to discourage the foolish. The gonging told him that this was a different kind of foolishness.

The warm sunshine on his scales almost made up for the bright light. Aneirin squeezed his eyes shut and cracked his lids open to adjust. He never enjoyed flying into the sun, and coming out of the dim tunnel wasn't much better.

"What's wrong with your eyes?"

He turned toward the voice. The human girl wasn't the usual offering. She was tall, red-haired and a bit chubby, truth be told. She seemed older, too.

"My eyes are fine. That should be the least of your worries right now, human."

"Right. I am chained to this post, about to be eaten alive because the idiots in my village think that a virgin sacrifice to a dragon will somehow cause it to rain and save the crops. It's a lot easier than getting off their lazy rears and building the windmills that I suggested to pump water and irrigate the fields. Plenty of water in the wells. Just need to get it to the fields."

"You know of windmills?"

"Of course. My father was the teacher and keeper of records till... he died last winter." A look of sadness crossed her face as the tone of her voice softened. "I had been teaching the children and recording the business of the town since."

"Why would your village want to lose someone as valuable as yourself?"

"Because why keep the girl whose father trained her for the job all of her life when you have the headman's son who drank his way out of university and needs a position? Plus, there was a shortage of maidens in the area."

"Shortage?"

"A lot of eligible girls decided to... remove themselves from consideration. I just wish I had taken my own advice," the woman said bitterly, "Anyway, just get it over with."

"Right, that can't be comfortable," he moved to the post, reaching out to the chain. The girl's composure broke. She squealed and tried to get away, stretching the links taunt.

He inserted a talon into the chain link at the top of the post and turned his paw. The link separated and the former captive slumped to the ground.

"You can get up now. You're free," The human didn't budge. Impatient, he repeated himself, "Girl, I am not going to eat you. No one is going to hurt you. Hey, say something?"

He reentered the study, carrying a tray laden with cheese, fruit, and bread, along with a pot of the good tea. Once he had realized that she had fainted, he cast a sleeping spell on her to keep her that way. Bitter experience had taught him that human females traveled better slung across the neck of a dragon unconscious.

The girl was up from the couch he had draped her on, having revived from her sleep. The red marks around her wrists caused by the iron cuffs he had removed had faded a bit.

"So, the afterlife has books," the girl said to herself as she traced her fingers along the spines of the books lining the shelves.

"I can't attest to the afterlife, but I am rather proud of my collection."

She turned, red shoulder-length hair whipping around, "Who are you?"

"Aneirin. Your host. Since I did not eat you, I decided to put together this dinner tray instead. Care to join me?"

"Eat me... where is the dragon?" She turned again, seeing the oversized door to the tunnel.

Eyes wide, she faced Aneirin again, "Noooooo..."

"Afraid so. Come sit and eat. The bread is just from the oven, and the butter is excellent. Much better than frightened virgins. At least, so I am told. And your name, fair maiden?"

Aneirin was pretty sure no human would name their child "Mab ast!". Plus, how could a daughter be a son of a bitch? He waved his hand to lock the door to the study before she got to it. That didn't stop her from tugging wildly at the smaller ring set below the larger one to try to open it.

After a minute of fruitless pulling and cursing worthy of the dockside at Stormharbour, the woman took a deep breath and turned.

"Dilys, Dilys Bard's Daughter. Of Mohald. I didn't know dragons could take human form."

"We don't advertise the fact."

"I guess you wouldn't be offering me a meal if you were going to eat me," Dilys replied as she slowly walked back to Aneirin. She stopped. "Unless you are planning to fatten me up for later?"

"You don't need fattening. I think the fact that I am offering you bread from my oven instead of putting you in it should speak for itself."

Aneirin was glad to see the fear leave her features. The flinty-eyed anger wasn't an improvement. What had he said?

"I am not fat! I'm big boned and well proportioned!"

Some things about females are universal. At least she's not frightened anymore, "I apologize. I meant no offense. I give you my oath that no harm shall befall you from me."

Dilys visibly relaxed, "It's said that a dragon never betrays his oath."

"Very true. Please, sit. The bread is not getting any warmer."

Sitting across from him, she reached for a piece of the warm bread. She buttered it and took a bite. The look of bliss on her face pleased Aneirin more than it should have.

"This is very good. And... I apologize for my outburst. Villagers often commented on my hip... appearance. Often cruelly," her eyes widened, "You have smoke coming from your nose."

Aneirin reigned in his dragon. What caused that flash of anger?

"It's a dragon thing. Nothing a good cup of tea won't solve," he replied, smoothly as he reached for the pot.

"Okay. So what's next? I know you promised that eating me is off the table, but you seem to be alone. Considering that the village was sacrificing virgins about every ten years, I am concerned about what happened to the others."

"What I normally do is take anyone like yourself to Wrexham. That's the town in the valley on the east side from the mouth of my cave. The people there think I am a wizard and wise man who occasionally comes across endangered girls. They are taken in and find a place in the community."

"Don't they see you transform?"

"Normally, they never know of my dual nature as I cast sleep on them whilst in dragon form. They don't awaken until I am well on my way down the path to Wrexham. I have quite a reputation for rescuing young girls from nasty dragons. The only reason that I didn't treat you the same is that there's a terrible storm over the town. I hate traveling in the rain. Plus, I was curious about you. I was surprised that you stayed conscious so long before fainting."

"I did not faint!"

The look of indignation was adorable, Aneirin thought.

"Then passed out."

"Of course, I passed out. I didn't get anything to eat all day. The headman didn't see the point of wasting food on me."

"So you were faint with hunger. You weren't scared at all," Aneirin replied with a slight smile.

"Perhaps a little." Dillys grimaced. "I was chained to a post for the express purpose of being eaten by a ravenous beast. Then, this giant clawed paw is reaching towards me. I think a bit of fear was called for," her expression turned curious, "So, this transformation process, can you do it again? I was sort of unconscious when you did it before. Excellent tea, by the way."

"I am glad you like it. And no, I have no desire to disrobe to satisfy your curiosity."

"Disrobe?"

"Did I look dressed in my dragon form?"

"Not that I recall."

"Well, don't you think the terror effect would be ruined if a blue-scaled dragon was running around in a tunic and trousers?"

Dilys went quiet. After a moment, she got a small smile on her face and replied, "True. Well, maybe later. About your books. This is quite a collection. My father's was a tenth of this, and he spent his entire life collecting it."

"I have many contacts among traders who pass through Wrexham. Plus, I can fly anywhere on the continent in a day or three."

"I noticed that Bettan's treatise on the formation of rocks is by the tray. What do you think of..."

Aneirin couldn't recall a more pleasurable evening as the two discussed a wide range of topics, from rocks, to physiology, magic, to astronomy. It ended when he realized she had nodded off while looking up a passage from Trevyn about the divisibility of matter. Smiling, he scooped her up and placed her on the bed of one of his seldom-used guest rooms, covering her with a blanket.

Looking out the window facing the Wrexham valley, the clearing sky wiped the smile from his face.

Dilys awoke feeling more refreshed than she had in weeks. She got up in search of a place to relieve herself and some food. The second door to the room led to a bathroom and a self-cleaning chamber pot.

The size of the kitchen and larder was amazing. One door opened to a room that was icy cold with hanging meat and poultry. Another was cool rather than freezing and contained produce, jugs of milk, and racks of eggs. She busied herself on a perfectly mundane coal-burning stove cooking eggs, bacon, sausage, and pancakes. She started biscuits and sausage gravy. There was no reason to let the drippings go to waste.

"I thought I smelled something good. You didn't have to do that. You are my guest," a deep voice rumbled from behind her.

Dilys nearly lost the pancake she was flipping at the sound of Aneirin's voice. She sat the pan aside and turned towards the sound. He had exchanged the belted robe of last night for a brown linen shirt tucked into green woolen trousers held up by a wide black leather belt. He had tied back the dark brown hair that had hung free last night. She realized for the first time that his eyes were the same sky blue as his scales. And he was clean-shaven, unlike the men of her village. She decided she liked it.

"I want to make sure that you don't get hungry and decide on me for a meal."

"No danger of that with how this kitchen smells and what's on the table." Aneirin clearly admired the heaping plates of ham, scrambled eggs, rashers of bacon, sausage, biscuits and gravy. "How did you know that I like pancakes?"

She blushed. "Actually I like pancakes. I thought you might too from the keg of syrup I found in the pantry."

"Good guess," he replied, taking the big platter of steaming pancakes from the counter and placing them on the table, "please have a seat."

Dilys couldn't recall a time when a man other than her father had pulled out a chair and made sure she was seated. She looked at Aneirin expectantly. He didn't touch anything, returning her gaze. He spoke after a few heartbeats.

"The tradition I was raised with was that the lady eats first. Please serve yourself, or I would be glad to serve you since you labored to make this fine meal."

After a moment of shock, she found her voice, "Thank you sir. The men of my village always got the first choice of what was on the table." She speared two pancakes and, after placing a scoop of butter on top, drenched the stack with syrup. The first bite was sweet, buttery, and delicious.

Aneirin took that as a signal to fill his own plate and ate with speed and gusto. Always with precise manners, he rapidly put away three helpings of a bit of everything on the table.

After carefully chewing and swallowing the biscuit he had used to wipe up the last bits of gravy on his plate, the dragon looked at Dilys. "I think this is the best sausage gravy I have ever eaten. In fact, I think this is the best breakfast I have ever had. I am not much of a cook."

Dilys was pleased with the way that Aneirin delighted in her cooking. She had built on the basics her mother had imparted to her before the winter cough had taken the woman. Her grieving father lost interest in eating and

Dilys mastered every recipe she could get her hands on to entice the older man to eat. At last she asked, "Don't you have someone to cook and clean?"

"I don't really need anyone. It's just me. Plus, I have to shift periodically. Otherwise, I feel like I am constantly itchy," he grimaced," Some of us don't care to shift. They cause a lot of travelers' tales about angry dragons."

"Why don't they shift? Sounds silly not to if they are uncomfortable."

"A lot of dragons don't like humans and being reminded of our human form. It has never made a lot of sense to me, but a fair number of my brothers and sisters feel that way."

"If I go to live in the village, could I come back to visit and read your books?"

Dilys saw Aneirin get a pained expression as he carefully replied, "You won't remember the books. Or me as a dragon. I will veil your memories. Humans can't know of our dual nature."

"But, I won't tell anyone."

"I know you would never intend to. But you might slip."

'What if I just stayed here? You like my cooking, and I am a great housekeeper!"

Dilys knew she was babbling. But she suddenly realized that last evening had been one of her best in recent memory. It had been the first intellectual conversation she had had since her father's passing. Even if she didn't recall the discussions or Aneirin's library, she would still have that void in Wrexham. She found that the idea of not remembering the dragon caused a pang she didn't understand.

"You don't know what it's like to be an educated woman in a small town. Most of the men think we're only good for looking after the home and having babies. The women think the same. If I mentioned Trevyn in a sewing circle, I would get blank stares. Or worse."

"Dilys, Wrexham is a bigger place than Mohald. More opportunities."

"It's not that much bigger. My father asked the Wrexham bard to teach me instrument making because Dafydd was the best musician in the province. He flatly refused. His letter said that education was wasted on a girl. Since they just go and get married."

"Dafydd thinks that?" Aneirin seemed genuinely dismayed, "He always came across to me as an intelligent and thoughtful sort. Although...he did seem to complain a lot about having to teach girls their letters. Now that I recall, he used that exact phrase over some ale last year."

"Aneirin, it's almost unheard of for a woman to be as well educated as I am in the hinterlands. My father took a lot of criticism from the village council for his decision to apprentice me as a bard. Dafydd will never complete my training, much less certify me as a journeywoman. The best I could expect from him is a marriage to the miller's son. That was his suggestion to my father."

"But you could go to the bard hall? Or university?"

"My father would have had to sponsor me in person. Or another master. It's possible he sent a request during his final illness. As of yesterday, there has been no response. He also secured me a university appointment through a professor he knew for the upcoming fall term."

"Problem solved then."

"Not really. Since I was to be sacrificed and had no heirs, all my goods and gold along with what I inherited from my father reverted to the town. I went from a well-propertied woman to your penniless dinner. Convenient that, don't you think?" she said wryly.

Aneirin grimaced. "That was just wrong. I really don't want you to leave. I have been lonely for...a long time. Books are a comfort. But it's not as much fun as being able to discuss them."

"Exactly! I have missed that since my father died."

"But you can't stay. The veiling magic doesn't work when another is nearby. Mohald will send another sacrifice. The drought is unlikely to break for at least a season. Possibly two. Those fools will just keep on repeating the same thing over and over again. It's ignorant insanity!" Aneirit roared. His eyes had taken on a ruby-red color. Dilys was pretty sure some wisps of smoke came out of his nostrils.

"I remember looking at the records. The drought seems to come in ten-year cycles?"

"Almost like clockwork. Brynmore's Study of the Seasons suggested that the Western Ocean influences the amount of moisture and wind it takes for clouds to push over the barrier range. It's why Wrexham gets so much rain, and Mohald and the plains around it do not."

"That's fascinating, I..." Dilys stopped herself with some effort. "The point I was trying to make is that the pattern of sacrifices are always tied to the drought. Mohard doesn't bother you otherwise. At least according to the records."

"True," he grimaced, "I do get the occasional batch of kids and would-be dragon slayers. A roar down the tunnel takes care of that."

She felt her face go hot. He smiled, "You tried to sneak into my cave before. Didn't you?" His eye color has moved back to blue. A blue with hints of gold.

"Well, once. On a dare. I was thirteen. We got to the entrance, and as soon as we got three feet inside, this horrible sound came out of the dark."

He chuckled, and the gold in his eyes intensified. "I have the mouth of the cave warded so I know when someone crosses the threshold. One roar usually does the trick."

"Well, it worked for me and my friends. Anyway, what if I told you I have an idea to break the cycle once and for all? It probably won't stop thrill seekers, but it would ensure that the area will no longer worry about droughts."

Aneirin sat up straight and looked intrigued. Perhaps even hopeful, she thought.

"Pray continue."

"There's a price," Dilys steeled herself.

"Hmmm, and that is?" His expression was unreadable, eyes guarded, and back to the blue.

"If I tell you and you agree. I get to stay here. Like I said, I will cook and clean. Just so long as I can keep using the library." Dilys cursed herself for letting her voice go desperate at the end.

"Dilys, I think that price is higher than you think. You can never leave here without me. There are countless libraries in the world, many far grander than mine. Admittedly, not many," he replied with a trace of smugness, "I haven't shown you the main stacks."

"There's more?" She couldn't suppress the awe in her voice. It would take her years just to work through what she had seen so far.

"Oh yes. Books are my hoard."

"I thought dragons hoarded gold and jewels."

Aneirin snorted, "It takes gold to buy books. My investments bring me far more than having my wealth sit in a cave. In fact, I could fund your schooling. Arrange an endowment for you to the university you were accepted to. I would pose as a friend of your father and deliver it myself."

"University was a way out for me and my father's dream. I visited the capital once with my father when he had business at the bard hall. Truth be told, I don't like cities and crowds. But thank you. It is good to know I have options. And I know that dragons always keep their word."

"Indeed. Now that you know you have options, are you sure you want to tie yourself to me for the rest of your life? If your idea works, then there is no going back. A bargain is a bargain, and once struck, the dragon in me will not let you back out."

Despite the harsh tone of his last statement, the hopeful look returned to his features.

He wants me to say yes, she thought. *The rest of my life? But what would my life be?*

The best she could hope for was working as a tutor to a noble's children while living in a smelly, crowded city. Despite her father's assurance that the larger communities didn't have the prejudices against learned women that their village had, she had seen how the few women bards were treated in the bard hall. One had told her that she was being 'retired' because she was getting married.

"Because a woman's highest calling is to support her husband and care for his children," Dilys could still remember the slightly older woman, Catrin's sarcastic tone, "At least my husband is getting a posting far from the guild hall so no one will notice that I will be teaching the children."

"I would rather have a life here, than a half-life somewhere else."

He seemed to visibly relax while continuing to sound neutral, "Very well. I will hear you out."

"This is amazing," Dilys looked around in wonder at all the tall bookcases in neat rows. Aneirin had led her to a lower cave full of bookcases so high that they had rolling ladders to reach the top. In front of the bookstacks were what at first looked like large chests on legs but on closer examination had several drawers each.

"What are those?" she asked.

"It's a system to keep track of all my books, scrolls, and artifacts. Every time I acquire something, I write down information about it and where it is located and file it here. I came up with it after I realized that I had seventeen copies of Alrick's Bestiary."

"I've been meaning to read that." Focus, Dilys told herself, "So what are we looking for?"

"We will need something to allow us to communicate while we are airborne. I ran across an artifact a long time ago that should do the trick."

He pulled out one of the drawers to reveal a row of yellow cards about the shape and size similar to an elongated gaming deck. Aneirin flipped through them. Finding one, he unscrewed the knob on the front of the drawer and pulled out a copper colored rod. He plucked out the card after marking its place.

"Why do you have that rod contraption?"

"The rod goes through the holes at the bottom of each one. It keeps them from falling out if the drawer is tipped over."

"Seems like a lot of trouble."

"Let's just say it's less trouble than the alternative,"

The look on Aneirin's face persuaded Dillys that there was a story there to pry out of the dragon later. He read the entry and nodded.

"It is a silver collar with a white jewel, said to have been made by Gemwaithcrefftwr himself for finding and talking to his mate. According to the trader that sold it to me, the inscription says that the wearer is able to find and speak with one dragon that is near to them. I assume that it acts as a tracker and voice amplifier."

"The seller told you that?"

"The inscription is in Ancient Draig. I have always wanted to study the language but have never gotten around to it. I could make out a few words that seemed to support the merchant's interpretation."

"Merchants say a lot of things trying to sell you something."

"True, He was selling it for next to nothing as part of an estate of the widow of a dragon that was killed by a slayer. It was probably part of the sales patter but the seller claimed the woman died right after her mate of a 'broken heart'."

"Well, it apparently worked. You bought it." Dilys chuckled.

"What worked was me haggling the price down to slightly more than the value of the metal. Plus, it's imbued with some odd magic."

"How does it work?"

Aneirin's face flushed with embarrassment. "Well, I have never had a way to test it. I originally got it as a curiosity and a prod to study Ancient Draig by translating the inscription. The day I got back, your village had the bright idea of sending me a sacrifice every three days for almost an entire month. I was barely getting in from Wrexham before another one was chained at the entrance. It gathered dust on my desk till things slowed down and I decided just to catalog it and work on it when the rains came back. Truth be told. I forgot about it."

"So I am your test subject?"

"Yes. Follow me."

The pair walked past lines of giant book cases. Dilys was starting to think she should have packed a meal for the trip when a torch flared, illuminating the entrance to a side tunnel.

"Ah, here we are. After you, my lady."

A new torch lit, revealing a space where Dilys could actually see the far wall. The room was more storage than library, with items spaced on shelves. Some of the items were quite dusty.

"You really do need someone to clean."

"I need to renew the cleaning ward. The side passages each require a separate incantation. I haven't been here in some time."

Dilys remembered from the old village records that "The month of sacrifices," when over ten maidens were given to the dragon only happened once, over six hundred seasons ago.

"You haven't been here in six hundred seasons?"

Aneirin turned, surprise on his face, "How did you know that... ah, the village records are quite complete."

Dilys blushed. "Yes, they are. That was the only time the village elders decided on quantity, so I remembered reading it. I have to say, considering the length of time, things don't look that dusty."

"The charms keep the dust down in the main space, so not much gets into the side chambers. Ah, here we are,"

He reached for a silver torque with a white crystal hanging from it. When Aneirin touched the crystal, it lit up with an inner light and the film of dust repelled from it, creating a cloud that engulfed the pair.

Dilys sneezed, but managed to get out, 'That's pretty."

"It is. Okay, the next step is to put this around your neck. Can you lift up your hair please?"

"Sure,"

Aneirn placed the collar, or torque, as she recalled a traveling merchant calling a similar item, around her neck. As soon as it touched her skin, the metal seemed to develop a mind of its own, the two ends jumping out of his hands and locking together. A shock went through her.

"Ouch!" They both said as one. Dilys decided he must have felt it too.

"Dilys must have felt that...Her flowing red tresses are so pretty."

"I sure did. And while I appreciate the kind words..."

"Did what?" Aneirn replied, puzzled.

"You asked if I felt the shock too."

"No I didn't."

"Yes, I clearly heard, you said 'Dilys must have felt that.' Then you complimented my hair out of nowhere. "

Aneirn grimaced, "First my grammar is far better than that. Second, I didn't say it out loud. I thought about it." The woman paled, then knitted her brows together.

"Aneirin keeps looking under my skirt."

He sputtered, face red, "I do no such thing, milady!" As soon as he spat out the denial, he realized the woman's lips had not moved. Until she started laughing uproariously.

"It doesn't amplify sound. It transmits thoughts." She sobered, "Can you read my thoughts?" Dilys looked concerned for some reason.

Aneirin said to himself, "Dilys can you read my thoughts?"

"No, I have been trying." Again, her lips did not move.

"Well quit trying. It seems like it only works to convey thoughts that are actually directed to the recipient," Aneirin replied out loud. "The trader said that the dragon had to both touch the crystal and put the torque around the woman's neck." He brightened, "This is even better than I had hoped. Not only will we be able to communicate airborne, but we can converse privately in the village. That will come in handy."

"Good. Let's get this off till we're ready to go." She lifted her hair up expectantly. Aneirin reached for the clasp only to find unbroken metal where the mechanism had been.

"Dilys... "

"This is very pretty and all, but please take it off," a trace of impatience tinging her voice.

"Well, about that. The clasp seems to have disappeared."

Dilys cursing echoed through the library.

The view from the air is amazing. Worth the chill. And the collar around my neck,

"It is, isn't it. And I promise you we'll figure out how to get it off. Even if we have to cut it free," Aneirin's voice boomed in her head. Dilys jumped, despite all the practice conversations the night before.

Her hand moved to the crystal hanging from the torque around her neck. She was sure the crystal was glowing brighter than the day before. Aneirin continued to assure her that it wouldn't let him read her inner thoughts, just things directed at him.

"Fair warning. You are broadcasting a lot. For example, I know I probably need a seat for the basket you are riding in. I never considered passengers. I use this to move books and supplies that I buy in the market cities."

"A seat would be nice."

The design of the carrier made it easy for Aneirin to step into a padded yoke across his shoulders in his draconic form. Heavy ropes ran from the ends of the yoke to four points of a wooden box, the top of which came to Dilys's breasts. It was half the size and shape of a wagon bed. "I am concerned about my thoughts leaking out."

"You have to think of me and focus the thought for me to hear it. I can't go digging around in your memories. I would not do that anyway."

She wasn't sure that they couldn't see what the other was thinking. She had caught bits and pieces of him appreciating the dinner she cooked last night. And the shape of her bum. She felt a mix of scandalized and smug.

Dilys looked back out. Her village was fast approaching. The trip that took almost two hours on foot, Aneirin could have covered in minutes. He has taken a roundabout route, claiming that he wanted to "stretch his wings,"

That stretching had led to a tour of some beautiful sights that Dilys has only heard about from travelers' tales and books. Agan, she caught traces of satisfaction from the dragon at her remarks about the scenery.

"We should be landing in a few minutes. Are you ready?"

"Ready as I will ever be. Let's do this."

Dilys was amused to see the villagers scatter as Aneirin's shadow crossed over the ground. She caught her breath as the ground seemed to rush toward her, almost losing her grip as the shock of Aneirin breaking his descent nearly drove her to her knees.

He landed at the top of the hill outside the town with a sheer cliff behind them. The view overlooked the village itself.

"No one seems anxious to see me for some reason," Aneirin remarked dryly, "Let's see if this works."

"PEOPLE OF MOHALD! Come forth to talk or be destroyed by fire in your homes." the dragon thundered. Dilys was deafened. She responded through the link.

"Think that was loud enough?"

"One must establish dominance early in a negotiation."

"I thought you were just going to tell them what to do?"

"Well, that too. I would like to avoid crisping some townspeople to get my point across."

For all the slights, disparaging remarks, and indignities Dilys had suffered at the hands of most of the villagers, especially the headman, she didn't want them dead.

"But you're not adverse to a little suffering, "Aneirin continued over the link, "I can hear that as well as your concern that no one gets killed. Well, time for the performance. Look suitably, downcast."

That was easy, Dilys thought, just thinking of how she felt when her father told her about Dafydd's response to his request that he teach her. She hopped out of the basket and made her way to the village. She tried to hunch her shoulders and drag her feet as she slowly approached the tavern. She had seen several people flee there, as the dragon had approached. The tavern was the oldest structure in the village and made of stone and a tile roof. A logical hiding place from a fire breathing dragon. One of the window shutters was ajar, an eye peering through the crack.

"Dilys? Is that you? The dragon didn't eat you?" Dilys recognized the squeaky voice of Poppy, the tavern keeper's daughter.

"No Poppy, it didn't. But I am its slave for life thanks to the elders."

"Hardly a slave," Aneirin's voice whispered in her head.

"Hush," she mentally replied as Poppy opened the shutter further and cautiously stuck her head out and whispered.

"Why is it here?"

"Because the village wanted the drought to end. He is going to end it."

Poppy went pale, "The village?" she gasped.

"No, you silly goose, the drought."

"So he is going to bring the rains?"

"He's going to make sure the crops get water. Is the town council hiding in there?"

"Yes."

"Tell them that the dragon wants to speak with them."

"Why does he want to speak to us? Were you not a good enough sacrifice?" a reedy voice sounded from the darkness.

Jared, Dilys thought. The growl coming from Aneirin was intriguing.

"Take it up with him. He wants to speak with the headman."

"No!" Dilys heard frantic-sounding muttering. Jared spoke again.

"We have elected you to act as an intermediary. The beast can convey his demands through you."

Dilys snapped, "What do you think I just said? Anyone still inside this building by the time I walk back to the hill will bake like bread dough inside the oven," She started walking back to the dragon.

Aneirin's chuckle inside her head caused her to look back. Villagers were pouring out of every door and window like the inn was already on fire.

"The headman, Jared, is the one with the red robe. Well-fed and balding. He's hanging towards the back of the crowd."

"He does seem shy," Aneirin remarked dryly.

"With you, yes. He was quite imposing when he decreed that I be sacrificed."

"Let's see if he can be imposing with me," Aneirin raised his head and bellowed.

"Jared, stand before me! Account for your village!"

Dilys could sense Aneirin's amusement that the crowd of villagers not only opened a path for Jared, but seemed to be pushing him forward. The pudgy man tried to reclaim his dignity by straightening up and adopting a haughty look. His facade was spoiled by the sweat forming on his brow. His voice quavered just a bit as he said,

"Dragon, was our sacrifice not pleasing to you? Would you care for more?"

"NO! My new slave is sufficient. Although, since you have given her to me I expect you to also transfer her gold and property to add to my hoard."

Dilys was surprised by the last. They had not discussed that part. From the look on Jared's face he was not expecting it either.

"But, but, you have never required that in the past."

"The wench will be the last sacrifice I require. I want her and all that she has in exchange for ending your water problems once and for all." The crowd murmured with a touch of excitement.

"No more sacrifices?"

"Will our crops be saved?"

"How will you do this?" Jared asked.

"You will. My slave will direct you in the building of windmills to pump the abundant water underground to the surface and direct it into irrigation ditches to nourish the growing crops."

"That's what she blathered about before we got rid... I mean, offered her to you."

"Perhaps you should have listened to her wise counsel and saved yourself a trip to my den."

"Well, we didn't listen to her then. Why should we now?"

"Because now your failure to comply will result in a scorched village and crispy villagers?" Aneirin replied, almost jovially.

Dilys was giving directions within the hour.

Aneirin noticed that the village headman and his cronies made a big show of walking about and bossing the villagers but actually hindered the progress. By the end of the second day, he had had enough.

"Why the shovels and pickaxes?" Dilys asked as she saw him load the tools into the basket along with the bolts of sturdy cloth to use as the sails for the three separate windmills that were being built to pump the water from existing wells.

"I think we need the village leaders to be more hands on and less in the way."

"You are going to make them actually work?"

"So you agree that they are not helping things progress?"

"Helping? No. Slowing things down? Absolutely."

As they took flight to the village, Aneirin swore that he could sense her pleasure and anticipation.

Dilys marveled at how precise Aneirin's flame could be. Assuring Jared that the hair on his head would grow back and that Dilys had poured the bucket over him before any real damage was done had been the highlight of her morning even more than the sight of the partially bald headman and his "council", cronies digging irrigation channels with the rest of the villagers.

Two days later Poppy approached Dilys to bring her some bread and cheese for the midday meal. Aneirin was "encouraging" the villagers by perching on the hill they had first landed on and messily eating a meadow beast he had hunted earlier.

"Does it do that in front of you?" Poppy asked with fear in her voice.

"No. I think he is doing that to frighten people. Thanks for the food."

"It's working. Everyone wants to get the job done so he will leave."

"I think we only have a few more days," Dilys replied.

"What will happen to you after that, Dilys?" Poppy asked softly.

Dilys was touched by her concern, "I am bound to the dragon for the rest of my days. It's not really so bad. Mohald will never have to worry about drought and maidens will be safe. That's enough for me."

"But...what does he make you do?"

"Cleaning and..." Dilys stopped herself, "And the like. The dragon takes me with him on flights. The views are wonderful."

"You are so brave. Dilys, I think that might be for the best. At least you are still alive."

"What do you mean?"

Poppy looked around to make sure no one was approaching, "When I was serving Jared and the council headman last night they were talking about your gold and the value of your property. Dilys, they don't mean to give it to the dragon."

"They didn't have any problem with my clothes, books and furniture." Aneirin had not complained about the three flights it had taken to move her things or the effort to move them into one of the many small caverns that the dragon used for storage. Dilys reflected.

"They talked about stealing you away while the dragon hunts for food and saying you have fled. They think that it will go looking for you. Jared sent for a dragon slayer the first day you returned. He told them last night that Rhys the Canny is a day away. Jared boasted that the man has never failed."

Dilys was shocked that Aneirin actually laughed when she conveyed the news through the link all the while schooling her features to hide her fear. Aneirin replied in her head, "Your concern is touching. Worry not. Play along. I suspect that treachery is afoot."

"If they kill the dragon then I am free and keep my property."

"Not if you are dead first. They are paying the slayer with some of the money they took from you. Dilys, they mean to kill you!" Tears rolled down Poppy's face.

Aneirin's voice rolled in her head, all humor gone "They are going to die. Take a care, Jared is approaching you."

Dilys called out to the approaching headman to warn Poppy that the man was coming up behind her, "Headman Jared. How may I help you?"

"Ah, Dilys. The work progresses well. Since we are close to completion, perhaps you can join me at the council house to oversee the documents transferring your gold and the value of your land that the dragon has demanded."

Before she could respond, Aneirin roared, "Slave attend me!"

"I must go," Dilys rose and ran toward the hill. She saw that he had the carrier ready.

"Get in, he said curtly. I want to review the work from above."

Aneirin circled the village lazily until he spotted a dust plume in the east.

"Ah, what I thought." A chuckle came over the link.

"What do you think? I have read about Rhys the Canny. You're not taking this seriously."

"I am taking it quite seriously."

Dilys had the strange idea that Aneirin was laughing, despite the words over the link, "Is there any reason you need to go back to the village today?"

"No, I already gave directions. The crews see that the work is almost done, so they are motivated."

"Good. I don't trust Jared. I don't want you out of my sight when we are in the village. By the way, we will have a guest for dinner. I expect him to arrive about a half-hour past sunset."

"A guest?"

"Yes. He loves breakfast. In fact, if you could replicate that wonderful meal you made me the first morning, that would be just the thing. Double the portions. He does have an appetite. I will help of course."

"Thanks, but I can manage." Dilys was glad he couldn't see her roll her eyes.

"The roast only burned a little!"

"Aneirin. It was a lump of coal by the time you remembered to check on it. I appreciate your willingness to help me, but you do seem absent minded when you are reading."

Dilys was thankful, for Aneirin insisted on carrying her personal property back the first day as she smoothed the wrinkles out of her blue linen dress. It was nice having a change of clothes. The outfit that she had been offered up in was a bit worse for wear. The biscuits were about ready to come out of the oven. Aneirin was "stretching his wings," as he put it, which kept him from the kitchen at least.

Stretching her legs, she trotted to the kitchen. Good thing, too, the biscuits were a perfect golden brown, much longer, and they would have been overdone.

She looked at what she called the window over the prep area. Magiced to show the view from the cave entrance, it displayed the setting sun t and the rising moons. She could make out Aneirin's form in the moonlight. The sight made her happy for some reason.

The second dragon caused the smile to morph into a frown. She wondered what this was about. During a conversation the night before last, Aneirin confirmed what she had read in Alrick's Book of Dragons that the draconian species tended to be territorial and solitary.

"Alrick is not completely useless. We tend to keep to ourselves, but we have strong rules regarding hospitality and visiting any dragon whose territory one crosses. Good visits are short visits."

She should have caught on to the dinner guest's draconic nature when Aneirin insisted on doubling the dinner portions. Dilys thought the dragon trailing Aneirin was a bit larger as the two dragons glided down to the flat area in front of the cave entrance.

Aneirin touched down, blue scales shining in the light of the risen moons. He moved into the cave entrance and out of view to give his companion room. The second dragon landed. The moonlight reflected off the second dragon's hide almost identically to the first. The teakettle's strident whistle diverted Dilys back to finishing dinner.

The dining room wasn't what Dilys expected from a solitary dragon. In fact, she had thought the door from the kitchen was storage. Opening it revealed a large room with a chandelier over a long dark wood table that would easily seat fourteen. The high-back chairs were cushioned, and the two end chairs had armrests. All the chairs had intricately carved backs in a leaf and vine pattern. A side table fashioned from the same dark brown wood continued the motif. The grain of the walls complemented the table. The brown panels were broken up with rich tapestries and what appeared to be external windows looking out over a mountain vista that had to be magiced the same as her kitchen window. The far end led to a set of locked double doors.

Aneirin had taken an almost childlike delight yesterday evening in showing her how the doors opened to the room where Dilys had first awoken. What appeared to be an unbroken line of bookcases actually hid the dining room entrance and opened out in an ingenious fashion.

Dilys chuckled at the memory as she put the third platter of sausage on the table. A quick glance at the surface confirmed everything was out and the places set. A muffled thump told her the entryway to the cave had shut.

She had yet to see Aneirin transform. Every evening, he insisted that she go ahead of him, shutting the giant hatch behind her and opening it after he was dressed. For a nearly thousand-year-old dragon, he was surprisingly shy. Dilys moved to the double doors and pressed the release hidden in the wood paneling.

The doors swung open to reveal Aneirin and a slightly larger and older version of Aneirin right down to the sky-blue eyes approaching the dining room. Both stopped.

"Dilys, let me make known to you my father, Cadwal. Father, Dilys, my..." Aneirin seemed at a loss to describe Dilys place in his household. She helped him out,

"Housekeeper."

"Mate," Cadwal said at the same time.

Aneirin whipped around and said the same words coming out of her mouth,

"What!"

"Son, I am so glad you found a mate. Books won't keep you warm at night." He made a show of sniffing, "Nor keep you fed. Smells wonderful, my dear Dilys." Cadwal appeared to follow his nose to the dining room table, leaving a thunderstruck Aneirin and Dilys in his wake.

Dilys was stunned into silence. Mate? She couldn't deny that Aneirin was an attractive man, smart, obviously well-read, and a wonderful person to talk to. The villagers her own age might qualify for one or two on that list, but none of them could be considered well-read or much for conversation.

Dilys regained the use of her legs and followed the older dragon into the dining room, Aneirin behind her. Cadwal was standing beside the chair at the head of the table where Aneirin usually sat. A growl sounded from behind her.

"Just testing you boy," Cadwal chuckled, moving to the other end of the table.

Aneirin strode to his place and pulled out the chair next to him that she usually sat at. Once seated, both of the men sat in turn. Dilys could see where Aneirin got his manners from.

"Father, what did you..."

"Only pleasantries during meals, boy, you know the rule." Cadwal turned toward Dilys, "it's considered impolite to talk about business or weighty matters at the table. You need to make sure that he follows that rule. As a boy, he was terrible about bringing scrolls to the dinner table."

Dilys quickly found that "the rule" didn't apply to her being interrogated by Cadwal about every aspect of her life to date. She might have been offended, but for the fact that almost every one of her answers led to a fascinating reminiscence of Aneirin by the elder dragon. She learned more about him during dinner than he had disclosed in the weeks she had known him.

"He was always a bookish lad. His mother, may Draco gently keep her soul, read to him even in the womb. It's not surprising that books became his hoard."

He tried to sneak into my workshop when he was about the age when you tried to sneak into his lair. He wasn't able to deny it since the enchantment I had laid on the entrance caused his scales to turn bright pink for a week." The idea of a pink-scaled Aneirin caused Dilys to laugh uproariously.

"Father!" His scowl was precious, Dilys thought as she laughed all the harder.

After the last of the sticky buns were consumed, Cadwal pushed back from the table and patted his stomach.

"An excellent repast, Dilys. My thanks."

"You're very welcome, sir."

"Please, call me Cadwal. I hope at some point you'll feel comfortable calling me father. Although, I would never think to try to take the place of your blood father, from everything you've told me, he sounded like a fine man who did an excellent job raising you. You can always tell the worth of a person by their children."

"Now that the meal is officially over with the ceremonial patting of the stomach, can you explain this mate nonsense?"

Dilys didn't know quite what to make of Aneirin's tone. Although the words sounded somewhat harsh, she sensed more curiosity than anger or frustration in them.

"Impetuous youth." Cadwal sighed. "Very well, the torque around Dilys' neck was created by a master craftsman and enchanter..."

"Gemwaithcrefftwr. I know. He created it so he could find and communicate with his mate." Aneirin huffed.

Cadwal shook his head and spoke in a whiney mimicry of Aneirin's voice. "'I don't see why I need to learn Ancient Draig,- father. It's a useless dead language father. I have better things to do with my time, my father.' Ring any bells, boy?"

"I will have you know part of the reason why I bought that trinket was to practice translating." Aneirin hotly replied.

"Ah, so how do you translate the inscription, my scholarly son?" Dilys could have bottled the sarcasm.

"The wearer is able to find and speak with one dragon that is near to them."

Dilys jumped at the snort and gales of laughter coming from Cadwal. Smoke started curling from Aneirin's nostrils. She jumped into the conversation.

"Cadwal, how do you translate it?"

"Ancient Draig Is a language where word combinations matter, as particular words can modify and change other words in the same sentence. I grant that Aneirin correctly interpreted the basic meaning of the words in the inscription. However, the particular words modified each other to create a very different meaning than what he thought." The elder dragon had the professorial tone down pat.

"So what does it actually say?" Aneirin snapped. Dilys was curious herself.

"Whomsoever places me around the neck of a human, if they both are found to be worthy of each other, shall be intertwined with each other, sharing everything, knowing each other's thoughts, and holding each other dear. Until the end of the dragon's days." Cadwal smiled. "In less flowery language, the torque identifies a dragon's mate. The magic links the pair and gives the human mate the same qualities and powers as the dragon the collar pairs them with. The process does take some time, but as I said before, Dilys, welcome to the family."

"Father, Dilys can't take it off. There is also the small matter of nobody asking her if she wanted to be mated to a dragon."

"Cadwal, you seem to know an awful lot about this collar," Dilys said, unconsciously stroking the metal around her neck. The older dragon's face flushed slightly.

"Well, Gemwaithcrefftwr reached out to me to help with the enchantments. The torque will only lock when it determines that the dragon and the person that he or she places it around the neck of are not only compatible mates but also have an attraction to each other."

Dilys felt her face flush. Aneirin looked back at her with confusion, interest. And something more. Finally, he cleared his throat and responded.

"Father, we definitely need to talk about this further. However, we have the more immediate concern of what we're going to do about the contract you've taken from the village elders to kill me."

"It's really quite simple my boy. I've grown tired of the Rhys the Canny character. Plus, I am running out of rogue dragons to slay. The Dragon Council hasn't sent me an assignment for over two years. Finally, my entourage is starting to notice that I'm not aging like I should. Time to go out in a blaze of glory."

Aneirin snorted. "I thought I told you the last time you wanted to go out in a blaze of glory was the last time for me. I know it's all pretend, but I really don't like fighting you."

"Son, I suspect this will be the last time. The Council has offered me a seat. That means I would have to give up my role as an enforcer. Plus, do you remember Caitrin?"

"Of course, I remember Aunt Caitrin. Don't be silly."

"She's decided that she wants a mate."

"Well, that's good news. I thought she was never going to, if I recall the words correctly, 'bind herself to another dragon.' I wish her the..." Dilys saw the exact moment when the realization hit Aneirin, "no, surely not?"

"Why not? I have mourned your mother for over two hundred years, and so has Caitrin, for that matter. They were twins, after all. We get along very well. She knows I will always love your mother and doesn't intend to replace her. Why shouldn't we enjoy some happiness in our declining years?"

"Father, please, we're immortal. We don't have declining years. Not that I disapprove or anything, but there's no reason to be melodramatic. I wish both of you all the best."

Immortal, Dilys thought. She knew dragons were long-lived. It hadn't shocked her to discover that Aneirin had been alive for centuries. But immortal? Then she remembered what Cadwal had said about the torque. "The magic links the pair and gives the mate the same qualities and powers as his or her dragon mate." Surely not. As she was about to ask, the elder dragon continued.

"So you see Aneirin, this will be the last time we spar before the humans. My thinking is that we...."

Dilys didn't want to interrupt the two dragons planning the staged fight for the village tomorrow but definitely wanted to ask Cadwal what the torque was going to do to her.

Cadwal and Aneirin had talked deep into the evening. Dilys decided that she must have dozed off at some point as she found herself laying on top of her bed after being awakened by sounds in the kitchen. She quickly washed herself, changed clothes and entered the kitchen to find that Aneirin was taking a huge skillet of scrambled eggs off the stove. Thick slices of fried ham and freshly baked bread were already on the table.

"Good morning Dilys. We just have enough time to eat and get back to the village. Father thinks he and his party will arrive at Mohald midday. Things should move quickly after that."

"Is all this really necessary? Couldn't Cadwal just disappear?"

"Funny you should say that. That's exactly what I asked him the last time we did this, although he used the name 'Aeron the Bloody' six hundred years ago. Truth be told, I can't fault his explanation."

"And that was?"

"That dragons can't let humans have an undefeated dragon-slayer. Even if the dragon-slayer is, in fact, a dragon."

"Ah, so you two are keeping the dragon mystique alive today?"

"Something like that. Please let me seat you."

"About the torque," Dilys began.

"Oh no dear, remember the rule? We definitely need to talk about it. I, for one, have a lot of questions for my father that went unanswered. He promised to join us for dinner tonight to answer anything we had to ask him. But for now, let's eat and get ready for the day."

He called her 'dear', she thought. How very interesting.

Flying in the cargo container with its newly installed seat was routine at this point. The only thing marring the trip was a persistent itch between her shoulder blades that she couldn't reach.

The morning was uneventful, other than Jared was entirely too smug. The fields closest to an existing well were showing visible improvement from the windmill aided irrigation. Dilys could see that eliminated the grumbling and encouraged the villagers to push harder to finish. Aneirin pretended to doze on his usual hillock.

"The last well will be dug by the end of the day." Cal remarked, wiping sweat from his bald pate. "Dilys, I thought you were daft to insist on building the windmill before digging the well. But you're right. It can haul up buckets of dirt just as easily as water. The time saved more than made up for the time building the windmill. Which we would have had to do anyway." He craned his neck." I wonder who's coming? That much dust would take a wagon and a couple of outriders to kick up."

Dilys turned and saw the dust plume. *The play begins..* "I better head back to the square. It's about midday. Don't wait too long or the food will be picked over."

Cal guffawed, "Picked over? Jared and his toadies would have the platters licked clean. Never fear, we will be there."

A white runner beast, high stepping hooves clumping on the road, the sun hitting its fur and tail strands caused the animal to almost glow, entered the square from the south road about the same time Dilys did. Cadwal, aka Rhys the Canny, was astride. Aneirin opened an icy blue eye to stare across the hard-packed dirt.

Dilys had to admit that as the man dismounted, resplendent in silvery armor, he cut an impressive figure, sword at his hip. On his back was a large shield that looked to be covered in dragon scales.

Aneirin yawned.

"I am Rhys the Canny and I am here to put an end to your reign of terror against the fair citizens of Mohald!"

Aneirin yawned again, jaw stretching even wider.

"Arise, you scaly beast! Defend yourself if you can!"

Aneirin looked to yawn a third time. Except this time, a gout of flame erupted from his open jaws, directed at the armored figure.

Rhys turned just in time for the shield on his back to deflect the dragon fire. Moving far faster than Dilys would have believed that an armored man could, Aneirin's father bolted to the right while whipping the shield from his back to his left arm. He turned to face his opponent just in time to shield himself from another blast of flame.

Aneirin reared up on his hindquarters, head tracking the dragon-slayer as he edged closer at an angle like a sailing ship tacking in the wind, except in this case the wind was dragon breath.

Cadwal had his sword out as he approched Aneirin. The dragon lashed out his tail. Rhys jumped up, narrowly avoiding being swept off his feet. The crowd in front of Dilys gasped, followed by some ragged cheers. She was regretting her decision to hang back behind the crowd as the villagers pressed forward, blocking her view. She knew she wasn't a good enough actress to react properly to the combat. Even though she knew it was a sham, for some reason, she was concerned about Aneirin or his father getting hurt. The consequence was she now didn't have a very good view of the fight.

Dilys couldn't see exactly what caused the crowd to scream and moan, but she did see Aneirin rise above, wings outstretched, and felt the blast of air on the down sweep, Rhys trapped in his talons struggling to get free.

As the pair rose into the midday sun. Dilys tilted her head up like everyone else. A sickly-smelling cloth slapped against her nose and mouth, muffled her cries for a brief second or two before she slumped into unconsciousness.

Aneirin craned his head around to judge how hi gh he and his dad were. It also gave him a respite from squinting his eyes as he flew into the sun. Looking down the village buildings and fields had shrunk to a child's play toys.

"Ready, old man?"

"Respect boy. And yes, let me go."

He released his father from his talons and let loose a stream of flame that washed over his father's transforming body. Pieces of armor and the shield fell away, blackened and glowing. Cadwal snapped out his own wings to break his fall, unaffected by the surrounding heat. Three wing beats later, and he was flying even with Aneirin.

"Nicely done," the elder dragon remarked. "Rhys goes out in a blaze of glory with only scorched pieces of armor remaining."

"Remember, that's the last time we're doing this. I will meet you back at my weir. I'm not comfortable leaving Dilys alone this long. I called out to her just now, and she didn't respond."

"If I remember correctly from Gemwaithcrefftwr, the range is initially not that great. We are quite high up. But go to your mate."

"About that..."

"Plenty of time to talk about it this evening. I plan to stretch my wings and then have a small nap this afternoon."

The infuriating old man flapped away, forestalling Aneirin's attempt to continue the conversation. He wasn't quite sure why he was so concerned about Dilys not responding to his mental call, but tucked his wings in so he could lose altitude and get back to her as quickly as possible.

Dilys awoke to the pain of something slapping the side of her head. Opening her eyes, she saw she was in the back of a wagon. Her head bouncing on the wooden floorboards caused the pain. The driver seemed to have a mission of hitting every possible bump in the road. From the clatter of hooves, she was positive that the wagon was going as fast as it could. Her hands and feet were bound together, the rough rope biting into her wrists and ankles. Bad enough, but being on her side, she couldn't do anything about the abominable itching between her shoulder blades.

"How far do we need to go?"

She recognized the voice as belonging to Marcus, Jared's favorite son, and her replacement as the village teacher and record keeper. For a wonder, he sounded sober.

"Just a little further. We need to be far enough away that the animals will have disposed of her carcass before anyone thinks to look in this direction. It shouldn't be a problem. I will make sure any searchers start out elsewhere."

"Do we really need to kill her? She's not bad looking, a little chunky, but brothel patrons wouldn't really care. We could brand her with a criminal brand, and no one would believe what she said anyway if we moved her far enough away."

"Don't go soft on me, boy," Jared snapped back, "too much trouble and too complicated. If that damn dragon had just eaten her like I planned, we wouldn't be forced to do the job ourselves. Thanks to her, I have a bunch of uppity villagers to deal with for the next few months. Worse, with the farmers' crops improving with that irrigation system, they'll be able to pay off their loans and I'll have one less lever to control them with."

Dilys seethed. She had honestly thought that Jared and the other elders were just resistant to change. She had never dreamed that Jared wanted the farmers to suffer and be unable to pay their debts in full so he could maintain control over the village. Her body vibrated.

The itching between her shoulders became intolerable. Her bonds seem to be shrinking around her extremities.

Not only that, her clothes seemed to be getting ever tighter. Just as she cried out from the pain, the rope snapped, and the fabric of her dress ripped apart.

She turned to try to push herself up, only to discover that the angle of her vision had changed. Dilys could feel herself on all fours, but instead of looking up at the pair on the seat in front of the wagon bed, she was looking down at two horrified faces staring back at her.

Startled, she struggled to her feet, only to feel herself lifted from the wagon bed. Looking around, she realized she had gone airborne because of the red wings sprouting from her back. She just stared at them as her body landed with a thump behind the slowing wagon, momentarily stunned.

"Gods! What did that dragon do to her?" Marcus wailed.

"All I care about is making sure we finish the job before she gets any bigger. Grab the other pike!"

Jared's command to his son snapped Dillys out of her momentary befuddlement. She eyed the duo rapidly approaching with bladed pikes in their hands. Resentment over years of slights, insults and cruel treatment of her over the years boiled up. She opened her mouth.

Dillys was glad they were far enough away from the wagon and team that the flames didn't hurt the animals.

Aneirin was frantic. Overflying the village, he couldn't pick up a trace of a response from Dillys. As he was about to land and demand some answers, he felt a tug from her to the south. Leaving the thoroughly terrified villagers, he flew in that direction.

He sensed pain at first, then confusion, then anger. He beat his wings as hard as he could. Then, there was suddenly a stab of horror followed by an odd sense of satisfaction.

The first coherent phrases over the link involve some rather creative cursing. The reason for the cursing became apparent as he topped the hill to view a female red dragon with a jeweled torque around her neck running in a field to the side of the heavily rutted road he had been following, flapping her wings in an apparent attempt to get airborne.

On the other side of the road, a pair of draft animals were grazing. Two lumps of what appeared to be charcoal were in the middle of a flame scorch. Aneirin landed.

"How do you make this flying thing look so darn easy?" Dilys demanded.

"Lots of practice. The best way to start is to glide from a height. You have to develop the muscles in your hindquarters and your wings to jump in the air and beat down to get airborne. Although running in the field and flapping your wings will build up your strength after a while."

The red dragon glared at him with Dilys' green eyes. Aneirin rather liked the combination despite the clear irritation they projected at present. She harrumphed.

"Well, how about a lesson? I am too big to fit in the wagon in this shape, and it's a long walk back to your home. Not to mention, I suspect the villagers will have some questions."

"Speaking of questions, what happened? Father's plan went without a hitch. He's probably back by now napping before dinner. I wasn't worried until I got close enough to the village and I couldn't make contact with you. I felt a pull, I presume from the collar," he noted that the collar had resized to her draconic form, and the jewels' inner fire flamed like a diamond in the sun, "I followed it, and here I am."

"And here I am. I don't care about your daddy's rules about dinner conversation. I want to get some answers. First, how do I shift back?" Concern tinged her voice, "can I shift back?"

"I am sure you can. What have you tried to do so far?"

"Ummm, I was sort of focusing on trying to fly. I hadn't really thought of shifting back before now."

As she spoke the words, she started to change. Her wings shrunk and disappeared, as did her scales blending back into creamy white flesh. Her hair grew out in the same red shade that her scales had adopted. Other things grew out, which Aneirin's human half appreciated as well as his dragon had appreciated how beautiful Dilys draconic form was.

"Gods!" she shrieked, "turn around this instant!"

Chuckling, Aneirin turned away and approached the wagon, hoping to find a blanket or something to appease Dilys' maidenly modesty. He shifted himself in order to avoid spooking the animals.

"What did you do that for?"

"You did want to see me shift. Plus, I didn't want to have to chase the wagon to try and find you something to wrap up in."

Finding a couple of blankets and a large empty feed sack, Aneirin turned without thinking to catch Dillys giving him an appraising look. Her face flushed as red as her draconic scales.

"Just seeing if my father's anatomy texts were accurate,"

"Of course you were." By the time he reached her, he had resumed his dragon form. "Wrap up in these. I will fly low as far as I can, but as I gain altitude to get to the cave entrance, the air will be quite chilly."

Dilys quickly wrapped herself. Aneirin noted her nose wrinkling at the smell of the fabric but was pleased that she didn't complain.

"Step in the sack."

"Why? I am in no mood to demonstrate why I never did well in the sack races as a child."

"It will make it easier to carry you with my forelegs. Plus, I have a feeling that you will be very hungry soon, and those horses look tough and thin."

"Hungry?"

"The first shift takes a lot of energy you need to replace. Pretty soon, you will be ravenous."

"I am feeling a bit peckish." She looked over at the horses with a predatory gleam in her eye.

"Okay, milady, Into the sack. There's a ham back at home that I promise will taste better than raw horseflesh. Trust me."

"Ham and eggs do sound nice." Dilys carefully got into the sack, clearly concerned about exposing herself.

Aneirin averted his eyes, but replayed her transformation from dragon to human. Just so he could give her pointers, he rationalized.

By the time they returned, Dilys was shivering so hard that Aneirin feared the sack would tear. The rumblings of her stomach had him questioning if she was going to start gnawing on her blankets. As soon as he back winged and came to a stop, she was out of the sack and running into the cave, her coverings askew and flapping.

The blanket draped woman was well into the ham and tearing off chunks of bread, washing each mouthful with a swig directly from a pitcher of ale by the time he made his way to the kitchen. Cadwal looked on with amusement while sipping from a tankard.

"She has a good appetite. I take it she shifted?"

"Yes, father. First, Hunger seems the same if triggered by magic or blood."

"I can't believe I am gorging in front of your father like this," Dilys voice echoed in Aneirin's head.

"This is First Hunger. From now on, you will be eating a lot more than you used to. It's perfectly normal." Aneirin replied through the link.

"This is probably as good a time as any to answer questions," Cadwal interjected, getting up and entering the cool room. He returned with a haunch of venison and a wheel of cheese that the elder dragon set before Dilys, who was now gnawing on the ham bone. "Son, fetch a cask of ale. She needs the fluids, and I am parched."

Dilys couldn't stop eating. The venison that she had planned to roast for supper tonight was quickly going the way of the ham. The cheese wheel was a third consumed.

She was so thirsty she was tempted to just put her mouth under the spigot of the ale cask between bites. Her body seemed to be digesting and redistributing the food and liquid as soon as it hit her stomach because she never felt quite full, although she was no longer starving. She relayed her questions to Aneirin through the link, who repeated them to Cadwal.

"Is the change permanent?"

"Yes, it is. Dilys is now a dragon. She can fly, breathe fire, and shift at will to her human form. She may develop her own affinity for an item to hoard, although I suspect that she will share your love of books." Cadwal paused, his features solemn,

"She will also share your immortality, although the death of either one of you will cause the other to fade and die. So be careful." He smiled. "She can also breed young dragons. With your help, of course." The elder dragon looked positively gleeful." You two need to get right on that. I want grandchildren."

"Wait, I am going to lay dragon eggs? Dilys managed to shout out between mouthfuls. Aneirin snorted. Cadwal laughed uproariously.

"That's one of the things that Alrick gets completely wrong. Female dragons gestate and bear young the same way humans do. The afterbirth hardens into shards on exposure to air. I suspect that is where the myth of dragon hatching comes from." Aneirin paused, looking thoughtful.

"Focus, son, I know that look." Cadwal looked over at Dilys, who was contemplating the bare bones of the haunch as she nibbled the last of the cheese. "I think there's another ham in the larder. Do you want me to get it?"

Dilys opened her mouth. A belch that seemed to go on and on came out. Her eyes went wide, her face going as red as her hair.

"I am so sorry that was rude. And no, thank you, Cadwal. I think I might be full."

"Perfectly understandable, Dilys. No need for embarrassment." Aneirin replied soothingly.

"Any other questions? No?" Cadwal asked.

"I'm sure I will have more questions tomorrow, but I think you've covered the basics," Dilys replied.

"I fear you will need to write them down and get word to me. I am leaving tonight instead of the morning. I am missing Caitrin, plus..." the older dragon almost leered, "I think you two need some privacy. Granddragons and all." He hugged Dilys first as the three got up.

"Welcome to the family. As soon as you have built up your flying muscles, you two have to come visit." Her new father-in-law gently kissed her forehead.

Cadwal embraced Aneirin, whispering in his son's ear, although Dilys could hear it.

"She's a good woman. I approve. Take care of her." Stepping away, he boomed, "And get started on the next generation!" As he walked toward the door, he turned and faced the pair.

"I almost forgot Aneirin. I nominated you to the Council to replace me as an enforcer. Expect formal notification in a couple of weeks. Farewell and congratulations again on your pairing."

Before Aneirin could respond, his father was out the door. A few minutes later, they could see him through the kitchen window, silhouetted against the larger moon. Aneirin sat and drew a tankard of ale from the cask on the table, offering it to Dilys.

"No thanks. Will you be doing the same thing as Cadwal? Hunting rouge dragons?" Dilys asked, concern in her voice.

"It's more than that. An enforcer carries out council decrees. He or she also mediates disputes between dragons, places orphans, and keeps an eye on the humans. It's considered a great honor to be appointed. An appointment you can't refuse. At least it pays well. Not that we need the coin."

He paused. "I would say that I am sorry that my poor translation skills have dragged you into this life. I regret your lack of choice. But it would be a lie if I said I was sorry we are bound together now." He reached out and grasped her hand. His touch sent warmth throughout her body. "I want you to understand that things will go at your pace," he snorted, "Not my father's."

The "we" wasn't lost on Dilys, nor was the profession of affection. She made a decision. Pulling Aneirin to his feet, she said in what she hoped was a sultry voice.

"Sir Dragon, I think you have a virgin sacrifice to attend to."

END

Under Hill, Under Moon

(A Magick America story)

By: Jon R. Osborne

"**S**wing at me again, Irish, and I'll bloody that freckled nose."

Ailsa glared at the man. He stood a head taller and had several stones on her. She balled her fist and set her foot. He also had two stones that left him vulnerable if he wasn't wearing a codpiece.

"What's the meaning of this?" Godfried Penders yelled from behind the counter. "Hendrik, why are you brawling with a slip of a girl?"

"She punched me upside the jaw!" Hendrik pointed an accusatory finger at Ailsa. "Don't think being a woman means--"

"He shoved me!" Her anger thickened Ailsa's brogue. Being Irish in the Dutch colonies was hard enough, but taking Jager contracts as a woman doubled the grief. "The big galloot--"

Godfried held up a hand. "I don't care who started it. Save it for the monsters."

"There's naught on the board but barrow rats and chicken-filching goblins." Hendrik wiped the side of his mouth with the back of his hand.

"Good thing I have a hunt contract fresh from a messenger falcon." Godfried slapped a parchment on the counter.

Ailsa stepped forward. Hendrik hadn't exaggerated. The other monster hunters had picked over the bounty board first thing in the morning. Fixing a recalcitrant spring in her dwimmergun cost Ailsa two hours, leaving her scanning the Jager notices for a mission worth more than a handful of kopers.

"What's the contract?" she asked.

Hendrik loomed over her. "Step aside, Irish. This is a Dutch colony; let a Dutchman do the work."

"That isn't how the Jager Guild works, and you know it," Godfried interjected. "This priority mission pays a premium for a quick response. Lives are at stake. I suggest you team up and split the contract."

Hendrik snorted. "Pair with that Irish--"

"Watch what you say, you rutting half-ogre." Ailsa clenched her fist again. "I'm not working with this oaf."

Godfried smacked his hand on the counter, the crack echoing in the empty guild hall. "There's children's lives on the line! We don't have time for you to bicker, and the other Jagers are already in the field."

"I can do it myself. I don't need a," he paused, working his jaw, "a green hunter getting in my way."

"I'm not unblooded," Ailsa protested. "I dinna fancy having to smell you the whole way to--?"

"Jonkers." Godfried slid the parchment to Ailsa. "See Alderman Eiderkamp when you get there."

"It's north, by Saeck Kill. I, we, can make it in eight hours if we hustle," Hendrik added.

"I know where it is. I passed it on the river during my last mission." Ailsa folded the parchment and tucked it in her buff coat. "I brought my day pack in case I found a close contract."

"This is going to be a long trip," Hendrik muttered. "Fine. I brought my gear for the same reason. Let's be off, and you can fill me in while we walk."

Ailsa grabbed her pack off a bench and slung it onto her back. She ran her hands over her equipment harness, ending her check at her dwimmergun. Hendrik strode for the door, a musket slung from his shoulder and a sheathed sword hanging from his baldrick. His brisk pace rustled a chainmail shirt against his gambeson.

Ailsa hurried to catch up. Mid-morning traffic filled the New Amsterdam streets with people, horses, and wagons. "You canna leave me behind so easy."

"Don't worry. I know a fellow who'll rent us horses. You only have to keep up until the Haarlem Gate."

"Who in their right mind would let horses to Jagers?" Ailsa asked. "They're as likely as not to end up monster food."

"My cousin. As long as I pay upfront and promise we won't ride them into a fight, he'll do it," Hendrik replied. "If we get them killed, we'll be on the hook for a dead horse, but horses will save us a couple of hours. You can ride a horse, can't you, Irish?"

"Aye, I can ride a horse." Her brogue crept back with the irritation of talking to the back of his head. "Can you read a contract?"

"I can, but why don't you fill me in?"

"Two children have gone missing," Ailsa replied. Glancing at the contract was enough time for her to memorize it.

Hendrik glanced over his shoulder, weaving around a farm wagon without looking. "I gathered as much. Do they suspect goblins?"

Ailsa shook her head. "Villagers and farmers have spotted elves lurking in the area. It's unusual for them to come this far south along the river."

"The contract says elves don't come south?" Hendrik returned his attention to the road.

"No, but I know a bit about elves." Ailsa quickened her pace to draw next to him. "Elves fascinated me in my youth."

"So you know elves grab women and children," Hendrik remarked.

"Those incidents are overstated and occurred in the early days of colonization. Save for the occasional trader, they've avoided human-settled land for the last two decades."

Hendrik halted and scanned a knot of men and horses along the gate that separated New Amsterdam proper from the fields and marsh of Manhattan Island. "I hope you realize the difference between mostly and always. Don't get me wrong, I have no desire to clash with elves, but if they did grab those children, we may have no choice. There's my cousin." He waved, and a man separated from the others.

The man cocked his head as he approached. "Who's the redhead, and does Judith know about her?"

"This is Ailsa. We have a Jager mission and need two horses to get to Jonkers with haste." Hendrik tipped his head toward the man. "Irish, meet my cousin Willem, one of the best horse traders in New Holland."

"Hello. A pleasure to meet you." Ailsa offered her hand even though Willem eyed her like a side of meat. "I'm a Jager, specifically a mechanick."

Willem shook her hand for a moment, then clasped it with both hands, staring intently into her eyes. "A tinker? Handy to have, I suppose." He reluctantly released Ailsa, turning his attention back to Hendrik. "Two horses? Fifty koper if you have them back by sundown tomorrow. Try not to get them eaten; I doubt you can afford it."

Hendrik dug into his belt pouch and handed over five silver coins. "I'll try not to feed them to any monsters."

"I could have paid for my own," Ailsa protested as Willem trotted off.

"I assume you will, but we can juggle coins later. Besides, Willem was starting to drool."

"Who is Judith?" Ailsa asked. As annoying as Hendrik was, at least he didn't leer at her.

Hendrik shifted his feet. "She's my, well, we, um, I'm courting her."

"Does she know you're courting her?"

"Of course! Well, yes, I hope so. Thank goodness, here come the horses." Hendrik took the reins of one of the steeds.

"Do you need a hand up?" Willem asked, handing over the reins to Ailsa.

"Thank you, but I can manage." They needed the horses, so Ailsa bit back a quip. She stepped into the stirrup and swung onto the saddle, thankful for equestrian lessons her mother had pushed on her in her youth. Once her foot found the other stirrup, she rechecked her gear.

"So I see." Willem favored her a grin full of crooked teeth before turning to Hendrik. "After the morrow, it'll cost you another 25 koper per day."

"Ho, you heading north?" a man called from a wagon.

"Aye, we are." Ailsa drew her horse alongside Hendrik, putting him between her and his cousin.

"Watch for bandits once you cross from the Haarlem ferry. Word has it a band of trogs are waylaying travelers," the drover said. "We had three wagons and a dozen armed men, so they let us be, but a pair might be tempting."

"Bandits?" Willem looked from the wagon driver to the horses.

"Too late to raise the price, cousin," Hendrik said. He patted the stock of his musket. "Don't worry; I'm sure we can discourage any ruffians."

"We'll bring them back. Dinna worry," Ailsa added. With a double-click and a nudge of the stirrups, she guided her mount toward the gate.

Hendrik cantered to catch up. "Good thing the warning didn't arrive ten minutes earlier. He would have doubled the price."

"Will these highwaymen pose a problem?" Ailsa asked. Monsters might spring out of the brush or even emerge from shadows, but a smart bandit could lay in wait with a musket, and no clever tinker magick would save her.

"I doubt it. Even renegade trogs know if they take to murder, the West Indies Company will hire enough muskets and mages to root them out. If we do run into them, let me do the talking."

Ailsa's cheeks flushed with ire. "You dinna think--"

"I'm not impugning your charm; some might fall for the whole bright eyes and freckles, but you're hardly intimidating." Hendrik waved away a fly.

"I'll show you intimidating," Ailsa muttered under her breath.

Either Hendrik didn't hear or chose to ignore the remark. They passed farmland broken by the occasional marshy pond in silence. Shortly before reaching Haarlem on the island's northern tip, they passed a crew of barrel-chested trogs shoveling gravel onto the freshly smoothed roadbed. A man sat on the wagon, supervising.

"It's no wonder they go rogue," Ailsa remarked once out of earshot. "The Company deals trogs a worse lot than even the Irish."

Hendrik shrugged. "I won't say you're wrong, but a lot of folk choose to indenture themselves to get a crack at a fresh start in the New World. The Dutch and Bourbons may get the easiest terms, but they choose all the same."

Ailsa peered over her shoulder. "It still dinna sit right."

Haarlem hunkered over the river separating Manhattan from the mainland. A road switchbacked down to the ferry landing. Hendrik and Ailsa broke into a trot, shouting to catch the boatmen's attention before they cast off and left the Jagers waiting.

"Hurry up, now!" a boatman called.

Hendrik guided his horse across the ramp, but Ailsa's steed balked, flaring its nostrils. Hendrik swung off his saddle. "Toss me your reins. I'll walk her across."

All eyes on her, Ailsa bit back a rejoinder. She patted the horse on its neck and whispered in a low tone. The horse whickered once before wheeling to canter a few yards from the dock. Ailsa turned the mare back toward the boat and urged her mount into a fast trot. The horse's hooves clopped on the wooden dock as the mare surged with a last burst of speed and leapt onto the broad boat deck. The ferry bobbed, and a pair of drovers who scrabbled out of the way at the last moment uttered oaths.

Ailsa patted the mare again and tossed Hendrik her reins before hopping down.

Hendrik handed her reins back. "All that fancy riding and you couldn't walk her across?"

"The ramp made her nervous, and I dinna want to end up in the river, if not for my pride, then because we canna afford the delay."

Once clear of the dock, the half-dozen boatmen took up oars, including a pair of trogs. As opposed to the road crew, these trogs worked alongside their human counterparts as equals. The ferry angled against the lazy current, ponderously gliding toward the far pier. Halfway across, Hendrik kneeled next to one of the trogs, exchanging a handful of guttural words Ailsa took for the trog tongue.

Once the waiting team caught thrown ropes and lashed the ferry to the dock, passengers filed off. Ailsa and Hendrik waited until last to lead their horses off the boat. Ailsa's mare followed her without fuss.

"You speak trog?" Ailsa asked once they mounted and continued north from Bronck's Puynt.

"I can manage the basics. I'm guessing you don't."

Ailsa flushed. "I'll have you know, I speak five languages, including Seethic."

"Elf-tongue? Why am I not surprised? Let me guess, you also speak Bourbon and Latin."

"You know bloody well any magicker is gonna speak Latin," Ailsa snapped.

"Don't get defensive, Irish. I assumed you'd learn bookish tongues; it's not an insult."

"You make it sound so." Was she overreacting? Trying to prove herself to a more experienced Jager? "I dinna pick up a dwimmergun on a lark. I went through Jager training in Ulster, the Alban Highlands, and the Black Forest."

Hendrik chuckled. "How many contracts have you closed? I don't mean barrow rats, but honest monsters."

"I just finished a hootbeer mission."

"One? You've completed one contract?" Hendrik shook his head. "The only thing more dangerous than a Jager on their first hunt is a Jager on their second hunt. The first-timer at least has enough sense to be scared. After that first success, they get cocky--oh, it wasn't so tough, and I lived! It takes a few hunts to drive home every mission, every monster plays out different."

"How many hunts do ye have?" Ailsa bit her lip, annoyed, and her brogue thickened.

"Twenty-seven."

"You dinna look so old," Ailsa said. "Are you sure you're na counting barrow rats?"

"A few years ago, we didn't have to travel far to hunt monsters. I'm surprised this contract is so close. I thought we'd pushed all the monsters deep into the wilderness."

"Jonkers isna downtown Dublin, or even New Amsterdam. Farms up that way are still hewing their fields--"

Hendrik raised his hand. "Hold on."

"Dinna shush--"

"We aren't alone, Irish." Hendrik scanned the trees uphill of the road. He called out, "Enoch, are you plotting to waylay Jagers? You know it won't end well."

Ailsa slipped her hand to the butt of her dwimmergun. She followed Hendrik's gaze but saw naught but trees and brush.

Hendrik unlimbered his musket. "Don't force me to prove I can see your bandits by shooting the one in the blue shirt." Guttural mutters sounded among the undergrowth and tree trunks. "Or I could start with you, but I'd hate to ruin your new coonskin cap."

"Fine. Wait." Grunted orders preceded a rustle in the brush. A huge man lumbered onto the road. "If I'd known it was you, Hendrik, we would have laid low and let you pass."

The brigand's broad chest and thick limbs marked him as trog-blooded. Unlike a full trog, his lower canines didn't jut up like tusks, but his smile displayed them prominently. He carried a musket low, its barrel dipped toward the earth.

"A new blanket warmer?" Enoch nodded toward Ailsa. "Cute, but a bit small for my taste."

"She's a fellow Jager," Hendrik replied before Ailsa could protest. "Children have gone missing up by Jonkers. Have you heard anything?"

"The sawmills? Lumberjacks spotted elves in the area," Enoch replied. "Chopping down trees riles them up, but big men with axes make poor targets. Maybe the elves vented their anger on the farm folk."

Hendrik nodded. "Robbing travelers and wagons vexes the powdered wigs at the Company. You and your band should find honest work before the West Indies Company puts a bounty on you. Besides, what are you going to steal on this road?"

Enoch shrugged. "Food. Powder. Coin. Whatever lets us live free."

"So this brings us back to the question--do you intend to try to rob us?"

Enoch grinned, baring the enlarged lower canines, marking his trog heritage. "No. Pinching your purse or looting your corpse isn't worth the cost in blood."

"And here I thought you were going to say it was because we're friends," Hendrik said.

"That too." Enoch chuckled and stood aside. "Safe journeys to you and your friend. Be careful; I hear there are brigands on this road."

"Take care, Enoch. Think on what I said. Buy a boat or wagon team and take up honest work." Hendrik urged his mount into motion but didn't return his musket to his shoulder. Ailsa's horse followed without prompting.

"Maybe I'll steal a boat," Enoch called before disappearing into the brush behind them.

After a hundred yards, Hendrik shouldered his musket. Ailsa nudged her mare abreast Hendrik's horse.

"What do you think?" She asked. The hair on the back of her neck finally settled.

"They'd be better off with a wagon. Half that lot would drown if they tried to pilot a boat."

"I mean what Enoch said about elves."

Hendrik grinned. He knew what she meant. "I'm not a fan of elves, but I bear them no ill will. Once in a while, they come into small towns or forts to trade, but there haven't been real problems with them for a couple of decades."

"Good. I'd hate to hunt elves. In my book, they dinna qualify as monsters," Ailsa said.

"Don't be sure they'd take such a charitable view. The Company effectively pushed them upriver and into the hills. They may consider us monsters."

Ailsa's mind drifted to her childhood books. "They're supposed to be in tune with nature and possess a wisdom that comes with their long lives. It dinna sound like someone who grabs children. They undertook the exodus to escape clashing with humans in the old world."

"They go across the Atlantic to get away from us, and a thousand years later, we turn up. I wouldn't blame them for getting pissed."

The horses' hooves echoed on a timber bridge over a stream babbling toward the river. Trees gave way to fields as they neared Jonkers. Beyond the farms, sawmills dotted the Saeck Kill River to the east, while the town proper huddled around the juncture of the Saeck Kill and the Noort River.

They reined in their trotting horses at the travelers' stable. A boy dashed out of the timber building, spryly vaulting the wooden rail fence. "Need your horses tended?"

Ailsa's mount shook itself. After hours alternating between a brisk walk and a trot, it welcomed the break. "We've ridden from Manhattan. Can you give them a good rubdown, feed, and water?"

"Yes, ma'am. Do you want to stable them overnight?" The boy's eyes landed on the insignia on her buff coat. "You're Jager?"

"Aye to both questions." She handed the lad her reins and dismounted. A man emerged from among the stable buildings, brushing his hands off and watching.

"I want to be a Jager when I grow up." The boy glanced over his shoulder. "My father wants me to take over the stables and caravan yard, but I want excitement, not a boring life here."

"Careful what you wish for," Hendrik remarked. "You'll live longer. Boring or not, it beats getting eaten by a grue."

The man cleared his throat loud enough to carry as he ambled around the fenced-in paddock. The boy started at the sound as though waking. "Right. That'll be three kopers per horse."

Ailsa pressed coins into the boy's free hand. "There's a seventh for you. Take good care of them. We'll likely head back south in the morn."

"Thank you!" The boy hurriedly pocketed the tip before taking Hendrik's reins.

"Where can we find Alderman Eiderkamp?" Hendrik asked.

"The biggest building off the square. If he isn't in the Common Hall, someone there should know his whereabouts."

"You here about the missing children?" the man asked, taking a set of reins from the boy.

"The Alderman put a contract on the matter." Hendrik collected a pack and a powder horn from his saddle. "Have you heard anything?"

The stablemaster spat a brown glob and worked his jaw. "I'd put my silver on elves. The Aquitaine fur traders are pressing in from the north, and once you go west of the mountains, there's the *autochoon* tribes. Box an animal in, and they lash out."

"Elves are na animals." Ailsa ran her hands over her gear before leaving the horse's side.

"I bet it was the schoolmaster. Everyone knows he hates children," the boy muttered.

"Don't speak ill of Master de Kloot. It isn't easy to convince a learned man to live on the edge of the frontier to teach letters and numbers to you ungrateful brats," the stablemaster snapped. "Lead in the horse and get together hay and water. I'll be right in with the other."

"Yessir." The boy guided the horse away without his former energy.

"Master de Kloot is strict with the children. It makes him unpopular, but he's never done wrong. Good luck with your hunt, Jagers."

A bored lookout watched them approach the gate in the palisade ringing the innermost buildings. The dirt streets gave way to cobblestones, and the buildings inside the fortifications mimicked those of New Amsterdam, as opposed to the simpler architecture of the surrounding structures.

"Someone makes good coin," Ailsa remarked as they crossed the open square.

Hendrik shrugged. "I suspect having a handy supply of lumber helps. As long as they have coin to make good on the contract."

The Common Hall loomed over the north side of the square, the shingled upper two stories rising above the stone ground floor.

Ailsa brushed her fingers on the stone blocks adjacent to the door. "These look old and too clean-cut for human masons, at least in the New World."

"What, are you a dwarf now?" Hendrik followed her through the door.

"Your Irish comrade isn't wrong," a man said from behind a desk near the foyer. "Elven ruins dot the area. They often make handy foundations for new buildings."

"Are you Alderman Eiderkamp?" Ailsa asked.

"No, I'm Johann, his secretary, as well as a few other hats. From your attire, I'd guess you're the Jagers from New Amsterdam? You made good time. I can answer any questions the alderman could." He gestured to chairs in the large room beyond the desk. "No need to stand."

"What can you tell us about the missing children?" Ailsa asked.

Hendrik plopped into the chair next to her. "As well as what prompted you to contact the Jagers as opposed to the Company."

"Three children have disappeared, two girls and one boy, all from different families." Johann held a journal in his lap but didn't open it. "Petra Konig, Stein Langbroek, and Thecla van Oorschot. The boy was eight, and I believe the girls were twelve or thirteen."

"You sound as though you dinna expect us to find them alive," Ailsa said.

"It has been three days since the first disappearance, Petra. The Langbroek boy disappeared the next day, then Thecla. We've warned families both in town and the surrounding farms to keep an eye on their children, especially when it grows dark, but this speaks to more than a child falling in the river or eaten by a bear."

"Where do the families of the missing children live?" Hendrik asked.

Johann opened the journal and unfolded a map on the adjacent table. He tapped on three outlines. "Two are near the Saeck Kill, but the Langbroeks live across the north fields here."

Ailsa studied the map. She pointed to a building halfway between the Langbroek home and the other two. "Has anyone spoken to the schoolmaster about the disappearances?"

"Izaak de Kloot? He reported when the second and third child didn't turn up for class. Master de Kloot confirmed all three had been at the schoolhouse the day before their disappearance." Johann cocked his head. "Why would he know more?"

"Perhaps he overheard the children talking?" Hendrik interjected.

Ailsa leaned forward. "He dinna report it when Petra vanished?"

"It's not uncommon for a child to miss a day of school," Johann replied. "You could find him at the schoolhouse or his home next to it."

"We only have a few hours of daylight," Hendrik remarked once they were back outside. "Let's not waste too much time with the schoolmaster."

"Children have more insight than adults credit them." Ailsa led the way, the map committed to memory. "If the stable boy brought it up, it's worth checking out. Even if the hunch is smoke and fog, your comment about him overhearing the children could hold water."

"Speaking as someone who had a Dutch schoolmaster, I'm not surprised the children don't care for him. My teacher was a strict disciplinarian, with a yardstick quicker than a Genoese fencer's rapier."

A woman sweeping the schoolhouse's porch glanced up at the Jagers' approach. "Can I help you?"

"Is Master de Kloot here?" Ailsa asked with a disarming smile. Hopefully, a fellow woman wouldn't put the lady on the defensive. "We're investigating the missing children, and we'd like to speak with him."

"Oh, you're the Jagers. Master de Kloot's inside." The woman opened the door.

Ailsa stepped into the single-roomed building. Precise letters written in chalk on a slab of slate mounted on the far wall listed lessons, practice assignments, and a Bible verse.

"I thought you were going home?" A pinched-nose man peered over his spectacles, knitting his brow a split second before slamming shut a book on his desk. "Who are you? This is a school."

"We're the Jagers the alderman contracted regarding your missing students," Ailsa replied. "Sorry to have startled you."

De Kloot folded his hands atop the closed tome. "Well, as you can see, they aren't here."

"We hoped you might have overheard the children talking about something that could give us a lead," Hendrik said. "There's little to go on."

"I'm sorry, but the students, while not as clever as they think, refrain from secretive chatter in my presence." The schoolmaster regarded them with pursed lips, as though he'd bitten a sour lemon. "I suspect the children fell victim to a monstrous predator or elves snatched them. Since you're Jagers, I'll leave it to your expertise and bid you good morrow."

"Thank you for your time." Hendrik took Ailsa's elbow and tugged her toward the door.

"We havena--"

"Let's scout around the victims' homes while we still have the sun."

Ailsa didn't resist as Hendrik guided her out. Once the door closed, she yanked her arm away. "What are you playing at? We hardly questioned him."

"We're not constables; we're Jagers," Hendrik replied. "We have naught but a hunch. If he's responsible, we'd need evidence. If he's not involved, we're wasting time."

"Excuse me."

Ailsa wheeled on the woman so quickly she stepped back, clutching her broom. "Sorry, I dinna mean to startle you."

"I don't know if this helps, but some of the older girls would go to the First Barn on the full moon."

"The full moon was four days ago," Hendrik said. "A day before the first disappearance. Do you know what they did there?"

The woman shrugged. "I imagine nothing serious, but in my day, we dabbled in a bit of hedge witchery. Reading cards, lighting candles hoping for our favorite boys to take a fancy, and warding off sickness or misfortune for a family member."

Hendrik shaded his eyes as he gauged the sun. "Should we start with the homes or check out this First Barn?"

"It's at the foot of the hill to the north, right?" Ailsa asked, receiving a nod from the woman. "While I doubt lasses playing at Granny Green Jen would stir up anything nasty, it's as good a lead as any. Thanks for your help...?"

"Kata," the woman replied. "I hope you find them."

"Me too, lass."

"Why would kids want to play here?" Hendrik asked as they pushed through the brush surrounding the dilapidated timber building after a ten-minute walk. "A good breeze could topple it."

The shutterless windows reminded Ailsa of a skull's eye sockets, and a quarter of the roof had crumbled away from neglect. Dense weeds testified to its abandonment. " If they dabbled in hedge witchery, maybe they wanted somewhere away from prying eyes."

Hendrik knelt and studied the weeds. "People have been here, but they may have been searching for the children. We followed their path through the scrub. This was once a wagon lane, but nothing big has passed through for a decade."

Ailsa picked her way up the eroded earthen ramp to the large door. It hung askew, digging a corner into the dirt. Shadows thrown from the late sun obscured details save for where windows admitted shafts of feeble light, and a gaping opening on the other side faced the woody hill. Ailsa shivered. "The door fell off the other end."

"Why build it here, away from the rest of the town, and then abandon it after going through the trouble?" Hendrik trailed Ailsa around the building.

Ailsa scanned the wild hedge pressing in, expecting to find something watching her. "I suspect they took advantage of the Elfstone foundation, same as the Common Hall." She paused where the stonework parted, and stairs descended into the earth. "Do you spy any tracks here?"

Hendrik squinted at the weeds and sidestepped around the stairway, backing toward the bushes. "Someone has been down there."

"Do you--"

Hendrik plunged into the brush, crashing through branches. Ailsa whipped out her dwimmergun and sidled to her left to get an angle on whatever thrashing creature Hendrik tussled with. A second later, he hauled a kicking woman into the clearing.

She yelled at Hendrik as he dragged her toward the barn. Hendrik's prisoner had pointed ears and large grey-green eyes—an elf. At first unintelligible, the elf's speech didn't conform to the dry text passages Ailsa studied in her youth, but pieces of words clicked into place as Ailsa matched sounds to letters.

Ailsa held up her hand. *"Stop. We are not going to harm you."*

The elf-woman froze. Either a human speaking Seethic surprised her, or Ailsa's mangled pronunciation confused her.

"Do you understand me?" Ailsa asked in the elven tongue. The elf nodded warily. *"I am called Ailsa. How are you called?"*

"Tell the man-bear to release me!" The elf wriggled in Hendrik's iron grip, but she was smaller than Ailsa and stood no hope of breaking free.

"If you speak her tongue, tell her to quit trying to bite me," Hendrik remarked.

"He will release you. Do not run." To Hendrik, in Dutch she added, "Let her go."

"You can chase her if she bolts." Hendrik opened his hands and stepped back, planting himself between her and the brush.

The elf scrabbled away several yards along the side of the barn. She eyed them warily while rubbing her upper arms. *"How did the man-bear see me?"*

Ailsa shrugged, hoping the gesture translated. *"Do you speak Dutch or French?"* She didn't bother asking about Irish, as trappers and traders dealt in the other two languages.

"Only a few words, and I make them as poor as you speak my tongue." Her tone carried no malice. *"I am called Luxnajd."*

"Why was she spying on us?" Hendrik asked.

"Why are you sneaking here?"

"I am searching for my sister. The town-living men took her."

"Her sister is missing. Sound familiar?" Ailsa asked. *"Children of the town are missing also. We are searching for them. What took your sister may have taken them."* Ailsa gestured to the dark opening leading underground. *"Do you know of that place?"*

Luxnajd's eyes widened. Her shivered mirrored Ailsa's from earlier. *"It is an under-hill. I was gathering my courage when you and the man-bear arrived."*

"She called it an uffo-knokk, an under-hill. Maybe she means cellar. We're sticking to simple phrases, so I might miss something in translation. She was afraid to go in."

"Well, we might as well check it out." Hendrik unlimbered his musket and readied it. "I'll go first."

Ailsa gestured for the elf to follow and trailed Hendrik down the ancient stone steps. At the bottom of the stairs, she drew a small brass and crystal globe from a pouch. Twisting the top half and reciting a brief formula, she pushed pneuma, magical energy, into the device. With a whir, the crystal incandesced with yellow light.

"*Are you a druwid?*" Luxnajd whispered.

"A druid?" Ailsa shook her head and held aloft the glowing mote-lamp. "*No, I use a different magick.*"

The glowing globe revealed a large chamber with four stone pillars supporting the timber floor above, the corners still falling into darkness. Ailsa shivered again, although only the three of them stood in the cellar.

"They are na here," Ailsa stated.

"Someone was here. They swept this patch of floor clean within the last week or two." Hendrik circled an area free of detritus. He stooped and brushed his fingers across the stone surface. "A candle burnt here. There's something else smudged into the stone." He dribbled water from his canteen on the floor.

Ailsa studied the faint curving lines on the damp stone. "Chalk markings for a summoning circle."

"Do you think the girls got more than they bargained for playing at witchery?" Hendrik asked.

"Hedge witches dinna get fancy with sigils and circles. Now, if one or more had the talent for magick and experimented with occult rituals, they could have summoned something." Ailsa turned to Luxnajd. "*Why would your sister come here?*"

"*Meline was curious about the town-people. We bade her to stay away, but she is young. She would sneak away, especially during the bright moon.*"

"I bet her sister was joining in the Granny Green Jen dabbling. She would slip away during the full moon. It explains the girls' secrecy, but dinna explain what happened to them."

Hendrik paced the cellar's perimeter. "Don't forget the boy, who I doubt the girls allowed to join into their little tea parties. Also, they vanished on different days. Bring your light over here."

Ailsa joined him at the foot of the stairs, Luxnajd at her elbow. Hendrik pointed to a curved symbol on the ceiling with a string of runes under it.

Ailsa raised the mote-lamp. "I've seen this glyph. It was on the book the schoolmaster slammed shut."

"*It is the old writing.*" Luxnajd shivered. "*I cannot read it. We write little now.*"

"Chalk one up for out-of-date study material," Ailsa muttered. She sounded out the carved script. "Uffo-knokk uffo-loukno--Under-hill, under moon. I suspect the original settlers built their bloody barn on top of an old temple or shrine, then someone mucked around with enough magick to open the veil to the Dwimmer-wold."

Luxnajd uttered the elven words. *"The world-between-the-trees."*

"Translate for those of us who don't speak magick or elven."

"Many of the monsters we hunt come from the Dwimmer-wold, an otherworld parallel to our own. Various magicks can open or tear a passage between the worlds. Based on the moon-glyph, I suspect this was a temple to an old elven moon goddess. Old texts attest to a Louxsna."

"Luxnane. The Shining One. I am called after her." Luxnajd stared at the symbol.

"Did a rift or portal open, and the missing children went through it? Or maybe whatever dwells on the other side dragged them through?" Hendrik asked.

"They dinna disappear at once, and there's no rupture to the Dwimmer-wold now." Ailsa stared at the carvings, as though they had more secrets to divulge. "We need to visit the schoolmaster again. Even if he wasna involved, he may know something helpful about these ruins and the markings."

Ailsa squinted against the evening light as she ascended. Four figures surrounded the stairway. A few blinks and her eyes adjusted. The men held muskets, ready but not aimed.

Hendrik bumped into her. "Gentlemen?"

One of the musketmen pointed. "They caught the elf!"

"I told you elves took the children!"

"Hold on, lads. She dinna take your wee ones. Her sister is missing as well." Ailsa glared at the men.

"You cannot trust the elves," an older man in a brocade-trimmed coat stated. "They truck with faeries and monsters. If her folk did not steal our young, she knows who or what did."

"What is happening?" Luxnajd asked wide-eyed.

"Stay calm. We will sort this out." To the elder, Ailsa said, "You canna take her. She dinna take the children."

"I'm Alderman Eiderkamp, and I've deputized these men. I have the authority under Company writ to hold her for questioning by tribunal or a Constantine confessor."

Ailsa's hand dipped for her coat, but Hendrik caught her wrist. "Alderman, we haven't found the children yet. Seizing the elf does nothing, and as my partner said, her sister is among the missing."

"Would she answer a summons on the morrow?" the alderman sneered. "We'll hold her in the blockhouse. Don't worry, once the confessor roots out her guilt and the location of the children, you'll get your commission."

"If anyone harms her, I'm holding you responsible," Ailsa growled. She softened her tone. *"Go with the town-men. Do not worry. We will make sure they do not hurt you."*

"Glare all you like, Jager." Eiderkamp nodded. "Lock up the elf."

The two largest men flanked the stairwell and seized Luxnajd's arm. As they dragged her in the direction of the town, she cried over her shoulder, *"Where are they taking me?"*

"Trust me." Ailsa fell into step behind the men, her eyes burning holes in their backs. Hendrik strode silently at her side.

As they passed through the gate, the alderman gestured toward the Common Hall, a few windows lit with flickering lamplight. "My secretary prepared a guest room for you. On the morrow, you can return to New Amsterdam."

"Not if we haven't found the children," Hendrik said.

"Of course." The alderman led the men half-carrying Luxnajd between them toward a squat stone structure.

Ailsa turned on her heel. "We could have helped her slip away."

"To what end, Irish? They may have shot her, and we may have killed one or more men if it came to powder and steel. The guild deals harshly with Jagers who cross the line between men and monsters without cause."

Ailsa's retort turned bitter before she could voice it. "Change o' plans. We're going back to the barn."

"It's nearly dark. I can get by fine in all but pitch black, but what's the point?"

"Under shadow, under moon," Ailsa replied. "The moon rises soon, and I have a hunch. The tear must open and close for us to miss it."

"We don't even know this tear lies in the cellar, Irish."

"We might as well check, unless you have a better idea." Ailsa stalked toward the palisade gate.

"Better idea? You've got me there."

Already, the dusk light faded, deepening the shadows on the path back to the barn. Ailsa fished out her mote-lamp and cupped the device in her hand, aiming it at the ground before her.

Hendrik's footfalls fell silent. Had he stopped or turned back? Ailsa peeked over her shoulder, stumbling over a root in the process. The tracker caught her before she toppled into the undergrowth. "Watch your footing."

The decrepit structure loomed through the trees, the weedy clearing around it dark. The windows watched their approach, and goosebumps rose on Ailsa's skin. She whispered, "How long until the moon rises?"

"No more than thirty minutes. I don't know what you expect to find, but we should wait until the moon breaks the horizon. If this rift between the worlds opens at moonrise, I don't want to stand in the middle of it."

"I canna argue with you."

"That's a change." Hendrik grinned and squatted on a fallen tree.

Ailsa's eyes flicked to every crack and rustle. She ran her hands over her equipment, ensuring everything remained in place, then repeated the exercise. Hendrik sat stone-still the entire time.

"The moon's up." He pointed to the east, but trees obscured the horizon.

Ailsa drew her dwimmergun, the pistol's heft giving her a small measure of reassurance. "I dinna know if I hope I'm right or wrong."

"Let me go first," Hendrik whispered at the top of the stairs.

"Now isna time for chivalry."

"Your light will blind me if you go first." He held his musket ready.

"Oh, right." Ailsa waited for him to descend half the stairs before following. She had to squeeze next to him at the foot of the stairway.

Shadows ran riot in the chamber, more than the pillars should throw. Strands of darkness wove between the columns and walls, absorbing the feeble light of her mote-lamp to throw an inky crisscross. Oblong bundles wrapped in black webs dangled among the shadows. A hand poked out of one, a shoe from another which wriggled.

"The children!" Ailsa forgot fear as she rushed forward.

"Irish, wait!"

Something sticky snagged her ankle. She shone her light at the floor, expecting to have snared her foot in a low web. An ebon line trailed off into the darkness. The strand jerked, yanking her foot out from under her. Ailsa dropped her lamp to break her fall with one hand while swinging her pistol toward the source of the line.

The lamp bounced off the floor and rolled, casting light for a split second on a lumpy, multilegged, spider-like mass. Above the multitude of limbs loomed a human face with bulbous black eyes. The creature tugged on the thread, hauling Ailsa a yard closer.

Ailsa leveled the gun in a two-handed grip and released pneuma into the weapon. A red glyph flared on the chunky cylinder. *BOOM!* Red and orange sparks trailed the bullet, which cracked against the stone wall.

BOOM! Hendrik's musket belched fire and smoke, and the creature squealed and hissed. Hendrik tore open a cartridge with his teeth and jammed it into his weapon.

Ailsa jerked her foot against the taut line, while she twisted the five-chambered cylinder into position for another shot. Her assailant responded by dragging her another yard across the floor. With another pulse of magical energy, her shot found its mark this time, eliciting an angry hiss. A shadow scuttled deeper into the darkness.

"Hey!" Hendrik's musket thundered, but the shot blasted splinters from the timbers above. Ailsa twisted to spy him wrestling for his gun against a snare of inky strands. Ailsa rotated her next shot into position and kicked the mote-lamp with her free foot. The brass ball clattered and bounced across the stone, stopping short of the new shadow-spider. The lamp wobbled, throwing swaying shadows from the webs onto the ceiling.

"Irish! Shoot the horn!" Hendrik jerked his powder horn from its strap and lobbed it toward his opponent. The horn stuck in the web, dangling a few feet before a bulbous shape, darker than the surrounding gloom.

Ailsa zeroed in on the silhouette of the powder horn cast by the mote-lamp. She exhaled as she channeled her pneuma, trying to force any extra potence into the charge. *BOOM!* A red-hot lead bullet cracked into the horn. For a split second, disappointment sapped her spirits, and then the powder flared.

The shadow-spider shrieked at the sudden glare, going from shadow to midnight-blue flesh and chitin. Free of the tug-of-war, Hendrik slammed another charge into his musket and fired. Black blood and gore erupted from the creature's head.

Something slapped the back of Ailsa's coat and her hair. A mighty yank jerked her onto her back, and she slid across the floor. She snatched a brass globe from the third pocket on her left and summoned magical energy. A blue-white glyph flashed on the device, and she lobbed it along the floor. A cloud of freezing mist erupted from the ball. Frozen strands crackled and shattered, halting the inexorable pull.

The mote lamp skittered past Ailsa, rolling to a stop under the shadow-spider. Ailsa rolled onto her stomach and aimed for the illuminated thorax.

CRACK! Her shot shattered the chitin on the underside of the creature. It collapsed onto the mote-lamp, smothering the light.

Two men stumbled from the stairway, one holding an oil lamp. "What in the name of Holy?"

"Give me your lamp!" Hendrik didn't wait for an answer before seizing the light. The wounded shadow-spider blinked and hissed against the glow as he closed.

Ailsa flicked another frost bomb, the ice glyph incandescing as it bounced against one of the creature's solid legs. *Crack!* Mist congealed into ice, trapping two of the monster's limbs. "How do you like it when someone snares you?"

Ailsa cranked her dwimmergun and fired as soon as the creature's body shifted from murky shadow to black-blue chitin. Hendrik's musket roared a second later. The beast's shattered husk sagged to the floor.

"What is that?" one of the new arrivals asked.

"They're what took your wee ones, na the elf." Ailsa went to the closest bundle and carefully pared away the wispy wrapping. A dazed elf girl blinked against the dim light. "Help free the other children."

"What is the meaning of this? I did nothing wrong!" the schoolmaster protested as two burly men escorted him across the square to the block house. Townsfolk lingered in front of the Common Hall despite the late hour.

Ailsa handed Alderman Eiderkamp a leather-bound tome. "He mayna have realized what he opened by mucking around with forbidden magick in an ancient site."

"Assuming he admits to conducting occult experiments." Hendrik tossed a leather satchel to the ground.

"I must commend you, Jagers," Alderman Eiderkamp admitted. "Once the confessor arrives, he'll question Master de Kloot about his occult tomes and eldritch practices. I'd think such an educated man would know better than to dabble in forbidden arts."

"Make sure you acknowledge our contract."

"Of course."

Two figures emerged from the throng. Luxnajd wrapped her arm around the younger elf. After the village healer's ministrations, the girl was wan, but could walk. *"Thank you for saving Meline."*

"Thank you for trusting us." Ailsa fought a yawn. With the adrenaline gone, she craved a bed. *"I hope we meet again."*

"As do I. Good hunting." Luxnajd led her sister away from the crowd.

Hendrik rubbed his eyes. "I don't know about you, but I'm beat. I'm going to bed."

"I hate to admit it, but we made good partners. Maybe we should team up again."

"Irish, I told you I'm courting someone."

Ailsa smacked his shoulder. "I meant hunting monsters, you great git."

"Well, you do have two whole hunts under your belt, and for a hot head, you keep your cool in a fight." Hendrik stifled a yawn. "Get back to New Amsterdam without taking a swing at me, and we'll talk."

END

Soul of Steel

By: Zane Voss

Duran skipped up the lane, something he did only when out of Master Rotez's sight. The blacksmith's apprentice grinned as the warm rays of sunshine bathed his face in light. To the west, the towering peaks of the Spine of Duanlesh would soon swallow the sun, but he enjoyed the feeling while he could.

He capered through the shadow of the tall windmill, accompanied by the groans and creaks of the spinning construction. He peered upwards at the edifice, entranced as always by the crimson runes etched on the face of the spinning shaft. They weren't glowing today, at least not bright enough he could see.

The elemental trapped inside must be getting some rest. Two days of rain filled the village's basin to overflowing.

He pitied the creature, shackled as it was to its labors, unable to roam free, play in the wind, or visit family. If elementals even had family. He considered that for a moment. Master Rotez had never remarked on the subject. Which was notable, as Master Rotez had a great many things to say about the mill, almost all of which were disapproving.

"Duran," he said recently as the two passed the mill, returning from the village, "imagine for a moment that I lured you into my smithy with the promise of a fantastic feast. And when you had eaten your fill, I forced you to work day and night at the forge bellows." This already sounded bad to Duran, but he continued to listen attentively. "And imagine that I only fed you sometimes. Occasionally, it's even enough. Other times, you go weeks between meals. I work you until you are nothing but skin and bones. And if I fail to pay attention to you for a while, well, you just die, and instead of taking responsibility, I blame you. How does that sound to you?"

"Very bad, Master."

"Exactly. That is what life is like for the elemental, chained to the mill, forced to spin the shaft to pump water every time the wind fails. All to sustain a village that never spares a thought for the creature keeping them and their crops alive every summer. I can't believe the headman paid that brute of a binder to snare an elemental. Although he was very clever in how he did it." The last comment came with a reproving grumble.

Thinking about that moment, he now wondered what exactly his master meant when he said there were better ways. He hadn't thought to ask at the time, so he resolved to do so on their next walk past the structure. In lieu of answers, he held his apprentice's pendant tightly for a moment, whispering a prayer for the helpless elemental. Tucking away the little iron hammer with its leather thong, he waved goodbye at the imprisoned creature.

Having dawdled long enough, he hurried on, wind picking at his tunic as he topped the hill. Behind him, further down the valley, sat the hundred or so houses and the handful of larger buildings of Triapi. With the breeze carrying away the ever-present smoke from the charcoal ovens, he could see a dozen figures in the central square.

Ahead lay the great stone dam and the recently refilled basin. Water cascaded over the spillway before rushing downstream to vanish under the great water wheel. On the far side of the wheel stood the imposing tower of the blast furnace and the much smaller buildings of Master Rotez's little corner of the valley.

The wheel turned, creaking and groaning as it was forced about by the simple pressure of water instead of the arcane magic in the windmill. A long shaft made from a single towering pine bole extended from the wheelhouse, supported at the far end in a heavily greased frame. From the bole, a trio of wide leather belts led to the smithy, the low-built puddling furnace, and the blast furnace.

The belts for the blast furnace and puddling furnace were loose, sliding around the bole without tension. But the last, serving the smithy, was turning steadily. The bellows drove air into the forge, burning the charcoal hot enough to turn the steel workpieces in his master's shop an eye-hurting yellow if left in the heat too long.

The steady thunk, thunk, thunk of a hammer striking hot steel echoed from the door ahead of Duran as he neared.

His heart quickened at the sound of his master's work as he took the last dozen paces to the channel.

The pace of hammering was fast, more so than usual. His master was slow and careful in his work. So, what could he be crafting today?

His boots, good quality if a little worn in places, made a hollow knock as he moved across the solidly built bridge. Water gurgled around the heavy timbers buried deeply into the bank. From the bridge, he could see the wooden box Master Rotez used to lift charcoal, iron ore, and limestone to the top of the towering furnace built into the hillside above the little hollow. A set of torturous stairs led from the ground to the top of the hill, but Duran greatly preferred the lift, scary as it was. Running on a set of cables and pulleys saved a lot of work in loading the furnace.

Preoccupied with the wondrous mechanical contraptions surrounding his home, it took a moment to notice the steady hammering ceased.

Attention refocused on his master's latest task, he crept closer to the shop, eager to catch a glimpse of the newest creation.

What could it be, he wondered, *perhaps a blade of some sort? A heavy spear tip meant to pierce the armor of the king's enemies?*

The villagers whispered about such things when his master wasn't around. But Duran, small and unnoticed, heard as he went about his errands. The villagers spoke of his master's past, of heroic deeds and mighty weapons wrought by his hands.

Duran walked lightly, careful to avoid the squelching mud. If his master caught sight of him too soon, he would be sent on another errand. There seemed to be no end of small tasks for him, mostly those involving the villagers, who seemed both relieved and insulted to be dealing with Duran instead of his master.

Approaching the smithy's wide structure, he felt the heat rolling from the open doors. The building was two stories, longer than it was wide, with the stone forge anchoring one short wall and the two longer sides both sporting a set of barn doors, opened wide to create a cross breeze.

Windows ringed the upper edge of the first floor. All tilted open to allow the hot air out. A staircase capped the far end, leading to the spacious, if plain, house on the second story.

Duran edged into the shadows beside the open door, listening to the renewed hammering inside.

He peered around the heavy oaken door into the smithy. Compared to most buildings in the village, this one wasn't dark and gloomy. Light spilled in the upper windows, joining that coming in through the two doors.

Racks held a brace of hammers, matched by another filled with tongs. Hard steel punches, forms, patterns, and all manner of mysterious tools covered every flat space and most of the walls. Duran didn't know what many of the items did: touching the precious tools was forbidden save during his lessons. Even Duran's lingering looks would prompt a warning rumble from his master. Mostly because the last time Duran dared to break the rule, he dropped a four-pound hammer on his foot, leaving it black and blue for weeks.

He finally summoned the nerve to poke his head around the door, taking in the entire smithy with its three anvils and the forge's sweltering orange radiance. The forge cast its own light alongside that from the windows, bathing the far half of the smithy in a strange double glow that reminded him of the light wreathing the windmill when it spun without the wind's aid.

Half the light faded in and out, with shoots of flame sprouting from the coals. The other half bathed the room in a deep shade of amber, which never flickered and was always only there or not there. In tandem, it seemed, Duran's pendant warmed against his skin, as it usually did in the half-light. It was quite a mystery to Duran how exactly the light worked. It was something he pondered regularly.

His master stood above the far anvil, back to Duran, making short, swift strikes on the object of his attention. Any time Duran was around his master, he felt intimidated, something he thought he and the villagers had in common. The smith was easily the largest man in the village. Tall, powerfully built, with broad shoulders draped in a leather apron. His hair was soaked with sweat, as was the cloth band tied around his forehead to catch the stinging liquid before it reached his eyes. The strap had always fascinated Duran, as the smith was the only man in the village he'd ever seen wearing one. The village women wore them at harvest time for the same reason, but many of the men refused. Only to end up blinking and scrubbing their eyes with dirty hands.

The forge gave an angry-sounding crackle, drawing a look from his master. The massive man gave a grunt, carefully placed his hammer on the anvil, and shoved a piece of steel into the pile of hot coals. Taking two long steps to the side, he reached into a barrel, scooping up charcoal for the forge. As it usually did, the forge's crackle seemed almost pleased as the fresh fuel was added. With another grunt, his master retrieved the steel and resumed his labors.

The steady tapping of steel on steel was slower now, with lighter strokes, probably because his master was nearly finished with his work, and Duran would soon catch a look. And indeed, he did. The simple horseshoe sailed through the air with a practiced toss, ending its flight in a wooden barrel of water, emitting a hiss of boiling water and a puff of steam as it clunked to the bottom.

Duran sighed in disappointment, wishing just once for some incredible contrivance or fearsome weapon to be birthed in the smithy, which he could breathlessly describe to the other children in the village. Should they deign to speak to him, that was.

"You are disappointed with the horseshoe, Duran?"

The boy jumped, startled by the question. "No, master, it is a very nice horseshoe." He shuffled his feet, aware he'd been caught sneaking when he should have announced himself and returned to his chores. But his master said nothing, simply brushing the scale from the anvil and returning his tools to the nearby rack. He stood for a moment, studying the hammer: blocky head with an angled peen on the reverse. Wooden handle worn smooth and shiny by years of use with sweaty hands. Duran hesitated, uncomfortable in the silence.

"Duran, there is great value in things that are merely useful and necessary. Horses need shoes. Without shoes, they slide or trip on bad roads. Without horses, there are no wagons. Without wagons, there are no traders and no way to get ore from the mines or our goods to the cities. Without our work, many things slow to a stop. It is hard on everyone, not just the horse and horseman. But through our good work, we keep things going. Keep life moving, just as the miller, and the farmer, and the miner do. Do you understand?"

"Yes, master." He said because it seemed right, even though he did not understand. There were many things his master said that he didn't understand. His master did not speak in the same way as the rest of the villagers, when he spoke at all. When he did, it was as if there were more he wanted to say, some deeper explanation of how the world worked that he simply could not put into words.

And when he did not speak, he seemed to spend most of that time thinking.

"There," His master motioned towards a table where a ladle sat, "take that back to Erik the Baker's wife. I replaced the rivets on the stem. She dropped it and broke it a few days ago. Collect three loaves of bread as payment. Then stop by Tomas' store. Pick up a pound of bacon and a basket of stew vegetables. I've already arranged payment."

Duran nodded, accepting the task, even though he knew Erik's wife had in fact broken the ladle on her oldest son's backside after he sampled a fresh apple pie without permission.

He just turned to head out the door when the whinny of an approaching horse drifted through the door.

"Wait."

Master Rotez strode across the cluttered room, passing into the bright sunlight. Following, Duran saw the horse and rider just as they clattered onto the bridge.

The man was old, like his master, with graying hair flowing from underneath the wide-brimmed cap he wore. A majestic gray beard flowed to his waist, nearly covering the tabard draped across his shoulders. He was almost as tall as Master Rotez, and well-dressed. A fine black cloak was thrown back over his shoulders, and neatly detailed saddle bags hung behind the saddle.

But most interesting of all, a long blade hung at his side. With a scabbard that positively *gleamed*. Duran had never seen such radiance. For a moment, it reminded him of the strange double-glow of the forge, but this was far more powerful. The silvervine glow was there, plain to see even in the daylight, and it took his breath away. Could this be one of the legendary elemental-bound weapons the village boys pretended to play with? One like what his master was rumored to have forged many years ago? If so, what did that mean?

This man was important. Very important. That much was clear.

"Rotez of Triapi, you are even older and more decrepit than I expected! My only luck is that you have not passed into the next world, as I half expected when I set out."

Duran braced for an explosion. The only times he heard such words were when the miners got very drunk and began arguing over rights to disputed seams of ore. But no explosion came.

"My dear Count Strover, I am sorry to have caused you such worry. You, however, have never looked so fine. Is that a velvet blouse? It looks quite luxurious. And your hands! They look so smooth and unblemished. What is your secret? Perhaps we could market it to the village ladies and finally make our fortunes?"

Duran's eyes bugged out at the words. A Count! Such insults would produce buckets of blood when uttered to any of the men in town. And this man carried an enchanted sword, no less! But the man just laughed. Uproariously.

"I see your wits haven't dulled in the slightest, Rotez! I am glad to see you, my friend!" Nearly vaulting from his horse, the man clapped forearms with his master before drawing him into a back-slapping embrace.

"And I you, Strover. But I confess I am surprised. I had no word of your coming."

For a moment, almost too quickly for Duran to catch, the Count's face darkened. But the jovial grin returned quickly enough for Duran to wonder if he imagined the look.

"I should have sent word, but the post is not what it once was, and I have been on an extended tour, so I was unsure of when I would arrive. And sometimes, the less the post knows of one's affairs, the better."

This time, the smith's face turned hard for a moment. Duran filed this information away to think on later.

"And speaking of having no word, who is this young man you have with you?" Duran withered under the great Count's attention. The man's blue eyes seemed to bore into him, demanding an answer which he could not force past the dryness of his mouth.

"My apprentice for the last year. Duran. He has served well, although he is only beginning to learn the craft."

The Count's eyes turned back to Duran's master, eyebrow twisted into an unreadable expression. "A most interesting development, Rotez. I shall have to hear more about your young apprentice. And we must catch up tonight! I have two bottles of the finest Dleanian brandy in my saddlebags and all the latest news from Court! But now I must go see the village headman for a time. May I join you for the evening meal tonight?"

"Of course, Strover. I was just sending Duran to fetch a few things. But be warned, I am no court cook. We eat well here, but simply. Hopefully, you will not faint from the offense to your royal lineage."

The count threw his head back and laughed again. He was still laughing as he mounted the horse and clattered back across the bridge.

Duran looked to his master only to find the big man staring at Duran. Like the Count, his master had piercing blue eyes. While the count was well groomed and cleanly shaved, Rotez sported bushy caterpillar eyebrows, and a wiry beard streaked with gray. It wasn't too different from the hazy image he retained of his father. But where his father's memory was tinged with lingering sadness, his master's regard brought about a host of competing emotions: foremost among them a powerful compulsion to measure up to his master's expectations.

The weathered and lined face was unreadable to Duran, but the eyes seemed to be searching his own for something which Duran couldn't fathom.

"Count Strover and I are old friends. We both served the King in the war."

Duran blinked, confused for a moment. Had he heard that, right? Serving the *King himself?* His confusion must have shown, for a twinkle sparkled in the blue eyes.

"I was not always a village smith, Duran. Now, run along with that ladle and complete your duties. We will dine with the Count tonight, so return promptly. No dallying today."

"Yes, master." Duran followed the Count's path over the bridge towards the village, ladle in hand. Yet he couldn't shake the feeling that the Count's arrival meant change was in the air.

Duran snuggled in the warm blankets, fighting against the pleasant feeling of a full stomach and the lull of sleep. Below his loft bedroom, a fire crackled and snapped in the hearth. In front of the fire sat his master and the mysterious Count Strover, who seemed to have known his master forever and had a host of hilarious—and scandalous—stories of the goings-on at court. Duran had no idea how so many fine court ladies could have the fondness for wine that the count claimed, but he supposed when someone never worried about where their next meal came from, they could spend all night in the court, which Duran guessed was akin to a very large tavern.

"How was your meeting with the headman, Strover?"

"Bhah. The man has no spine. He gave the answers he thought I wanted to hear. No more. His greatest concern was seeing me on my way as quickly as possible while never committing to anything."

"And what did you want to hear from him?"

A deep sigh whispered up from the room below. "I wanted some idea of where the village stood on the Imperial succession. But he gave me nothing. Which means he will go with whatever seems most advantageous when he is forced to make a choice."

"The succession? What is there to take a stand on? Crown Prince Gryan will be King, yes?"

"He should be King. According to the Writ of Succession and the Decree of Floston. But that might not be the way it works out when his dear father passes from this world."

"A civil war?"

"It increasingly looks that way, yes. The Duke of Porclan has been quietly gathering support. And not just among nobles, but merchants and commoners too.

"What makes this all the worse is that they have a point. The Prince is worthless. He spends his time partying. There is a Court ball *every night*, Rotez. Every. Night. He drinks himself into a stupor so deep his female companions are unable to even rouse him for his most preferred activity. He cares nothing for affairs of state. The Imperial Council makes all decisions and hopes he never comes to their meetings. When he does, it is a whirlwind of order and counter-order that makes no sense and does nothing but anger everyone involved. He will be a disaster as King, frankly."

"So what is it that you want, Strover?"

"He should abdicate. His cousin, the Duke of Reakil, is as competent a lord as you can find. Not in the direct line of succession, but since Crown Prince Tikir and his entire family mysteriously fell out of a window, we have no other options."

"But he will not abdicate."

Another sigh. "No, he will not. The last councilor to mention it received a beating from the Royal Guard, excuse me, a random street tough actually, brutal enough that he retired to his summer estate to recover."

The fire crackled, filling a gap in the conversation.

"Is the Duke of Porclan so difficult to accept? He is well outside the line of succession, but his father was a good man. A great man, even. I would not have forged one of the Five Armors for him had I not thought so. He would have been a good ruler, even without the question of averting a civil war. Like many, I mourned at the news of his passing. Is his son so different?"

Duran nearly gasped in shock. Master Rotez forged the Five Ducal Armors of Duanlesh! This was far beyond even the village boys' wild imaginations!

"I am sad to say that in this case the son inherited few of the virtues of his father, save that of martial ability. He is a capable leader, even regaining some of the outer villages and trade routes lost to the Torvian hill tribes during the war. He inspires loyalty among those closest to him, but mark my words Rotez, he is a snake. I can't prove it, but I am certain he was involved with the Crown Prince's death. And he uses his position at Court to subtly encourage Prince Gryan's more… decadent excesses. His own guard is far larger than the law allows, almost an army in itself. Well supplied and well trained. And he has been accumulating mercenaries recently at a pace that has every man able to carry a sword flocking to Porclan."

Duran heard a deep swallow as if the Count downed his entire glass of brandy in a single gulp.

"Why are you really here, Strover? Triapi is a minor, unimportant village. Sure, we produce some iron ore, coal from further up the valley, and a few trade goods, but what of it? There are a hundred villages just like this between here and the capital. And yet you find your way here with these tidings. Why?"

"Because whether you want it or not, the war will come to you too, Rotez."

"No." His master's words were harsh, filled with a multitude of emotions, chief among them anger. A matching angry crackle echoed from the hearth. "I served the King without question, plied my trade for my country, and did things which I regret to this day. For that I was granted my freedom. My King would not call on me as long as I lived, and any King of Duanlesh is bound by that writ. I will not go."

"Porclan knows where his father's armor came from, what it is, and who made it. His Captain of the Guard is coming here to fetch you. Within the month."

Silence once again descended between the two men. This time a sullen, brittle stillness so different than the companionable comfort of earlier.

"I am sorry to bring you this news, Rotez. Believe me, it's the last thing I want. But I needed to warn you so you could at least prepare to leave."

"Leave?" The anger in Master Rotez's voice was hot enough to heat the room all by itself. "This is my home, Strover. Where I was born. Where my father taught me to wield a hammer. Where my wife…" His voice cut off, thick with emotion.

Silence hovered for seemingly an eternity. So long that Duran's eyes grew heavier, the faint hint of wood smoke easing him toward sleep. His breathing settled into a deep rhythm, and his thoughts became soft and indistinct.

A sudden gurgle snapped him awake, followed by the hollow thud of a bottle being returned to the table.

"What of the boy? I hadn't expected to find you with a young apprentice."

"Duran is a good lad. Dutiful, clever, and much smarter than most give him credit for. He sees much and says little. People tend to underestimate him."

"Hmmm… That reminds me of someone I used to know. A certain master smith, I believe. Does he have family?"

"His father died in a mining accident years ago. His mother fell ill two winters past. She fought. Fought hard, but just couldn't get over it. He stayed with several families after. But the people here aren't too prosperous, and another mouth to feed is difficult for most. And well, the boy was grieving. The local head of the mining guild asked if I would have him on to do odd jobs as a favor. And well, he just stayed. I took him on formally as an apprentice not too long after that."

"He has the sight?"

"Yes. Much to my surprise to find a simple miner's son here in Triapi with sight at least as clear as my own. Did you see his face when he caught sight of your sword?"

"Poleaxed, he looked."

"Aye. He can even see the fire elemental that likes to lurk in my forge, and it's a young one. Not one in five binders would be able to see it. He will be a very gifted smith should he choose to follow that path. Or perhaps even a war mage should he find one able and willing to train him.

"I haven't met a war mage in near a decade. There's none at court, at least that I have seen."

"Probably a fortunate thing, should your fears come to pass."

Quiet filled the cozy room again, warm drafts of air coiling around Duran in his nest. His drowsy eyes drifted closed.

"What will you do, Rotez?"

"I don't know, Strover. I don't know."

Duran hurried along the beaten path, trying to match Master Rotez's long strides. It was nearly noon, and the village headman expected everyone to attend the assembly.

In the square ahead he could just make out a low buzz of conversation from the gathered crowd. Duran couldn't remember a time when so many were packed into the square, not even when Father Treal died, and the village gathered in prayer to mourn his loss.

Master Rotez stopped suddenly, causing Duran to pass him by several paces. The apprentice turned to find his master's gaze wasn't on the crowd or the headman perched on the balcony of his well-adorned manor. Instead, he was turned to the side, staring down one of Triapi's narrow alleyways.

Rejoining his master, he peered down the alley to see two figures in fine green and black cloaks. They stood at the far end of the passage, one leaning against the wall of the baker's shop. The men faced away, idly holding the reins of their horses.

"Riders?" He whispered to himself.

"Yes, from Porclan, to judge by their colors." Duran twitched at Master Rotez's comment, not expecting to be heard.

The boy stared at his master, who in turn watched the two riders with an intensity usually reserved for uncooperative metal and stubborn mules.

"Master," he finally spoke, "is something the matter? Are we in danger from the Duke of Porclan?"

The man's eyes dropped to his own, and Duran felt as if he was being judged for every misstep and mistake in his short life. Part of him wanted to quail, but another part, the one that said this was important, refused to bend, to let the gaze's weight exert its force on him. Instead, he looked back, resisting the urge to look away.

"So you were listening to Count Strover and I."

Duran flinched, finally dropping his eyes at the accusation.

"No, don't be ashamed. I should have expected it, and I will not punish a boy for being curious. The Count's visit was extraordinary by your standards, and you've a right to know, I think." Sighing, he looked back at the two riders.

"Duran, things may become dangerous soon. For me. For us. It is not your fault. You will be held responsible for some of my sins, even though you are only a boy, merely because of your association with me." He sucked in a deep breath. "Unless you leave."

"Leave?" Alarmed, Duran's hand found the hammer pendant underneath his shirt.

"Yes. Leave my service and go into another trade. Porclan would likely leave you alone if you do. You would be free of obligation to me and I would ensure you are well treated."

"Master, I... I don't know..." Duran's mind whirled, unsure of what to say. He looked into his master's eyes and saw... kindness? Concern? He wasn't sure exactly what to call it, but the tinge of worry and regret in the expression was something he could understand.

He glanced again at the two riders, now passing a small flask back and forth between them. Uncertain, he squeezed the pendant, closing his eyes and breathing deeply to settle his mind. After a second's reflection, he felt warmth radiating from the little hammer.

He carefully pulled the leather thong from his shirt, allowing the small talisman to settle into his right palm. It was nothing special, just a crude black iron shape with a small hole punched in the haft for the leather.

Warmth flowed from the little token to his hand. A silverine aura, much like that surrounding the Count's sword, slowly unfurled itself around the metal. He blinked, doubting his eyes. But if anything, the glow intensified.

He looked up to find Master Rotez's gaze on the pendant wide with surprise, leaving no doubt in Duran's mind the glow was real, not imagined.

"It is your choice, Duran, no one else's. But you must choose."

"Master, you have been..." Duran's breath caught in his throat, suddenly constricted with emotion. He gripped the pendant again, steeling himself with resolve. "Since my mother. Since she died, you have been very kind to me. I had nowhere else to go. And you took me in. No one else would do that. I want to stay. I will not leave you."

The pendant gave a last pulse of heat, almost burning Duran's hand, before fading away. Suddenly exhausted, Duran dropped it back through the neck of his shirt, returning his attention to Master Rotez.

His master studied him again, this time without judgment. After a long moment, he spoke again.

"Your mother was a good woman, and your father a good man. I, too, lost my parents as a boy. It makes for a hard life, with no one to call family. I was taken in by a Forgemaster, just as I took you in. He was a far better master and a far better man than I. But despite my shortcomings as a teacher, your parents would be proud of the young man I see in front of me."

A half sob burst from Duran's chest as tears threatened to well up from his eyes. A calloused hand held his shoulder with surprising gentleness, and he leaned into the offered comfort.

The two stood that way for a few moments in a pool of peace like Duran had seldom experienced since his mother died.

The moment of calm shattered as the headman's shrill voice quivered down the lane, calling the townspeople to order.

A deep sigh revealed his master's irritation with the bothersome headman. "I suppose we should go see what our fearless leader has to say today, eh, Duran?"

Duran snickered in response. The comically skinny headman and his strident voice were a frequent target of mockery by the village children and, it seemed, by the adults as well. The master and apprentice, standing side by side, joined the milling crowd in front of the headman's showy two-story house.

"My friends, my friends, thank you for coming!"

"As if we had a choice." Someone muttered. Tittering laughter spread through the throng, earning the group a brief scowl visible even to Duran in the rear. The moment passed, and the headman's lean face returned to its usual slimy smile. As the headman fiddled nervously with his cloak, Duran realized it bore green and black trim, the colors of the Duke of Porclan, instead of the usual blue and white of the Duke of Creal.

"My friends, I have an important announcement! We have distinguished visitors who will be staying with us for a few days, no more than a week, certainly. This is a sign of the great favor in which Triapi is held, for we have none less than the honored Wrelt, Captain of the Guard, in service to the Duke of Porclan!" With a flourish, the headman stepped aside, allowing a tall, armored man to stride to the balcony.

The man, nearly as large as Master Rotez, stepped to the railing, a wide smile fixed on his handsome face. Like the headman, his cloak was trimmed in green and black.

He only half caught the headman's words, as the moment Wrelt stepped into view, relentless waves of nausea overwhelmed him. A sickly glow of angry red and orange surrounded the man. Duran fought against the gorge rising in his throat, and his stomach began a wild somersault. His vision blurred at the edges as sweat broke out across his body.

A rough grip on his shoulder snapped him from the trance, holding him enthralled. Looking up, the sight of his master's composed face soothed him.

"Steady now, Duran. Try not to look directly at him."

Blinking away the tears in his eyes, he looked around, expecting others in the crowd to be in the same state. It took only a moment to realize not a single person seemed to be affected by the sickening glow. The crowd muttered among itself, clearly puzzled by the headman's announcement.

"Porclan?" Erik the baker muttered.

"What will the Duke say about an unannounced visit from another duchy's Captain of the Guard?" Another asked.

"What is going on here?"

"What a sharp set of armor he has, yeah?"

Duran tried to do as his master said, peering at the captain from the corner of his eye. Towering over the fawning headman, Wrelt lifted an arm to wave dandily at the crowd. The fine set of lacquered scale armor covered his body almost completely, outwardly normal save for its obvious quality. Decorated with green in a pattern, it seemed to flow about him in a wave. As he moved, silver trim on his shoulder plates caught the weak sunlight, sending sparks of light across Duran's vision. The crest of the Duchy of Porclan, a raging boar's head, was half-visible on his left shoulder, worked into the half dozen scale plates covering the area. To top it off, a long sword hung in a gilded sheath on his right hip.

He's left-handed, thought Duran idly.

"Greetings, people of Triapi! It is my pleasure to visit your lovely village. My men and I are making our way through the country and wish to spend some time among you, the people who make up our great Kingdom. I thank you for your hospitality and look forward to meeting you all in good time. I will not keep you any longer, as I am sure you have valuable tasks to perform. Tasks that I am very eager to hear about."

Duran shivered, for as he uttered the last line of the short speech, he looked into the far rear of the crowd, directly at Master Rotez.

Duran followed his master closely as the man's long strides carried him across the bridge and into the smithy. Duran narrowly avoided a collision as his master stopped just inside the open doorway.

"Duran, listen closely. We must prepare to leave quickly if needed. I have badly underestimated the danger from Porclan. This Wrelt is no friend of ours nor of the village."

"Master, what is he? What was that feeling?" Still shaken, Duran shuddered in memory. Rotez turned towards the forge at the far end of the smithy, staring at the banked fire bound within.

"That man is wearing a suit of armor with a demon bound to it." His master's voice rumbled through the room, seemingly filled with anger and regret in equal measure.

"A demon?"

"Yes. You know, elementals can be bound to physical objects. Like the elemental bound to Count Strover's sword or the one chained to the town's windmill. But you must get the elemental to bind with the object. Enticement is the usual method, but not always the most reliable. Sheer force is another, although only the most powerful binders can do this dependably. One method can be counted on to work every time, at the cost of your very soul, should you be willing to pay the price. The ritual blood sacrifice of a human life releases enough energy for even a weak binder to force an elemental to bond to an object. But this changes the elemental, warps it so that it is never the same."

Duran jumped at a sudden, slow clap, closely followed by more. He darted behind Master Rotez as a dark shape filled the far doorway. Wrelt, Captain of Duke Porclan's Guard, cast a long shadow in the afternoon sunlight, one that seemed to dampen the light in the entire smithy. The featureless shape made the man seem even more sinister as Duran's roiling queasiness returned.

"Quite the story, Rotez of Triapi. I am sure it serves well to frighten your young apprentice or the odd villager into line. But I am of sterner and better stuff and not alarmed by your tales. To think that the Captain of the Guard of Duke Porclan is consorting with demons or those that made them is ludicrous. In fact, it verges on the very edge of treason. For how can a Duke be so ignorant of his Captain's activities, especially if he is meddling with dark forces? Are you treasonous, Rotez?"

The man meandered through the door, turning to pass along the far wall, examining the collection of punches and tools carefully, as if he cared nothing for Rotez's response.

A response which failed to come, as Master Rotez only stared at the man. Wrelt glanced back, a small smile twisting his face before returning to his study of the tools. Much closer now, Duran could see the man's long blond hair pulled back into a knot at the back of his head. A few strands of fine hair had escaped the knot, framing a sharply chiseled face with a misshapen, hooked nose. A faint scar trailed across one cheek, adding to the man's vaguely sinister look.

"Or perhaps it is that you are mad. After all, you have no way of proving your claims, which are patently absurd. That must be it, the ravings of a madman."

Master Rotez remained silent.

Duran whirled at a rustle behind him. Two men clad in the uniforms of Porclan's guard, perhaps the riders from earlier, stopped in their approach to the smithy. Truly afraid, he turned to find another guard in the doorway Wrelt had entered. Confused and struggling to contain the growing terror strangling him, he began to shake in fear.

His Master's strong, steady hand found his shoulder, imparting instant reassurance and comfort.

"Steady now, lad."

"Ah, so he can speak." Clearly done with his inspection, Wrelt spun smartly to face master and apprentice.

"Of course I can. You were just clapping at my elaborately detailed yet quite mad ramblings earlier."

A scowl rippled across Wrelt's face before vanishing in a moment. "Hmph, perhaps we should take you into custody and take you for treatment for your condition. For someone who has served his King and country with such distinction, I am sure I could convince the Duke to provide the necessary resources. He is a generous lord, after all."

"Is he? Then perhaps he would be generous enough to abide by the King's Writ of Release. I owe the King and country nothing more. I have made my contribution, and I wish to be left in peace for the remainder of my life."

"If you don't cease your insolence, that won't be very long!" Spittle flew from Wrelt's lips as he screamed the words. The armored man's eyes seemed to flash with an inner fire, making the dark armor seem even more sinister. Duran cowered, afraid of the man, despite the steadying hand gripping his shoulder.

"Wrelt, listen to me carefully. It is unfortunate that the Duke put you in this position, both with your armor and sending you to fetch me. Neither are good for your health. But you have a chance to save your soul, at least. The warped elemental bound inside gives it incredible powers. You are tougher, faster, stronger in the armor than a normal man. You have more endurance. You heal quickly. You feel *alive*. In fact, it has probably gotten to the point where, if you take it off, you can barely hear yourself think over the craving to put it back on. But it is warping your soul, Wrelt, and you must take it off, or it will consume you. This is how the Jaealian mages created their monsters, and I do not want that for you."

"Lies!" Wrelt shouted. "You will come with us, or you will regret your impudence! Seize them." The three guards stepped forward at their captain's command.

In less than an eye blink, Master Rotez *moved*. His comforting hand shoved Duran to the side, clear of the two guards drawing short swords as they rushed the door. The opposite hand whipped out, closing the haft of a huge fifteen-pound mining hammer propped by the door.

One guard, faster than his companion, darted through the doorway with his sword already drawn back for a swing. Duran saw the man's expression shift from wicked anticipation to utter terror as his master spun, smashing the hammer down on the man's left shoulder. The audible crunch of breaking bones was quickly drowned out by shrieks as he dropped to the floor in a puddle of pain.

His companion skidded to a stop in a cloud of dust, safely out of the reach of the long-handled sledge.

Master Rotez had already moved on. He stepped backward, allowing the smooth oak to slide through his hands, taking the sledge in a shorter grip. Mid-turn, he used the iron strapped handle to parry a flashing chop from the third guard. The man let out an alarmed yelp as Master Rotez used his immense frame to shoulder the man backward. He crashed into the door frame and rebounded, only to meet a sharp sideways blow from Master Rotez's sledge to the head, collapsing bonelessly to the floor.

Another swift turn brought Master Rotez around to face the remaining guard hovering in the doorway, marginally more fortunate than his two fellows. The man hesitated, hovering over his now silent comrade. His eyes flickered to Duran, who backed further away towards the warmth of the forge, wide-eyed at the drawn sword twitching his way. With the big smith halfway across the room and Duran retreating further, he glanced down to check on his now silent companion, seemingly sure of his safety.

At least until Master Rotez landed a kick squarely on the bucket beside the large center anvil. Half-filled with quenching oil, it emptied itself in a thick rain. It thoroughly drenched the green and black-clothed guard from head to toe. He stumbled backward from the door, blinking his eyes to clear them of the thick oil. Wiping his face clear, he had a fine view as Master Rotez struck the anvil at a shallow angle with his sledge, kicking out a shower of sparks. Alone, the sparks would have never been enough to light the oil. But in tune with the resounding clang of hammer striking anvil, Master Rotez's voice rumbled a strange phrase. His voice seemed to fill the smithy with a swirl of light, one that flowed and swirled along with the arcing sparks.

With an audible whoosh, the guard disappeared within a tower of flame.

He barely had time to scream before the thrown sledge smashed into his chest, catapulting him out of the smithy into the dust of the yard. He lay still, burning fitfully.

Duran sighed in relief. The guards would trouble them no longer. But then he heard the scrape of a boot behind him. Realizing he lost track of Wrelt while watching the short battle, he rushed to his Master, only to be seized roughly by a cold, armored gauntlet. Duran tried to squirm away, earning him a stunning blow to the head for his efforts.

"Be still, boy, or you'll earn far more than that."

Head lolling, Duran felt an icy shape press against his throat. Realizing Wrelt held a knife to his neck, he recoiled, pressing against the armored shape behind him. But this was no better as the armor sent waves of nausea through him. He struggled with the impossible task of holding onto the remains of his lunch while keeping his throat intact.

The armored man yanked him backward, away from Master Rotez. The gauntlets dug into his shoulder, holding him tight against the nauseating armor. Wrelt backed clear across the smithy, right into a rack of tongs beside the forge. Duran yelped as a hot line burned itself across his throat, followed by a stunning blow to the side of his head.

"I said quiet! That's enough, Rotez! No closer!"

Duran blinked his eyes, trying to focus on the blurry form of his master, who stood no more than three yards away. As his vision cleared, he realized something was very different. During the handful of seconds, it took Master Rotez to dispatch the three guardsmen, his face was calm, focused, and maybe even a little sad. But now he looked angry. *Very* angry.

It dawned on him that Master Rotez was angry not at the invasion of their home, not at Wrelt's demands, but was furious that Duran's life was being threatened. Dangerous as his situation was, warmth spread through him at the thought, pushing away the nausea. Under his shirt, the little pendant grew warm once again.

"If you want this boy to live, you'll back up Rotez. I'll not warn you again! What do you think you can do against me, anyway? My armor will protect me. I've taken blows like that before and fought on. The power infused into this armor is beyond anything you've ever seen, old man! Beyond even the power of the Five. Why the Duke wants you when he can have ensorcelled armor like this, I'll never know. But I will do my duty, nonetheless."

"Your duty, Captain? Your Duke is contravening a Royal Writ in order to retrieve me. Three of your men are dead already. And your armor? What do you really know about it? How it was made? When was the last time you took it off for more than a few minutes?"

"I… That's not important! Back up, turn around, and kneel on the ground. I'll tie those strong hands together so we don't have any further misunderstandings, yes?" Duran winced as Wrelt gripped him even more tightly. Duran shivered in fear: Wrelt's voice had taken on a hysterical edge that sounded far less confident than his words indicated.

Master Rotez held his thickly calloused hands out to the sides, taking four steps backward. But instead of turning to kneel as ordered, he reached up above the heavy beams above. Tall as he was, he had to rise onto his toes to reach, and Duran heard the scrape of something sliding across the wooden beam. Master Rotez's hand reappeared, holding a dusty hammer.

Extending the tool, he tapped it gently on a nearby anvil. A pure, clear tone rang throughout the smithy. Duran smiled at the tone. He couldn't explain it, but the vibrant sound was the direct opposite of the feeling Wrelt's armor provoked.

Wrelt's body stiffened as he and Duran reached the same conclusion: this was no forging hammer. The solid shape was a powerful war hammer. The broad head gleamed even through a layer of dust. Inlaid lines of silver chased around the rounded body from the flat head to a spike at the rear. Inscriptions marked the length of the dark wooden handle, capped with a steel butt plate.

"Wrelt, you are a victim of a terrible crime. Your Duke has sentenced you to endless madness if we don't act soon. You have your oaths to your Duke, I understand. But I have oaths of my own. I will not permit this demon to exist. Please let me help you. We can do this together."

"The Duke would never consort with such powers! You will surrender, or the boy dies!"

In sharp contrast to the warmth of his pendant, Duran's back grew painfully cold, pressed against Wrelt's armored torso. Waves of nausea pounded him, barely fought off by the strength of the pendant around his neck. The two competing sensations roiled back and forth inside him, waging a silent war for his soul.

"That hammer will do you no good, Rotez! I am a Captain of the Guard. I have trained in the arts of battle for my entire life. My armor is imbued with elemental power you can only imagine. Whatever magic you've bound in that lump of steel won't save you. Or your little apprentice here. And if you try to stop me, perhaps the Duke won't be receiving his prize after all." Wrelt's voice turned sickly sweet as if he relished the chance to defy his orders to take Rotez alive.

"Did you know, Wrelt, that a Binding Smith can convince elementals to bestow a great many different properties to its host? I can see from the way you move that your armor is much lighter than it should be, no doubt a benefit from the elemental chained inside. Your silent approach earlier is another benefit, no doubt. Many things are possible, like swords that remain sharp for years, arrow points that strike with the weight of my hammer, or a spear tip that can pierce even the finest steel."

As his Master spoke, Duran's nausea eased, or rather, was pushed out. He gulped a deep breath of air, still conscious of the blade at his throat. Outside, the sun was descending, its last few rays swallowed by gathering clouds. But inside, the smithy was growing brighter. To his left the forge was bathed in a roiling orange and silver glow, far brighter than Duran had ever seen.

Distract him! Master Rotez needs your help! He cried wordlessly to the elemental.

"I'm not interested in your…"

"You see, Wrelt," cutting the Captain off, "the steel has a soul as real as mine. As real as yours was. The best binders work with that soul to create something truly incredible. Your armor is a perversion of that bond. Instead of dealing fairly with the elemental to bind it, or better yet, simply asking, the monster that created your armor enslaved an elemental, denying it free will and compelling it to an eternity of servitude. And what is even worse, they failed to give you something very important, Wrelt."

"What… What do you mean?" Wrelt's voice was strange. Strained, angry, and yet confused, as if Master Rotez held it in thrall with his very words. Or perhaps it was the radiant light flowing from the oddly quiet forge just behind Wrelt that had him befuddled.

"I'm sorry to be the one to tell you this, but I think you should know. Your very fine suit of armor doesn't cover your face."

Wrelt's body twitched as if he was struggling to make sense of the statement. Before he could muster a response, the forge erupted in flame and the angry crackle of hot coals, bathing the smithy in light both magical and visible.

For a moment, Wrelt shifted his knife hand to meet the new threat.

That moment was all Master Rotez needed. His right arm blurred as it whipped forward, hammer streaking through the air to strike Wrelt's face with a sickening crunch. Duran darted away as the body clattered to the ground. He found himself wrapped in Master Rotez's arms, the big man kneeling on the hard floor, holding him as sobs wracked his body.

"You did very well, Duran. We're safe now."

Time passed. How long, he couldn't have said. Finally, the sobs faded.

Reluctantly, Duran stepped back from the warm embrace.

He glanced at the unmoving, armored shape half-folded up against the wall. He wiped the remnants of tears from his eyes, noticing he'd smeared blood from his neck on his Master's shoulder.

"What will we do now, Master?"

"First things first, Duran. We need to get that cut cleaned. Then deal with this." Sighing deeply, he motioned at Wrelt's crumpled figure. "After that, we get to the real work. We find the one who did this and make sure it won't happen again."

Underneath Duran's shirt the pendant smoldered.

END

Compact

By: Arlen Feldman

You didn't have to make it across the desert. Most didn't—they'd find a sprite or occasionally something more powerful, join with it, and return home with just enough power to live their lives.

Even this early, Kieran was already sweating under the blazing sun, his shirt sticky under the heavy pack he carried.

But Ander, his mentor, had made Kieran race around the village with ever-heavier packs. Kieran had hated him for that. Ander was already considered a coward, and Kieran, his pledge, was seen doing nothing but running.

But now he understood. He'd seen Serbus—whose massive fists Kieran had encountered more than once—lying gasping against a rock, pouring precious water over his head to cool off.

As Kieran jogged past, he wondered if Serbus would even make it home. Not everyone did. And nobody made it back without joining, ever. Nobody but Ander.

The whole village had turned out for the Assigning. It was a picnic for most and a chance for people to show off. Kieran had entered the village square through a gate made of wispy rainbows and then dodged shooting stars from a mock-battle between last year's pledges. There were tables stacked with a dozen different types of food that never ran out— the plates constantly refilling.

Kieran wasn't hungry, though. He was just barely old enough to be assigned a mentor, and he was smaller than every other pledge. It wasn't a competition—supposedly. But your joining defined your whole future life, and none of the pledges was willing to risk that. Even the thought of eating made him feel sick.

He walked past a table where Ander, the blacksmith, was showing off his wares— some day-to-day pots and implements, but also cunning animals made of wood and bent metal. Iron didn't accede to magic, so these all had to be made by hand. Ander's work was very popular, especially amongst those with smaller joinings. The majors, of course, didn't need to bother with iron or pots at all.

Kieran would give anything to have a major joining. To have power and respect—and maybe some fear—from the bullies he'd grown up with. But that meant getting a strong mentor. Again, everyone said there was no particular reason why a pledge would end up with the same joining as their mentor, but it seemed to happen more often than not. Yet another thing about magic that people didn't really understand. Or, if they did, something they weren't willing to talk about.

Kieran was starting to feel like an ant under a lens. The shadows under the white boulders littering the desert were sharp, and the reflections made his eyes water. Ander had said that it was better to move in the mornings and evenings, and rest during the day. You didn't, of course, risk traveling at night.

He found a space amongst a group of rocks that would provide him with some shade and cover. Kieran checked all around before lying down, using his hands to make as comfortable a spot as he could on the gravelly sand. He took a small drink, swirling the tepid water in his mouth before swallowing it.

It was then that he saw the sprite. It was a mottled gray humanoid, maybe a foot tall, with four semi-transparent wings fluttering like mad behind it as it pushed a rock twice its size for its own purposes.

It would be so simple to capture it and be done. It would be a small power, but a power. A year ago, when he'd first become a pledge, Kieran would have leapt at the chance. But not now. He knew how to get through the desert. He smiled, watching the little creature working.

From behind him, Kieran heard a rustling sound as though something heavy was trying to move quietly. Kieran pulled back his legs so that he was entirely hidden behind the rocks. The sprite looked around warily.

Serbus crept within a few feet of Kieran's hiding place, moving as stealthily as the large boy could manage, a large rock in his hands. Kieran had a mad urge to yell out and scare away the sprite, but even as he thought it, Serbus threw the rock. It connected with a sickening crunch, crushing the little creature. Serbus ran over in delight, grabbed the sprite, and held it up to his face.

The creature wasn't dead. It was making a weak chittering noise. Serbus used a finger to take blood from the sprite and touched it to his tongue. Then he said the words.

By the compact, thou and I are joined.

There was a flash. A blue glow from the sprite enveloped Serbus, who went rigid for a moment, then laughed. It was so strange to see the huge, scary Serbus laughing with the joy of a child as sparks shot from his fingers— even as he dropped the lifeless body of the sprite to the hot desert floor.

Emotions warred in Kieran—horror, jealousy, disgust. He knew that he'd have to do this if he wanted magic, but not against a defenseless sprite. He would face a creature that could fight back.

Both Kieran and Ander were yelling. Josim and Serbus, standing next to their new mentors, were laughing. Even some of the adults were laughing.

"There aren't enough mentors," Priam was saying. "The drawing was completely random." As if anyone believed that. Priam, head of the village, proud and incredibly powerful, looked slightly abashed. Ander, who never lost his temper, stood inches away from Priam, who backed up a step.

"Can you even mentor me?" Kieran asked after they had bowed to the inevitable, and Kieran had followed Ander to the smithy.

Ander bit his lower lip and stared at Kieran for what seemed like an age. Finally, he sighed and nodded.

"Aye, lad. I can train you. It won't be like the others— no magical shortcuts. But if you listen to me, I can tell you how to get past the desert and the cliffs and into the forest. If you join, it will be with something powerful—something as capable of killing you as you are of killing it."

Kieran had felt the faintest sense of hope rekindle in his chest. He'd known about the desert, but this was the first time he'd heard about cliffs. Or a forest. How did Anders know about them? The smith may not have power, but he had knowledge, and that was something. Maybe Kieran wasn't destined for the failure that his friends and, hell, even his father had always assumed for him.

Pilox was dead. Something big had ripped him to shreds. Kieran's stomach somersaulted at the sight and smell, and he had to turn away, taking several long breaths before he was sure he wouldn't lose what little food he'd eaten that day. Kieran considered, briefly, trying to bury the other boy, but whatever killed him could come back. Of course, if it were something powerful…

But no. Ander had told him he needed to get to the forest for a major power. Even with a more powerful species, the ones that roamed the desert tended to be old or runts. Kieran held his breath and dragged Pilox under the shade of a rock, which was pointless but made him feel better. After a few agonized moments, he took Pilox's water

Not long after, he passed two of the girls, Radia & Quell. Quell ignored him, but he was almost positive that Radia had winked at him. The thought of it buoyed him up for the next hour as he worked steadily east.

Despite the heat, he perspired less than expected, probably due to the lack of liquid inside him. Kieran emptied Pilox's waterskin, dropped it to the ground, and froze; something was there, a few dozen yards ahead on the path.

But it wasn't moving. He took a few cautious steps forward, and when the shape still didn't move, he went over to it. It was the body of a wyvern. They didn't often come out this far, but whoever joined with it would be very powerful, no matter what Ander said. Kieran hoped that it wasn't Josim. Josim and his gang were bad enough. Josim, with a major power, was the stuff of nightmares. Kieran swore to himself yet again that he wasn't coming back without a major power of his own.

The sun was higher in the sky now and he'd have to stop soon, but he wanted to put some distance between himself and the wyvern's body. He jogged forward for a while, then crested a gravely dune and stopped, awestruck. They were still miles away, but the gray cliffs stretched away seemingly forever. From here, they looked sheer, high, and completely impassable.

But Ander had shown him how to get past them.

Just because Ander was the only adult in the village without magic didn't mean he was defenseless. The boys were sneaking up on him, where he slept on a cot outside his workshop. As children, they didn't have magic either, but they had sticks and rocks.

"Look out," Kieran yelled. He'd regret that later if the other boys caught him.

Ander was up and moving faster than seemed possible. Josim swung a thick stick at Ander, who caught it as though it was nothing and pushed, sending Josim flat onto his back. The other boys rushed in. Kieran heard the crunch as Ander's fist made contact with someone's face, followed by a scream of pain. Another boy—Serbus—went sprawling.

Kieran charged in and grabbed at one of the boys attacking his mentor. Next thing he knew, Kieran was on the ground, clutching his gut. The boy who had hit him was shoved backward by Ander, windmilled, and then tripped over Kieran, winding him a second time. Gasping for breath, Kieran watched as Ander slammed two other boys into each other as though they were toys.

But there were too many attackers. A rock hit Ander in the forehead and he stumbled backward. Josim was back up and swinging his stick towards Ander's back.

Then, there was a flash, and everyone froze in place.

Priam was standing there, hands outstretched, looking furious. Even Kieran, wheezing on the ground, found that he couldn't move.

"Explain," said Priam, ice in his voice. He gestured, and Josim slid forward as though pulled by ropes until he stood before the village elder. Another gesture and the boy could speak.

"He's a coward. It's not right…"

"Enough." If anything, Priam looked even angrier. "All of you, out of my sight." Another wave of his hand, and everyone could move again. Two of the boys, who'd been frozen in motion, fell over. They all looked down as they walked away. Except for Josim, who glared at Priam before turning and strutting towards his home.

Priam gave Ander a measured stare and the slightest nod, which Ander returned. Then Priam just disappeared with a tiny crack of sound. Priam was one of only a handful of people in the village with the power to do that. Rumor had it that he'd joined with a dragon, but he refused to say. Watching the display of power, Kieran hoped more than ever that he'd join with a strong spirit during the trials—or else Josim and his cronies would make his life a living hell.

Not that he had much of a chance with Ander as a mentor. Despite his early promises to train him, Ander had him doing pointless exercises, mostly running with weights. It was all so unfair. The pain in his gut brought all of the anger back to the surface. Why had they assigned him a mentor who wasn't joined at all?

Ander limped over to him and held out a hand. Ignoring it, Kieran climbed to his feet and went into the house. Even that made him angry—every other house used magic to make it comfortable and light. Ander's house was hand-built, *the rough-hewn space lit by smoky little lamps. Kieran threw himself into a chair and held his stomach, which still ached.*

After a few minutes, Ander came in and took a chair himself. His forehead was bleeding, but he still wore the crazy-calm look.

"Are you hurt badly?" he asked.

"I'm fine."

Ander nodded. "Thank you for the warning."

Kieran grunted.

"If you hadn't given it, they might've killed me. They've tried before."

Another grunt.

"And then you would have been given another mentor. One who is joined."

That shocked Kieran out of his anger for a moment. He looked directly at Ander. Honestly, it hadn't occurred to him. For half a second he regretted calling out the warning, but then it passed. Ander hadn't chosen to be a mentor; he had argued against it. It wasn't the blacksmith's fault, and Kieran wouldn't have been able to live with himself if he'd not tried to help.

As if he could read Kieran's thoughts, Ander suddenly grinned. It made him look twenty years younger.

"Well, I'm glad you warned me, no matter what."

Unable to stop himself, Kieran grinned back, then frowned. "You're bleeding. Should I get someone to heal you?"

Ander touched the wet spot on his forehead. "It's nothing." He fetched a damp cloth and pressed it to the wound on his forehead.

"Don't you wish you had power of your own?" Kieran suddenly asked, a question he'd been bottling up for weeks. "To heal yourself. Or finish your house, or make better food or, or…everything? Even if you'd joined with a sprite, you'd be able to…" He trailed off.

Ander listened to Kieran's rant with a slightly bemused expression but didn't say anything for a while. Finally, he sighed. "I wanted magic, strong magic, more than anything else in the world. But I wasn't willing to pay the price."

"Price? What price?" Kieran felt completely confused.

"Never mind. It's getting late. Let's leave off your training for today and get an early start tomorrow."

The *easy* way past the cliffs was a thirty-mile hike through the desert, then making your way through a marshy bog full of things wanting to kill you—only a few of which were worth joining with—and twenty miles back.

Unless your mentor was a blacksmith. Kieran pulled the collection of iron spikes and the hammer out of his pack. He and Ander had snuck out on a dozen nights to practice climbing at some nearby rocks. But the cliffs were another thing entirely—hundreds of feet, mostly sheer. Kieran took a deep breath and then started to ascend.

"What do you know of the compact?" Ander asked suddenly, after breakfast.

"It's the agreement between humans and magical creatures that cedes humans the right to magic." Kieran recited the exact wording they'd all been taught in school.

"And what do the magical creatures get out of it, do you think?"

Kieran blinked. He'd never thought about it. "Uh, protection, I guess. We stay out of their lands. Except for during the joining, of course."

"Of course," said Ander, his voice calm as always. "Now, how many pullups can you do?"

He had to be more than halfway. Surely, he was more than halfway. He hammered in another spike and tied off the rope that would theoretically catch him if he fell, using the knot that Ander had drilled into him. Kieran's arms were burning, but if he trusted the spike and his knot, he could lean back and rest.

He leaned back. The spike held.

Kieran couldn't see the top of the cliff from where he hung, but he could definitely see the ground far below.

If he could ignore his precarious position, the view was amazing. Kieran could see for miles and watch the other pledges crawling across the desert like ants. He'd seen Radia, no longer with Quell, fight and defeat an Indus and was glad for her. There were a couple of unidentifiable bodies and he wondered who they were. He hoped that one of them was Josim. Somehow, he doubted it.

Kieran drank some water and went back to climbing.

"How did you end up becoming a smith?"

Kieran was pumping the bellows as Ander turned several billets in the coals, waiting for them to heat to the proper temperature.

"My father was a smith. He taught me, and when I came back without…it just seemed natural. Besides, I've always enjoyed the work."

"And your father. Did he have…? I mean, was he joined?"

Ander snorted. "Oh yes. He was very powerful. When the big cockatrice attack happened—that would be a few years before you were born—my father and Priam were the ones who fought them off. He loved showing off the scars from that."

The smith took one of the billets from the fire and started shaping it on the anvil with smooth, heavy blows from his hammer. But he looked wistful. "He was a hard man, but I miss the old bastard."

Kieran thought about that for a while. "I don't miss my father. Not at all."

"I noticed that you hadn't gone to visit him."

"No point. Either he'd be too drunk to notice me, or he'd spend the time telling me how worthless I was." Kieran's voice was even, but he was suddenly pumping the bellows hard.

"Slow down there, boy," said Ander quietly. "You'll burn through the billet."

Kieran forced himself to slow down and took a deep breath.

"It's my fault that he only joined with a sprite. He had to get back to my mother because she was pregnant with me. But then she died, and he had to raise me by himself with hardly any power."

Ander stopped hammering and turned to face Kieran, his eyes flashing orange in the light of the forge.

"I was on the same joining as your father. He thought he was a big man because he was only sixteen and had married. Not his choice, of course—once it became clear that your mother was expecting. She was a pretty little thing and smart. It was a shame that…well, it was a shame."

Kieran stopped pumping the bellows. He'd never heard anyone talk about his parents before.

"But I'll tell you this." Ander raised his hammer and shook it towards Kieran like a toy. *"Pregnant wife or not, your father wouldn't have turned back if he hadn't run out of water. He was lucky he even found a sprite."*

Kieran left the ropes and climbing gear at the cliffs. He'd need it for the climb down. Although, if he joined with something powerful, perhaps he'd be able to float down. Better still, perhaps he'd just be able to reappear back in the village.

One of the many things Ander hadn't been able to tell him was how quickly you could use your power. Did it come all at once, or did it take its time? Or did you need time to learn how to use it? Different people who'd joined with the same type of creature seemed to have different skill levels, so it might require practice. Or maybe different people were just naturally more talented? And jumping off a cliff as a first major test of power seemed a little foolhardy, so he'd likely need the climbing gear no matter what.

Of course, if he were killed by whatever creature he attempted to join with, he wouldn't need the climbing gear either.

The forest didn't come right up to the edge of the cliffs. There was a broad rocky plateau. A few scraggly plants were growing in cracks, but Ander had cautioned him against eating anything he didn't recognize. The forest was visible in the distance, though.

Kieran ate the last of his travel rations and started walking. It wasn't until he'd almost reached the forest that it occurred to him that someone else could use his climbing ropes to get up the cliffs. But it was far too late to go back.

It took a while for Kieran to realize it, but Ander mostly didn't use magical objects either. As the village smith, he could pretty much demand any price for his work, including magical items to make life easier—glow-bulbs, pots that kept food warm or cold, anything. He could have had magic users improve his home or create a self-pumping bellows. But he didn't.

"I made my choice," was about all he said on the subject. *"I like to rely on what I've earned."*

The forest was an entirely different world, dark and sinister. After twenty minutes inside, Kieran was completely turned around. The whole place fairly buzzed with insects. Unseen creatures made a cacophony of songs, croaks, and screams. Even the trees creaked and whispered. He felt watched from all sides.

Kieran stumbled onto a path, a game trail maybe, and decided to follow it for a while. It led to a stagnant pool. He looked around, but it seemed deserted, so he risked cupping his hands and taking a drink. The water was a bit sour, but otherwise seemed okay.

He reached back to grab his waterskin just as something huge exploded out of the water, right where his head had been a moment earlier. He windmilled backward as a head full of teeth spun toward him. Kieran managed to pull his knife out of his belt and slashed at the thing, grazing its thick hide and making it retreat slightly.

A moment later, two more heads burst out of the water. Kieran managed to block one with his knife, but the other sank its teeth into his arm. He screamed and stabbed blindly, burying the knife deep into the head, which let him go, emitting a high-pitched scream. Kieran just managed to pull his knife free, rolling backward out of reach of all three heads.

It was a hydra. He tried desperately to remember whether the thing could leave the water. He knew they were very powerful but almost impossible to kill—particularly with just a knife.

Fortunately, the thing decided that Kieran was not easy prey either. The three heads disappeared beneath the surface. Kieran pushed through tree branches and brambles to distance himself from the hydra. He finally stopped, bleeding and breathless, next to a huge old oak tree.

Some are genuinely mean and evil. Some are smart and wily. But most magical creatures are just that, creatures trying to live their lives who happen to have magic. They'll defend themselves, though. Or eat you if you seem like an easy meal.

Surprisingly, Ander knew a lot about the various magical creatures that lived in the desert and forest. He made Kieran memorize characteristics, including how they defended or attacked.

He'd mentioned this to Radia in the marketplace, and she'd been genuinely surprised.

"My mentor hasn't said anything about that. I don't think she knows much about the different creatures."

For once, Kieran felt proud of his mentor. He also wondered if he'd underestimated Ander in other ways. Few of the other boys were doing the physical training that he was and as his arms and chest swelled with muscles, the bullying dropped off. And how many of those in his joining year knew how to get past the cliffs?

But if that was all true, it was also true that Ander hadn't joined. Why not?

Kieran heard it before he saw it. It sounded like a titanic struggle. He eased his way cautiously between some trees that edged around a large clearing. Close to the center, a horse was trapped in a pit and desperately trying to free itself. Except that it wasn't a horse; it was a snow-white unicorn.

The sun chose that moment to break through the clouds, sending a beam of light to bounce off the golden horn. The unicorn was huge, with rippling muscles straining against its prison. Blood spattered its flank, and an ugly wooden spike protruded a foot beyond its side.

The creature was simultaneously the most beautiful and the scariest thing Kieran had ever seen.

Ander hadn't talked much about unicorns, but everyone knew there wasn't a more magical creature. Unlike most magical beasts, unicorns were smart and actively used their magic. In a straight-up fight, Kieran wouldn't stand a chance of joining with a unicorn. But trapped and distracted? In his mind, he pictured himself drawing his knife, sneaking up on the creature, and slitting its throat. But he left his knife where it was.

After a while, the unicorn stopped struggling. It must be close to exhausted. Kieran watched it, then picked up a thick branch and crept into the clearing.

He got within about ten feet before the unicorn sensed him. It turned its head to face him. The horn looked deadly-sharp, and the icy blue eyes seemed to bore into him.

Kieran held up a hand. "It's okay," he said, trying to keep his voice calm. "Trust me."

The unicorn shook its head and made a sound deep in its throat but held still. It either understood him or was too tired to fight. Either way, it let Kieran come right up to it without attacking.

The spike looked rotten. The trap must have been old. Kieran grabbed the end of the spike and snapped it off as close to the unicorn's flank as he dared. The unicorn snorted in pain but didn't move.

"I'm sorry, but this is going to hurt." He slid the branch underneath the unicorn until the end rested on the other side, then he took a couple of deep breaths and lifted.

A year ago, he wouldn't have been able to move the branch at all. As it was, all of his strength was just barely enough to raise the unicorn a couple of inches.

It was enough. The unicorn's powerful back legs suddenly kicked, pulling itself off the spike. Although Kieran couldn't quite see how it managed it, the creature kicked two more times and was suddenly out of the pit. Kieran sighed with relief.

But then the unicorn rounded on him, the point of the horn pointing right at him. Before he could speak or move, the powerful head thrust the horn deep into Kieran's shoulder.

Kieran screamed and tried to pull away, but the horn's spirals held him in place. It was agony.

And then there was a voice in his head.

Do you expect gratitude, human?

He wanted to protest, to say he expected nothing. But that was a lie. He *had* expected gratitude, or at least not to be attacked.

The voice in his head laughed. *Perhaps you should expect the same mercy from the creatures whose power you steal with your 'compact'?*

Kieran thought he was going to pass out from the pain. He wanted to argue—to explain what he'd always been told—the compact was *between* humans and magical creatures. But right then, he couldn't bring himself to believe it. He wondered how anyone could.

But at least he hadn't killed and stolen anything. And, if he was going to die, he was going to face it head-on. He forced himself to raise his head and look the unicorn straight in the eyes. Then he noticed someone coming up behind the unicorn.

"Look out," he yelled.

In a second, the horn had come free, leaving Kieran in fresh agony. The unicorn reared, and iron-shod hooves dodged Josim's spear and smashed into the boy's head. Josim went down and lay still.

The unicorn turned and stared at Kieran with those icy-blue eyes for a long moment. Then it turned and galloped off.

"You're back. You're alive!"

Kieran grinned at his mentor. "Sorry. Had to take the long way back."

"The long way? You've been gone for a month." He pulled Kieran into a fierce hug, then let him go when he heard the wince of pain.

"You're hurt?"

"It's nothing." Which wasn't exactly true. The wound in his shoulder was still painful, although it was healing. "But I could use something to drink…"

Ander then insisted that he sit, eat, and drink and didn't ask him any questions until Kieran finally pushed away his second plate.

"I didn't think it was possible, but I can't eat another thing."

That got a laugh from his mentor, followed by an appraising stare.

"So, did you find a powerful creature to join with?"

"You could say that. I ran into a unicorn."

Ander stiffened. "A unicorn?"

"Yes. It was trapped in a pit, unable to move."

"And did you 'join' with it?"

"No. I helped it escape."

Ander breathed out, "Did you now?" His expression was curious, but then he turned away deliberately and walked to his favorite chair. Kieran watched as his mentor made himself comfortable.

"Funny thing," Kieran said finally. "The unicorn had iron horseshoes."

"That is funny," said Ander. His tone was bland, but there was the slightest twinkle in his eye. "So, tell me. Why didn't you join with him?"

"It wasn't worth the price."

END

Sins of the Scarlet Rage

By: Michael K. Falciani

"I cannot believe you are taking the word of that nitwit at the gate," Kildare complained, eyeing his brother pointedly. "Did he look trustworthy to you?"

The lean hunter riding next to him shook his head. "Not particularly, no," Zedaine waved offhandedly.

"Then why in the bloody hell are you listening to him?" Kildare demanded, absently patting the neck of his chocolate-colored mare. "By the gods, no wonder we keep having problems. You think everyone is truthful."

Zedaine shot his older brother a look of disapproval. "That's nonsense. Everyone we met on the road said the same thing. The Deacon is the only decent-sized inn within the walls of Golwick. Did you want to spend another night out under the stars?"

"Pfftt," Kildare grunted with a wave of his hand. "Better the stars than a place named The Deacon," he scoffed. "Sounds like some kind of religious purgatory. Besides, your guard friend back there said it caught fire a few days ago."

"Minot damage, I'm sure," Zedaine replied.

Kildare wiped a line of sweat from his brow, muttering to himself. "There has to be someplace else. Golwick isn't that small of a village."

"Let's give the religious purgatory a look, at least," Zedaine chuckled. "If it doesn't meet your lofty standards, we will seek lodgings elsewhere."

"It's probably a lice-riddled cesspit," Kildare grumbled.

Zedaine gave his brother a long stare. "You have been in a sour mood since we left Reefhaven. I miss them too, you know."

Kildare gave Zedaine a sharp look. "What are you talking about? I don't miss anyone."

"Yes, you do. You miss Gwen," Zedaine stated simply. "I know how you feel. I can't seem to get Lisle out of my mind. They were…decidedly unique women."

Kildare inhaled as if to refute his brother's words but chose to hold his tongue instead.

Knowing he had hit close to the mark, Zedaine kicked the sides of his mount, moving his dappled stallion at a trot toward the center of town. Less than a half mile from the village gate, a three-story building came into view. Hanging above the entrance was a white sign depicting a faded picture of a black biretta.

"There it is," Zedaine nodded, casting a backward glance at his brother.

"Doesn't look like much to me," Kildare drawled, shading his eyes with his hand.

"The place might surprise you," Zedaine continued.

"Ever the optimist," Kildare grumbled. "The paint is chipped on one side—there is lichen growing on the roof, and the back wall is all burned." He sighed. "I told you; this place is a cesspit."

The elder sibling climbed off his mount. "Get the horses to the stable, I'll check the place out. I need to use the privy anyway."

"Leave me a drak to tip the stable boy with," Zedaine said, leaping from his saddle.

"Here's an obol," Kildare grunted, flipping his brother a circular coin. "You want to leave a silver. Take it from your own money pouch."

"No one likes a miser," the big hunter sniffed, catching the bronze coin easily.

"Shut up, Zedaine," Kildare snarled, walking inside the building. "I'll only be gone for a few minutes. For once in your life, stay out of trouble."

Zedaine chuckled under his breath and made for the stable on the eastern side of the inn.

Ridley walked between the trio of armed men, trying to keep her hands from trembling.

"Pick up your feet, girly," barked the burly guard to her left. Dressed in a stiff leather cuirass, the man nudged her shoulder, moving her along. "Don't try any of that mystical nonsense either."

Hands tied behind her back, Ridley stumbled, nearly falling to her knees. Glancing upward through eyes swollen black, she saw the three-story structure of The Deacon looming less than fifty yards away. The fifteen-year-old girl knew who waited inside. A cold fear clutched at her chest, and she came to a grinding halt, her legs refusing to budge.

"What's this?" snarled the sergeant from behind her. "Get moving, else I'll drag you the rest of the way."

"Please, Vole," Ridley begged the man behind her, "there must be some other way…"

"I said move!" Vole barked, shoving her forward.

Ridley crashed to the ground, hot tears streaking down her face. "I won't go in," she cried, her voice breaking. "You cannot force me too…"

"Damn you girl," Vole roared, grabbing a fistful of Ridley's hair. "Get on your feet and move your ass, or I'll bleed you here in the street!"

Ridley tried pulling away from the sergeant's grip on her hair in a futile attempt to escape.

"Please," Ridley sobbed. "I beg you. Let me go back. I won't do it again, I swear…"

"The hell with this," Vole hissed, drawing his knife. "It's high time we teach this bitch…"

"Well, this is a sight to see," Ridley heard a voice say, cutting through the sergeant's bluster. "What heroes they have here in Golwick,"

Ridley looked up and saw a tall man dressed in brown hunting leathers walk from around the side of the building. He was strong and lean, his chestnut-colored hair tied in a shoulder-length ponytail behind him. A sword hung neatly at his side in a mud-spattered scabbard that had seen better days. He seemed calm, relaxed even—save for his eyes. Those dark orbs were hard, home to an anger Ridley could sense from her position several yards away.

"Keep your distance," the third guard said, placing a scarred hand upon the hilt of his sword. "We are under orders."

The man's gaze shifted to the speaker, and a smile crept its way onto his face. "Tell me," he began, casually removing one of his riding gloves. "What crime has this child committed that it would take three soldiers to force her into submission here in the middle of the street?"

"Piss off," the sergeant snarled, his hand still gripping a fistful of Ridley's hair.

The hunter cocked his eyebrow and stepped closer, removing his other glove. "I don't think I will," he said. "You see, I despise bullies. I have no tolerance for them—never have."

"If he takes another step, gut him," Vole ordered, narrowing his eyes.

"Hold on now," the hunter offered, coming to a stop, his hands raised in front of him. "Let's be reasonable about this."

"This is none of your business," the first guard warned, placing a hand upon his knife.

"I am *making* it my business," the hunter replied, his voice hardening.

The three guards glanced at one another, uncertain what the stranger meant.

"Hold this for me," the hunter said, suddenly tossing his riding gloves at the two guards flanking Ridley. Both men, moving reflexively, snatched the gloves out of the air.

Ridley felt the hand gripping her hair push her forward. Off balance, she fell into a face full of mud. She was aware of the sound of flesh striking flesh above her, followed immediately by two bodies crashing to the ground.

Regaining her focus, Ridley twisted herself into an upright position. She saw the stranger standing protectively over her, his hands balled in fists. On either side of him lay Vole's two guards, bleeding and unconscious.

"Those are my cousins, you bastard," hissed Vole, drawing his sword. "You will die for that."

"I doubt it," the hunter replied, moving past Ridley.

Faster than her eyes could follow, Ridley saw the hunter lash outward, striking Vole in the face with a lightning jab. Stunned, Vole rocked back on his heels. An eyeblink later, he was struck by a roundhouse that knocked him from his feet. His body crashed to the ground, joining his cousins in the realm of unconsciousness.

Ridley's savior turned around.

"Are you alright?" he asked.

"I…I think so," Ridley managed to stammer, rising unsteadily to her feet.

"Give me your hands," he grunted, taking out a knife and slicing through the ropes that had bound her.

"You…should not have interfered," Ridley muttered, rubbing at her wrists, looking fearfully at The Deacon.

"Why not?" the hunter asked in confusion. "Did you enjoy being dragged through the streets?"

Ridley forced herself to remain calm. "No," she admitted. "But…," she glanced down at Vole. "These men—they work for Sir Pierce."

"Who is Sir…" his question trailed off. "What happened to your face?" he asked, "It is nothing," Ridley began to say, wiping away the mud as best she could.

She heard the door to the inn open behind them. In a panic, Ridley turned, seeing a second man, similar in appearance to the hunter, staring at the scene in front of him.

"You have got to be *shitting* me," he snarled, rubbing at his temple.

Glaring daggers at her savior, the newcomer stepped down the stairs and walked over next to them. "I was gone for less than two minutes," he raged at the hunter. "Can't I even take a piss without you mucking things up?"

"Kil, they were…" the hunter began.

"Shut up Zedaine, just shut your goddamn mouth!" Kildare snapped. "I don't care if they were going to flay the skin off a newborn child…I told you to stay out of trouble!"

"Please, sir," Ridley cut in. "It wasn't his fault. Your friend…"

"My brother," Kildare corrected, still seething.

"Your brother saved me."

Kildare looked at the girl for a long moment and then back at the smirking face of Zedaine. "Let me guess," Kildare said finally. "These men work for whatever idiot runs this village?"

"Apparently," Zedaine agreed, glancing for confirmation at Ridley.

"Of course they do," Kildare snarled. "I'll bet you a gold falcon we can no longer stay here at The Deacon, can we?"

"Not likely," Zedaine smiled.

Kildare began to swear under his breath.

"What is the big deal?" Zedaine asked. "We will stay someplace else."

"Because, you calf-brained moron," Kildare snapped. "I just paid for our room!"

Ridley swore Zedaine had to press his lips together to keep from laughing. "That is unfortunate," the big hunter managed to say.

Kildare eyed his brother dangerously. "You just—can't help yourself, can you?"

"You would have done the same," Zedaine replied.

"I doubt it," Kildare huffed, gesturing at the downed soldiers. "Did you even try talking to these poags, or did you lead with your fists?"

"What do you think?" Zedaine quipped.

The elder brother looked from Zedaine to Riley and sighed. "Is there somewhere else in this godforsaken village we can stay?"

"Yes," Ridley answered. "The Candlelight Inn."

"Where is it?"

"Just outside the walls, on the southern edge of Golwick," Ridley answered.

Kildare scowled at them both.

"You didn't want to stay here anyway," Zedaine offered.

"I didn't want to be run off after I paid either," Kildare snapped back.

"Well," Zedaine shrugged. "It turns out that you were right. There *is* another inn here in Golwick. That should make you feel good."

Ridley saw Kildare's face turn red, clearly fighting against the desire to explode at his brother.

"Go…get the horses," he managed to choke out.

"Yes…um…about that," Zedaine said innocently. "I'm going to need another drak," he deadpanned. "I'll have to pay the stable boy again…you understand."

Kildare gave his brother a look of such rage, that Ridley thought he would suffer a bout of apoplexy right there in front of her.

"Don't be surprised if I murder you in your sleep tonight," he hissed, stomping southward.

Ridley saw Zedaine smile broadly at his brother's exit, laughing softly to himself. "You'd best go with him, lass," the hunter said finally. "I'll catch up shortly."

She looked down, seeing the three men lying on the ground. "Thank you," she murmured, knowing his help had only staved off the inevitable.

He nodded at Ridley. "We will get to the Candlelight Inn and see what we can do about his mess."

Ridley felt her heart sink in her chest.

There is nothing anyone can do to protect me from myself, she thought as she started after Kildare.

The trio arrived at the doorway of the Candlelight Inn a quarter of an hour later. It was a neat, two-story structure with a half-dozen rooms located on the second floor. A stone fireplace rose up from the middle of the common room, its chimney extending to the roof. Upon their entry, Kildare noted a pair of worried faces inside, near the bar.

"Ridley!" shouted a middle-aged woman, rushing forward.

"Aunt Tess, Uncle Rex," the red-haired girl shouted in relief, running into the woman's embrace.

"How did you…never mind," a stout man began to ask before engulfing them both in a bearhug. "I'm just glad you are safe."

The three stood in the middle of the common room, holding one another for the span of several heartbeats.

"How about a drink?" Kildare asked, striding up to the polished mahogany bar.

"How about you sod off!" Rex barked, reaching behind him, gripping an oak cudgel.

Kildare frowned. "I think you…"

"You'll not be taking my niece to that filth Pierce again…I don't care how many of you he has!" the innkeeper roared, lifting the cudgel over his massive shoulders, swinging it at Kildare.

Kildare easily stepped aside, letting the oak club fly harmlessly past.

"There's been a bit of misunderstanding, friend," Zedaine offered, easing up next to his brother.

"Uncle, stop," Ridley said, moving between them.

"No," Rex snapped, raising his cudgel once more. "Those soldiers came when I wasn't here last time. Your poor aunt had to watch as they dragged you away. Never again! If it's a fight they want, they are going to get it! Now move!"

Ridley stood her ground.

"Oh, I like him," Zedaine smiled. "He's a brawler, that's for certain."

"You like everyone, you milksop," sniffed Kildare. "That's why we're in this mess."

"Nice attack, too," Zedaine admired, nodding at Rex. "Well timed, good balance—I bet you were a soldier once."

Rex blinked at Zedaine and lowered his cudgel. "Who are you?" he asked.

"Uncle, they helped me escape," Ridley explained. "Zedaine here downed Vole and two of his men. Kildare…well, he…"

She stared at the elder brother, at a loss for words.

"I objected to the whole thing," Kildare put in, giving her a scowl. "Unfortunately, my brother thinks more with his heart than his head, so here I…"

Kildare stopped speaking and lifted his nose high, inhaling deeply. "Is something burning?" he asked.

Tess swallowed softly, flicking her gaze toward the back of the inn.

"There is a stew cooking in the oven outside," she said, shifting her feet.

Kildare moved to stand in front of Tess, his dark eyes narrowing in suspicion. "That doesn't smell like stew."

"Kil?" Zedaine asked, catching the scent.

"In the backyard," the elder sibling nodded, striding through the common room.

"Wait," Tess shouted, "customers are not allowed to go back there!"

Ignoring her, the brothers left the room, exiting through the back door.

They stepped into a well-kept, cobblestone yard. There was a small brick-and-mortar building used for cooking adjacent to the inn. A babbling brook wound through the verdant grass plain behind it.

"That smell better not be what I think it is," Kildare muttered to his brother.

Zedaine said nothing. He entered the cooking structure a step ahead of his sibling.

Inside, their suspicions were confirmed. To the veteran warriors, the smell was unmistakable. Sickly sweet, it could only be the scent of burned human flesh. Lying in a charred mass on the ground was the nearly incinerated corpse of a man.

Kildare turned to his brother. "What the hell did you get us into?"

The five sat around a wooden table in the common room, each with a drink in front of them. The windows were closed, but Kildare sat at a vantage point where he could see if anyone was approaching from the village road. He glanced at Ridley who was looking down at the floor, refusing to make eye contact with anyone. He had become suspicious of the girl, and he wanted answers.

"First off," Kildare began, shrugging off his leather cuirass. "Who's out in the oven?"

Rex cleared his voice. "That is Boynten, younger brother to Sir Pierce."

"Pierce," Kildare murmured in thought. "Why does that name sound familiar?"

"Did you rap him on the head with your club first before incinerating him?" Zedaine asked Rex, unaware of Kildare's musings.

Rex shook his head. "Of course not. The missus and I retired early last night. Ridley was left to close things up. She's fifteen now…ready for more responsibility…and our patrons had all gone home for the evening…or so we thought."

Kildare turned his gaze to the red-haired girl next to him. "What happened?" he demanded, his tone cold.

Ridley shrunk under his words, clearly afraid.

"By the tits of Chara, you have the bedside manner of a picador bull," Zedaine said in annoyance. "Why don't you try turning her upside down and shaking the information out of her?"

"What?" Kildare protested, throwing his hands up. "It was a simple question."

Zedaine shook his head. "Tone matters—so does body language. You look and sound like one of the men that dragged her off."

"I can't help it—this is how I talk," Kildare snapped. "By the gods, when did everyone become so sensitive?"

"Try again," Zedaine suggested. "This time, think of her as a little sister."

Kildare placed both his hands on his head and pulled at his hair. "This is ridiculous," he groused.

"Just do it," Zedaine insisted.

Letting out an exasperated breath, Kildare slammed his hands on the table next to Ridley. "Would *someone* tell me what the hell happened to the man in the oven?" he demanded.

"By the gods, what is *wrong* with you?" Zedaine hissed.

"What?" Kildare protested. "You said treat her like our little sister! Saracen is a badass; she would yell back at me."

"I said *a* little sister, not *our* little sister," Zedaine growled back. "Of course, Saracen would yell back at you, she's used to you acting like a jackass!"

Kildare stood from his chair, a thunderous look on his face. He moved over to the window. Gazing outside, the taciturn warrior saw nothing on the road. In his head, he saw a pair of brilliant blue eyes that had haunted him for more than a fortnight.

Gwen, he thought, knowing Zedaine had been right earlier. He missed the fiery swordswoman more than he cared to admit. Kildare closed his eyes and focused on easing his mind. He'd told Gwen once when facing stressful situations, it was critical to remain calm. He knew, at this moment, he needed to follow his own advice.

Exhaling deeply, he turned away from the window and sat back down at the table. "I apologize for my tone," he began, looking at Ridley. "My brother is right about me; I am a jackass sometimes."

He placed his index finger under Ridley's chin and gently lifted her green eyes to meet his.

"However, if I am going to help you, I need to know what happened to Boynton. I am not angry with you, but this information is important."

Ridley swatted his hand away. "Don't touch me," she barked, her green eyes flashing in anger.

"My apologies," Kildare said. "I still need you to answer my question."

Ridley glanced over to her aunt, who nodded with encouragement.

"Boynton was waiting behind the inn last night," she said, her voice quiet. "He'd been here in the common room for most of the afternoon. I don't know how much wine he had, but it was enough to where I suspected he was drunk."

She paused, taking a drink of her cider.

"He left a few minutes before we closed," she continued. "He must have doubled around to the back of the inn and hidden inside the oven house. After my aunt and uncle retired for the evening, I went outside to dispose of the trash. That's when…"

She stopped as tears began to streak down her face.

"You are safe here," Zedaine encouraged her, coming to sit next to Ridley, careful not to touch the girl. "You can talk to us."

Ridley wiped away her tears with a sleeve and looked imploringly at Zedaine. "He grabbed me from behind," she said, her voice breaking. "He said…that I'd become a beautiful young woman."

She stopped once more, her breathing labored. "He said he wanted one kiss…one kiss and he'd go."

Ridley was crying now, unable to speak through her tears. Her aunt slid next to her and placed an arm around her shoulders. "These men are here to help you luv. I know how difficult it is. I want you to be brave, like you were last night."

Tess's words calmed Ridley and she pushed on. "I told him, 'no.' I said he needed to get off me…but Boynton refused. He started kissing my neck, licking me with his tongue. I remember he was laughing like it was some kind of game."

Ridley's eyes flicked to her aunt again. "I fought against him as hard as I could Tess, I swear it. But he was strong…by the gods he was so strong. I tried to call out, but he put his hand over my mouth, still laughing in my ear."

Ridley paused a moment before speaking again. Her voice was so quiet the others had to lean close to hear. "He put his other hand under my dress," she breathed. "He said I would love it. By Chara, I…I was so afraid."

"Did you get away?" Kildare asked softly.

Ridley hesitated at his question.

"Yes," she answered, a touch of anger in her voice. "I managed to bite the hand over my mouth. He yelled out and struck me across the face. I fell to the ground as he stood over me, cursing in pain."

She stopped, her face still.

"I saw him then, as he was. Not as Boynton, brother to our knight protector, but a spoiled child who'd grown into a man. He was petulant and angry because I wouldn't give him what he wanted."

She looked up at Kildare, her green eyes cold and distant. "He placed his hand on his belt. He said, 'I know how to treat a slut like you. You'll be begging for my cock come this time tomorrow.'"

Ridley's eyes flashed angrily at Kildare. "That's when it happened. That's when I killed him."

"*You* killed him?" Zedaine asked, eyes widening.

Ridley's face twisted in rage as she took in both brothers. "Yes, I did. I'll never let another man touch me again. No one will speak down to me anymore."

Ridley's eyes changed from cool green to hot amber as she stared back at Kildare in malevolence. "Including you, you arrogant bastard! How dare you touch me!"

"How did you kill him?" Kildare rasped.

"Like this," Ridley spat, raising her hand toward Kildare.

"*Ignis!*" she shouted.

A torrent of fire shot from her palm and struck Kildare directly in the chest.

"Ridley, no!" screamed her aunt, reaching out toward the girl.

"It's too late," shouted Rex, grabbing his wife, pulling her protectively behind him.

Flames of orange and yellow engulfed Kildare, thick enough to where his face was obscured. The magic lasted for no longer than a few seconds as Ridley's rage played itself out. She dropped to her side, horror filling her eyes.

Rex and Tess stared across the room.

"It... it's not possible," Rex stammered, his eyes wide.

"Goddammit, that stings," cursed a voice.

Standing in front of them was the sour face of Kildare. He was hale, save for the faint scorch marks on his chest where his tunic had been.

"I'm going to need a new shirt," he muttered.

"So, that's how you did it," Zedaine said with a nod. "You're a fire mage. Damn powerful one by the look of it."

"You...you're alive," gasped Tess, taking a tentative step toward Kildare.

"Yes," the elder sibling said offhandedly. He lifted the collar of his cloak, examining it closely from the side. "Damn me, this is singed too," he muttered.

"How did you survive the fire?" Rex asked, clearly stunned.

"I'm a vessel," Kildare shrugged, dropping the collar of his cloak.

"What, by Dourn's beard, is a vessel?" Tess asked, her mouth wide.

"I can absorb magic," Kildare answered, waving away the question. "Tell me Ridley, has your power ever manifested itself before yesterday?"

Ridley stared at Kildare, shocked that he was still standing. "I...yes, once, last week, at the Spring Festival."

"What happened?" Zedaine asked.

"Aren't you angry with me?" Ridley asked, ignoring his question. "I mean...I just tried to kill you."

"Pfftt," Kildare waved, sitting back down to his cider. "People try to kill me all the time. I wasn't in any danger. Besides, I suspected you could use magic. I wanted to provoke you into it. I am sorry I touched you, but I needed to see what would set you off."

"But, how did you..." Rex left his question hanging.

"Live?" Zedaine finished. "Like he said, Kildare is a vessel. He can absorb magic."

"A finite amount," the elder sibling put in dryly, reaching into his pack. "And it hurts like hell." He withdrew an olive-green tunic from the pack and draped it over his head. "Ridley, I need you to remember. What happened at the Spring Festival?"

"I...it was stupid," Ridley admitted. "I got angry over something trivial."

"What was it?" Tess asked.

Ridley hesitated a moment and then let out an exasperated breath. "You know the baker's son, Alac?"

"Bloody hell," Kildare said, rolling his eyes. "Tell me we aren't here because of some teen-age drama."

"Kil, that is enough," Zedaine chided. "We were that age not so long ago. I remember you pouting for a week because your crush, Althea, didn't respond to that love letter you sent her."

Kildare's eyes went cold. "Shut up, Zedaine. I was eleven years old. By the gods, how is it you can remember every little misstep in my life, but you cannot recall your own name half the time?"

"Alcohol, mostly," Zedaine quipped.

"Just drop it," Kildare snarled, leaning back in his chair.

"I'm just saying," Zedaine continued. "When you are young, these things become important, don't they, Ridley?"

"Yes, though I feel silly over it now," Ridley answered sheepishly.

"Tell them what happened," Rex encouraged.

Ridley nodded. "Alac kept asking me all week if I would dance with him at the Spring Festival. I finally said yes, and he begged me to save the last dance of the night for him."

"Did he turn you down?" Tess asked sympathetically.

Ridley shook her head. "No. Alac was walking across the village green straight for me as the festival was ending. That's when it happened."

The four adults listened intently.

Ridley's face twisted in annoyance. "That strumpet Ginna stepped in front of me, kissed Alac, and dragged him into the dance area."

She paused and cast her eyes downward. "I know it was stupid to get so upset, but I…I lost my head."

"When did your magic manifest?" Kildare asked.

Ridley flicked her eyes toward her uncle. "I ran away from the festival, I did not care where I went, I just needed to get away from everyone. Before I knew it, I was standing behind The Deacon, all by myself. I could not get the image of Ginna kissing Alac out of my head. I wanted to scream as loud as I could. The anger was building inside me until it felt like I was going to explode."

She stared hard at Kildare "I needed to get it out. I raised my hands and howled in rage. That's when I set The Deacon on fire."

Zedaine let out a low whistle. "So, that was you?"

"Yes," Ridley admitted. "It was an accident, I swear it."

The inn fell quiet for a few moments as they mulled over the information Ridley had shared with them.

"Did anyone see you?" Kildare asked.

"Yes," Ridley answered, her shoulders drooping.

"Who was it?" Kildare pressed.

Ridley looked at her aunt and uncle, who nodded encouragingly. "Sir Pierce was inside The Deacon," she said softly. "He was seated upstairs in his private suite. I saw his sickly pale face glowing in the light of the fire through the window. He was watching me. I didn't know what to do, so I ran."

"Sickly pale face?" Kildare said, eyes wide. "Sir Pierce," he whispered in thought. His hand slammed down on the table. "Johanssan Peirce," he shouted, looking at his brother. "That bastard from Agenhelm, remember him?"

"It does sound familiar," Zedaine mumbled.

"He was one of the bodyguards in Gauth," Kildare explained. "Always going on about how his uncle worked for…"

He trailed off, his eyes going wide.

"Shit," Kildare said, looking at his brother. "I know what he wants."

"What *who* wants?" Tess asked.

"Sir Pierce," Kildare answered. "Tell me, innkeeper, does Pierce strike you as the kind of man who is happy with what he has? Or is he bent on attaining power?"

"The latter," Rex replied. "He only took over here in Golwick last winter, and he is constantly talking about expanding his influence to the towns south of us."

"Who appointed him in Golwick?" Zedaine asked.

"The Duke in Adian, or so I heard," Rex answered, narrowing his eyes. "At the behest of a foreign counselor—I forget his name. Wargar, or Warman…"

"Warlan," Kildare hissed in recognition. "That snake…why is Artimus listening to a word he says?"

"You know how Warlan is," Zedaine shrugged. "Ever the opportunist. He probably weaseled his way into the duke's good graces."

Kildare let out a deep breath. "No. Warlan has been furious since…" he hesitated a long moment, "he was displaced from the palace. Warlan knew exactly what he was doing. Pierce isn't here to protect the people of Golwick. He is here to recruit an army."

"An army?" Tess scoffed. "Golwick is not known for its warriors."

"That's not true," Zedaine disagreed. "I've met several fine soldiers on my travels that hail from the southern Rhone. How many soldiers did Pierce have when he arrived?"

"No more than five," Rex answered.

"How many answer his call now?" Zedaine continued.

"Sixty," Rex offered. "Maybe more. But they are new recruits, half-trained boys, most of them."

"Recruiting takes time," Kildare agreed. "But his strength is growing. I'd wager by next summer, he will field several hundred. In another year, a thousand, especially if he expands his power to the southlands."

"That's a pittance compared to the armies that serve in the coastal cities," Rex said. "Adian alone has five-thousand soldiers."

"Even with a thousand soldiers," Tess added. "Pierce could not conquer Aiden."

"You are right," Kildare agreed. "A small army alone could not threaten the larger cities."

He paused, rubbing his jaw. "But Golwick was also home to a famous wizard."

"Who?" Rex asked.

Kildare glanced at Zedaine. "A powerful mage. One that had mastered at least three spheres."

"Why are you looking at me," Zedaine frowned. "I don't know who you are talking about."

"Yes, brother, you do."

Kildare nodded at Ridley. "Look at Ridley. By the gods, I should have guessed it the minute I saw her."

"She's a pretty lass, certainly," Zedaine stated. "Fair of face and figure, but I don't see…"

"Look at her hair," Kildare insisted. "Bright red with streaks of orange…"

"Scarlet," Zedaine whispered, his eyes wide. "Well, I'll be damned."

"What are you talking about?" Ridley asked.

Kildare turned to Rex and Tess. "You aren't her aunt and uncle by blood, are you?"

The innkeeper and his wife glanced at one another. Tess wrapped her arms around Ridley. "No. Ridley came to us from the local priests. Someone, a woman, dropped her off fifteen years ago at the monastery, and we agreed to take her in."

"I've always known I was adopted," Ridley said. "Aunt Tess and Uncle Rex raised me knowing I was not of their blood."

Kildare raised his hands defensively. "I make no judgments young lady. Quite the opposite. They are good people, and you are lucky to have them. I speak, however, of your birth mother. If it is who I think it is, she was a mage of great power."

"Who was she?" Ridley asked.

Kildare looked at Zedaine, who cleared his throat. "A woman we only know through reputation," the hunter explained. "She tried to conquer the city of Windholm once, but she was thwarted in the attempt by a wizard even more powerful than she."

"What was her name?" Ridley breathed.

"Her given name at birth was Kadira," Kildare answered. "But she was known throughout the Rhone by a different name. The Scarlet Rage."

"The Scarlet Rage…" Ridley's voice tapered off. "I still don't understand. What does Sir Pierce want with me?"

"Up until last week, I doubt he knew you existed," Kildare sighed. "Now, however, you would be the crowning piece to his army."

"His army?" the young girl gasped.

"Aye," Zedaine nodded. "A fire mage would be a powerful ally to have if he had designs on conquering the Rhone."

"Whether you like it or not, Ridley," Kildare said. "He and his sixty soldiers will be coming for you."

The silence inside the inn was broken only by the high-pitched chirping of crickets wafting in from the air outside as dusk began to fall.

"What…what can we do?" Tess asked fearfully.

Zedaine looked at Kildare, who scratched his chin absently.

"Don't even think about it," Zedaine warned. "We've been exiled."

"*We* won't be welcome there," Kildare noted, "but Ridley would be."

"What are you talking about?" Ridley asked.

It was Zedaine who answered. "There is a place where you would be safe," he explained. "More, it is a place of learning. You would be taught to harness your magic by masters of the craft. It is far from here, but you would be out of danger."

"Where is it?" Rex asked.

Zedaine let out a sigh. "The city of Brisbane. It is home to a magic academy second to none in Quasa."

"That sounds wonderful," Tess said in relief. "When can she go?"

"It is not that easy," Kildare put in. "The road is long and filled with peril…and that is *if* Ridley escapes from Golwick unscathed."

Rex and Tess exchanged looks and turned their eyes to Kildare. "I think we are getting ahead of ourselves," Rex said. "I don't mean to question your logic, but this theory of yours—it's just speculation. There is no way you can know what Pierce is doing in…"

"Riders coming," Kildare interrupted, his eyes looking out the window.

"We often have guests at this time…" Rex began.

"It is a column of soldiers," Kildare cut him off. "Two score, at least."

"Let me see," demanded the innkeeper, striding over to the window. "Damn me," he swore. "That is Pierce, riding in the front."

"You were saying?" Kildare grunted sarcastically at Rex.

"What do we do?" Ridley asked, her earlier fear returning.

Kildare looked at his brother and shook his head. "We aren't going to get that relaxing stay, are we?"

"How much magic did you absorb?" Zedaine replied in answer, picking up Kildare's cuirass, tossing it at him.

"Not enough to make a difference," Kildare frowned, catching the leather armor. "Maybe a burst or two, but no more than that."

"It could be worse," Zedaine said, his voice calm.

"How could it be worse?" Kildare snapped, draping the armor over his head.

"It could be raining," Zedaine suggested.

"I hate you sometimes," Kildare growled. "Go. Take your bow and get on the roof. Use the stone chimney as cover. I'll try and keep them in front of the inn."

"Want me to start feathering them right away?" the hunter asked, moving up the staircase leading to the second floor.

"I'll talk to them first," Kildare answered, "see if we can avoid a confrontation. Just don't shoot me this time."

Zedaine shook his head. "That happened once, and you deliberately got in my way."

"Tess," Kildare continued, ignoring his brother. "You and Ridley get our horses and move them behind the inn."

"But, what if…" Tess began to say.

"There is no time," Kildare barked. "They will be in shouting distance soon. Go! Do it now!"

Tess glanced at her husband, who nodded. She and Ridley shot out the front door and did as Kildare commanded.

"What about me?" Rex asked.

Kildare clapped the innkeeper on the shoulder. "You and I are going to go outside and talk to Pierce. Let's see if we can persuade him to bugger off."

"You think he will listen?" Rex frowned, moving behind his bar, grabbing an old wooden shield.

Kildare snorted. "Better get your cudgel, too," he answered dryly.

Pierce was in no mood for excuses. Already his brother had failed to bring the red-haired fire mage to him. Now Boynton was missing. If that were not enough, three of his soldiers had been accosted by a single man who had kept the girl and her powers away from him.

Pierced had suffered enough delays on the account of this girl. No longer. Now, he and fifty of his men stood in front of The Candlelight Inn, ready to take the mage by force if needed.

"Biggs," he grunted. "Take a squad around back. I don't want them slinking away into the night."

"Yes sir," a stocky officer wearing the white armband of a lieutenant nodded, waving to his men.

"Dontell," Pierce continued. "You and your squad come with me. Kill anyone that stands in our way. No harm is to come to the girl, understand?"

"Aye, sir," the lanky Dontell barked, flanking his commander.

"Let's go," Peirce ordered, dismounting from atop his short-haired charger.

Pierce and his men moved toward the front door. They were twenty paces away when the door swung open. Out walked a lean man dressed in hunting leathers, armed with both a brace of throwing knives and a sword. Next to him was Rex, the innkeeper, touting a stout oak cudgel and an old wooden shield.

"That's close enough," the stranger said, his face implacable.

"You don't give the orders here," Dontell shouted. "Kill him," the lieutenant ordered. "I'll have his tongue for speaking to Sir Pierce like…"

Dontell's voice was cut off as a steel knife slammed into his throat. Dontell fell, choking on his blood.

"I said that's close enough," the stranger repeated, fingering a second throwing knife.

"You son-of-a-bitch," snarled Lieutenant Biggs. "At them men…"

The sound of an arrow cutting through the air hissed from overhead. A fraction of a second later, it tore through the lieutenant's armor, slamming into his heart. Biggs toppled to the ground, his lifeblood spilling out of him.

"I will say it one last time," the stranger shouted. "Come no further, else more of your men will die."

Pierce held up his hand, stunned at the deaths of his men. The throw of the knife—the accuracy of the arrow—these were no common warriors. He eased closer to his charger, realizing he needed to be wary.

"Who are you?" Pierce shouted, staring at the man.

"An emissary from Brisbane, here upon the king's business," the stranger replied.

"King?" Pierce scoffed. "What king?"

"Medyha Whitelance," the stranger answered. "I believe you've heard of him."

Pierce felt the hairs on the back of his neck rise. "The battlemage?" he spat. "Aye, I know who he is. Unfortunately for you, your king has no jurisdiction in this village."

"Be that as it may," the stranger continued. "He has sent me to collect this man's ward," he nodded toward Rex. "I am here to complete that task."

"Rex," Pierce said, speaking to the innkeeper. "Who is this man? Does he truly speak for you?"

"He does," Rex replied.

"I would rethink that decision," Pierce warned. "Send your niece to me, and we will be on our way."

"No," Rex answered, placing his hand upon the stranger's shoulder. "She is not going anywhere with you. I have agreed to place her under Kildare's care."

"Kildare?" he rumbled, looking again at the stranger. "You would trust the traitor of Gauth with your niece's fate?" Pierce shook his head. "Leave the child to me. She is my loyal subject and under my protection. Ridley can stay here in Golwick, as she should."

"Your protection?" Kildare snorted. "What kind of protection have you offered the girl? To drag her through the streets against her will? Why, just last night, she was attacked by a ruffian in this very inn. The soulless wretch tried to have his way with her. You might know him. He was an oafish brute by the name of Boynton."

There was a ripple among the soldiers at the news.

"What do you mean, was?" Pierce demanded.

"I knifed him in the back," Kildare shrugged. "Can't have a rapist running around the village. His corpse is rotting in the field with the rest of the trash."

"You're lying," Pierce roared. "The guards at the gate said you only arrived in Golwick this afternoon."

"I rode out before dawn," Kildare said. "Had to bury the little shit before he smelled up the place."

Pierce narrowed his eyes in anger. "It was you who accosted my men on the road," he accused.

Kildare shook his head. "No, that was my brother. He is something of a vigilante. I tried to talk him out of it, but you know how thickheaded younger brothers can be."

The knight's lips curled in a sneer. "Boynton was supposed to escort Ridley to me last night," he said. "He is a man of honor. You think to sully his reputation with these lies of debauchery?"

"He was a pig," Kildare snorted back. "The little shit got what he deserved. Best you run home, sir knight. Go suckle at the teat of that imbecile Warlan. You tell him Ridley is under my protection."

"And if I refuse?" Pierce snapped, his pale face hardening.

Kildare snapped out his sword and twirled it around his body in a dazzling display of swordsmanship. "Then I will wash this village in your blood."

"Kill him! Kill them all—save the girl!"

Five squads of men surged forward, racing at Kildare and Rex.

"Now Zee!" thundered Kildare, slamming his sword into the ground in front of him. His hands a blur, the fiery warrior threw the remaining knives he had secreted upon his person. Four of Pierce's soldiers went down, tripping up several others.

Zedaine was vaguely aware of his brother's charge into battle. He was more concerned about killing the last of the knight's lieutenants.

Nice of the officers to wear those white armbands, he thought to himself. Thanks for making it easy.

Spotting the last lieutenant, Zedaine pulled back on his bow and shot. The arrow sped through the air and slammed into the man's chest, spinning him from his feet.

Next, protect Kildare's blindside, he said to himself. Zedaine knew his brother would be hard-pressed in a few moments, but the initial attack would be to his advantage as the inexperienced attackers often crowded one another, hampering their ability to fight. Glancing down, he saw Kildare had already slain two of the knights' soldiers while Rex was smashing a third from his feet.

Where did he serve, I wonder, Zedaine thought, fitting another arrow to his string. With those shoulders, it had to be with a heavy infantry unit, he mused, seeing an attacker trying to get behind Rex. Zedaine shot and fitted another arrow, seeing his previous target drop. He loosed a second, then a third, each time felling one of the attackers.

Zedaine flicked his gaze to the back of the enemy lines. Pierce was there, hiding behind his horse. The big hunter snorted in contempt.

Coward, he thought a split second before a bolt ricocheted off the stone chimney he was standing next to.

Ducking behind the chimney, Zedaine snorted to himself. Maybe he's not a coward, just smart, he reasoned, ruefully.

Peeking out from behind the chimney, Zedaine spotted the problem in the fading daylight.

Crossbowman, he sneered. The bolter was busy fitting another bolt to his bow. Wasting no time, Zedaine stood and loosed his arrow. It struck the man in the temple, dropping him instantly.

Didn't see that coming did you… he thought triumphantly until two more bolts went whizzing past his head. "Shit!" He screamed aloud, dropping back once more. "Kildare, retreat!" Zedaine bellowed, fitting another arrow to his string.

Phase two, he thought, sneaking a peak over the top of the chimney. One squad was flanking the inn to the east, trying to make their way behind the building. Another was mirroring their actions to the west.

That's me, the big hunter nodded to himself, knowing Ridley and her aunt were likely behind the inn.

"West side!" he shouted, letting Kildare know which squad he was focusing on. Taking a deep breath, Zedaine pulled back on his bowstring and loosed another arrow.

"Kildare, retreat," Kildare heard his brother yell from the roof. "Fall back," the blood-soaked warrior ordered to the now laboring Rex. Kildare parried a clumsy thrust from a stocky soldier in front of him and stabbed the man under the armpit. Bright red arterial blood poured from the wound. "Go!" he shouted, moving back from his position.

Rex, bleeding from wounds on his arm and face, raced for the door, Kildare hot on his heels. Reaching the entryway, Rex dove inside while Kildare slammed and bolted the door behind them.

"West side," they heard Zedaine's muffled shout.

Holding his hand upward, Kildare focused his will.

"Sicut Ferro," he whispered.

The inn doorway glowed white for a moment, before fading back to normal.

"Your job is to hold this room as long as you can," Kildare barked. "Keep their attention here. When they breach it, don't be a hero. Fall back to the courtyard for our last stand."

"Where are you going?" Rex panted.

"I'm attacking the squad flanking us on the east of the building," Kildare responded.

Rex nodded, as the sound of iron weapons began banging on the door. "Guard the windows only," Kildare warned. "I've reinforced the entrance so they will not be able to get in through the door."

Kildare ran from the room to the backyard. He looked up to see the terrified faces of Ridley and Tess. "Be ready to ride," he shouted, tearing around the corner, heading east.

"Is Rex alive!" Tess shouted, panic in her voice.

"For now!" Kildare answered, turning the corner. He came face to face with a dozen hard-eyed, armor-clad soldiers. "Let's dance," Kildare sneered, moving to attack.

Zedaine had changed his tactics. When the opposition was out front of the inn, he was aiming to kill. Now he was shooting to disable. Cries of pain and anguish often led to confusion and a slower response time in the enemy ranks. So far, it had worked. He had feathered four more of the soldiers, pinning them behind the rough cover of a growth of trees. He had been able to incapacitate the last two crossbowmen, though the bolter's final shot had grazed Zedaine's arm moments ago, drawing a line of blood.

Unfortunately, Zedaine had run out of arrows.

He was torn between dropping into the courtyard and helping his brother or staying in place on the roof, keeping the squad on the west side bogged down and out of the fight. The decision was made for him moments later when one of the soldiers peeked out from behind the trees.

"He's dry," the soldier yelled, waving his fellows forward.

Cursing inwardly, Zedaine ran to the back of the building, slid onto the back stairs, and leapt into the cobblestone yard. Drawing his sword he sprinted around the west side of the building, immediately exchanging blows with one of the soldiers. He blocked a thrust and cut the soldier down with a murderous riposte. A second soldier charged. Zedaine dodged the man, striking a blow with his fist across the man's face, knocking him down.

Despite his initial success, Zedaine was forced to give ground under the press of the remaining soldiers. Still, he fought, killing a second man and knocking another from his feet.

The back door swung open and the broad-shouldered innkeeper, covered in blood, rolled into the courtyard.

"The common room is overrun," he gasped, trying to regain his feet.

"Rex!" screamed Tess, running to her husband.

"Go Ridley!" Zedaine shouted, ducking under an attack. He heard the galloping of hooves over the earthy terrain and knew the girl had listened to him.

Pouring through the doorway were a dozen soldiers followed by the glowering countenance of Sir Pierce. Kildare, too, had been forced to retreat, though there was not a scratch on him. Knowing the west side was lost, Zedaine abandoned his fight, retreating into the courtyard with Kildare. The knot of defenders stood huddled together, their only defense the brick-and-mortar oven house at their backs.

Glancing back, his only solace was in knowing Ridley had escaped.

Ridley, kicked at the mare's sides, wanting only to put as much distance between herself and Sir Pierce as possible. The man terrified her, even more than his brother Boynton had.

She chanced a look back, seeing Pierce standing on the back landing of her uncle's inn. He was smiling, laughing at the defenders, just as his brother had laughed at her last night. The memory of the sound rang in her ears. Without meaning too, she slowed her mount, looking back once more. She closed her eyes and heard a cacophony of voices fill her head.

"Did you enjoy being dragged through the streets?"

"One kiss and I'll leave."

"I want you to be brave, like you were last night."

"You'll be begging for my cock come morning."

"I'm sorry I touched you, but I needed to see what would set you off."

"No more!" she shouted inside the stillness of her mind.

Opening her eyes, she kicked at the mare's sides, turning the horse around.

"Impressive," Pierce acknowledged, seeing dozens of his men killed or incapacitated. "What would it cost to employ the likes of you two?"

"Ten thousand gold coins of kiss my ass," Zedaine barked, standing his ground.

Pierce smiled without humor. "How about you?" he asked, looking at Kildare. "Surely you are not as irrational as…your brother."

"I promised you I'd wash this town in your blood," Kildare responded. "I'm a man of my word."

"That is, unfortunate," Peirce said, shaking his head. "However, I can see you've made up your minds."

The knight looked to his men. "Kill them." He pointed at Kildare. "The one who brings me his head will become my new captain."

"Wait!" came a cry from behind them. Looking back, they saw Ridley, leading Kildare's mare, walking back to the courtyard.

"Dammit girl, I told you to run!" Zedaine hissed.

Ridley ignored him.

"You came here for me," Ridley said, leaving the mare behind the oven house. "Here I am. I will go with you, willingly—but you must let the rest of them live."

"You are in no position to dictate anything to me," Pierce snorted. "These men have cost me half my force. They are going to die."

Ridley stopped. She stood no more than a few feet from Pierce, who towered over her. "Don't make your brother's mistake," she warned, her voice steady. "He wanted what he couldn't have. It cost him his life."

"So, I've heard," Pierce replied. "He was only supposed to invite you to the Deacon, but his avarice for you got the better of him. It is of little importance. The man responsible for Boynton's death is about to die."

Ridley straightened her back and looked Pierce dead in the eye. "Kildare didn't murder your brother. I did."

Pierce began to laugh. "You? A pittance of a girl? How could you have managed to kill Boynton?"

Ridley gave him a cold smile. "The same way I'm going to kill you."

"Get in the oven house!" Kildare ordered, shoving Rex and Tess inside. Ridley raised her hands.

"Zedaine, go!" Kildare thundered, standing in the doorway.

The big hunter darted inside the stone structure at the same moment Ridley unleashed her magic.

"Ignus!" Ridley shouted.

A great burst of flame exploded out of Ridley, incinerating everyone in the courtyard. On and on it went, scorching the stone of the inn with its incredible heat.

Her power lasted no longer than a few seconds, but it was enough to kill every remaining member of the knight's guard.

Save one.

Standing before Ridley was Sir Pierce himself, untouched and unspoiled.

"We will make the cites of the Rhone beg for mercy," he said, his eyes full of malice. "With you at my side, I will raise an army capable of taking Adian itself!"

"How?" Ridley gasped, shocked that he stood before her.

"A gift, from your mother," the knight mocked, taking a sapphire pendant out from under his tunic. "A magic item from another age, to ward the wearer against magic."

He reached out his hand. "Come with me child, let us tarry no more…" he stopped, his breath catching in his throat. Ridley saw the tip of a knife burst from the front of the knight's chest.

A hand grabbed a fistful of Pierce's hair and yanked it backward.

"I told you, you twisted shit," Kildare's voice rasped. "I'm a man of my word. I'll wash this town with your blood."

Pierce's eyes were incredulous. Stunned, he tried to turn, but Kildare twisted the knife. Screaming in pain, blood frothed from the knight's mouth, and Kildare let him fall to the blistering cobblestone. The knight let out one last sigh and closed his eyes forever.

From behind Ridley, Zedaine helped Tess ease Rex to the floor of the oven house. Ridley looked back at Kildare in astonishment.

"You've got to stop ruining my shirts," he complained, plucking at the remnants of his olive-green tunic.

"You fought well," Kildare said, complimenting the innkeeper early the next morning.

"I hope to never have to do it again," Rex mumbled, clasping Kildare's hand.

"Must you leave so soon?" Tess queried from the seat next to her husband.

"Word will get out," Zedaine replied, belting on his traveling pack. "Others will seek to take advantage of Ridley's power. The sooner we get her to Brisbane, the better."

"By mid-morning, the rest of the Golwick is going to wonder what happened to their leader," Kildare added. "Whatever remnants of his men survived will talk. Don't be surprised if you have a slew of visitors today."

"A fire broke out in our oven room," Tess said evenly. "Pierce stayed for a drink but left near sundown. We haven't seen him since."

Kildare smiled. "Now that, I believed," he said with a wink. "Keep it simple. Where did Ridley go?"

"To visit family in Adian," Rex said somberly. "She'll be gone for a few months learning the ways of the big city."

"That will do," Zedaine nodded.

From the back room came Ridley, dressed in a green tunic and dark brown riding pants. A navy-colored cloak was draped over her shoulders.

"Say your goodbyes lass," Zedaine said.

"Take care, luv," Tess said, embracing the girl, her voice shaking.

"I will," Ridley promised, tears streaking down her face.

"Be safe, child," Rex added, wrapping his arms around his niece. "Don't forget about us."

"Never," Ridley replied with a brave smile.

Kildare cleared his throat. "It's best if we leave now, before the sun rises. I want to be well out of Golwick before anyone notes our departure."

"How long will it take to get to Brisbane?" Tess asked.

"Perhaps a ten day," Zedaine answered. "Depending on the tides."

"We will return after dropping Ridley off and have that meal you promised," Kildare said wryly, glancing at his brother. "I'm looking forward to a bit of downtime—if this lummox can manage to stay out of trouble."

"You cause more issues than anyone," Zedaine scoffed. "Remember that time in Gallanse? It was a bowl of soup!"

"It was my bowl of soup," Kildare drawled, heading for the door.

"Damn near started a riot," Zedaine continued, shifting his gaze to Ridley. "Let's go lass, we've a long way to travel."

With a last squeeze, Ridley said her farewells and followed the brothers.

Tess and Rex waved goodbye and stared after them long after the trio had left.

"How can soup start a riot?" Tess asked, thinking on what Zedaine had said.

"No idea," Rex smiled, embracing his wife.

The sun peeked over the horizon some ten miles from Golwick when Zedaine pulled his dappled stallion alongside Ridley's gray charger, Pierce's former mount.

"You alright?" he asked.

"I...I don't know," Ridley confessed.

"Talk to me," the big hunter said. "What's troubling you?"

Ridley let out a sigh and pulled the sapphire pendant Pierce had been wearing out from under her tunic. "I…I took this from Sir Pierce's corpse before you dragged him away, but, I'm not sure it belongs to me."

"It is a valuable magic item," Zedaine said. "You should keep it."

"I thought, maybe you or your brother might want it. You two did the lion's share of the fighting, after all."

"I don't need it," Kildare said, riding up beside them. "I've enough protection from magic already."

"You keep it," Zedaine repeated. "It is your legacy from your mother."

Ridley fell silent for a moment, thinking on his words. "Do you think I will turn out like her?" she asked, terrified of what the answer might be.

Zedaine gave the girl a frown. "Kadira was a terrible mage who bears the responsibility of killing hundreds of innocents. You are a fifteen-year-old girl, just starting out in the world."

"I…I don't want to end up a murderer," Ridley confessed.

"You won't," Kildare answered simply.

"How can you be so sure?" Ridley asked. "This…this power I have. It is terrifying."

Kildare raised an eyebrow at his brother. "Tell her," the elder sibling said, kicking his horse into a canter to scout ahead.

"Tell me what?" Ridley insisted.

"You were raised by two people who loved you," Zedaine answered. "You came back to save us all when you didn't have to. That is who you are Ridley. You are far from the self-serving, power-hungry mage Kadira turned out to be. You've a noble heart beating in your chest. Don't let the sins of the Scarlet Mage worry you. I've seen you in action. You are ten times the woman she will ever be, magical power or not."

Ridley stared at him as Zedaine dropped back to cover their tracks.

She looked out over the horizon and saw the dawning of a new day as Zedaine's words echoed in her mind.

"You are ten times the woman she will ever be."

"Hell, yes I am," she said to herself, sitting up a bit straighter in the saddle. Ridley cast her gaze out over the landscape, riding north toward her destiny.

END

Savages

By Casey Moores

Captain Guillaud knelt in a field and scanned the nearest trees of the great forest. Experience told him to listen as much as look, so he closed his eyes and took in the sounds. Wind rustled the grass and the many branches. Water rippled along the wide, but shallow stream. It was the last barrier before they entered the forest itself. Birds whistled and fluttered, undisturbed by the impending devastation. There was even the low hum of the myriad insects that hounded his company.

His calves already ached from the short march. Soon enough, he knew, they'd warm up and work themselves out. He wriggled his shoulders inside his thick blue coat in anticipation of the much longer and faster march through the forest.

"I don't like it, Captain. I don't like it one bit." Though there was no sign of any Fersangian troops, Sergeant Castel kept his voice low out of habit.

"It's quiet enough… and in the normal way," Captain Guillaud said in a similar low voice. He opened his eyes and glanced at Sergeant Castel. "We can take it now, while it's unoccupied, or we can take it later, when it's filled with thornwire, poppers, and chain guns. Which would you prefer, Sergeant?"

"Well, sir, when you put it that way." The sergeant crouched with a wide-eyed, suspicious expression. His fingers twiddled with his thick, black mustache and he chewed his lip. "Still… lots of stories about this forest. There's a reason there are no towns nearby, and not a single road passing through. One of the last guarded ones, they say."

"Not to repeat myself, but I'll take tall tales to a hail of bullets," Guillaud said. "I don't mean to ignore your concerns, Sergeant, but even if there is some great beast that defends the forest, or some band of nature-worshiping savages, I can't imagine either will be a match for modern weaponry. And it's modern weaponry our enemy will carry. Every moment we delay is a moment they'll get further. It'll be a fight at some point, and we need to take every inch we can now, while it's easy. You know as well as I how much those inches will cost later, when the storm begins."

"Didn't say I wasn't coming along, sir—just that I didn't like it. Of course, sir, I realize if we didn't do anything we enlisted didn't like, we'd never get out of bed in the morning. Ready on your call, sir."

Guillaud nodded and raised an arm into the air. He snapped his fingers. "Kip!"

A tiny winged man dressed in tight blue clothes zipped up and floated in front of him like a hummingbird.

"Sir?"

"Head back and pass along that we're crossing the river." The captain glanced at his timepiece. "Ahead of schedule, make sure you say that. Return straight away. Dismissed."

"Sir."

The fairy saluted and zipped away.

"Well, Sergeant, let's get on with it. Move quickly, but keep our eyes open, yes?"

"Yes, sir."

The captain waved an arm forward and jogged toward the stream in a half-crouch. He splashed softly through the water, doing his best to avoid sharp or slippery-looking rocks. In no time, the company entered the forest.

A far distant thunder swirled through the trees.

Rain will be good for the forest, but I hope there isn't too much wind or lightning.

Holg crouched by a set of bushes and cupped his leathery gray hands. His dark, smoky snout twitched. Drawing in a deep breath, he focused energy through the plant to the nourishment below. With tender care and direction, he encouraged it to grow wide, luscious green leaves. Just as carefully, he released his connection to it and backed away. If he cut the line too quickly, the plant would wither. He withdrew completely and the bush remained vibrant and full.

He backed away from the delicious treat he'd created and whistled to the nearest birds. As long as the sounds of the forest remained, his breakfast would not suspect its fate. Smooth as the wind, he moved to a good vantage point, lowered himself, and prepared his bow. No deer in the entire forest could resist such a snack.

The sparrows were a chatty lot on that particular day. They caught his attention when he heard them discussing large numbers of outsiders camped all around the forest. He relaxed his bow, shouldered it, and strolled up to join the discussion.

"Outsiders?" he asked them in a series of chirps and whistles. "What kind of outsiders?"

"Many kinds," a red-breasted robin tweeted in response. "Big and little, hairy and scaly. Some even fly. Some have magic."

"Most carry sticks of thunder and fire," a hummingbird chirped, almost too fast for Holg to understand it.

"All around, you said?" Holg asked. He'd always had trouble envisioning how incredibly vast their forest was, but he knew that it was too large for any number of *any* creature to surround it.

"Many from the sunrise," the robin tweeted, "and many from the sunset. A few from the High Star as well, but not from the Great Lake. Not everywhere, but many large flocks."

Mostly East and West, then, with a few from the North.

"Does the Circle know?"

"If the wind wills it," the hummingbird chirped.

Holg rolled his eyes. Birds had a claws-off approach to almost everything that wasn't gossip, predators, or food. Their kind *could* have been a great web of scouts and spies for the Circle. According to the Lord of Verdure, they once had been. For no discernible reason, they'd stopped acting in that capacity hundreds of years prior.

"Yes, if the wind wills it," Holg said to be polite.

The thunder was growing louder and more frequent. The storm would be on them soon.

He rustled around in a pouch and withdrew two fat mealworms.

"Would you like one?" he asked the robin.

The robin jumped off the branch and flapped toward him. He jerked his hand back as the robin approached.

"One now if you'll go tell the Circle about the outsiders," he said. "And the other one when you come back to tell me you've told them."

"We already know," someone said. Holg recognized the voice of Cozmur, the Lord of Verdure. "Savages from outside are invading."

When he turned his head, he found the entire Circle rushing through the forest. They were heading east toward the stones. The large, black-haired High Lord led the way, followed by the slender Lord of Sylvans and the hairy, muscular Lord of Beasts. Not far behind, the four Elemental Lords crowded together as they always did. None of them demonstrated any awareness of Holg.

Amidst Holg's distraction, the robin swept through and snatched the mealworms from his hand. When he turned to watch it, he found Punas, the Lord of Insects, skulking a dozen yards away behind a tree. The old, wrinkly-faced man leaned out and nodded a greeting.

"Holg, you've got to get everyone to safety," Cozmur said. The tall, gray-haired man looked at him with pained, pleading eyes. "We're off to the Circle to create some protections for the forest. You must help safeguard the other creatures until we can do so."

"Verdure, come along!" the High Lord said without slowing or looking back. "We'll need your wards while we perform the real magic!"

Cozmur twisted away from Holg. "Coming, High Lord!"

"Yes, my Lord of Verdure," Holg said. "I will do what I can to protect the forest creatures. You must hurry, before the storm gets here."

"That's no storm," Cozmur said. He stalked away after the other Lords and Punas followed him. "If it were, Air and Wind could handle it. It's a war, Holg. The outside world has found us."

"What's a *war*?" Holg asked.

It was too late, Cozmur had hustled away.

The other Lords despised Holg because of his heritage. As the spawn of one of the dark, pig-faced beasts that plagued the edges of the forest, most of the other Sylvans hated him as well. Only Cozmur and Punas had ever shown Holg any kindness. They were the only ones who did not blame Holg for the evil that had planted him inside his mother. The evil which had later returned to…

Unbidden, his only memory of his mother appeared in his mind. Her pale, still face lying in the grass. He had cried and cried for her to hold him, to feed him, to pick him up off the cold forest floor. She had done nothing but stare at him with those fading green eyes for what had seemed an eternity. The pains in his stomach had become torturous, his face had turned to ice, and his throat had burned from thirst when some unseen savior had arrived. He still wondered who, or what, that had been.

Focus. Do as the Lord of Verdure asked and see to the forest creatures.

Holg cleared his mind and drew in a long, deep breath. His hand slid into a pouch on his left side and withdrew two clumps of brown fur. With a clump in each hand, he stretched his arms apart and lifted his chin.

"Draassanc and Raamat, goddesses of the forest, grant me your favor!" He recited the words of the ancients, invoking their power. He held his arms as wide as he could, tilted his head back as far as his neck allowed, and repeated the words. The longer he chanted, the harder he focused on submitting himself in mind, body, and spirit to the will of the ancients.

His skin bulged and rippled. The bones popped and shattered. Needles erupted from inside every inch of his body and pressed outward. His teeth crushed together and his jaw broke into pieces. His toenails tore away as thick, boney daggers pushed them out.

Having completed his transformation into a large, brown bear, Holg barreled toward the western edge of the woods. As he ran, he spotted two fat deer trotting up to the bush to feast on the leaves he'd made. In his new state, he'd never catch them. Besides, he no longer had the time.

What a waste.

Breakfast would have to wait.

Captain Guillaud's body stung everywhere from the assault of some unseen needles in the foliage, but he forced himself to drive onward. He knew he must set the standard for his men and show no sign of pain or fatigue.

"My Captain, with respect to the men, are you sure we couldn't stop for a moment to catch our breath?" Sergeant Castel asked.

Guillaud continued forward, but turned his head back to talk to the Sergeant.

"I know I'm driving us hard, Sergeant, but the further we get before we meet the Fersangian dogs, the less we'll have to fight through later."

"You've said so, sir, but if our men drop from exhaustion before we can fight, the dogs will walk right through us," Castel replied.

Well behind and to the left of Castel, on the company's far left flank, Private Rossi collapsed.

"You mean like that?" Guillaud asked and pointed.

Castel spun about, searched for a moment, and then cursed.

"I'll deal with it, Captain," Castel said. He stomped toward the unconscious soldier.

Guillaud paused and inspected his company. At the far right end, Private Napo grabbed at the air with a goofy grin on his face. Right next to him, Privates Lucien and Louis struggled with each other. He hurried toward the fight to find them tossing lazy, ineffectual punches at each other, faces screwed up in hazy anger.

Something fluttered through the corner of his vision. He froze and focused on where it had been. In a flash, he saw a small, winged creature zip away.

"Company, take cover!" he ordered. "Fairies!"

His men dropped in a cacophony of breaking branches, rattling metal, and cries of excitement. One soldier fired his rifle into a tree.

"Hold your fire, men!" Sergeant Castel called.

"On the contrary, men," Guillaud said. "Eyes out and rifles ready! Shoot anything that moves. Anything with wings or eyes, shoot it!"

Leading by example, he drew his pistol and searched for the tiny winged demon he'd spotted. He caught movement up in the branches of a tree. He fired.

On cue, the men of his company poured lead into the surrounding forest. He stormed over to Louis and Lucien and clapped both on the back of the head with the butt of his pistol. They staggered away from each other and regarded him with drunken eyes and hanging jaws.

"Come on, men, it's just pixie magic," he said. "Snap out of it and get it together."

All around, breeches snapped open and shut. The fire became more sporadic and random, but continued. Tiny gusts of wind swirled about as hummingbird-like creatures zipped around. Taking care not to aim at his own soldiers, Guillaud did his best to shoot at the fairies whenever they paused. Every so often, one of the tiny creatures dropped out of the air.

A croaking sound drew his attention to a short, plump green fairy belching noxious fumes on a poor, hapless private. Before Guillaud's eyes, the man's skin turned black and rotted away until nothing was left except a heap of dark dust. The captain shot the fat fairy before it could waddle to another soldier.

Small objects crunched into the leaves on the forest floor, proof that more of his men's bullets were finding their marks.

A bullet clipped his right arm. Before he shouted at his men to watch their aim, he realized it had come from the forest. He spotted large puffs of black smoke. The forest creatures were firing old-style muskets. Barely audible over the din of the gunfire was the clomping of hooves. Through the smoke, trees, and branches, centaurs charged around the sides of his company. Each would fire, trot along while reloading, and fire again.

"In the trees, men! Centaurs! Return fire and watch the sides!"

Where he and his company had fired sporadically in the air to deal with the fairy threat, now they took careful aim to take down the large, easy targets. A few centaur muskets found their marks, but far more of his company's rifles found theirs. Moreover, his company had greater numbers and fired at a much greater rate. It was not long before the centaurs retreated.

His men shifted their attention back to anything that looked like a butterfly or bird. At that moment, a loud snort presaged a warthog dashing into their lines. With a chorus of growls, a pack of wolves rushed in on their left flank. The company broke down into a great melee with the vicious animals. Captain Guillaud satisfied himself that his sergeant would rally the men against the wolves, and he went after the warthog.

It rumbled through the ranks, driving its tusks left and right. It gored whoever it could and barreled into others. By the time Guillaud caught up, it had left a channel of bloody stomachs and broken bones.

He fired his pistol into its back. When it spun to face him, he fired again. The bullets had no apparent effect on the beast. Three other soldiers fired their rifles at point blank range into its sides, but it remained fixated on the captain. Which was exactly what Guillaud wanted.

It charged toward him, head down and tusks pointed. Guillaud slashed it across the face as he danced to the side. It thrashed its tusks after him, but missed. He cocked and fired his pistol again. More soldiers unloaded rifles into it. It finally wavered and collapsed. The nearest men cheered.

Guillaud jogged down the lines to where the wolves had been and found Sergeant Castel and the other soldiers had driven them off. Maybe a dozen of his men had been bitten or scratched, but a score of wolf corpses showed they'd won the engagement with distinction.

A great roar echoed through the trees. Guillaud searched for the source, but ducked at the sight of more musket fire. Crashing through branches, a great, brown bear loped out of the woods. Its claws slashed the first man it came to and it latched its jaws onto the head of the next. With a horrific crunch, the soldier twitched and went limp. A nearby soldier raised his rifle, but the bear flung the lifeless body at him and the shot went wide. The beast swiped its massive paws at whoever it could find and lurched toward whoever it could bite. Fewer soldiers got shots on the bear— most contented themselves to scatter away from it.

Guillaud pushed past the retreating flood of men to find a pathway of death trailing off to their right flank. Ahead, the bear slammed a soldier so hard against a tree that the wood cracked. The man dropped.

The captain fired his pistol, once more drawing the ire of a forest beast on himself. This time, he had no one to support him. The bear turned slowly, dropped its paws to the ground, and released another great roar for the captain's benefit.

A neat line of rifle fire broke out from the forest from the south. The bear recoiled in agony as dozens of bullets slammed into it. It swung its head back toward Guillaud and flicked its head, as if to say, "Another time."

It rolled to its right and bounded into the darkness.

Guillaud recognized the voice of Lieutenant Lefevre of Fourth Company shouting orders.

"Sorry to intrude, Captain Guillaud, but I didn't think your men should have all the fun," Lefevre said. The tall, blonde elf strode up and saluted. "A mean bit of fun from what I can see. I will have my guérisseuse see to your men."

"You have my appreciation, Lieutenant," Guillaud said. "May I ask to the whereabouts of Captain Holyoke?"

"Went all soul-brained, sir," Lefevre said. "Mad as a death mage. Tried eating Private Flamiche. We nearly killed him trying to restrain him."

"Fairies," Guillaud said with a sympathetic nod. "It seems the forest is not as empty as the War Staff thought."

"Nothing in this war is as the War Staff thought, my Captain."

"Watch your words, Lieutenant," Guillaud said in a low voice. He looked around at his ragged company as they collected themselves. "This is still but a pleasant stroll compared to an assault on Fersang trenches."

"With respect, Captain, these things always have a way of getting worse over time. Never better."

Guillaud nodded and sighed. Lacking a decent response, he cracked his canteen open and took a long, welcome drink. Returning his attention to his men, he cursed himself. Were it not for his prideful drive to push through the forest as fast as possible, he wouldn't have gotten so far ahead of the other companies. A lot of his men had paid the price.

"Well, Lieutenant, now that you and the other companies have caught up, we should continue with haste. Fersang soldiers won't dawdle, so neither can we."

Holg stumbled through the trees in a rush. He had done what he could to help fight off the invaders, but there had been too many and their weapons too powerful. If he'd gotten to the fight sooner, he might have helped organize a better, more successful attack. However, he doubted the result would have been much different.

His hide carried dozens of the metal stones their weapons threw. They were like the muskets the centaurs carried, only far better. The pain in his left side became unbearable as he lumbered along. He decided it was time to shuffle off his blessing.

Confident he was well clear of the humans, he notified the forest goddesses he no longer required the form they'd provided. Invocation was the difficult part; revocation was easy. On the other hand, it was no less painful.

The bones cracked and collapsed in on themselves. The claws ripped themselves from his fingers, taking skin and fur with them. His nose and teeth crushed backward into his face. His outer flesh and hide tore away from his body as if he were being flayed. After a few minutes of pure suffering, the hide was loose. He found the seam in the belly and tore his way out.

The great upside to returning to his normal form was that he sloughed off most of the injuries. His shoulder and side were still bruised and aching, but the metal stones had remained in the bear hide. Fully returned to his half-orc form, Holg took a few moments to catch his breath and stretch his reformed muscles.

"You were much more handsome as a bear."

Holg spun to find the same red-breasted robin he'd spoken with earlier.

"Yes," Holg said, "I've been told that. But the gifts are temporary and besides, my injuries were pretty bad."

"Injuries?"

"Yes, I was injured by humans."

"Humans?" the robin tweeted. Its head cocked back and forth to the sides. "You mean the Lords? Or the forest folk?"

"No, these are different humans. The outsiders which *you* were telling *me* about."

"Was I?"

Flighty birds…

"Yes, you were." Holg looked out along his intended path. East, to reach the stones and warn the Circle that his efforts to slow the invaders failed. He looked back to the bird. "Do you think you could help me with something?"

"What do I get from it?"

Holg chuckled and shook his head. He reached back down into his pouch and retrieved two fresh mealworms.

"One now, one later, as I offered before," Holg said.

"Before?" The robin's head twitched sideways.

"Anyway, I need you to fly around and warn all the other forest folk, and the fairies, and the forest creatures and the sylvans… everyone. Warn them that a great evil is moving into the forest. Anyone who hasn't left their home, anyone who hasn't worked this all out for themselves." He held out one of the mealworms. "Can I trust you to do this?"

"Of course," the robin tweeted. It hopped off its branch and swooped low across Holg's hand, snatching the mealworm. It flew away into the trees.

Holg took off at a run. It was a long way to the Circle. As he ran through the great forest, he found various signs of destruction at random intervals. Small hamlets were blackened and crushed, clearings had been blown out of thick wooded areas, and dead creatures of all kinds lay everywhere.

With a scream and a loud *crump*, a tree to his left exploded in a shower of splinters, sparks, and a hail of sharp metal stones. He realized the small metal stone-throwers the humans carried were the smallest of their horrible weapons. The booming sounds, which he'd thought were thunder, were the sounds of much bigger weapons firing large explosives deep into the forest. There was no pattern to where they fell. He prayed to the ancients that none would hit him on his way to the Circle.

After Guillaud had seen to the injured and accounted for the dead, he reformed the rest and resumed their march into the forest. He was careful to maintain contact with the other companies. As they went, they discovered more and more evidence of the artillery barrage that had been laid out in front of their advance. His heart ached at the senseless destruction the War Staff had wrought. Fersang had not been in these sections of the forest yet, and most reports had known it. The artillery barrage had simply been a mindless modus operandi. The War Staff always threw shells in advance of an assault, so it had for this advance with no consideration of effectiveness or for whatever lived inside.

First, he discovered a few clearings where the shells had burst the trees into charred, splintered messes. It was a real-life projection of his thoughts. Shelling the trees had accomplished nothing worthwhile except the potential for blazing fires and handfuls of dead animals.

In one spot, he found the burst of fire and metal had occurred in the middle of a collection of the forest folk's hovels. Guillaud had never known humans lived in the forest. There had been rumors of tribes amongst the trees, but all assumed they were bloodthirsty savages if they existed at all. Stories called them feral, and none removed from the beasts they lived among.

This was not the hamlet of feral, savage people. These had been the hovels of a small group of families surviving in harmony with their surroundings.

He found two children, blackened and broken, lying among the rubble. Dead adults were spread around as well. A child's bare feet stuck out from a collapsed home.

Guillaud lifted the wreckage off and the child beneath made the slightest of movements. As he eased the child out, she struggled to draw breath. Her eyes flew open and her face turned to terror when she saw him. From the neck up, she thrashed about and struggled. The rest of her remained limp. She began choking. With great concern, Guillaud looped his arms around and cradled her.

"Guérisseur!" Guillaud shouted. He craned his head to find the nearest healer.

Her head spasmed and bounced in agony. Before anyone could help her, she gave a final cough and went still.

"I wonder if the War Staff knew the forest was so full of life," Sergeant Castel said, having arrived by Guillaud's side. "Or whether they cared. But then, I find myself wondering if the War Staff knows anything at all."

"That's enough, Sergeant," Guillaud said. "Quiet your tongue before I'm forced to cut it out."

Guillaud himself had wondered the same thing for months. Nonetheless, he also knew that no matter how much a thing needed to be said, nothing good ever came from enlisted men speaking the truth.

Holg pushed through throngs of forest folk, sylvans, animals, and fairies. They'd crowded around the Circle and spoke in hushed, despairing tones. He edged his way around a satyr who cradled a naiad baby. Its parents were nowhere to be seen. A few steps past, a group of squirrels crowded around a real brown bear. Continuing through, he spotted a small clearing where the group had made space. A sobbing female tree elf knelt by a male, who lay dead in front of her.

A *boom* sounded from somewhere ahead. The entire assemblage froze and went silent. After a brief delay, the forest creatures scattered away from the Circle in a mad panic. Holg threw his arms up defensively and waded through the stampede. He stumbled a bit as a honey badger ran between his feet. A passing centaur sideswiped him and he fell against a family of human forest folk. The mother screamed and sheltered her two small children while the father became enraged and shoved Holg away. Holg tumbled over a fox, which carried on without a word.

Sprawled on the ground, Holg got jabbed by a deer's hoof. With his hands over his face for protection, he curled into a ball and endured a long series of kicks, stomps, bumps, and claws. Through the gaps in the fingers he caught sight of the High Lord's golden robes. Face screwed up in hysteria, the High Lord ran off like all the others and knocked aside more than a few to do so. Further out, he saw some of the other Lords fleeing as well.

When the crowd had thinned enough, he cautiously regained his footing and continued toward the Circle. The stones were quiet and empty. A shallow, fresh crater had sprung up in front of one of the stones. Against that stone lay Cozmur, the Lord of Verdure. Holg ran up to his side and found that he was weak, but still breathing. His robes were torn and charred in a few spots, exposing flesh, blood, and bone.

"My half-orc friend," Cozmur said, followed by a gurgle and a cough. "I'm sorry… I failed the Circle. I failed the forest."

"Easy now." Holg took Cozmur's hand as he examined the Lord's injuries. He felt certain he'd used up all of his favor with the ancients when he'd become the brown bear. Nonetheless, he drew in a breath of air. In a soft whisper, he called out to the ancients and beseeched them to grant him one last favor for that day.

He was shocked when the energy of the earth flowed through him and into Cozmur. The bones set themselves and the flesh closed up all over his body. Aside from the dried blood and tattered clothing, one would not have known Cozmur had been injured at all. The Lord of Verdure's eyes went wide as his face went flush.

"Holg, by Draassanc and Raamat! What favor you have gained!"

Holg shook off the question, as he was not sure of the answer. "What happened, my Lord of Verdure?"

"I failed, as I said. I thank you for your healing, but it might have been better that you let me perish. I failed them all."

Cozmur stood with unexpected ease. By his expression, he was even more surprised than Holg.

"How?"

"I was to protect the Circle while they worked their great magic. The High Lord was drawing tremendous favor. More favor than any being has collected in all of memory. He was going to channel it to the Elemental Lords, and they in turn were to channel it through the Lords of Sylvans, Beasts, and Insects."

The two stood alone among the Circle. The Lords and all the other creatures were now long gone.

"To what end?"

"They planned to imbue all the creatures— the Sylvans, the Beasts, the Insects, all the creatures gathered here, with the essence of the four elements. We would've destroyed our enemies with paragons of Fire, Earth, Water, and Air! But we did not, because I could not keep the Circle protected. I raised the trees, thickened their branches, and yet the great thunderstones of the outsiders came straight in. I failed… and the Lords escaped while they still could. It's all over now."

The Lord of Verdure gawked in every direction with confusion on his face, as if he couldn't make up his mind on which way to go. Every direction seemed bad by Holg's estimation. As Holg looked around, he found a large stag with an impressive rack of antlers had wandered up to the stones. It stared at them with a powerful, noble presence.

"Transform the creatures into the Elements?" Holg asked. He became transfixed with the stag. He could not recall ever having seen such a stag before, but it was familiar nonetheless. It was remarkable in its fearlessness. All other creatures had fled.

"Yes, they would have been invincible!"

"Could you have changed them back?" Holg asked. "Simple transformations dispel themselves, but that kind of magic… wouldn't they have been changed forever?"

"It was necessary! It was the only idea we had. Well, not the only one, but the best one. The only one that would've worked according to the High Lord, and he knows best about these things."

Ask him about the other way.

Holg felt the words in his head…knew the thoughts were not his own. The stag flicked its head.

"Is there another way?" Holg asked.

"Well… my thought was to imbue the trees with the power. There is no history of them ever having done so, but I've had dreams— all my life— that the trees could come alive and defend the forest. The High Lord told me it was nonsense."

The High Lord was nonsense! We've kept this forest safe for thousands of years, yet these humans came and declared themselves its protectors.

Holg was certain the stag was speaking to him. With the words forming in his brain, he realized it was in a voice that he recognized. At the same time, the wind shifted and he caught the scent of the stag. All the pieces came together in his head. The stag before him was the creature who'd saved him all those years ago when his mother had died before his eyes. Holg had lain, not much more than a baby, starving and freezing on the forest floor. He'd stared, helpless, at his dead mother and had nearly died himself when the stag had arrived and saved him. Afterward, he only remembered being well-fed and warm until he'd grown up enough to take care of himself.

The greatest mystery of his life stood before him. It stared, still as a stone. No more thoughts came to Holg, yet he somehow understood what needed to be done.

Holg nodded.

"Lord of Verdure—"

"Cozmur, please, Holg. I've told you before. Besides, I do not deserve the title. Come now, we must flee as the others have. There's no hope."

"Cozmur, my only friend… tell me of your dreams. Tell me of the trees."

"It's foolish really…"

"Tell me!" Holg shouted much louder than he'd intended, as if he'd intoned the stag itself.

Cozmur recoiled in bewilderment.

Holg caught himself and relaxed. "I'm sorry, my friend, but you must tell me what you've seen. It might be the answer."

"I don't see how. There's no favor left in me, and the other Lords are gone. There's no way to make it happen, if it were even possible. But… the dreams were simple. I saw the trees harnessed by a great being, a being of tremendous favor, who seemed to draw all the favor of all the gods and goddesses, more than just Draassanc and Raamat, through him. Absurd, I know, but that was the dream. They drew all that favor into the trees and the trees came to life. And not like those sleepy treekin or the dryads, no. The trees marched through the forest like great wooden golems and crushed the forest's enemies. That was my dream."

Holg felt warmth soaking through his feet and filling his body. He smiled and took Cozmur's hand. The stag screamed and beat the ground with his hooves. Cozmur turned to see it for the first time. His jaw went slack and his shoulders dropped. Holg shook Cozmur's arm to regain his attention.

"Then that is what we will do."

"Captain Guillaud, our spies report we have advanced much further than Fersang. If we can maintain the pace, we'll meet them much closer to their side of the forest. The War Staff orders all Lutetian companies to advance as far as possible until nightfall and then dig in until morning. They say the forest will be ours by midday tomorrow."

The captain could not restrain a twinge of joy at the news. He might have driven his men hard, but it had been necessary. He knew his decisions had led to the deaths of many. However, if it meant more ground gained, he could have potentially saved the thousands it would have taken to claim that ground from Fersang.

A great crack echoed through the forest, followed by a great thump. Guillaud turned to find a tree had fallen on a group of soldiers in Fourth Company. Some cried in pain, some in alarm. Guillaud ran over to help but stopped short as the cries became shrieks.

The branches of the fallen tree were wriggling about and winding their way around and *into* the nearest men. A line of wood wrapped around a private's leg and dragged the man toward the trunk. The rest of the company swarmed the tree with axes and bayonets. Some grabbed at the entangled men and pulled. Some hacked at the tree's limbs. A select few fired rifles with no apparent effect.

The shrieks and screams took a higher pitch and an edge of dark despair as all the efforts to free the men failed.

Guillaud had heard the agony of men dying en masse on battlefields. He'd heard them cry for their mothers, beg for help, scream about lost limbs, and plead to be shot so their misery could end.

He had never heard men make the sounds these men made. Their faces twisted and writhed in terror. They thrashed about and bent in unnatural, impossible ways. One by one, their bones cracked and they ceased moving. Those who fought in desperation to free others found themselves caught in the vines and branches of this evil wooden beast.

A second crash sounded as a different tree fell into another section of Fourth company's ranks. The nightmare repeated.

A chain gunner team unleashed a deafening stream of bullets into the trunk of the fallen tree from just a few yards away. Guillaud watched, dumbfounded, as the tree slowly rose and swung sideways like a massive club into the chain gun crew. The men were smashed into a bloody mess, and the gun's ratcheting stopped.

Another tree fell, this time into Guillaud's company.

And another.

"Retreat!"

The word escaped his mouth as loud as he could shout it before he knew he was saying it. His heart turned icy and black in despair knowing he had just surrendered all the gains they'd made. But, for the life of him, he could think of no way to counter this new threat. They hadn't brought any fire mages into the forest for fear of catching themselves in a blaze. There were no Bigs to support the offensive as most had died in the early days of the war.

He ran to the first tree and fought to free the closest ensnared man. The man had been working to free another man who was now lifeless and moving only under the thrash of the tree's branches. Guillaud hacked with his sword against a winding vine snaking around the surviving man's leg. The leg snapped, crushed by the branch, as Guillaud chopped through the last bit of wood. Another branch reached toward them as he dragged the man away. He hauled the man to safety and stepped lightly through a growing field of vines.

"Leave the others," he shouted. "Save yourselves while you can!"

Though he wished he could sprint out of the forest, he could not abandon his new charge. As best as he could, he half-carried, half-dragged the man through the safest looking spots. They'd spent hours marching in. He had no hope they would ever escape this new enemy, but he had to try.

Cozmur collapsed in exhaustion.

"It's not working. I can't feel any favor flowing through me. I'm sorry Holg, but I continue to fail us. The High Lord was right, this would've never worked."

The entire forest sang through Holg's mind. It was not *favor* that flowed through him. It was everything. All the energy of the forest, every plant and living creature, even the soil itself breathed power through him. He could feel the trees swinging themselves about, thrashing around, reaching out with their branches and crushing every outsider they could. He saw through the eyes of birds flying overhead and watched the outsiders flow away like blowing sand. The great masses that had swept into the forest on three sides now flooded back out in a frenzy.

A snort brought him back to his senses. As if torn from his mother's arms, his great connection with the forest broke. Depression rushed in as he felt his insignificance. A moment earlier, he had been a god. The Great God of the Forest, reaping vengeance on its invaders. Now he was just… Holg. A twisted, half-orc abomination who was despised by sylvans and forest folk alike.

The stag brushed its muzzle against his face. Once again, he understood. He reached up with both hands and grasped the stag's thick mane. He doubted he could jump onto the giant stag's back, but he tried.

As if floating on air, he flew onto it with ease.

It took off like an arrow through the trees. It bounded over large rocks, fallen trees, and shallow streams in great leaps. Holg held on for dear life as the creature ran hard and fast. He glanced up at the low sun to see they were headed south. He lost track of how long they traveled.

At one point, his hand ran out of strength and slipped. He braced for a fall, certain he would fly off the stag and smash into the ground. Instead, he remained firmly attached to its back, held on by some unseen force.

They broke out of the forest into the field of tributaries at the base of the massive falls that sat between the forest and the Great Lake. The stag rumbled through the sand, mud, and water as if running on solid ground. It ran to the base at the north side of the cliff face and stopped.

It snorted a few times. It was not even breathing hard.

Holg took in the new surroundings and wondered at the stag's purpose. The stag snorted again and waved its muzzle at the bushes that ringed the base of the falls.

Holg smiled and reached out to the ancients. He felt the connection reattach to him through the stag and into the ground. The connection went deep, deeper than it had before. Energy flowed through him. He pushed the energy into the bushes. Then, he guided them as their branches wended their way into the rocky cliff. First, they found the smallest of cracks and grew inside them.

Piece by piece, tendril by tendril, the tiny shoots expanded and stretched into the tall stone formation. Chunk by chunk, the stone cracked apart and water burst forth. In time, the entire cliff crumbled and collapsed. Water gushed forth in a great wave. It smashed against the promontory of the forest and routed to the sides. The shallow streams that followed the east and west boundaries of the forest turned into great raging rivers.

A thunderclap echoed from storm clouds to the south. A torrential downpour erupted from the clouds and added to the flood.

The stag climbed to safety on the northern bank and knelt. Holg climbed off. The stag swung its muzzle toward the half-orc and gave one last huff before leaping over the river and running into the trees.

Holg stood on the bank and watched the water flow. Though he was drenched, he had never felt warmer in his life.

Soaked and exhausted through to his soul, Guillaud heaved the private onto the far bank of what had become a turbulent flood. He dug his arm into the mud and dragged the man up with the last of his strength.

Only a few had made it out. He had no idea if any in his company had survived.

"Well, I guess that's done for the day."

Sergeant Castel crawled toward him along the muddy hill.

"Sergeant, good to see you," Guillaud could hardly hear himself speak. His voice was cracked and not much more than a whisper, but the sergeant nodded.

"And you, sir. Try again tomorrow, I suppose the generals will say."

Guillaud couldn't help but give a hoarse, hollow chuckle.

"I don't think so, Sergeant. Even the generals must realize this forest will not be taken. Not by us, not by Fersang, not by any army that will ever march. The powers that protect this forest cannot be overcome by any force of arms. And I'm glad for it. I'm glad there's a place in this world that's found a way out of this terrible war."

END

Dragon Trap

By: L.N. Hunter

Archmage Screwpole stormed into his chambers, pausing only to fling hat, cloak, and staff into the waiting hands of his long-suffering apprentice, Oyk. She calmly placed them on their stand, pleased that the cloak didn't have the collection of food and drink stains that usually accumulated during one of Screwpole's outings. She might be able to skip the tedious chore of washing his robes that evening.

Oyk let the archmage bluster and rant for several minutes before interrupting him. 'So, master, how much money did you persuade the board to give us?'

Screwpole threw his arms in the air. 'None, damn their minuscule, barely functioning, insignificant minds. Not a groat. Those short-sighted buffoons don't give a fig for the pursuit of knowledge.'

He slumped into a chair, holding out his hand for a glass of wine. 'Chancellor Marmaduke said the Faculty of Performing Arts has to take precedence because—apparently—it's *vital* that the university puts on a good show for the king's visit at the end of the year. Which means there's not a sausage for Thaumaturgical Philosophy. According to Smarmy Marmy, his so-called concert could launch the career of many a playwright or actor. As if careers matter in the grand scheme of things, pah!'

'Indeed,' Oyk sympathised, handing him his favourite Esmiyan Merlot, while taking care that he didn't spot her eyes rolling—she was taking no chances regarding *her* chosen career. Wizarding didn't have the most enviable reputation in the Kingdom of Estalia, but it guaranteed steady work, at least if one was prepared to tolerate Screwpole's idiosyncrasies.

She held up a parchment. 'Sir, this was delivered while you were out. Some farmers in a village not a dozen leagues from the city say they have a dragon infestat–'

'Dragons!' Emptying his glass in a single gulp, Screwpole launched himself from his seat. He slapped his hat on his head and grabbed his cloak and staff. 'Well, what are you dawdling for? Bring the books. Come on, come on—don't dither.'

After a brisk walk to the city's coach yard and a brief but noisy negotiation with the head ostler, the archmage grudgingly handed over two groats. Screwpole and Oyk squeezed themselves into a rickety stagecoach. The coach was already occupied by a severe-looking matron with a bun tied so tight her eyes were watering and a wet fish of a girl who appeared to be her daughter.

After three hours' bumpy wagon ride, during which the matron smoked four foul-smelling cigars and her daughter stared at Oyk without ever seeming to blink, Screwpole and his apprentice disembarked outside *The Bedraggled Phoenix*, the tavern in which the parchment indicated they could find the farmers.

'Good riddance,' Screwpole muttered, as the carriage disappeared off to the next village. He blew his nose, no doubt trying to expel the stench of the cigars, then inspected his handkerchief, grimacing at what he found.

He let Oyk brush the road dust off his robes and smooth them, before he strode into the tavern and boomed, 'Archmage Screwpole, the greatest wizard in the land, has arrived. Now, where's this wyrm of yours?'

Silence.

Screwpole glared around the room. 'Well?'

Oyk tugged on his sleeve and whispered, 'May I try?'

When the archmage gave her a grudging nod, she said, 'Good farmers and townsfolk, you sent a missive to the University of the Mystical and Mundane, asking if we could investigate your problem with a dragon.'

'Ahhh,' chorused the tavern's customers. 'Dragon!' one said. 'Why bain't you say so, instead of blethering about worms?'

Screwpole inhaled, but Oyk defused an impending outburst with a light touch on his arm.

'I wonder if one of you kind sirs could escort us to the site of the most recent—ah—visitation?'

A short, ruddy-faced man drained his tankard in two gulps and sauntered across to the newcomers. 'Follow I.'

Screwpole harrumphed, Oyk bowed politely, then both followed the man.

'I be Farmer Costigan, and it be I farm the vermin has been pillaging. Stealing horses and destroying fences. Burned down I barn, too, it did.'

'Destroying fences, you say,' murmured Screwpole.

'Good sir, would those fences be made of metal?' Oyk asked.

Costigan laughed. 'You'm think I could afford metal fences? Nay, lad—er, lass. Them be wooden, though I did treat I-self to some new-fangled *nay-ils*.

Do you'm got nay-ils where you come from? Clever things they are, holding the wood together.' He paused. 'Oh, they do be metal, I suppose.'

Screwpole asked, 'Is there much metal around here?'

'Well, there be horseshoes, and these nay-ils. And my plough, that I keeps in the barn.'

'The barn that burned down?' Screwpole said.

Costigan nodded.

'And was your horse shod when the dragon took it?'

'Aye,' said the farmer, 'she were. Funny, dragon left my other horse alone. I hadn't shodden en, since she weren' a working horse.'

'That's your problem, metal. This dragon's feeding on the stuff.'

Costigan stopped walking.

'Don't be daft. Everyone knows dragons eat'—he flicked a glance at Oyk and blushed—'maidens. Sheep, too. Not metal.'

Screwpole drew himself up. 'My good man, I have been studying diverse draconic species for over thirty years, and while I do not claim I know *everything*, one thing of which I am certain is that you have attracted a *Draconis ferroneous*, or ferric dragon. Probably a rather sickly one at that, if it's desperate enough to feed on a handful of nails and horseshoes.'

He turned to Oyk. 'Fascinating. This will be an education, girl. Ferric dragons are among the rarest, and if we can capture a living specimen, we'll–
'

'Living? I wants the thing dead!'

'Good lord, we can't possibly destroy a creature like this, at least not immediately. However, rest assured we will capture it and remove it from the area.' Screwpole continued, almost to himself, 'I'm not sure it's possible to kill such a beast.'

Oyk said, 'Mr Costigan, you were taking us to your farm?'

'Oh, ar. We be almost there.' He pointed. 'There'm barn, what do remain o' en.'

Screwpole clambered across the charred wood, as nimble as a youth in his eagerness.

'Look here, I warrant that's where your plough was,' he called from behind a pile of debris. 'The dragon focussed its energy on this area and ignored everything else. And your stables—only one stall damaged.'

Oyk whispered to a frowning Farmer Costigan, 'He gets this way when he's on the trail of a dragon. But don't worry, he knows what he's doing.'

Costigan's expression suggested he wasn't totally convinced.

Screwpole returned wearing a wide grin. Smuts of soot decorated his face and his robes—laundry was back on Oyk's list of chores.

'This is it—a real dragon. The creature left behind some footprints, yea big.' He held his hands about ten inches apart. 'It's a juvenile, no more than five, maybe six, feet tall; about twenty long.'

He rubbed his hands together. 'It'll be easy to capture—a far-ready cage and some metal for bait.'

'A what?' said Costigan.

Oyk said. 'Folk wisdom is that dragons travel by flying. A few can glide short distances, but in truth, none can fly particularly well. They move from place to place through the *quantum*.'

Costigan's brow wrinkled.

'The mathematics is complicated, and involves a stretchy sheet with heavy balls rolling across it and wyrmholes joining parts where the balls make particularly deep pits in the sheet...' She noticed Costigan's eyes glazing over. 'But you don't need to understand any of that. All you need to know is that dragons sort of disappear from one place and instantly appear elsewhere, and are attracted to heavy things. Ferric dragons are especially attracted to metal. Anyway, it's possible to create a complex spellbound box which can trap such a creature. We call it a *far-ready* cage because the dragon comes from afar, and we have to be ready to snap the cage shut when its inside. It won't be able to escape thanks to the structure of the trap's walls.'

Costigan looked like he wanted to ask a question, then shook his head and closed his mouth.

Meanwhile, Screwpole was pacing across the farmer's yard, pausing to look at the sun every now and then, and progressively inscribing a large circle on the ground with a charred stick.

'This'll be an excellent place for the trap.'

'What?' Costigan's eyes widened. 'I don't want no dragon here. En did enough damage last time.'

'Ah, my good man, that's precisely why here is a good place.' Screwpole gestured towards the ruined barn. 'The dragon can't make things worse, can it? Look, the creature's probably more scared of people than you are of it— that's why it chose your farm out here, instead of, say, attacking the smithy in town, with all its lovely iron. We need somewhere quiet—such as here— and it helps that the place is familiar to the dragon.'

Costigan's shoulders slumped.

Screwpole clapped him on the back. 'Think about it, man. Your farm'll be famous as the place where we trapped a dragon. People will come from miles to visit. You'd better start planning a range of souvenirs—ornaments, tea-towels, hats with dragons on them, jerkins embroidered with *I saw the dragon and survived!*—you know the sort of thing.'

Costigan's gaze drifted into the distance as if he were watching groats pouring from the sky, and a smile spread across his face.

'Now, Oyk, you've got the book of knowledge, haven't you? Let me see the chapter on far-ready cages.' He snapped his fingers irritably. 'Come on, hurry up. I haven't got all day.'

Oyk hauled the massive book from her backpack and handed it over.

Screwpole scanned the pages of the heavy volume, mumbling, 'Iron… yes, gold… hmm, sevenfold weave, birch, yew, purified water.'

He snapped the book shut.

'Mr Costigan, we need as much iron as the town can supply. And gold—do you have any gold?'

The farmer scratched his head. 'Mayor Grumbleton's got a heavy chain, and en's wife's do 'ave some jewellery. I think them be gold.'

'Good, good. Let's head back into town and collect everything.'

'You can't have my chain!' Mayor Grumbleton placed a heavy hand over his chain of office.

Oyk tilted her head to one side. 'Mr Mayor, would you rather get rid of the dragon terrorising your town, or hang onto a shiny gee-gaw which is sure to attract the creature when it becomes more desperate for sustinence?'

The small amount of skin visible between Grumbleton's shaggy hair and his voluminous beard paled. He removed his chain and handed it to Oyk, calling, 'Miriam, bring down your rings and necklaces. It's for the good of the town.'

Screwpole grinned. 'Once we catch this dragon, your town will be famous. You'll soon have enough money to buy a chain twice as heavy, and sufficient jewellery to bury your wife in.'

Shortly after similar conversations with the blacksmith, the town carpenter and the baker, a wagon heavy with iron, several types of wood, a portable forge and charcoal for the forge set off for Costigan's farm. The baker provided the three large pork pies and six custard tarts which Screwpole consumed over the duration of the brief journey. Oyk had to make do with the occasional crust discarded by the archmage. Mr Costigan accompanied the wagon, because it was his farm. Master Jones, the blacksmith, followed, to work the forge. Mayor Grumbleton joined them to ensure he was part of the story that would make the town famous. And several other townsfolk tagged along, because this was the most exciting thing to happen hereabouts in living memory.

Screwpole set the townspeople to gathering wood to build a box atop the wagon, while he got the blacksmith to melt the gold along with the ash of several types of wood for strength, and draw it into fine strands.

Wearing a worried expression, the mayor asked, 'Won't all this metal attract the dragon?'

Oyk said, 'The beast almost certainly senses its presence, but it won't come here with all this activity going on.'

The archmage glanced upwards and mused, 'It's probably watching even now. But we'll never see it, because it's on the other side of a wyrmhole.'

Mayor Grumbleton gulped, and spent the rest of the afternoon surveying the skies, despite being told that this type of dragon tended not to fly, while everyone else got on with the heavy work.

They completed the far-ready cage just as the sun started to set. Everyone stood back to admire the gold strands woven in intricate patterns around the box twinkling in the evening light. Screwpole got some townsfolk to raise one end of the trap while he propped it open with a stick. He and Oyk collected the remains of the iron and piled it into the wagon, then the archmage tied a thin rope between the largest piece of metal and the box's prop.

'That should do it,' Screwpole beamed. 'In his haste to gobble the iron, the dragon will dislodge the pole and—snap—he'll be trapped.

'Um,' said the mayor, 'will that box hold a dragon?'

'Of course it will, man,' Screwpole said smugly.

'But...'

It was left to Oyk to explain again. As she described how the ensorcelled metal strands in the box's walls interfered with the quantum modes of travel typical of dragon species, she could almost *hear* her audience's minds congealing and grinding to a halt. Looking at the blank expressions surrounding her, she sighed and said that the archmage's magic—she hated that word, being the sort of person who preferred a scientific explanation for everything over arm-waving mysticism—would trap the beast inside the far-ready cage.

Screwpole clapped his hands to get people's attention. 'Well done, everyone! The dragon's not going to come while we're here making a lot of noise, so can I suggest we all go home and return tomorrow morning?'

Costigan headed to his farmhouse while the others went back to the town.

Screwpole turned to the mayor. 'I wonder if there's a pleasant hostelry hereabouts which might have a pair of rooms for a hard-working and important wizard and his barely adequate apprentice. Perhaps such rooms would be donated free of charge for services rendered … Dinner included?'

Several hours after dawn the following day, Screwpole finally hauled himself out of bed and thumped on Oyk's door. 'Get me some breakfast, you lazy excuse for an apprentice. Bacon, eggs, mushrooms, and anything else that'll fit in a frying pan. And a coffee, strong. Now!'

Oyk had been awake for those several hours and more, busying herself with her master's book of knowledge, looking for any details about capturing dragons that she might have missed. She placed a feather between the pages, closed the book, and headed to the inn's kitchen to obtain breakfast.

The irritated cook explained that breakfast was over ages ago, but once Oyk handed him a handful of coins, he was happy to fry pretty much everything in the kitchen that could be fried, along with some things that shouldn't. Oyk ate an apple and sipped a cup of fine Khaleskan coffee while she waited, then took a tray containing a steaming mug of coffee and the plate piled-high with fried cholesterol steeped in a lake of yet more cholesterol up to her master.

She paced back and forth impatiently while he consumed enough food for three people, then they set off for the farm. Her ears were aching by the time they reached it—Screwpole waxed long and lyrical about how rich and famous he'd be when he brought a dragon back to the university. The chancellor was sure to want to show the beast off to the king, and there would be a much more equitable division of faculty funding, oh yes…

Farmer Costigan was leaning on an axe handle by the far-ready cage when they arrived. The box lid had dropped, but everything was still and silent.

'Mr Wizard, I don't think your trap worked. There'm nothing inside.'

Screwpole paled, then rushed to put an ear against the wall. After a moment, he muttered, 'I think I can hear… Maybe, there's… I'm sure there's something inside. There'd better be something inside.'

'You'm need windows,' Costigan said, lifting his axe. 'I could knock a small hole in en.'

'No!' Screwpole and Oyk yelled simultaneously.

'Any gap in the walls, and the beast will escape,' said Oyk.

'Well then, how'm we know if en's in there or not?' Costigan grumbled.

Screwpole put his thumbs in his lapels, preparing to give a lecture. 'It's all to do with probabilities. The trap was open and now it's shut, so there's probably a dragon inside. If we put another pile of metal outside the box, and it's still here tomorrow, there probably isn't a dragon outside. Dragons are solitary creatures, so the probability of there being a second one in the neighbourhood is low. We can extrapolate from several days' observations until the probabilities combine to result in an acceptable threshold of relative certainty. Q.E. and therefore D.'

Farmer Costigan stared at him blankly, then rapped on the side of the far-ready cage with the handle of his axe, and shouted, 'Be ye in there, dragon?'

'Oh, don't be silly, man,' Screwpole snapped.

A huge voice rumbled, 'Possibly…'

Costigan went pale, and Screwpole's mouth dropped open.

Oyk said, 'Erm… Hello, are you really a dragon?'

The deep voice said, 'I might be, or I might not be. I don't know. What is this thing you call a dragon? I am Behofnungiskranticaldera. What are you?'

'I'm Oyk, and this is my master, Archmage Screwpole, and we're joined by Farmer Costigan.'

'What's an oik?'

'We're people. Oyk is my name. Can I call you Hoff?'

'If you want. I don't think I've met a people before, just things that squawk and scream. But if peoples are things that can think and talk, I believe I might be a people, too. By the way, Oyk, if it's not too much trouble, might I ask why I'm in this dark place, and why can I not leave it?'

Archmage Screwpole cleared his throat and shook his staff in a threatening manner, the effect somewhat muted by the fact that the dragon couldn't see it. 'Beast, you will terrorise this area no longer! You cannot escape from our far-ready cage. We will take you back to the city to study.'

'Terrorise? I've terrorised nothing.'

Oyk said, 'What about Farmer Costigan's barn and his horse?'

'What's a barn? And a horse?'
'The things you destroyed while you were searching for metal.'
The box was silent for a moment.
'Oh. Oops. Sorry.'

The horses pulling the wagon to the city were nervous and difficult to control, so the journey took half a day. Archmage Screwpole sat up front with the driver, who seemed only marginally less skittish than his horses, while Oyk perched awkwardly on the back of the wagon.

She spent most of the journey in conversation with the dragon, explaining the concept of ownership.

'So,' the dragon said, 'Farmer Costigan is a people and he *owns* the creature which had metal on its feet, but that creature isn't a people. Do all peoples own all non-peoples?'

'No, it's more complicated than that. Mr Costigan bought the horse and looks after it, and the horse does work for him.'

There was a moment's silence as the dragon digested her response.

'Does Archmage Screwpole own you?'

'No!'

'But he looks after you, and you carry out work for him. You don't seem to be related, so I must conclude that he paid money for you, which means he's your owner.'

'Yes, I work for him, but he didn't buy me. He's supposed to pay me an allowance, I guess, though he charges me an equal amount in rent for staying in his house. But he doesn't own me.' She added, under her breath, 'And I'm not so sure about the looking after, either.'

'I don't see much of a difference from here.'

As she muttered, 'It's not the same thing at all,' she tried to think how her place in society differed from that of Farmer Costigan's horse, at least, the one that hadn't been burned to a crisp. Being apprenticed to a wizard was probably more interesting than pulling a plough—but then there were the days and days of preparing potions or carefully copying spells from dusty books. And the archmage's endless droning about his exploits. And the equally endless chores.

Maybe she *would* be happier as a simple farm horse.

Her sigh was echoed from inside the far-ready cage.

'Actually, I don't see much of anything from in here.'

'Sorry. My master says we can't risk you escaping and doing more damage.'

'But now that I know about peoples and owning things, I'll be more careful. I know I have to give a people some sparkly things in exchange for their metal, and I know not to burn the things the metal is attached to.'

'Maybe you can explain all this to Archmage Screwpole when we get to the city.'

'Is it far? I can normally tell exactly where I am because of the Earth's magnetic field, but that's cut off in here. It's as if I'm blind—though I suppose I am, trapped here in the dark.'

Oyk shifted guiltily.

Finally, the wagon arrived at the city gates, and was escorted by a regiment of the King's Guard to the Grand Palace. People lined the streets, cheering the archmage, who bowed and waved to everyone. They all ignored Oyk.

Screwpole was told to wait in an outer courtyard.

Eventually, the king bustled out of the palace, accompanied by his senior advisors and mages. He was short and scrawny, but wore elegant elevated shoes and a heavy cloak to hide his inadequacies. However, he was unable to hide his disappointment when he saw the wagon.

'One expected to see a dragon,' he whined, 'not a dirty old wagon.'

Archmage Screwpole bowed so low his beard brushed the ground. 'Your majesty, I'm sure an educated person such as yourself is aware that if we make so much as a pin prick in this far-ready cage, the beast will escape. And who knows what damage he might do? Sire, I'm afraid your majesty will have to settle for conversing with the dragon, at least until we establish how to kill it.'

'Kill it?' Oyk and the dragon shouted simultaneously.

Screwpole pretended he hadn't heard and continued, 'It is a magnificent beast, and we can learn much from it before that happens.'

One of the advisors muttered, 'There's nothing in the wagon. There's no such thing as dragons.'

The king sniffed, then strode to the wagon. 'Dragon, are you in there? This is your king.'

A voice rumbled, 'Yes, I am in here, though I would prefer not to be. Did you say you're my king? I didn't know I owned a king. This is all very confusing. Are you a people? Do I own other peoples and things? Do you?'

'Ah, your majesty,' Screwpole oozed, wringing his hands, 'the dragon doesn't understand the ways of civilised beings and clearly has never encountered a king before.'

The king dismissed him with a wave of an elegantly manicured hand.

'Dragon, I am the king, and I possess everything I can see. And if I say so, I own you.'

'But you can't see me, so…'

The king turned to his advisors. 'This isn't good enough—I need to lay my eyes on this beast. Can you restrain it if this covering were to be removed?'

Screwpole gasped. 'Your majesty, I strongly recommend against this course of action. It is only the spellbound box that keeps the dragon here.'

'Piffle. My senior mages are more knowledgeable in the affairs of the world than a mere thaumaturgical philosopher. The problem may well be beyond you, but my experts will solve it. Won't you, chaps?'

His advisors looked at each other, then bowed towards the king, nervously mumbling, 'Yes, of course, sire. Permit us a moment's consultation.'

All Oyk could see for the next half hour were the bowed backs of the advisors as they huddled together, holding a frantic whispered conversation. There was much waving of arms and sending of serfs to retrieve various volumes of lore from the city's libraries.

The king had left after five minutes, telling his advisors to inform him when the dragon would be ready for viewing.

Archmage Screwpole muttered, 'Idiots, the lot of them. Come, Oyk, let us retire for something to eat—I believe we missed lunch on the road.'

Oyk said, 'I'll wait here to see what happens.'

'Suit yourself.' Screwpole marched off.

The activity in the courtyard increased, with several burly men turning up with shovels. As they dug a deep pit, supervised by some of the advisors, another group of people started to mix and boil what appeared to be tar under the supervision of the rest of the mages.

Partly to get away from the smell of boiling tar, Oyk went across to the wagon.

'I'm sorry about all of this.'

The dragon said, 'It's not your fault. I've learned quite a lot about peoples from in here, more than in the rest of my life. I'm not sure I like them, and I understand why my kind has avoided them. There seems to be too much owning of stuff and even other peoples. No one seems to be allowed to do what they want.'

Oyk sighed. 'You have to work to be free.'

'Before you trapped me, I was free—none of this work thing, and able to fly wherever I wanted. OK, so it does appear that I accidentally caused problems for peoples, but now that I know, I can do better.'

Oyk said wistfully, 'I think I'd like to fly away from here. And away from the archmage.'

Just then, the group of advisors turned towards the wagon, while one rushed off to find the king.

'Out of the way, serf,' the leader said to Oyk. 'Your dragon's coming out.'

Oyk ran off to locate Screwpole, and by the time they returned, the advisors had laid a gold chain around the hole in the ground, which had been filled with the tar. The links were covered in intricate engravings, which Screwpole inspected.

'You can't seriously think this'll hold the dragon,' Screwpole blustered.

'Watch your tongue, old man,' said one of the advisors, pointing at the sticky mess. 'This is black hole thaumaturgy; nothing can escape it. Modern, sophisticated techno-magic can do much more than your clumsy, old-fashioned enchantments.' He chose to ignore Screwpole's snort. 'Once we tip the dragon in, the beast will be unable to move.'

'What's the chain for?'

'Decoration.'

Screwpole blinked. 'Oh, I see… I wonder if I might have my reward for catching the dragon before you do anything else.'

'Very well,' said the leader, handing over a large bag of groats.

'Come along, Oyk, we're leaving.'

'I want to stay.'

Screwpole shrugged. 'If you want to share in my wealth, you'll come, otherwise I'll free you from your apprenticeship, and you can do whatever you damned well please.'

'But…' said Oyk. 'What about your desire to learn from Hoff—I mean, the dragon?'

'No,' snapped Screwpole. 'I've had enough of your insolence. I'm rich now and have no need to teach an impudent layabout such as you. The only reason I took an apprentice was to avoid paying a housekeeper, and I can afford three or four of those now. Pick up your belongings before the end of the day or I'll have them thrown into the street.'

Oyk's shoulders slumped as she watched her erstwhile master stride out through the palace gates.

She turned to see the lead advisor nod towards several of the hole-diggers, who began to push the wagon towards the tar-filled hole. A thought struck her, and she quickly pulled the book of knowledge from her backpack and thumbed through the pages.

She went pale, and ran to the advisor. 'Excuse me, sir, but there might be a flaw in your calculations. That hole seems too large, and the pressure of the tar might cause it to collapse into a wyrmhole rather than your intended black hole.'

The advisor tilted his head back so he could look down the full extent of his nose. 'Piffle, boy. Wyrmholes don't exist. Now, get out of the way.'

Oyk bristled at being called 'boy,' but merely muttered, 'You didn't think dragons existed until we arrived with one.'

The wagon toppled into the hole and slowly sank, the air inside it causing large bubbles to form on the tar's surface and burst, letting loose a foul stench.

Everyone peered into the hole, waiting for something to happen.

And something did happen, but not in the hole.

The wall of one of the buildings adjoining the courtyard exploded. Within the cloud of dust and grit, Oyk caught an impression of enormous red wings and a long sinuous neck and tail.

Everyone ran. Some screamed in terror, while others saved their breath for sprinting. Everyone apart from Oyk, who stared at the beast.

'Hoff?' she whispered.

He turned his enormous head towards Oyk and nodded.

He stretched out a claw to snag the chain around the tarpit, gathering it up to pop into his mouth. When it slid down his throat, he licked his lips and pushed back on his haunches as if to launch into flight. Then he lowered himself and glanced at Oyk. 'Well, coming?'

'Oh yes!' Oyk ran towards him, then darted back to grab the backpack with Screwpole's book of knowledge. She raced to the dragon, scrambled up the offered forelimb and settled into position on Hoff's shoulders.

The first mighty flap of the dragon's wings knocked down more of the courtyard's walls. Two more flaps took him above the palace.

'Look, there's Archmage Screwpole,' Oyk called, pointing at a running man.

The dragon dropped down and snagged Screwpole's money bag with a claw. He flipped it into his mouth and swallowed, before soaring high again.

Then, with a pop, he and Oyk vanished into the quantum realms.

END

Soul Invictus

By: John D. Payne

As raindrops pattered onto the roof of his tent, Sergeant Camillus Furia Rufus, sat on his wooden trunk opening his leather pouch. He dropped in a clay vial, which clinked as it struck lightly against a lone silver coin. Gingerly sliding in the small black crow's feather, he closed the purse and tucked it into his belt.

He shivered. Best not to think about it too much. He had his orders. And it was almost done in any case. So he did as any soldier should and set aside his doubts and fears, focusing his attention entirely on the work of his hands.

With precise, measured strokes, he ran his finest oiled stone carefully over his blade. Not the heavy, sickle-curved falcatus, unfortunately. No, its work was done. Time for the ugly little pugio now. Rufus grimaced. Orders, he reminded himself.

A sudden draft of bone-chilling, late autumn air alerted him to the tent flaps behind him being opened. The wind was heavy with the night's rain, and it bit right through the scales of his

lorica squamata armor. He was glad to hear the wet slap of the flaps falling closed, once again sealing in the meager heat offered by the flickering flame of his little terracotta lamp.

The lamp was crafted in the shape of a frog, which was supposed to bring luck, particularly in matters of fertility. It had been a gift. From Aletha. Rufus's jaw clenched involuntarily, and his fingers gripped both dagger and oilstone hard, knuckles growing white.

No. He was no slave to his emotions, not like these barbarians. Control. He unclenched his jaw and relaxed his hands.

The legionary behind him coughed politely. Rufus didn't bother turning around. He knew which man he had sent for.

"Report, Novius Fabius." Rufus spoke quietly. Voices could carry far in the night, especially when both squads had their mouths closed and their ears open.

"Sir, the Deirans continue to receive reinforcements." Fabius's voice was tight, rigid, formal. "Although, at this distance, it is difficult to say for sure, many of them we judge to be of Minnaeus by their dress and bearing."

Rufus tested the edge of the newly honed dagger against his thumb and nodded. "So, our brothers have lost the beaches."

"Sir, it would appear so."

He tucked the whetstone back in his purse and sheathed his dagger. It slid in smoothly, like a duck diving soundlessly into the water for a belly full of slugs. With a quiet grunt of satisfaction, Rufus turned around.

Novius Fabius stood near the tent's entrance, his pathetically thin beard making him look even younger than his sixteen years. But the oldest man in either squad besides himself was only twenty-three. Rufus was just past thirty, which made him one of the dozen old men remaining in the legion.

"How many now?"

It was dark in the tent, but not too dark to see the young soldier blanch as pale as a Deiran. "Sir, the enemy's combined forces now outnumber us at least ten to one. Perhaps as high as twenty." His face twitched in something that might have been meant as a smile. "The same odds the Emperor's Guard faced in the Eastern Provinces, so the stories say."

Rufus raised his eyebrows and exhaled through his nose, feeling his long moustaches blow outward with his breath. "Indeed."

Novius Fabius gave him a look that all but begged for some scrap of hope. "Do you think they will tell stories about us someday, Sergeant?"

It was a disgusting display of timidity, and his first inclination was to give the boy the back of his hand, and then perhaps a taste of the vinewood rod that was the symbol of his office. The Legions were no place for the weak, as his Centurion Lucius Brennuss had taught him. The memory of that terrible first beating had Rufus reaching up to touch the scar, but he covered for it by stroking his moustaches instead.

Yes, firm discipline was the way to instill strength in a Legionary– or cull him, before he got his contubernales killed. And yet. Perhaps his years in Deira had taken the steel out of his spine. Or maybe it was this strange, macabre, rainy night. But he pitied the boy.

"Yes," Rufus said, rising to his feet. "They will tell stories about us, I am sure of it. And not just back home. For generations to come, Deirans will whisper, when nights grow dark, of the terrible fate that befell their kinsmen in the high mountains of Ghel."

Fabius grinned, his eyes shining. "Yes, sir!"

"The situation may appear dire to the untrained eye," Rufus said, drawing his head back to gaze down his nose at the young soldier. "But all of this is part of the Emperor's plan. He will crush the rebels and bring Deira to heel. And you will have the honor of being the terrible instrument of his wrath."

"I would very much like that, sir." He paused. "Thank you, sir. I must confess I very much needed to hear this from you."

"We all falter at times, my son," Rufus said gently. He clapped his hand on the younger man's shoulder. "But we stand together. Always. Against a foe of flesh and blood or against the fear that gnaws at every man's heart. Side by side, shields raised, weapons out."

He let go of Fabius's shoulder to lift an admonishing finger. "Remember!"

The soldier instantly stiffened to an even straighter posture and fairly shouted the words that had been drilled into him repeatedly, the motto of the Legions. "We never let go of our own!"

Rufus gave an approving smile. "Well said, Novius Fabius. You have learned well. And tomorrow morning, you will teach that barbarian rabble the meaning of those words to their eternal regret."

"Yes, sir! With pleasure, sir!"

"Good man. Now, we have one final preparation to make before sunrise."

Fabius cocked his head to one side. "Shall I gather the squads, sir?"

Rufus shook his head. "No." He gestured to the small stool and table, the only furniture inside the tent. "Sit."

The young soldier looked puzzled but did not hesitate to obey.

Standing in front of him, Rufus pulled from his pouch a small clay vial, hardly bigger than his thumb. He pulled out the cork stopper and handed it over. "Dip your finger in that. But don't taste it."

The boy's eyes grew wide, and his skin was once again as pale as a corpse. "Poison?"

"No." Rufus chuckled. "But it tastes foul."

"Oh. What is it?"

"Something from Yall. Certain herbs prepared for our soldiers to bring us ultimate victory."

At the very mention of that benighted place, Fabius shuddered with dread. "Sir, I prefer not to have anything to do with . . . them. Frankly, I don't see why the Emperor doesn't order us to wipe them all out."

"There is a place at the table for all within the Empire." Rufus reached up to stroke his blonde moustaches. "My own Baiowarian ancestors fought with all their might against it, and now we fight with all our might for it. Because a place was made for us here."

"Yes, sir. But that's different."

"Whether with spears or shamans, all peoples contribute their strengths to the Empire, that it might grow ever stronger. In this case, these herbs were prepared by priests who serve in the cult of the Unconquerable Spirit." Rufus let that sink in for a moment before continuing. "Would you turn away the aid of the Emperor's own servants?"

"No, sir," Fabius quickly answered. His eyes were still wide, though, and he grasped the vial gingerly, as if it were a venomous spider.

"Good. Now. Your finger." He pointed. "Dip it in."

Fabius met his eyes for an instant, searching them for reassurance— or perhaps some sign of treachery. Whatever he saw there, he broke off the gaze, dipped his finger into the clay vial, and then held it up.

"Now what, sir?"

"Touch your finger to your forehead. No, a bit higher. Just below the line of your hair. Yes. Now, just below your eyes. Good. And finally, just in front of your temples. That's it. Well done." Rufus gave the boy a smile and a nod.

"That's it?"

"That's it."

Rufus pointed, with the needle tip of his dagger at the cork stopper, which Fabius immediately stuck back in the vial. Some of its contents had smudged the young soldier's fingers and he looked as if he wanted to wipe his hands on his cloak, but he thought better of it and stopped himself. Good. Rufus tossed him a piece of rag to wipe off the last residue.

"In fact, that's it for both squads. You were the last."

Fabius smiled awkwardly. "I had no idea, sir. I mean, nobody said anything."

"They were instructed not to," Rufus said. "And they followed orders, just as a soldier should."

"Yes, sir."

Rufus gave the boy a hard look and let silence grow long and oppressive. "Sometimes I think we forget that. We've been in this land too long, become too much like these savages. Our legionaries see these Deirans wandering wherever they like, doing as they please." He snorted, the wind of it blowing his long moustaches up and out.

A corner of Fabius's mouth quirked up a bit. "It is contagious, sir."

Was that intended as a comment on Rufus's non-regulation facial hair? His eyes narrowed, and his fingers tightened on the grip of his pugio, and for a moment, he thought of striking the insolent child down.

The right of Baiowarians to wear their moustaches had been purchased with blood, and with blood that right was defended. There was no comparison between this hard-won honor and the failures of discipline that had become increasingly commonplace in the expeditionary legions.

Formerly commonplace, he corrected himself. But no longer. Not after tonight. The thought gave him satisfaction enough to temper his anger, and he smiled.

"Contagious only if we tolerate it. And the time for such tolerance, if ever there truly was time for such, has come to an end. Now is the time for . . . sacrifice."

Fabius nodded and shivered. Perhaps it was the bone-biting wet cold of the autumn night, still whistling in through the chinks in the tent's armor. Or maybe it was the look he had seen in his sergeant's eye. Good. A legionary should fear his superiors. Rufus himself had stood his ground more than once because he was more terrified of his sergeant or decanos than the screaming horde charging in, howling for blood.

With the lightning speed of a serpent's strike, Rufus stabbed his pugio into the cork stopper of the vial still held in Fabius's hand. With a start, the boy bit off a strangled yelp, and the vial would have dropped to the ground if it weren't affixed to the tip of Rufus's blade.

Rufus showed his teeth. "Tell me, son. You helped dig the trenches for our fortifications here, correct?"

"Yes, sir," Fabius said, mastering himself enough to step forward and resume an air of attention.

"What did you find?"

"Sir?"

"When you dug." Rufus pulled out the cork stopper and dipped a finger into the dark mouth of the vial. "In the earth. What was down there?"

The young legionary looked uncertain. "The usual, mostly. Roots, stones, that kind of thing."

Rufus looked down and, with his wet finger, painstakingly traced the sigils he had committed to memory on the blade of the pugio. "Mostly?"

His feet shifted, and he coughed. "Also... Bones, sir. Many bearing weapons and armor. We all found them. The hill is covered with them. Layers and layers."

Rufus nodded absently. "Generations of soldiers and warriors. They may not look like much, but these desolate rocks lie on strategic crossroads between half a dozen nations. Men have fought– and died– here for centuries."

Fabius shivered again. "I believe it, sir."

A lone horn sounded from the center of the encampment, its brassy echoes somehow mournful in the still of the night.

With a grunt, Rufus looked over his handiwork and then restoppered the vial for the last time. "And do you know what made the difference? What separated the victors from the vanquished?"

The young soldier's eyes darted about as if reviewing mental logs of their conversation, looking for the correct answer. "Training, sir? Discipline?"

Taking a deep breath and releasing it, Rufus met Fabius's eyes and held them. "Will. The will to pay the price."

Then he punched the pugio straight into the younger man's throat, severing his windpipe in a single, brutal strike.

The young soldier's eyes went instantly round with shocked surprise as betrayal, anger, confusion, and fear all flitted across his face. A gurgling choke escaped his lips, along with a spurt of bright red blood.

The ugly noise echoed several times from the next tent over. Eleven times, as each of the remaining soldiers instantly died the same death as Fabius. The vial from Yall had seen to that.   Fabius reached clumsily for the dagger, but it was slippery with blood and his already weakening fingers could get no purchase on it. He managed to loosen it, which resulted in a spray of arterial blood. Rufus stepped to one side.

An idle part of his mind wondered if the others, lying in their bedrolls, were all aping these useless actions. The little Yaltese priest had said only that their deaths would be linked, which left it an open question.

A moot one, in the end. They were dead, all of them. Even if some of them, like young Fabius, had not yet accepted it. In truth, they had all been doomed since before they had even begun to march to this outpost. Their fates had been sealed the very moment the Legate and his Adjutores had inscribed their names in the rolls of this newly created Legion.

Rufus stepped to his cot and squatted to open the wooden trunk at its foot. Sitting atop his second-best braccae and tunic was a dented and battered old brass signaling horn. It was in the style of the Eastern Provinces– no longer than his arm and nearly as straight as a tuba.

Gingerly, he removed it from the trunk, careful not to disturb the dark smudges showing where he had painted occult symbols on the brass instrument using a finger dipped in the Yaltese vial. Months of planning, instruction, and secrecy all came down to this.

An unasked-for laugh bubbled out of him, and he nearly threw the wretched horn down and jumped on it. "Madness," he said aloud. "This is madness, and I must be mad to go along with it."

He glanced at Fabius, but the dead man offered no counsel. He just sprawled there in a thickening, sticky pool of hot blood.

Rufus shook his head and sighed, feeling his moustaches float in the wind and fall over his lip again. Holding the horn in one hand, he dug into his purse and pulled out his first coin, his only remaining coin, the one with which he had accepted service in the Imperial Legions.

The Emperor stared up at him, his eyes commanding, his majestic head crowned by long, straight rays of light. There was something in the confident set of his shoulders, the not-quite smile that played on his lips that always reassured him— even before he had joined the cult of the Unconquerable Spirit. Rufus rubbed his thumb reverently over the face of the coin, feeling the well-worn ridges decorating its edge.

He turned the coin over to see a fist clutching a handful of stinging nettles together in the familiar impromptu scourge used by soldiers to warm themselves in cold-weather campaigns. He traced his thumb in a circle around the edge, where the motto was inscribed: "We never let go of our own."

Rufus nodded and tucked the coin away. He lifted the horn to his lips, and after a moment's hesitation, he blew.

In his fifteen years in the Legions, he had of course, been exposed to signaling horns of nearly every description— cornua, tubae, litui, buccinae, and even boar-headed Deiran carnices. This horn was smaller than all of those, but he had expected that in the confined space of the tent, the sound would be overpowering.

Instead, it was sweet, sad, and richly mellow. Poignant, like the sun sinking mercifully low to end a brutal day of battle. The soft, mournful notes were distant somehow as if they had traveled a long way to get there. And perhaps they had. Rufus gave it one more blow, as he had been instructed, and replaced it gently in his trunk.

After securing the trunk, he stood and turned to regard the corpse. Even though he had been told what would happen, Rufus was still surprised to see Fabius open his eyes and sit up.

"On your feet, legionary."

Fabius looked confused, but rose— or rather, one of him rose. There were two now. One lay pale and still with a gaping wound in his throat. The other stood, apparently unharmed—except that his form was somewhat translucent, so that Rufus could see the front flaps of the tent behind him, untied and waving slightly with the night wind. That, and the man's eyes darted about like a newly caged bird searching for a way out.

"Attention!" Rufus barked in a commanding voice that, by long experience, he knew could cut through both literal and mental fog to bypass a legionary's brain altogether and instead grab hold of his spine.

Though he looked rather hazy, the standing Fabius snapped into a martial posture as straight and rigid as a javelin. As with any weapon, he would need to be carefully inspected before use.

"Report, Novius Fabius."

"Sir! I am dead, sir!" He paused. Though he did not attempt to meet his sergeant's eyes, obvious perplexity and furor roiled across his face before he continued. "You— you killed me, sir. I remember . . . the blade . . . Oh, gods!" One hand reached unconsciously for his unmarred throat.

"The legionary will remain at attention!" Once lost, control was difficult to regain. Rufus knew that for living soldiers, and assumed it was true for the dead as well.

Fabius's hand came back down to his side, and he returned to good order, better order, in fact, than he had been able to display in life. There was not a whisper of sound, not a single blink of an eye, not a movement of the chest for breath.

Rufus grunted approval and nodded. "Your memory is good, Fabius. You are dead, and I did kill you. But you are still a soldier in the Emperor's Legions, and I am still your commanding officer. So take care to show the proper respect."

"Yes, sir!" His voice fairly rang from the tent walls.

"Very good. Now, gather up the squads. I have orders for them."

The spirit of Novius Fabius glanced at the loose-hanging tent flaps and then simply vanished. After a few moments, it reappeared, accompanied by eleven other apparitions, each belonging to one of the men Rufus had killed by proxy a few minutes ago.

In three decades of honoring and making sacrifices to his house's Manes and other Dii Familares, he had never seen a spirit nor even suspected that he was in the presence of one. And now, his tent was full of them–all newly slain, and all by his hand.

The Yaltese priestess had sworn to Rufus, and all the other officers and principales that the ritual would protect them. Obedience, she promised, would beget obedience. If they faithfully followed their own instructions, then the slain men's spirits would be bound to serve within the hierarchies of the Legion.

Looking into those dead men's eyes, Rufus wondered if he had just midwifed a squadron of malicious lemures, hungry for vengeance.

His body told him to scream, empty his bladder, and flee – perhaps all at once. But with the self-discipline drilled into him by years of merciless martial conditioning, he suppressed those instincts. Although he had no experience with Those Who Dwelled Below, he knew how men and beasts reacted to displays of weakness and strength.

"Attention!" he bellowed.

The dead legionaries saluted and stood in two ranks, ready to receive his orders. Each of them was clothed, armed, and armored– despite the fact that three or four minutes prior, many of them would have been in their bedrolls. And like Fabius, they all appeared unwounded and in good health, aside from being as sheer as the thin gauze veils of an Attaric temple dancer.

Rufus took up his vinewood rod and stood before the assembled spirits, giving them each a long, hard stare. All of them, to some degree or other, evinced the same kind of disorientation as Fabius. But as in life, they were wise enough to keep their eyes forward rather than trying to meet his challenging gaze.

"Legionaries. Why are you here?"

They stirred a bit at the question, looking nonplussed, but none was foolish enough to hazard a response. Taking up the rod was an unspoken promise that any incorrect answer would be met with immediate discipline. (Although Rufus had no idea how he would administer correction to the incorporeal, he saw that Legion training endured beyond the mere limits of mortality.)

Of course, experience with sergeants and centurions had also taught them that if no one answered, they might all be punished. One of them would have to grasp the nettle. Unsurprisingly, it was Fabius who opened his mouth.

"Sir, the vial of–"

"Wrong!" Rufus roared, loud enough to shake drops of rain from the tent flaps. He pounded the vinewood rod into his palm with a resounding, meaty thunk. "You are here because it is the Emperor's will that you be here. The Legions are the Emperor's, and you are the Legions'. In life or death, you belong to us."

Rufus stalked down the line, regarding each spirit with a grim smile. "None of you are conscripts. You took the coin. You signed the contract. Twenty years of service we were promised, and by all the gods, we will have our due!"

The newborn spirits blanched, rendering some of them virtually transparent. But they kept in good order and had the sense to keep their mouths shut.

"Now," Rufus said with a crocodile's grin, "some good news. I told every last one of you that this Legion– and this squad– would be victorious. That our triumph would be the stuff of legend, song, and story. Some of you believed me. Some of you did not. But now I can finally tell you *how* we shall gain the victory."

At this, the men perked up. They did not go so far as to attempt to speak to each other, but their eyes darted to either side in anxious excitement.

After a long moment of electric anticipation, in which the only sounds were the creaky wheeze of the night wind and the sullen spattering of cold autumn rain on the tent roof, Rufus judged that the dead soldiers had waited long enough.

"Since before most of you were born," he began, "the Legions have struggled to pacify this barbarous land." It was a much more expansive vision than he had ever given his men before– or ever would again. But he judged it necessary for them to understand and execute their crucial strategic role.

"It is the same mission we have accomplished in countless other grateful lands, including the Baiohaemum of my ancestors." Rufus stroked his moustaches in reflection. "The Legion brings order, and the Empire brings prosperity, culture, and civilization."

Unsurprisingly, given the Legion's actual experience in Deira, the ghost soldiers began to murmur and shift about in nervous agitation, some overlapping each other slightly. Rufus lifted his chin and bulled ahead lest he lose their attention.

"Even this miserable nation of bandits, thieves, and pirates would cease their useless strivings against the might of the Legions– given the proper resources. And time. But, thanks to the Minnaean invasion of the Far North provinces, we have had neither," he said, biting off the bitter words. "And the Deirans know it."

"Following the doctrine of our own Fabius Maximus, Shield of the Eternal City, their aim has therefore been to delay and deny rather than defeat. And like the Lingerer, they have not triumphed, but they have endured. And waited for the chance to take advantage of a fatal mistake."

Rufus smiled. "Which is how they were drawn into our trap."

It was strange to see hope on the face of a dead man. Stranger still to see it on the faces of eleven men he had just murdered. But Rufus was glad to see it. Fear of the vinewood rod might get a soldier to take the field, but he needed more than that to stay and to triumph. And these men surely had a long, brutal campaign ahead of them.

"The Deirans and their allies believe themselves poised for a great victory when the sun rises tomorrow, but instead, they have sealed their doom. This very night, we turn the tables on them. They have liked to harass and retreat. But there is no haven where they can hide from you, no place of safety you cannot penetrate. This night, the Ninth Legion becomes an invisible, unconquerable scourge, the instrument of the Emperor's chastisement."

Rufus stopped his pacing and turned to face two ranks of soldiers. They looked so fierce and resolute in the warm glow of his little terracotta frog lamp that it was almost hard to remember that they were dead. Except that Fabius both stood before him and lay on the floor, stinking of blood and death.

"Your irresistible insurgency will cover our western flank, allowing the Legions to concentrate and utterly destroy the Minnaean threat. Your valiant sacrifice saves not just our position in Deira but the entire Empire."

At this, the spirits cheered. He supposed some of that was his speech, but the larger part was the men seizing courage wherever they could find it in a desperate, confusing, terrifying situation.

Alone among them, Fabius looked thoughtful. In life, he had not thought the boy to be anything particularly special, but he had the guts to speak up when his fellows did not and the good sense to keep thinking when others celebrated. Perhaps, like his venerated ancestor, his gifts were only found– or only recognized– in extremis.

"Sergeant?" Fabius's spirit wore a carefully, respectfully neutral expression. "Sir, I don't understand how we are to strike at the Empire's foes." He licked his insubstantial lips. "Without our bodies, how can we harm them?"

The other men glanced around at each other, the tide of jubilant optimism immediately receding.

Rufus nodded. "An excellent question." One for which he had been waiting. "I do not have the answer. But it is time for you all to meet the one who does."

From his purse, Rufus pulled a single shining raven's feather and held it in the flame of his little earthenware lamp. As the oily feather shriveled, melted, and finally burned, an unpleasant, acrid smell quickly filled the tent's confined space. Then something worse assaulted his nostrils: ripe carrion.

Death, after his years in the Legions, was a familiar enough companion that Rufus knew it had many component smells. The corpse of Novius Fabius, for example, emitted two primary stinks: the bright, sharp, coppery smell of freshly spilled blood and the dark, clinging, almost warm stench of emptied bowels.

But these two were washed away completely by the sudden, overpowering, sweet reek of mass murder. He had encountered this scent only once, but he never forgot it. Moldering corpses, too many to bury, exploding with decay. Bodies heaped so high and wide that the buzzards and ravens could not pick out their soft bits.

Rufus gagged on the putrescence for the first time in this bizarre night unable to maintain his composure. The spirits of his men stirred and murmured, though whether they were reacting to his own weakness or to the stink of the grave, he could not say. Could a spirit smell? He did not know.

From just beside him came a cold, hollow voice. "You have summoned me. And here, obedient to your commands, I have come. What do you desire of me, Sergeant Camillus Furia Rufus?"

To his left stood a pale, still man. He was lean and muscular with close-cropped dark hair and sharp features. He wore a long black cape which appeared to be made of ravens' feathers. The cape covered him completely; Rufus could not see his hands, but something told him the pale man was armed and dangerous.

He hesitated. The priestess had revealed little about what would happen after he and the other principales burned their respective feathers. A powerful servitor would appear. They were not to trifle with the servitor but should show it respect. The servitor would instruct the spirits of the dead soldiers on how they were to fulfill their new mission. This, and nothing more.

The pale man stared at him. Not moving. Not blinking. His eyes glittered, hard and black and empty of emotion.

"What shall I call you, spirit?"

"I have been called many names." He shrugged. "You may call me Crow if you like. It is not important. What do you desire?"

Rufus took a long, slow breath. What did he desire? The inescapable conclusion of all his calculations was that the servitor would kill him, as he had killed his men. That his spirit, like theirs, would be bound to this mission, to harrow and break this land until the seeds of civilization could be planted here.

The world of the living had little to offer him at this point. His sweet Aleeta had left him, running off like a thief in the night to follow the newly-crowned pretender. Seven years he had given her. Seven years, and two sons.

He thought of all the favors he had called in, all the bribes he had paid to legitimate their union. Once they reached the age of inheritance, those two sons would have been Citizens. And now all they would inherit from him was red hair and a cleft on their chins.

"What do you desire, Sergeant?" the servitor repeated.

To serve the Emperor. "Venerable Crow." Rufus gave the pale man a sober nod of respect. "I desire you to answer a question posed by one of these soldiers."

At a gesture, the spirit of Novius Fabius stepped forward. "How are we to fight the living?" With one step backward, he resumed his place in the front rank.

The otherworldly servitor calling itself Crow smiled. "As newborn babes, you are unprepared to understand the answer. Although you will learn much in times to come. For now, perhaps a brief lesson?"

Crow looked to Rufus, who nodded for him to continue.

"Will belongs to the living." The pale man did not move, but his eyes flicked to each of the spirits in turn, capturing each's attention in an instant. "But even those deprived of their living will may still be the instruments of another's will. And may fashion of living will instruments of their own."

Rufus grunted. To an old soldier, it sounded familiar enough.

"Belief is power," Crow said. "More precisely, a surrender of power. A grant of will. Ergo, one always has that portion of power given by the living through belief or even expectation."

Crow turned to Rufus, and his cloak parted, releasing another wave of malodorous effluvium. It also allowed the passage of one gaunt arm, sheathed in black feathers, stretching out toward the sergeant's vinewood rod.

"If I may?"

Wordlessly, Rufus handed over the symbol of his rank. The servitor's immaterial fingers grasped the rod and took it from his hands.

"See? Freely given, and therefore easily taken." Crow lifted the rod above his head, and every pair of dead eyes in the tent tracked it like hungry canines following the movement of a juicy bone.

A chill ran down Rufus's spine, and it had nothing to do with the autumn night, the frigid rains, or the drafts stabbing through the tent's seams.

"An instrument of will," the pale man purred, turning the rod over in his hands with loving tenderness. "Ready to be repurposed."

So this was it. To be slain with his own weapon. Ignominious, perhaps, but for the glory of the Empire he could bear it. He assumed a posture of parade rest. Back straight, chest out, chin up. He had taken the coin. He had made his choice. Not an execution, but a sacrifice.

"Fascinating," Crow murmured. "The power we give to such scraps of wood or metal. Or bone. Material, yes, but it is intention that makes them tools. Symbols. Weapons."

Rufus ground his teeth at the servitor's needless cruelty. He surely knew by now that his victim was expecting the death blow, and yet he dallied. Rufus had not made his men suffer such pains of anticipation. They deserved better; they were legionaries. And he was now ready to join them.

"A very thorough answer." Years of experience dealing with casually brutal superiors aided him in keeping the impatience out of his voice. "Thank you, Venerable Crow. And now, I believe we have work to do."

"There is indeed work to do." The pale man's glittering, pitiless black eyes turned on him with an unblinking focus and intensity that underscored his inhumanity. "A much greater work than you know or could know."

The longer this dragged on, the more Rufus found his hands unconsciously itching for his little pugio. Better yet, his reliable old falcatus. This thing looked like a man. Could it die like a man?

He clenched his teeth and reminded his anxious body that this was not the time to fight. Soon, he would rejoin his men. Then their slaughter would be gloriously unrestrained, no longer held back by the foolishness of silly politicians who clad themselves in silks and scarlet while hoarding coppers like misers when it came to matters of military necessity. Starting tomorrow, the Ninth would lay a doom on this place fit to shock and terrify every enemy of the Empire, including those fools in the Senate. The thought brought a smile to his face.

"Your part in this work," said Crow, "though small, has been important. And you have played it well, better than most. Thank you." With one hand touched to his chest, Crow bowed his head low in what appeared to be sincere respect and gratitude.

Despite the unexpected warmth of the gesture, Rufus felt acutely uneasy. Then, as Crow straightened up from his bow, the sergeant realized what it was. The servitor's bow had sent a ripple of movement through his black cape, revealing it to be not made of feathers but of living ravens– wings, beaks, talons, and all.

He tried to keep the shock off his face, but something of his unease must have shown since Crow took notice. He smiled a very familiar smile– that of a bully taking delight in the discomfiture of his prey.

"You like my pets?" Crow turned this way and that in a slow and graceful dance, seeming to be entirely absorbed in watching the responses of his living cloak of ravens. "I had better, once. But I don't hold that against you, my beauties."

The pale man spoke directly to the birds now, like an indulgent mother intent on spoiling her last child. "No, I don't. You're just so fresh and new. Minutes old, some of you. Poor dears, no wonder you're still confused. You think you're legionaries, but you'll learn. Oh, yes you will."

Crow looked up at Rufus's slain men, who looked distinctly ill at ease. Then the pale man held up the vinewood rod, and each of the dead soldiers snapped instantly to attention. "You'll all learn." He stretched out his empty hand toward Rufus. "Lesson the first. Kill this man. Tear him into pieces and eat him."

The spirits turned their eyes on their former sergeant, but there was little hint of recognition now, let alone respect. With odd little hops and twitchy head movements, they began to advance toward him, their fingernails lengthening into long, black talons as they came.

Rufus swore and reached for his sickle-curved falcatus. But he kept it in its scabbard, in part because he hoped he wouldn't have to use it. "Get back to your ranks, you miserable curs. If I have to lift a hand to a single one of you, you'll all be sorry." Also, partly because he wasn't sure the heavy blade would have any effect on these spirits.

It certainly didn't appear to make any significant impression on them. They hopped forward, shrieking and fluttering their arms. Black feathers had begun to sprout out from gaps in their armor and clothing wherever skin should have been visible.

"I said get back," Rufus bellowed, pulling out his pugio. "What in the name of the Emperor do you think you're doing?"

The pale man smiled sadly. He was still holding up the vinewood rod. "They can't hear you anymore."

"They had damn well better listen up if they know what's good for them." Despite his best efforts, the spirits were backing him into a corner. He still had his falcatus for all the good it would do him.

Crow shook his head. "They're not yours anymore."

"They were never mine, damn your eyes." Rufus swept his blade back and forth, trying desperately to keep his corner of the tent clear.

The spirits, now looking more like ravens than like men, jostled for position and cawed as if to egg each other on. Behind them, the servitor who called himself Crow watched them with amusement and parental pride.

"Legionaries belong to the Emperor," Rufus growled, wondering how long it would take him to cut his way out of the tent. Too long. "We are his instruments. That was the whole point of this. That's why we were all willing to sacrifice not just our men but ourselves as well. That's why this worked."

"Not precisely," said Crow. "In fact, not at all. You were never really in control. But it's moot. These spirits are mine now, to command and to use as I see fit."

"Not likely, you bastard. I'll never do your bidding. No true Legionary will."

"Yes, well." Crow clucked at the excited but so far ineffectual spirits, making shooing motions and looking slightly embarrassed. "It takes them a little while to get used to their new role. Just one reason why the first time is always a little awkward. But in time they learn, most of them, anyway."

The pale man met Rufus's eyes. "Then there are those like you. The indomitable ones. I truly wish we could use you, but you said it yourself. You'd never take orders from me. And so, your sacrifice is . . . declined."

Rufus screamed as the first talons tore at his flesh. He swung his falcatus in a practiced series of powerful chopping strikes that should have sent heads and limbs flying, but he couldn't seem to connect with anything. The raven spirits, on the other hand, had no difficulty tearing into him with beaks and claws, seeking out the soft bits, flaying him very much alive.

As he sank to the earth, one red thought blazed through his dying mind. "You think you can dispatch a servant of the Emperor so easily? Just wait until I get to the other side."

END

Test of Trust

By: J.F. Posthumus

Chapter One

The Silver Stein had been an entirely new experience for Kaista, complete with interesting and different foods. She'd chosen a variety of dishes that had sounded tasty. Upon receiving her order, Kaista returned to the room she shared with her mentor across the alley at the Broken Wing.

As she neared the door on the upper level where their room was located, she discovered it open. Her mentor would never have left it ajar. She stepped cautiously and quietly into the quarters they shared. Her eyes fixated upon the body on the floor. Shadows moved in the room's corners.

Kaista knew death. She had seen it. The fixed anguish on her mentor's drained face froze her blood. But fear became fire. Her senses flared, and the presence of others became known to her. Her body spun, throwing the bowls of spiced rice,hot stew, and the small goblet of wine she'd been carrying. The killers ducked and put their hands up to avoid the worst of the barrage. She was back in the street, running mindlessly through the unknown city.

"That way! She went that way!" The deep voice yelled from behind her.

Shoving her hair from her face, Kaista kept running, darting around shoppers and through merchant booths in the bazaar. Fortune had allowed her to escape. Spotting what appeared to be a large stone church nearby, Kaista raced for the walkway. Few churches would turn away an innocent, and fewer still would dare harm her within a holy building. The clergy typically preferred to decide who would die upon their altars instead of allowing outsiders to choose for them.

Her feet thudded against the stone path as she raced for the large doors with a crest painted upon them. Her eyes glanced again at the symbol. It didn't depict any of the gods she knew, so she prayed it wasn't a deity who allowed open murder within the sanctity of the church walls.

If the god of luck smiled upon her, her pursuers would not dare enter the church.

There were rows of pews made from dark wood with blood-red cushions. The center aisle was covered by matching red carpet. The light tap of her footsteps against stone echoed and was the only sound heard inside the elaborate room. As she searched the interior, she realized no statues or paintings of any deity were within the building. A large stage occupied the opposite side of the room, with only a small pedestal off to the right side dotted with rows of lit candles along the back wall.

Nothing else occupied the stage.

The sound of steps from outside carried through the door. Kaista didn't have time to figure out what any of the decorations meant. She ran down the aisle, glancing furtively over her shoulder. On each side of the aisle were doors that must lead deeper within the building.

Someone has to be within this building. Anyone. Kaista tried to assure herself. She headed for the first door to the left of the stage, pulling it open, and darting inside.

Kaista came to a crashing halt at the door's threshold when she collided with a person's chest. Startled that she hadn't noticed anyone in the way, she glanced up. Her body reflexively took a few steps back, placing her outside of the door she'd attempted to come through. Her eyes widened. A deep fear gripped her and squeezed until she thought she could no longer breathe. She managed two trembling steps backward on the stage before the elf gripped her shoulder and urged her toward him. His skin was dark as ebony and his curious glowing orange eyes studied her. He'd tucked the sides of his thick silver hair behind his pointed ears. She had no doubt he was a dark elf. Legends of the evil docelfar spread wide and far, and each one described them as cruel beings. This elf matched those depictions perfectly. Except no one had told her how much they would look like the surface elves, how they would look like her, aside from the difference in skin and eye color. His skin was smooth and blemish-free. Ageless. Ethereal.

He wore black robes trimmed in intricate purple embroidery with tiny, delicate flourishes. Kaista swallowed hard, but remained silent. She was fairly certain she wouldn't be able to speak, even if the elf bade her to do so.

A frown marred his otherwise perfect features as he looked from her to the main entry doors behind her. She heard the doors open, and anger flared in his eyes. She felt his hand tighten briefly upon her shoulder before relaxing again.

Drawing a shaking breath, she stepped closer to the strange dark elf. She'd rather have her fate decided by the docelfar than the men who had killed her mentor. She turned to face her pursuers. Her mentor would have chastised her for giving an unknown her back, but she felt it was the safer option.

The men stood a few feet from the entry doors, close to the second row of pews. "You can either come with us, or die here," the center man said, his black mask muffling his words. He lifted his chin, nodding toward the elf. "Our quarrel is not with you, Elf. You can go." The trio all seemed to puff up slightly, implying their confidence. The center man fixed his gaze back at her.

"I'll not go with you," Kaista shouted, finally finding her voice. She flinched at the echo of her words around the room. "I'd rather die at the hands of this elf!"

"You presume I would kill you," the elf said, clearly. "Instead of finding a better use for your talents."

Kaista looked up at the elf, eyes widening in shock at his words. Her entire life she'd been told a dark elf would kill anyone from the surface without thought. She opened her mouth to speak, but no words fell out. She snapped her mouth shut but couldn't pull her gaze from his brilliant orange eyes, eyes that seemed to burn into her soul and see her every thought.

The snap of the bow string broke whatever spell the docelfar had cast upon her.

She turned in time to see the arrow stop abruptly halfway across the room before clattering to the floor. The archer's body jerked once before he collapsed to the floor, a dark pool forming around him. She stepped backward, stopping when her back pressed against the dark elf's chest.

She felt warmth seeping into her, spreading through her body, calming her, and easing her shivering.

"This is not your concern, elf," the group leader stated, ignoring his fallen comrade. "She murdered her master."

"I did not!" Kaista took a step forward, her hands clenched into fists. The elf's hand on her shoulder halted her advance. She turned, looking at him. "I have killed no one! I swear it!"

"Be calm, child," the elf said gently.

Kaista sucked in a breath at his words. Did he believe her?

A warming calm washed over her. She drew in a deep breath and let it out slowly. Relaxing her hands, she allowed the elf to pull her back, closer, against him. She felt as if she could trust this strange dark elf.

"You can leave, or you can die," he stated. "The girl will be staying."

As the docelfar spoke, he moved her to his right side.

The surviving pursuers glanced at each other before turning to the docelfar.

"You can't protect her forever, elf," the second said from behind his black mask.

Kaista watched in morbid fascination as the docelfar's hand rose in what seemed like slow motion. His fingers curled into what reminded her of claws.

Magic flared around his fingers, filling his palm. It twined around his skin, curling outward.

He gave the magic a command.

"Death," he hissed.

Kaista watched as the magic obeyed its master.

The sickly green light twisted and curled around the two figures, seeping into their mouths, noses, and ears. The wisps formed and coiled around the men in thick green ropes that held the pair tight as it bathed them in an eerie glow.

The masked duo clawed at their throats, the whites of their eyes turning green as the magic sank into their eye sockets. They writhed and clawed, fighting for breath. Failing, they sank to their knees and collapsed to the floor.

Kaista watched, unable to move. Her skin rippled with chills, fighting against the heat rising in her chest, but the warmth was too great. Despite the unnerving calm claiming her body, she'd never forget the scene that had just played out before her.

"Come, child. We will speak in private," the dark elf said, gesturing towards the door.

Kaista nodded, bowing her head. He led her through the door where she'd collided with him.

On this side of the door, Kaista could hear voices. She followed her rescuer along several hallways, passing many docelfar. None approached them despite their curious expressions. Now relatively safe, her body ached, grief and uncertainty settling into her bones. Her eyes darted around, trying to discern everything.

Anything to keep her body from shaking like a leaf in an on-coming tsunami.

They neared a plain wooden door at the end of a corridor. The docelfar opened it and led her into an outer office. She followed him across the room to the next door and into the innermost office. *This elf who had saved me*, she realized, *must be someone of power within this building.*

She stood in the middle of the room.

"Sit, child," he said in the same gentle voice.

Nodding, she settled into the chair to her left. Politely, she asked, "May I ask your name, sir?"

"When you raced into my guild, I judged you to be around eleven or twelve." The docelfar watched her with an unblinking stare while continuing, "Now, after a moment to contemplate the matter, I'd place your age closer to sixteen."

Petite, even for an elf, and shorter in stature than most her age, she could understand his initial mistake.

Kaista kept her silence.

"I am Lord Xantos Zaurahel," he declared, leaning back in his chair. "Tell me what transpired and why you chose an assassin guild as a place for sanctuary."

"I am new to this city, sir. I thought this was a church."

Xantos shook his head slowly, a bit surprised at her answer. "No, it most definitely is not a church."

She said, "I suppose that does explain a few things."

When she said nothing more, he sighed. "Let's attempt more simple questions. What is your name, and where do you hail from?"

"Kaista It'taun. I'm from the Eastern Lands. The port city Kuudzhu. It's in Tapne," she replied, not meeting his eyes. "My master was Pellias Yinsys."

"Why were those men chasing you, Kaista?" Xantos asked, keeping his voice gentle. When she seemed unable to answer him, he posed her with a different question. "Why were you and your master in Fellhaven?"

"We were at the Broken Wing Inn. They have very limited options for food. Master Yinsys sent me to acquire our meal from The Silver Stein. When I returned with our food, those men were in his room, and Master Yinsys was dead. I turned and ran when they came towards me." A chill ran up her spine, shaking her to her core. A tear cascaded down her cheek. "I… I ran. I saw this place, and it reminded me of the churches in Kuudzhu, so I came here hoping to find sanctuary."

"Be at ease, young one," Xantos said, leaning forward in his chair slightly. "There will be time for sorrow later. The answers you give will shape your future. Possibly even revenge for his death. I see potential, and I do not waste such a valuable commodity."

"I'm sorry," she whispered. "He was my uncle."

Wiping her eyes, she cleared her throat and looked up at him.

"When I asked why we were leaving Tapne, he told me that lies from someone with a forked tongue were often whispered into the ears of those easily manipulated." Kaista shook her head, her brows furrowing in confusion. "I didn't understand it. I asked him again later when we were on the ship. He never explained what he meant."

"Perhaps he believed someone in a position of power had been told an untruth about him," Xantos mused. "Did anything strange happen before you and he fled your homeland?"

Kaista's brows furrowed. "Mother did ask me if anything had happened between us. That no shame would be placed upon me if it had."

"What words did your mother use?" he asked. His eyes narrowed slightly at the implications of such a statement. "Her exact words, Kaista."

"My mother asked if Pell had ever said anything disrespectful towards me or any other lady. 'Pell does enjoy the ladies', Mother said, 'is he treating you well?'" Kaista bowed her head slightly. "Mother was always concerned about me. She didn't like that I was placed under her brother's tutelage instead of my aunt. 'It isn't proper for a lady to learn from a man,' she would say. She loved her brother but was always concerned about my wellbeing."

"Did she ever question if he was improper towards you?" Xantos asked.

"No. She trusted her brother. He was several years older than she. According to Mother, he had a hand in raising her and finding her husband. My father," Kaista replied. "My uncle was a *meiji*. He was our shogun's favorite. Whatever happened, it wasn't something easily dismissed."

Xantos raised his brows at the girl's statement. "The *meiji* are the Eastern Lands sorcerers. Their childhoods were spent strengthening their mental shields and ability to concentrate." he explained. "Upon the age of seven, they were placed into apprenticeships to be further trained in controlling the elements and 'spirit world'. Not quite necromancers, but only because they didn't dip into the darker aspects of that particular branch of the Craft. Your uncle would have been a master to have been given an apprentice."

There was nothing that she could think to say to that.

"How old are you?" Xantos queried.

"Sixteen."

"How long were you apprenticed to your uncle?"

"Upon completing the ceremony on my seventh birthday, I was placed into apprenticeship with him," she replied. Tipping her head to the side, she studied him. "You are familiar with my homeland?"

"Oh, yes, child. I am known there amongst certain factions," Xantos said with a smirk. "My reach is extensive, for I've had many centuries to develop my network."

"Ah." Kaista glanced down at her hands before looking at him. "Have I answered your questions?"

"You've been able to give me a start," Xantos stated.

As he stared at her, she shifted uneasily. She couldn't tell what he was thinking or feeling towards her. The longer he seemed to study her, the realization she was effectively alone in a new land without a protector or guardian dawned on her. She also had zero knowledge of the city or the mysterious Xantos.

If she returned to the inn without a protector, harm would certainly befall her. She suspected death would be a welcome respite compared to what might happen to her.

"You are here without a master. Without protection." His words echoed her thoughts. "There is a contract for your death. It is unsafe for you to leave the guild."

"Then where am I to go?" she asked, fear and panic creeping into her thoughts.

"You were being trained as *meiji*. Though none in these lands can continue that particular training, others can teach you the use of magic. As for where you will stay, you may come with me to my estate. There you will be safe from attack and can continue to be taught magic, as well as learn about these lands."

"Why are you willing to help me?" she asked quietly. She recoiled, preparing to be struck for questioning his intentions as her uncle would.

"That is a fair question," Xantos said, settling back in his chair again. " Asking intelligent questions is the only way for one to learn, Kaista. Since you do not know me, I will explain. I am helping you because you are a young woman in need. To those of my race, that alone means you should receive aid." Xantos paused, allowing his words to settle.

Blinking a few times in surprise, she found herself relaxing somewhat at his comments.

He gave a slight nod. "In the docelfar society, women hold the power. They are to be respected, and should one be in need of help, they are to receive it. Especially those of nobility… or great power."

"What will become of me?" Kaista asked.

"That is not for me to decide," Xantos replied sagely. "I will give you the knowledge you require to thrive within these lands. I will resolve your problem with the contract on your life. The price for that is nine years as my employee."

"You will be my liege lord, then?" she asked, meeting his eyes.

A liege lord held complete control over those beneath them. They dictated where the person went, what they did, who they saw.

"I will be your employer," Xantos corrected her. "Once you turn eighteen, you will be given assignments to carry out. After the time has concluded, you will be free to do as you please. Continue as an employee, leave to make a life for yourself within Fellhaven, or even travel the lands as you desire." He paused before adding thoughtfully, "You may not return to the Eastern Lands, though, as it will be unsafe for you."

"You will not choose my husband?"

Xantos shook his head. "No. Unlike in the Eastern Lands, here you have the freedom of choosing your own mate. May it be a lover or a husband. But there is time for that discussion later. For now, you must make a decision. Accept the terms given, or take your chances in a foreign land with a bounty on your lovely little head," he concluded.

Kaista bowed low at the waist.

"I accept your proposal," she said as she straightened. "I will do as you ask and strive to bring honor in your name. I pledge loyalty to you and your House until my death, even should I choose to leave your service after the aforementioned years."

"Time will bear out your claim. Until then, I will have people sent to retrieve your belongings from the Broken Wing. They will collect any personal items from there," Xantos stated. "That will include your uncle's items, as well."

Opening a drawer, he pulled out a small silver bell and rang it twice. The door opened to reveal a man standing in the doorway, he stepped into the room, closed the door behind him and bowed, but remained silent, awaiting Xantos' commands.

"I need you to send some people to retrieve all belongings and personal effects from her room at the Broken Wing," Xantos said briskly.

At Xantos' pointed look, she said, "Room 6 at the Broken Wing Inn."

Xantos gave a brisk nod before continuing. "Her uncle was assassinated, and she is now under my protection. Take the needed steps to ensure everything goes smoothly."

Then man's eyes glanced toward Kaista, and he gave a single nod. "It will be done, milord. Do you also wish me to investigate the death of this uncle?"

Xantos gave a nod. "Thank you, Everyn."

"Will you need anything else?" Everyn asked.

"Not at the moment. We will discuss your findings later," Xantos stated. "Including the answers from the earlier incident."

"Yes, milord. I'll assign people immediately," Everyn replied.

With a final bow, he turned and departed the room. Xantos waited until the door closed before standing. Crossing from behind the desk he held his hand out to her.

"Come, child," he said. "It's time for you to get settled and begin anew."

She inwardly cursed her hesitancy before taking his hand. But it seems not to bother him. He gestured with his free one, summoning a portal.

This made Kaista gasp once, before falling silent. She realized that her hand was squeezing his tightly.

"You will find safety within my halls, Kaista, as long as you follow my rules," Xantos assured her. She nodded, and felt herself relax. "We will discuss those rules while I escort you to your chambers."

Kaista gave another nod as they stepped through the portal together.

Chapter Two

A year had passed, and in that year, she'd been given a new home, new instructors, and a new life. Kaista embraced it all, for to do otherwise would be to bring dishonor upon herself and her employer. The freedoms offered beneath Lord Xantos' roof and the lands beyond were completely foreign, but she also embraced those.

Stepping into his office, she bowed deeply from the waist before rising and crossing the distance to his desk. He gestured towards the chairs.

"Your instructors report you have excelled at your lessons," Xantos stated without preamble.

"Thank you, milord," Kaista replied, uncertainty ringing in her words.

"In a week you will have been a ward for a year. In the next year, you will be an adult, and as such, you will begin your nine years of service," Xantos said.

Kaista noted that he did not clarify if she would remain in his care.

"Yes, milord," she said when he didn't continue.

A small smirk flashed across his face. "You have not broken your oath during this past year, despite the fact you are often headstrong and rather capricious." Kaista ducked her head, her cheeks warming at his words. Xantos nodded before continuing. "Despite your youthful mannerisms, I have a task for you."

Kaista inhaled sharply. She looked her lord in the eyes, but didn't dare say anything for fear of him changing his mind.

"A dignitary has been in contact with me. They wish to have a peaceful night's sleep without interruption. They sleep quite lightly, so you must keep absolute silence in the room. You will also need to ensure their complete safety. Your instructors state you have the skill to perform both tasks." Xantos paused, studying her intently. "It is not an easy task, nor is it something to be taken lightly. The task can become tedious, but many tasks will have that challenge."

"I understand, milord," Kaista said, trying to keep the excitement from her voice. In the Eastern Lands, no female would have been given such an important assignment. "How long does the dignitary wish to sleep? Where will I be performing this task?"

"No more than six hours. I have the address for you on a scrap of parchment. You will read it and then destroy it."

"Very well," Kaista replied, holding her hand out for the address.

She stared at the paper scrap for several long moments. The Royal Chambers at the Turtle Back Inn. The location? Kerunand. The capital city of the Deltheyan Province. A city she'd never visited.

Committing the location to memory, she closed her eyes and visualized the words written on the parchment, ensuring it was burned into her memory. Opening her eyes, she held the paper in the palm of her hand. Without speaking, a flame sparked to life, consuming the parchment, leaving only ash in her hand.

"When do I leave?" she asked, closing her fingers around the ash.

"Since you will be traveling by magical portal, you will leave after the evening meal. Had you no such resource, you would have a trip of nearly two fortnights."

"What about the return?" Kaista asked.

Xantos gave a small dismissive wave. "A return portal shall be made available to you at the inn upon the completion or failure of your task."

That was a relief, although she didn't believe she would fail. Die trying, perhaps, but not end with failure.

"Do you wish me to report to you upon my return?" she asked, a little disappointed she wouldn't get to explore the city.

"I expect to be aware of all details upon first light."

Bowing at the waist, Kaista remained silent.

He would probably be scrying her throughout the entire task, she thought. No pressure on her at all.

After a single nod, he said, "You are dismissed."

Rising, Kaista bowed again before turning and leaving. She would need to complete her daily chores quickly, so she would have time to prepare for the evening's assignment. With a bounce in her step, Kaista hurried off to finish her day's tasks.

Chapter Three

Upon walking through the portal, Kaista's first impression of Kerunand was that it smelled terrible. She was impressed by the clean, tall buildings and bright colors. Banners and strange lanterns caught her eye in every direction. But, oh that smell!

While the smell was not terrible, it differed from anything she was accustomed to. She was not used to the aroma of cooking fat, horses, cats, or so many unwashed humans jumbled together.

There were also too many orcs around for her comfort. She could smell the acerbic, heady miasma of orc flesh clinging to the air. None were close, but many had traversed this road in the past hour. Far too many Frightened and excited humans as well, which made the odors so much more pungent.

She removed a bit of dried elderberry leaf from her pouch and held it under her nose. The fragrance freshened her senses to a tolerable level. Steadying herself, Kiasta began the short walk to the inn. She kept the leaf under her nose until she walked into the lobby.

The Turtle Back Inn was painted in green hues, with a large dome for the ceiling. So there was something to the name. Kiasta wondered if the lobby would be decorated with images of turtles or the same green hues of the exterior. To her delight, the lobby was colored with hues of blue, the lighting cleverly giving the walls the illusion of rippling water. The wide desk looked to be made of piled rock, with dried seaweed draped over the stones.

A pair of human female clerks stood behind the desk and said in unison, "How may we serve?"

"The Royal Chambers. I am expected."

The clerks wore identical gold and green silk uniforms. Their haircuts were also the same short bobs that ended at their earlobes. One had blue eyes, the other brown.

The brown-eyed clerk smiled. She said, "Ah, Mistress Kiasta, a pleasure to have you here. The Royal Chambers can be found at the opposite end of the inn. The double doors atop a flight of four steps. You are instructed to knock thrice before entering. No one is allowed to accompany you, for we must keep our post."

Kiasta nodded her understanding and walked on, ascending the short staircase and knocking thrice.

"Enter," commanded a familiar voice.

Schooling her features, she opened the doors and faced Xantos. He was standing in the foyer, dressed in long, simple robes from his neck to past his feet. There were no other beings that she could see, either in the foyer or past it into the large bedroom.

Yellow and blue flames danced low in a large fireplace. The bed was enormous and could likely fit five with ease. Two chairs, a washstand, plus a small couch and a single short couch to her right in the foyer made up the rest of the furniture. There was, in contrast, an abundance of decor.

. She looked back to Xantos.

"I expect no less than five good hours of sleep," Xantos said in a flat voice. "Six if you can manage so."

He turned and went to the bed. "Am I permitted to sit?" she asked in what she thought was a respectful tone.

"You can do whatever you may, as long as it is in silence," he answered while sliding onto the bed. He turned away from her, laying his head on one of the dozen pillows piled at the headboard.

Kaista waited for a few moments before quietly walking along the walls, as close as she could get without disturbing anything. Silently she placed the strongest silencing spell that she knew as she walked.

The magic filled the room., Once she had pointed to all four corners and returned to the one she originated from, the "lines" were made, and the spell completed. She closed her eyes and gave herself a few moments for her body to adjust to the shift in magical pressure.

There was a considerable difference between the spells she'd learned in these lands and the ones learned from a master *meiji*. However, over the past several months, tomes from the Eastern Lands had made their way into her hands via her instructors. She never once questioned where those books originated from, or how they came into Xantos' possession.

Turning towards the door, she knelt, her skirt billowing around her legs. She took out the medallion strapped to her leg. A tool from Xantos, which she had borrowed for this job. He had charged it with his own energy, so she would be able to use the spell. Her lips moved as she called upon the realms of the spirits, speaking the name of one of the ancestral guardians that would protect anything the summoner requested on the material plane.

As she felt the cool touch of the spirits, she opened her eyes to find gray and silver wisps spinning in the air. A tall being wearing plate armor, a helmet with tiny little horns, and a katana took shape.

The face was purely masculine, and she felt his voice in her head. <"What is your demand, *nyama*?">

Nyama, she thought, surprised. It was a title given to a feudal lord's wife. A title of respect and honor. The warriors of the feudal lords would never refuse an order given from a *nyama*.

Silently, she replied back, "Guard our liege lord from any attack. Gift unto him a peaceful sleep."

There was a moment of pause and she watched as the guardian studied the sleeping Xantos. He finally bowed his head before placing himself in front of the door.

<"As you wish, *nyama*,"> the voice said, again in her head.

Kaista stood, and turned away, running her hands along her sides, seemingly to straighten any wayward wrinkles.

With that accomplished, Kaista felt she had done all she could aside from physically patrolling. So that is what she did. The hours passed without anything of even mild interest occuring. During the third hour, she had to slow her pace on five occasions before her footsteps became audible. Worse, she had nearly knocked over items at least twice. The first two hours had passed without incident.

At least the silence didn't bother her. The soft hum of her connection to the guardian in her mind kept the silence from being overwhelming.

As the fourth hour crawled into being, Kaista let herself take in the decor around the room in fine detail. The more she observed, the higher her wonder went. Were these pieces part of the room on a regular basis? Or did they adjust the decor to the client? Had Xantos brought the myriad pieces in himself? If it was the last, how long had he been here before she arrived?

Nothing but time ahead of you, unless the situation changes, Kaista, she thought in the voice of one of her instructors. *Observe and see what conclusions you can intelligently make on your own.*

There were six pedestals in total scattered around the bedroom. All seemingly made from the same stone, worked by the same artist or similarly minded artists. Likely then, part of the inn's inventory. Also, they were a dull white in color. Not much of that existed in Xantos's manor that she had observed.

As to the decor, Kaista cautiously examined every piece. Tapestries of scenes within seas and oceans. A single bell carved from sea shells. The largest pedestal held various sized decanters of liquid. A sheathed dagger hung over the fireplace.

Moving on, Kaista came to a pedestal with flattened scrolls, held in place by a small stone carving of a turtle. Past that, a painting of a small party being interrupted by six beings dressed in masks, all armed. Several feet below that painting, the next pedestal had a thick ledger, open to a pair of meticulously well written pages. Behind the book was a lit candle, burned perhaps a third of the way down. The steady flame illuminated the pages and writing.

Coming back to the collection of decanters, Kaista noticed that a pair of tiny jars had been obstructed from her previous viewings. In the first jar was crushed purple leaves that she believed to be from a nightshade plant found in the Great Forest. Shaking the thought from her mind, she tried to discern what might be in the second jar. An inch of white powder was the answer.

What in the nine hells was the purpose or theme of all this? Kaista tried to reason.

She made another slow patrol around the room, walked a little closer to the items as she went. To her mind, some of this had to have been placed in the room specifically for or by Xantos. But why?

She had occupied the fourth hour of her task with this arduous but ultimately futile effort. Coming into the fifth hour, still no disturbance, she decided to examine even further.

Since the jars behind the decanters of liquid compelled her, Kaista examined them first. After long minutes of study, she decided that her first thought was correct. Leaves from the Great Forest's type of nightshade, which secreted a nearly tasteless poison when infused in alcohol. The powder was likely a poison, although she was not familiar with it. The smell of it was bitter but somehow also nutty.

Again she wondered if these came standard with the room, and why either would be there at all. She did not open any of the decanters, no matter if the room had been silenced. The smell of alcohol could be enough to wake Xantos, or most elves. Kiasta was confident that she properly identified at least half of the liquids. The other half were likely to be other spirited drinks that she simply wasn't familiar with yet.

The dagger was another peculiarity. Its design was Western influenced, curved, with very modest filigree on the hilt. No language was etched anywhere on the surface. The blade slid silently from the scabbard when her trained hands withdrew it. Until the last inch, she saw nothing of significance.

But the last inch of the blade was treated with poison. The kind her instructors had only recently brought to her and the other students' attention. The skill required to make it was very significant, and the poison was quite toxic.

Kaista replaced the blade and hung the dagger back in its place.

Although she did not anticipate the scrolls or ledger to be of any interest to her, at half past the hour she decided to glance them over, out of approaching boredom.

Two of the scrolls were tied with black ribbon. The third, though, was not tied at all. In fact, it was slightly unrolled so she could read part of its contents. Her eyes latched onto her family name of It'taun and she quickly scanned the few sentences written.

The It'taun family resides in Kuudzhu, Tepne. Beneath the Shogun Sessai Shimazu. A family known for producing strong meiji, *Kaista It'taun is not considered an outcast. Her uncle, however, has been officially declared 'outcast' and only death by his own hands will return honor to his name.*

There was more, but it vanished into the rolled section of the scroll. Kaista closed her eyes, thinking upon what she'd just read. All her life she'd been taught the rules of being a *meiji*, how to keep the family honor, and not bring shame upon the family name. Unfortunately, there were many methods one could bring shame upon oneself without involving another. Even an apprentice.

There was great temptation to pick up the scroll and read the rest of what was written, but that would be wrong. If Xantos had desired for her to read the contents, he would have handed it to her.

She shook her head. No, she would not bring his distrust upon her by reading his scrolls.

With that, she carefully, quietly, rolled the scroll up and pushed it against the other two scrolls. It remained in place and she gave a curt nod.

Curiosity did not stop her from glancing at the pages of the journal.

This time, the information was the same she'd heard frequently from her instructors. She was a pleasant student determined to learn all she could. Obedient. Perhaps a bit too trusting, though she was learning to not trust everyone as the days passed. She desired to learn everything possible and expand her knowledge about not just magic, but the cultures of the docelfar, and those of various provinces of the Central Lands. Her desire to learn the more common languages, including docelfar, intrigued her instructors.

Kaista could not argue the comments about her impulsiveness, stubborn streak, or dogged determination. Or, as an instructor put it, she 'was like a snapping turtle that refuses to let go when something doesn't go the way it should'.

Reading everything her instructors had often said to her made her smile. She was pleased to know they weren't simply saying those things to appease her. Or to use it as a method to manipulate her into doing what they wanted.

Amusement fled quickly as she reached the bottom of the page. The words seared into her mind as she read them.

Mistress Kaista is an apt pupil and doesn't show the loss of her former master openly. One can see it at times, but she tries to hide it well. Upon further investigation, the cause for Master Yinsys' flight from the Eastern Lands has been discovered. Despite that Master Pellias Yinsys was a favored meiji *of Shogun Shimazu, until shortly before he fled the Eastern Lands, his favoritism with the shogun did not prevent his need for departure. Master Yinsys forgot-*

Forgot what? Kaista's mind screamed. What could her uncle have done that would have caused the shogun to remove all protections from being a favored *meiji*?

Her fingers itched to turn the page and read more, to learn what had truly happened. Drawing a deep breath, she turned her back to the book and crossed the room. Sitting on the small sofa, she closed her eyes, refusing to even see it.

Finding her center was difficult. Nearly impossible. Her mind reeled on what she'd read and everything in her wanted to know the rest of the story. But she could not -would not- turn that page.

For several minutes, she attempted to lose herself in the book.

When the guardian moved swiftly to one side of the room, Kaista almost felt relieved. Something, anything to occupy her time. She slipped off the sofa to see what had alerted her \
summoned aide.

A small panel, which Kaista recognized as a servant panel to deliver food or other supplies without disturbing a guest, slid up. While she was still approaching, a small clawed hand reached out to push the servant door up further.

The guardian grabbed the hand and forcibly pulled the kobold attached to it out of the small compartment. The kobold thrashed against the strong grip and used the long fingernails of its free hand to tear at the guardian's chest and face. Large, unbleeding gashes appeared on the guardian, who acted as though it was mildly annoyed. The free hand was soon grasped, and the kobold was held up by his arms in front of the guardian. The kobold did not speak, but bared its teeth and snapped at its captor.

Finally, Kaista was upon the pair. She grabbed the kobold's chin and forehead, wrenched it violently to the right. The snap from the neck was louder than she was comfortable with. Still twisting the dead kobold's head, Kaista looked over to the bed, her eyes wide with worry.

Xantos had not moved. His body did not stir in the slightest. With a sigh of relief, she took the corpse from the guardian and stuffed it back into the waiter chamber. Closing the panel took more effort than she expected, because the kobold's hand kept flopping down where the panel had to close before she could get it all the way down. On the third attempt, she tucked the hand under the corpse and was able to fully shut the panel.

No movement or change from Xantos.

Once she had silently traversed back to the sofa, Kaista found little trouble finding her center. Calm eased across her body.

Five minutes after the sixth hour began, Xantos rolled towards Kaista. His orange eyes glowed between his barely opened lids.

"Good," he said clearly.

Feeling as though she were going to jump out of her skin, Kaista managed to not yelp in surprise, or fall off the sofa. Her movements were jerky as she stood and bowed to Xantos. Turning, she bowed to the guardian she'd summoned.

Silently, she said, *You may go. Thank you for your service.*

The guardian bowed low to her before vanishing in a swirl of mist. Kaista gave a slight nod of satisfaction before turning her attention back to Xantos.

She asked aloud, "Did you rest well, milord?"

"My rest was undisturbed, if not uneventful."

He spun on the bed and stood with fluid ease. The wide smile he favored Kaista with was not, to her inexperienced mind, comforting. It was full of glittering teeth and spread further across his face than any she had seen before. The orange eyes had a bright glint that she was also unfamiliar with.

"Your rest was… eventful?" she managed to ask.

"Indeed," he confirmed while he walked to the decanters and began pouring himself a drink from the smallest one.

The unmistakable aroma of well-aged elderberry wine floated in the air as he topped off his glass. Casually, he used his free hand to pluck the dagger from its hanging spot at the mantle.

"Do you like the dagger?" he asked. His eyes fixed on her.

"It… it's an interesting weapon," she said without too much stuttering. She hoped.

"Were you intrigued with the poison used on its tip?" Xantos continued, amusement tinged his voice.

"I found it confusing, to be truthful," she replied. "The dagger is not part of the room's decor provided by the hotel, is it?"

Xantos laughed. A full rich sound that startled Kaista.

"The pedestals are provided by the hotel," he explained, "all else came from my estate."

Everything suddenly made sense to Kaista. The poisoned dagger. The contents of the containers. Even the scrolls and ledger.

"This was partially a test, wasn't it?" she asked cautiously. "The dagger and poisons were to see if I could attempt to harm you."

After a long draft from his glass of wine, Xantos nodded.

"The decor is meant to encourage betrayal, or worse," he confirmed. "A test that you have passed above most others before you. You should understand by now. The docelfar are a people mostly preoccupied with opportunity and acquisition. Nor are they alone in that. I must know where I stand with each of those I chose to employ. The higher the regard, the greater I must be able to rely upon them implicitly. This is one of the tests I use."

"Worse? What is worse than betrayal, milord?" Kiasta asked, giving little regard to the rest of what he had said. She would never have want to harm him, so this and any other test were unneeded. But if he wanted to test her, he would.

Before answering, Xantos placed the dagger on the pedestal with the decanters. He poured a second glass from the same container his wine had come from and handed the glass to her. He waited until she took it to speak again.

"On at least two occasions, the subject of the test attempted to seduce me. Whether to curry favor or lull me into a false sense of security? I know not. They did not live long enough to confess their intentions."

Kaista nodded and took a sip of the wine he had given. It was heady and sweet. The bitter aftertaste was smooth, a testament to its age and the care given.

"I must tell you, the extra step of the summoned guardian was a new factor," he continued, "A silence spell is often employed by those capable of such. The addition was clever."

"Thank you," she said, although she could not look him in the eyes. Her skin felt flushed.

"Do you have questions for me, Kaista?" he asked. He set his now empty glass on the pedestal.

"Do you know what happened with my uncle?" she finally asked. "It has been almost a year to the day."

"I do. The short version is thus: Your uncle was approached by Ishyi Eilsalor, a feudal lord in the southern region of Tepne, for your hand in marriage. Your uncle refused. Eilsalor, a favorite of the shogun of Tepne, approached the shogun. He claimed your uncle had coerced you into having an affair with him. Your uncle fled the Eastern Lands to save you, as well as himself, despite knowing the dishonor that would befall him. His assassins were sent to not only kill him, but return you to Eilsalor. Who would then force you into marriage."

Kaista stared at Xantos, uncertain of what to say. Or even how to react. She lifted the glass to her lips and took another, longer sip.

"If you wish to have the full story, the scrolls and ledger will reveal all. I grant you permission to read over that which is pertinent to you and your uncle."

She nodded. Lowering the glass, she studied the liquid within it, wondering if something had been added to the wine.

"There is nothing but wine in your glass, Kaista," Xantos stated.

She looked up at him startled.

"You need to feel confident enough to ask any question on your mind. That will save you more often than your weapons."

He gestured past her. A portal formed. The view was familiar: his office lay on the other side.

She looked from the portal to her benefactor.

"Why are we going to your office?" she blurted.

Xantos nodded again.

"Because we are done here, and the documentation I am allowing you to read needs to be returned to my office when you are done. So, we shall sit in that room while you learn what you wish to learn. My chefs are also far better suited to a fine morning meal than the hotel staff will ever be. I imagine the wine, strong as it is, to be more than you are accustomed to as the first sustenance of the day. Some food will improve your constitution, so you may finish that fine vintage."

A smile bloomed across Kaista's face. "Thank you."

Taking a few hesitant steps, she determined she wouldn't fall over just from walking. Collecting the permitted items, she turned and followed Xantos through the portal.

"Indeed," Xantos said as they stepped through. "Thank *you*, Kaista."

END

Dust in the Mouth

By: William Joseph Roberts

Draven had marched along a well-beaten game trail over the rolling hills of Angara for weeks. Just ahead in the dimming evening light, the fiery glints of the setting sun reflected in the frothing whitecaps of the rushing stream. Weary and worn from his long trek, he had hoped for a trout or some other easy prey as it drank from along the water's edge.

He quietly knelt and retrieved two fist-sized stones from the ground, then, crouching low, he moved as if transformed into a wolf stalking its prey. Slowly, he pressed forward around obstacles to find an opening in the undergrowth, off the side of the game trail.

There before him, bathing in the frigid mountain stream, a voluptuous beauty sat stark naked on a worn boulder at the water's edge. Gooseflesh rippled upon every part of her supple white flesh. She faced away from him and looked in the direction of her camp, which lay beneath a rock ledge that protruded from the face of the mountain. A familiar scent drew his attention to where a hare or river rat roasted over the fire.

Draven turned his attention back to the woman. Long, dark hair hung down her flawless back, brushing the well-formed top of her curvaceous rear. Draven could barely make out the familiar tune the river vixen hummed over the rushing torrent of the mountain stream. Lifting one of her ample breasts, she continued to wash, unaware of his presence.

He watched from the concealment of the underbrush. Both the scent of cooking meat and the sight of the softly pale olive flesh struck long-denied chords of hunger within his soul.

"It is impolite to spy on another unawares, such as you do," a wizened old voice said from behind him.

Draven whirled to face the unseen voice. Beneath the boughs of an ancient grandfather oak, an old man sat cross-legged on a bed of thick heather.

"By Morrag's beard. You startled me, old man," Draven said quietly as he stared. The ghastly white of his clouded eyes seemed to glow from behind his large, hawkish nose, which was the dark brown color of tanned leather.

He wore ragged and muddy furs draped over his shoulders and hung loosely over his gaunt frame. "Who are you? And how do you know me to be a warrior? I could be a huntsman or a simple beggar, and you would never know, for you cannot see me."

"Naught but an old blind pilgrim on his way to the temple of Surath-Durgra," the old man said in a dry, raspy tone. "As for your second question, my boy. To these old ears, you tromped through the forest like a wild bull. A huntsman is quiet, soft of sole, and mindful of his surroundings. Now, if I may ask you a question, young warrior."

"By all means, Seer, ask away."

"Why do you spy on my daughter?"

"A man would be a fool not to gaze upon true beauty when he comes upon it. I merely admired from a distance, and did not soil her with my touch."

The old man smiled and laughed with a heavy breath. "I cannot blame you, son. My very own lustful gaze has caused me more trouble than I have cared for during my years." He let out a bellowing bout of laughter, then stretched forth a withered hand. "Help me back across the river. Come, share our fire and sup with us, young warrior."

Help the old man he did. Through the briar and brambles at the water's edge they emerged, startling the girl, who stood and stared, doe-eyed, before realizing the warrior was aiding the old man across the flowing waters.

After a time they sat and supped and shared the roast rodent. The old man introduced himself as D'Bia of the Azkateri, a people from far to the east. His daughter he named Branwen. She looked up at Draven, then averted her eyes shyly and stole glances of interest. The thin silks she wore left nothing to the imagination. Each delicate and soft curve of her pale olive skin called to the flames that burned within Draven's heart and loins.

Feeling somewhat obligated to contribute to their meager meal, Draven passed his wineskin to her, and she eagerly let the sweet liquid pass between her parched but otherwise thankful lips. He removed his cloak and draped it over her shoulders. She thanked him. D'Bia told of how they had traveled from far in the south with a trade caravan.

"Three days ago, we were set upon by bandits," the old man growled. "If not for my Branwen's sharp eyes and quick wits, as sure as we sit before you now, I would be dead, and she'd be a slave or whore." D'Bia spat to the side.

"Then, for your kind hospitality, let me guide you to your destination," Draven demanded.

"We could not impose upon another during our pilgrimage," Branwen said softly. She looked up at him with innocently imploring amber eyes that melted Draven's heart. "We must endure the trials which both the goddess Surath and her king consort Durgra impose upon our mortal shells in order to seek purity by the time of our arrival."

He hung on her sweetly spoken words, which gently glided on the air as brightly as the fresh golden honey of an early spring harvest.

"Perhaps your goddess set me upon this path to find and guide you through the wilderness. I have neither obligation nor set path before me," Draven announced. "I am free to wander the world and experience all it offers. By the Morrag and his witches three, I willingly pledge my blade and my arm to the two of you, to see that you arrive at the end of your pilgrimage otherwise unmolested."

The next morning, Draven set a fair pace, scouting ahead, while Branwen guided D'Bia along the game trails of the Angaran forest. By early evening, the trio tread upon the open grasslands of rolling hills bordering Nos'Bigyle lands. Beneath the boughs of a poplar grove, they stopped to camp for the night. Draven gathered wood for a fire as Branwen tended to her father and settled him in for the night. By luck while gathering wood, Draven stumbled upon a growth of root vegetables that he sliced and placed on a stone amid the hot coals and flames.

Quietly crouching beside the fire, Draven stared into the hellish red glow of the coals as he stirred them about, careful to evenly heat the stone.

"You are a kind soul, warrior," Branwen said, placing Draven's cloak over the old man as he dozed. "Not many would go out of their way to help a stranger without expecting something in return."

"It was merely luck that I happened upon the two of you when I did," Draven said. "My course has not been steadfast in months. I set my rudder by the winds of change, to sway to and fro as is necessary."

She smiled and looked away into the orange glow of the fire. "You speak as if you were a poet as well as a warrior."

"I've never been anything, really." Draven took a long breath. "I've learned many a thing in my time, but never will I be a master of any skill or trade. The fates see to it that my stars change and a new adventure begins before I can settle down. I sometimes fear that I am cursed to wander the world for eternity, never able to find my peace in one place."

"Then let us test the fates," she said excitedly in a hushed whisper. "When we reach the temple and join our brethren, you must stay and join us."

Branwen sat behind the fire-haired warrior, resting her breasts against his stooped back. She draped her arms over his muscular shoulders and neck, holding him in a firm embrace. "We will not go hungry in the service of the Surath-Durgra." She nuzzled the side of his face and nibbled on the tip of his ear lobe. "It is said that *all* the hungers of man and beast alike are satiated and fulfilled in the service of the earthbound gods," she whispered into his ear.

Draven leaned to the side and drew Branwen down into his lap, where he embraced her, smothering her with a passionately deep kiss before the long howl of a wolf in the distance struck at his soul.

A low growl escaped Draven's throat as he located the direction of the howl. Lifting Branwen with ease, he placed her back onto her feet, then stood and pushed a heavy stone into the girl's hand. "Stay close to the old man, and try not to move unless you have no choice. Let them focus on me. If you move, you become prey."

She swallowed a dry gasp and nodded before returning to her father's side and kneeling on the ground where he slumbered.

Draven withdrew his dagger from its sheath, and gripped its familiar form in his right hand, while wielding a makeshift cudgel of firewood in his other. He circled the small campfire, keeping his back to the flames. Shadows danced and leapt about amid the ancient poplars in the dimming light of dusk. His gaze scanned the dimly lit forests that surrounded them.

The howls grew closer, the darker the sky became. Movement darted about at the edge of the firelight. Leaves rustled on all sides.

Draven could hear Branwen's frightened breaths over the pounding of his heart. He circled around the fire to his left and froze at the sight of two burning green orbs in the black distance. They moved and swayed with the hypnotic dance of a stalking predator.

Two other pairs joined the first, followed by three more that had flanked them. Gooseflesh rippled up his neck at the wolf's long howl from his left, then the growling charge of the pack into the dim firelight.

Draven batted away the first and dove beneath the second beast to leap at him, sticking the creature in the haunch with the blade of his dagger, before rolling back to his feet in the face of another massively wooly beast that stood as tall as the warrior himself. He swung and dove at the creature, landing a crunching blow to the side of the wolf's sensitive snout.

All but one of the husky beasts kept their distance. Some whimpered, some limped, but the pack continued to circle. Draven roared and stomped the ground. A massive wolf with fur as red as fresh blood answered his war cry. The mottled dark fur of the beast's face made it look as if it wore a black-masked helm, like a warrior prepared for battle.

Draven sprung backward as the great wolf lunged for him. He swung the cudgel in a circle above his head and brought it around with all of his might, only to have it stopped as if he'd stuck a stone wall. The beast clamped down on the makeshift club and shattered the seasoned branch as if it were nothing more than a twig.

"Alkahi!" Draven roared at the forest as he stepped back from the beast. "Call home your pet before I send him to sit at the side of your cousins in the nethers of the great Underdark!"

The beast charged again, only to be met by both blade and fist alike. It whimpered and staggered from a powerful left hook to the side of its head.

It's jaws snapped, barely missing, as Draven stepped aside and forced his blade down into the gullet of the heaving beast. Its body constricted and wrenched as it reflexively attempted to expel Draven's arm. He twisted the blade wildly about on the inside of the retching monster, carving out the beast's innards. The massive red wolf heaved and contorted, then suddenly slumped and went limp before it dropped to the ground and slid free from the warrior's blood-soaked arm.

Sorrowful howls erupted from all around them. The pack paced and barked at the warrior who had felled their leader.

Draven griped the leader by the scruff, cut its massive head free, and held it high for all to see. He roared and howled at the pack, stomping ferociously at the ground as he leapt toward other members of the pack. With reluctant whimpers, the wounded animals grumbled and growled, then slowly, they melded back into the darkness of the night.

Draven broke the top of a large sapling and mounted the massive head atop the living pike. He roared, then cried out to the things that lurked in the dark of night. "Neither man nor beast nor god alike matters to me. I swear to the universe that you will all bleed equally by my hand should you cross me!"

His menacing gaze swung around. Without another word, he stoked the fire, then rolled the carcass to the side, and with a quick flick of his blade, he separated fur from flesh.

By early evening, three days later, Draven strode into the outer courtyard of the temple of Surath-Durgra. Columns and statuary of gleaming white marble burned with the hubristic reds and oranges of the setting sun. A loud drumming gong resounded throughout the courtyard. A midnight black beast of a man who stood at least two hands taller and better than four hands wider than Draven struck an intricately cast bronze gong. It hung suspended by chains between two of the white marble columns. The two heavy wooden doors of the temple entrance opened, and attendants dressed in loose-fitting wraps of white fabric emerged from within.

Attendants ran to welcome Branwen and her father. Branwen explained the exploits of Draven the Red Wolf during their journey and begged that he receive a hero's welcome.

And so he was led away by a half-dozen women that, to the best of his knowledge, were each from a different land. One had the midnight black skin of the Tuathakan jungles far to the south, another with the buttery-colored hair and complexion of a woman of the ocean-going Angeraine. There was a redhead of the Juentheim, a hawk-nosed brunette of the Azkateri, a deep brown goddess of curves with eyes as dark as the pitch of night and a petite, flat-faced lass half the size of the others of the Bergarum people from the frozen deserts far to the north.

They led him deep into the temple to a steamy chamber of cerulean blue tile, where each disrobed before stripping him of his garments. He slid into the soothingly hot water, where they bathed, oiled, and pampered him beyond anything he had ever experienced in his short eighteen seasons.

Once finished with him, the six carefully dressed him in a white linen wrap and brought him into a torch-lit great hall. Dozens of onlookers stared at him in complete silence as he entered the spacious chamber.

The scent of roasted pork hung heavy amid the pitch-scented air. Eight long feast tables were arranged in the hall's center to face one another, forming an octagon. At the head of the room sat the old man, D'Bia, in a throne-like seat, dressed in rich red velvets and expensive furs. To his right sat Branwen, dressed in a silken gown the color of a man's blood. The thin layers of the gown did little to hide the voluptuous curves of her body. Each of the six attendants nudged Draven forward to be seated at the head table next to Branwen.

"I thank each of you for your service," Branwen said as she stood and nodded a bow to the attendants. They reciprocated the bow with giggles and blushing smiles as they rushed to take their seats around the hall.

D'Bia arose with an outstretched hand as a gong resounded from deep within the temple. Musicians plucked at harps and tapped lightly at drums as a mass of roasted meats—ribs, shanks and the like, surrounded by enough exotic fruits and vegetables to feed a small army—carried in by two muscular men upon a thick wooden plank. A pack of boys rushed ahead of the pair to place the supports in the center of the tables. Once set in its place, the two hefty men exited the room. The small army of boys began to serve the meal to those seated at the tables, starting with D'Bia, Branwen, and Draven.

"From His great hall on high at Jut'athal'akan, where *He* slumbers and awaits the next coming, may He bless us again on the morrow as we are now, with full bellies and the protection of His great embrace," D'Bia said aloud as he held his goblet high, then drank deeply.

Draven followed suit and choked on the heavy, coppery tang of the sweet drink, but swallowed so as to not offend his hosts.

At one point midway through the meal, a small man in finely colored silks, equal parts jester and bard, plucked at a small harp while he sang and joked and poked fun at the audience gathered about the tables. The meal continued for some time, with light chatter, laughter, and the music accompaniment before the first of the attendees rose.

Two beautiful young women, one of the Angeraine and the other of the Reklaw people who dwell in the hills south of the valley of the Mauga, Draven's homeland, tugged at a strapping lad not much older than they. They teased and beckoned him to follow as they embraced one another, then disappeared from the room.

Branwen leaned over and laughed as they watched the young man arise and leave the hall. "It looks as if the evening's real festivities have begun." She giggled and flashed a knowing smile at Draven.

"By the grace of Del and Corimaen," Draven cursed. "The lad may be at the edge of death's door by the time those two are finished with him."

"That is quite a goal to strive for, is it not?" Branwen said, then toasted Draven.

"Aye," he said, returning her toast with a clank of goblets. "Aye, it is, and it is quite a good goal."

They quietly finished their meals, each giving the other teasing glances as they watched the others slowly slip away by ones and twos. When only a few remained, and the kitchen boys had returned to collect the meal's remains, Branwen placed her hand over Draven's thickly calloused hand.

"Come, let us not miss out on all that the evening offers." She smiled wide and stood. Hand in hand, she led him from the room in pursuit of the ones who had gone before them.

They ducked through the low entryway into a long, dark hallway. The scent of lavender roses hung heavy in the air. Draven could feel the effects of the wine as they strode forward into the darkness, where the corridor arched to the left. The air seemed to undulate with the slow, rhythmic beat of drums and moans that emerged from the end of the corridor as they approached.

Braziers burned at five points around the circular room, the acrid smoke rising high overhead to the tiled dome of a ceiling above. Two gilded thrones sat atop a raised dais to the left and overlooked a massive bathing pool that occupied most of the room. Linen wraps littered the floor, leading to the steaming surface of the water. Stairs climbed either side of the wall that backed the pool and ended at a platform twenty feet above the writhing mass of nude bodies below.

Branwen looked back over her shoulder as she released Draven from her grip and slipped the red silk gown from her shoulders, where it fell in a heap on the tiled floor of the chamber. She flashed a teasing smile at Draven, then descended the steps into the pool.

Eagerly, Draven let his cloth wrappings fall free as he pursued her into the waist-deep water of the pool. He caught her up in his grasp and pulled her tightly against his bare, muscular chest. The warm scent of vanilla filled his nostrils as he sniffed at her long, dark tresses. Others pawed, kissed, and groped at the pair, and his hunger intensified as he tasted her neck, then spun her about and pinned her against the carved stone wall, where he partook of her full, thick lips. Draven rose for breath and glanced upward at the strange carving. *A seal of the cult's elder god, no doubt,* he thought, but he had other matters to attend to.

Branwen looked up, following his gaze. "There are many other benefits to being a believer," she said softly. She pulled her wrists free and draped her arms around his thick neck. "The old ones," she said, nodding behind herself, "they hold our eternal souls in balance among the universe, to be devoured by the void, or born again on this unholy plane."

She tiptoed and kissed him so deeply it felt as if she drew his soul from his mortal form.

A trio of other attendees stumbled into the pair, separating them. A pert and healthy blond all but climbed onto Draven's form. He pushed the blonde aside and went back to Branwen, wrapping his thick arms about her tiny waist, as he lifted her high and ravenously suckled at her breast. Her back arched as she let out a long, entreating moan.

The world suddenly lurched and spun out of control. Her breast crumbled to dust in his mouth, then became whole once again. He tightened his grip, holding on to her to steady himself, but only heard the dry crinkle of leather over the cacophony of rushing wind that roared in his ears. The universe coalesced and reformed into reality as he released his grip and dropped the shapely lass into the steaming pool. Pushing her away, he leaned back against the great carved seal.

"Come, lover," Branwen said in a sultry tone that rattled in his skull. "Tell me, what is wrong? Don't you like me? Embrace me and submit," she beckoned.

Sight and sound alike failed him, and the universe became a dark, perpetual silence to Draven. He retched at the overwhelming scent of electric purple ozone that felt as if it danced across the entirety of his being. An indescribable inky blackness became the eternity of existence in the absence of all other things.

Reality snapped back at her gentle touch. Branwen stepped closer. Pressing herself against him, she wrapped herself around his thigh. Draven shook his head and attempted to clear the charm that had overcome him.

"What are you?" Draven growled.

Branwen pulled herself close and, standing on tiptoes, gently kissed Draven's spasming brow. "Quiet, lover," she said with a shush.

"I asked you a question, witch!" Draven roared as he attempted to push her away. He could feel the strength of his limbs ebb away, and they began to fail him.

"Your soul is stronger than any I have encountered in a millennium," Branwen said with awed reverence. "Jut'athal will be pleased. Guards! Take him to the cells while we await D'Bia's arrival." She reluctantly untwined herself from the warrior and stepped away. Draven struggled to stay where he was, slumped against the stone wall. He watched helplessly as Branwen strode to the dais and sat on one of the thrones. She beheld all who bowed in reverence to her commanding gaze.

In moments, two large guards rescued Draven from slipping beneath the water's soothing surface and carried him to a holding cell with no other exit than the steel-grated entrance the pair tossed him through. He lay there for some time in the near darkness, unmoving, surrounded by the sounds of shuffling feet on stone as they moved about the cell.

"Welcome to the rest of your life, warrior," a smooth voice said with a shaky laugh. "Do not fear for your limbs, my good man; they will work again in no time at all. Each of us who remains here has been face down in that same place at one time or another. Jaleel, the one in that dark corner over there, didn't learn the first time, and thrice did he find himself face down in that spot."

The disembodied voice laughed and grew closer. "Slowly," the voice said as a figure knelt beside Draven and rolled him onto his back. "They take us out occasionally to meet their god or some such thing. One past inhabitant of this place speculated they were beings of another realm. Then again, he also talked as if they were daemons or succubi sent from the lowest pits of the twelve hells."

Draven strained with every ounce of his being to sputter and form his lips into words his talkative cellmate could understand. "What is Jut'athal?"

The young man smiled down at Draven. Old eyes stared out from a smooth, boyish face. "That, my friend, is the mystery of this place, but from what I have ascertained, Jut'athal is the God-thing these cultists serve and worship." He spat to the side. "Something along the lines of 'service leads to immortality' or some nonsense. You look as if you've been about the world a time or two. I'm sure you've run across the type in the past."

Draven sat up with the young man's help. "Branwen mentioned introducing me to her god."

"Oh, did she now?" The young man scoffed. "You should feel a might privileged, my friend."

"I don't think that's something I care to stay here for."

"Neither do I," the young man said, laughing as he extended his hand. "I am known as Callum the Atlantean. Poet, minstrel, and scribe to those with the silver for such luxuries."

"I am Draven of the Mauga," he said, then forced his arm to do his bidding with all the power of his will. He reached up and locked arms with Callum.

"It's a pleasure to meet you, Draven of the Mauga."

Some time passed before the effects of the charm fully wore off, and Draven climbed to his feet. He tested the cell for any weakness.

The only light in the room filtered through the barred window set in the thick wooden door. The walls were of solid stone, carved into the bedrock. The locked door must have been two inches thick. He tugged and tested the rings set into the stone walls and connected the shackles to the chains that dangled down the cold-hewn surface. One such ring they found to be loose in its setting. Callum and Draven worked at the ring, and then with their combined might, the spike released its grip and pulled free from the stone.

The other prisoners cowered in the room's darkest corner, out of sight should one of the guards look in.

"This should be all we need to pry the hinges on that door. But what of the guards?" Draven asked.

"Most times, the guards are nowhere to be found," Callum replied. "We've been lucky to be fed at all, but it seems to me there is more noise from above as of late. And the guards have been more active in the last two days. So there's no telling when they may be back."

"Then let us be swift." Draven strode toward the door. "It is time to leave this forsaken hole."

Using the freed spike, the pair dugat the iron bars set into the window of the wooden door. Removing two of the bars, Callum held onto them for later use. Able to reach his arm out through the portal, Draven lowered the chain, and hooked the crossbar that restrained the cell door, which he lifted and freed it from its cradle. The door creaked open.

Silently the pair pressed forward, down the carved stone corridor, back the way they had been brought, and stopped at the first turn in the path. Draven calmed himself and slowed his breathing to little more than short, shallow gasps. They both went rigidly still as they listened intently to the festivities above.

"Do you know how we'll get past that?" he said, pointing toward the revelry with the iron bar.

Draven held up the chain and let the shackle drop before Callum. "Aye, I know exactly how we'll get through that. We'll cut our way through it using whatever we have at hand."

He peered around the corner of the corridor, then turned back to Callum. "We've two guards only a few feet away, but they look to be sleeping." Draven looked Callum over, then to the weapons that they each held. "Here, lad, you strangle the life out of one of them, while I snap the other's neck." He handed Callum the chain, took one of the cold iron bars from his hand, and rounded the corner without another word.

The pair moved swiftly, both upon their quarry in the breath of a moment. Callum wrapped the chain around one's neck and pulled backward with all his might. The other guard turned and drew his sword just as Draven's calloused hands gripped the man's skull and snapped his neck as if it were a piece of dry tinder. He clasped the guard's short sword before the man could hit the floor and sliced across the other guard's throat in one swift movement.

"Come, let us hurry from this place," Draven said. He turned and continued down the corridor in the direction he knew led back into the great hall. Both men gagged at the heavily sweet odor of rot and decay.

"What in the hells is that stench?" Callum coughed, covering his face in the crook of his arm.

"Nothing for us to concern ourselves about, if I have my bearings right. We've to climb these stairs, then cross the great hall to a corridor that leads directly to the outside." He turned back to Callum and smiled. "How fast can you run?"

"Fast enough to keep up with you, at least," he said, then flashed a challenging smile back at Draven.

The red-haired warrior leapt forward at a blinding pace and climbed. Callum reached the top and skidded to a halt beside Draven.

"How convenient," a large guard said with a sarcastic smile at the pair. "Our mistress sent us to fetch you back to her." He motioned with outstretched hands to either side at the dozen other guards armed with crossbows who stood about the great hall. "Please. Do resist. It's been some time since my men had more than stuffed targets to fire at."

Draven glanced at Callum. He nodded, and both men dropped their newly acquired blades to the hall's stone floor.

Flies swarmed about them as they were urged into the room by the guards that circled behind them. The scene in the great hall had changed, from the decadent magnificence of earlier, to a grotesque disfigurement. Rotten fruits, molded by what looked like time, lay alongside the fettered carcasses of man and beast. Clouds of black flies swarmed over everything. The buzzing of wings and the sickly wriggle of maggots resounded as a deafening discord within the chamber. Atop the tables, cadavers of questionable origins lay flayed open and left to ferment over time, forming into oozing puddles of putrid rancor that collected on the cold stone floor below.

Callum involuntarily heaved, the sound adding to Draven's own discomfort as the guards led them toward the inner sanctum. Draven growled and spat, cursing under his breath at all the gods that came immediately to mind.

The guards marched them into the inner sanctum, where D'Bia and Branwen sat on the thrones atop the dais. A massive guard stood to one side of the thrones, and with rhythmic regularity, stamped the butt of his glaive on the floor. Joined by the wooden beat, a low-toned drum echoed through the chamber, its resonance droning, beckoning to all within earshot. Most figures stood stoically among the shadows of the dimly lit chamber, while a few shifted and swayed in time to the drumbeat.

D'Bia stood and stepped to the edge of the pool, its waters now stained dark with the blood of the bodies that floated aimlessly about. He turned his white-eyed gaze upon Draven and laughed.

"You have such great energy, untapped and raw as it is; the power within you is majestic, my son. My master will be very pleased."

A guttural chant emanated from deep within D'Bia's throat and joined the cadence of the room. Others joined in, humming to the tune, as the old blind seer sang a deep, throaty chant. At the point of their crossbows, the guards urged their prisoners along to the stairs leading to the upper platform.

Branwen's voice continued the low chant as D'Bia spoke the unknown words of a long-forgotten tongue. The guards shackled Draven at the platform's edge overlooking the pool below. The cold steel grip of shackles upon his flesh was an intimate reminder of his past indiscretions. He smiled as he held up his wrists and gazed at the metal bindings.

"Hello, my old friends. We meet again." Draven laughed so loudly as to overpower the measured time of chant and drums, then let out a whooping howl.

D'Bia began a new incantation as the beat and throaty chants continued The old man's white eyes glowed brighter with the pronunciation of each ancient word. The skin of his face cracked and began to flake away, as if a thousand years had suddenly reclaimed their grasp upon him. Dry, desiccated flesh fell away from the bone in places. His robes showed the ages since their creation, rotten and moth-ridden as they were.

"Blessed be the grace of Del and Corimaen," Callum cursed.

"Krull!" Draven shouted, then began to growl and stomp to the time of the drumbeats. "Sorcerer or daemon, makes no matter to me, beast! You'll bleed the same by my hand!" Draven roared and let out a barking howl that echoed through the chamber.

Branwen stood alongside the old man with her arms raised. Her eyes began to glow as she joined him in the sing-song incantation. Her voluptuously beautiful nude form sloughed away, leaving the husk of a rotted corpse behind as the pair praised and called upon Jut'athal the Ancient, Jut'athal the Magnificent, Jut'athal the Old One Himself.

A great rumbling shook the platform beneath Draven's feet. The roar of falling rocks became a cacophony of noise that drowned out the rhythmic beat of chants and drums. Flashes of purple light reflected in the blood-filled pool below. The undead undulated in the dark waters. Decayed and bloated flesh writhed about atop one another in an orgy of necrophilic ecstasy.

"Kill the lich and his queen!" Callum shouted, then elbowed the guard who restrained him. He took up the guard's sword—a large curved scimitar—and skewered the second guard atop the platform, then with one mighty swing, he cleaved through the iron chain that bound Draven to the floor.

Draven lept from his perch into the bloody waters below. Without hesitation, he pounced upon his prey. Grabbing the first ghoul by the head he twisted its head. With a sickly snap of bone and sinew, he decapitated the animated corpse, then smashed its fleshy skull into the face of another fiend.

With his bare hands Draven rent flesh from bone, and two more things dropped to float helplessly in the darkened pool. Guards charged into the fray, surrounding the wild warrior. He started to bellow a shrieking war cry when a blinding flash of purple light filled the room, and a portal came into being. Frantic screams of another guard echoed throughout the chamber.

He dropped his sword and pounded at a slick black tentacle that extended into the chamber from the great abyss beyond the portal. It grabbed another one of the guards, knocking his sword into the air to splash near Draven. Gurgled screams and the cracking of the man's ribs accompanied the chanting and drums before the appendage dragged the man through the iridescent purple portal.

Draven dove beneath the surface of the red-stained waters. His grasp found its mark, and he burst forth from the water. The leaf-bladed sword in hand, he began to cut a path through the roiling throng of undead. With quick, accurate strikes, the short blade found its mark and cut down ghoul and guard alike.

Reaching the edge of the tiled pool he gripped the ankle of the thing that had once been Branwen. The she-creature's foot was held fast to the ground, as if staked through with an iron rod. Neither D'Bia nor Branwen attempted to evade; instead, the sing-song incantation continued to repeat from the depths of their seemingly hollow forms.

Another of the inky black tentacles shot forth from the portal and wrapped itself around the warrior's leg. Blood rushed to his head as he spun about and dangled upside down before the great maw of the beast that emerged from the portal. Its muzzle splayed open into four equal sections, like the budding of a flower, to reveal thousands of teeth lining the inside of the thing's gaping jowls. The stench of a thousand dead souls flooded the inner sanctum as the thing roared its arrival.

Draven struck at the appendage with his sword, stabbing deep into the thing's rubbery, black flesh. It jerked him about so violently that the sword flew from his grip. Digging deep, he drove his fist into the gash made by the sword and gripped the thing from the inside. He reached with his other hand into the opening and forced it wider.

The beast let out a primordial shriek, unlike any earthly beast Draven had ever heard. The sound sent waves of gooseflesh rippling up the back of his neck. The tentacle let loose of his leg and retreated through the portal, dropping him headlong into the pool below.

Without hesitation, Draven climbed out of the water's sticky depths to face the largest guard he had ever seen. The man towered above Draven with shoulders at least twice as broad as his own. The honed blade of a massive great axe sang a wailing tune as it sped in a killing arc that grazed the lip hairs below Draven's nose. The fire-haired warrior pounced upon the massive guard before he could recover and swung about his neck to land on the man's broad back. He dug his heels into the man's kidneys and, holding onto the guard's throat with laced fingers, pulled with the entirety of his being. The guard reached overhead and flung him down into the water.

He scrambled to get his head above the waist-deep water, but before he could turn, a mighty fist came down onto his shoulder. It felt as if an anvil had been dropped onto him from a great height.

Dazed, he spun and pounced at the guard once again and slammed his fist into the guard's thick jowl. The mountain of a man staggered, and before he could shake the fog from his head, Draven was upon him. His hands clamped around the guard's throat, Draven chortled like a madman as he and the giant plunged back into the ruddy pool.

Draven burst forth from the water again, the titan's great axe in hand. A scream immediately drew his attention upward. Above him dangled the nude, flailing form of a young woman. She beat at the thick black tentacle that gripped her legs with no result. It lowered the girl into the maw of the great beast and with the suckling sound of a thousand ravenous pit fiends, the being consumed both flesh and bone.

"We have to flee!" Callum shouted from the far side of the chamber. He kicked at a guard, drawing his blade from deep within the man's gut, where it had lodged.

"No!" Draven shouted. "We can't let that thing loose upon the world! We have to stop it here and now!"

He let out a roar deeper than that of a great saber-toothed beast and more shrill than the cry of a harpy eagle, then charged for the stairs that led to the upper platform. With little effort, he swung the great two-bladed axe in a wide arc that cleaved another of the guards in twain. Careful not to slip in the spilling entrails, he retrieved the man's spear and continued up the stairs.

"What do you propose we do?" Callum shouted from across the room.

"We kill the wee beastie!" Draven reached the upper platform and stared over the edge at the exposed top of the creature extending from the portal. He hefted the spear in his right hand to test the weight of the thing, then hurled the missile downward, plunging it deep into its rubbery flesh. Black ichor flowed freely into the already dark pool as the thing howled and thrashed about.

The creature screeched with a sound like the lost souls on the winds of the nether.

The black tentacles of the thing lashed out, grasping for anything within reach. The remainder of the guards fled as the god-beast snatched and devoured two more of them.

Draven crouched low as another of the thing's appendages reached onto the platform. It swung about and connected with a frightened worshiper. The strike sent the man flying into a wall, cracking his bones. The worshiper crumpled to the ground in a heap.

Draven reeled forward, blindsided by another limb as it whipped about in search of prey. He shook the fog and spinning stars from his head, forcing himself back to his feet.

"By all the gods," Callum shouted. "Draven! Kill the Lich!"

A mighty laugh drew Draven's gaze back to the platform, where heavy muscles flexed beneath a guard's ebony skin. He spoke in a tongue full of clicks and forceful grunts, which Draven did not understand. In an overhead swing, he slammed a great maul down. Draven leapt out of the way, and the weapon crashed into the stone floor. The man swung it around in a wide arc with a single hand, bringing the castellated hammerhead around at Draven.

He ducked and rolled to the side just as the hammerhead struck the platform's edge, knocking a number of the stones loose to drop into the pool below. With muscles bunching, the guard reversed his strike and brought the bladed edge back in another blow.

Draven lunged backward, arching his back, and he could feel the wind of the blade as it passed by his naked groin.

He dove forward at the black warrior's feet, gripped the man by the ankle, and lifted with all his might. The ebony guard tumbled backward. Draven grabbed the great axe and swung it in a killing stroke that chopped through the guard's chest and into the stone floor.

"Kill the Lich!"

Draven worked the axe free from the chest of the corpse and stepped to the edge of the platform to take in the scene before him. Callum batted at undead things that lunged forth from the pool. D'Bia the lich and his daughter-queen continued their chant to the god-thing that slipped ever farther through the portal.

"Hurry and kill the bastard already!" Callum yelled as he severed a ghoul's leg at the knee.

Draven stepped back to the wall of the upper platform, then he turned and sprinted over the crumbling edge. He soared downward across the distance with the great axe raised high and brought it down on the lich. The blade found its mark and split cleanly through the ancient skull of the lich king, stopping only at the abrupt meeting of steel and the cold stone floor. The desiccated corpse of the old man slipped to either side and fell away to the floor.

The world exploded into a dissonance of bestial aberrations as the portal closed upon the great god-thing. The remaining tentacles fell limply to the ground, augmented by momentary muscle memory that sent contorted spasms through their dying limbs. The head of the great beast slid down and separated at the carved stone wall that had been the portal to some unknown hell dimension just moments before. Thick ichor and entrails forever stained the waters an inky black, overflowing the pool of the inner sanctum.

Draven stood tall and gazed down on what remained of the old man. *Perhaps that was who he was once before the evil of the undead took hold of him. Perhaps,* he thought.

"They stopped," Callum shouted. "You did it! "

Draven held up the great axe and examined the edge of the blade. He brushed his thumb against the edge, seeing it still keen despite its striking stone surprised him.

Motion to his left caught his eye, pulling him out of his contemplation. He looked up to find Branwen sprawled out, moaning and writhing in pain on the cold stone floor. Even now her shapely nude form called to a hunger deep within him. A wave of dizziness and nausea washed over him. He leaned over and placed his hands on his knees to steady himself but could not take his eyes from the woman.

Branwen sat up and turned to face him. She leaned to one side, arched her back, and presented her pert round breasts. "You have freed me of my curse, warrior. The throne is yours, and I am your eternal prize."

Draven watched, transfixed on her thick, full lips as a teasing tongue darted out and licked their deep red surface. All the world suddenly fell away except those plump, ruby lips.

"Come to me, my love. Come to me and rule by my side," the lips said softly, sensually.

"She's bewitching you! Draven! Kill her!"

Draven shook his head and looked over in the direction of the familiar voice. Callum struggled to free himself from the grip of one of the beast's spasming limbs.

"By my side for all eternity," the soft voice sounded as if whispered into Draven's ear. "My love…my king."

Draven turned back in the direction of Branwen's voice. She sauntered toward him slowly. Her round, enticing curves bounced gently with every step and begged for his touch. He wiped at his eyes and shook his head, but it did not clear the fog from his mind.

"Become one with me, lover," she said as she gently took him by the chin and tipped his head upward to look into her eyes. "Together we shall rule all."

Draven laughed. With all his might, he slammed his fist into the side of his head to clear his muddled mind.

He blinked and stared up at the desiccated, leathery flesh of the corpse bride that held his chin in her hand.

"I will not be shackled by you, nor by anyone!" He jerked his chin free and kicked her in the chest with his bare foot. She stumbled backward from the forceful blow but regained her footing and began a low guttural chant.

Without hesitation, Draven lunged forward, bringing the great axe around in a whirlwind arc that split the lich queen in two, from her right shoulder to her left hip. Before the halves could slip and separate, her cadaverous form shattered, crumbling to dust that exploded into motion. A dust devil formed and undulated on the stone floor. It danced and swayed in time to a cackling scream that drifted out of the room as smoke on the breeze.

"Del and Corimaen protect us," Callum said as he approached.

"Oh, aye," Draven said with a grunt. "And the Morrag's witches as well."

"I'm indebted to you, Maugan," Callum said as he flipped his sword, gripping it by the blade. He held it out to Draven and knelt. "You've freed me from a fate worse than death itself. I pledge my fealty and my steel to you, Maugan. Bound to you by my willing honor and oath."

Draven gripped the handle of the blade and took it from the man. He admired the intricately engraved details along the fine steel lines, then flipped it in his hand. Holding it by the blade, he handed it back to Callum. "I'll not be master of any man, whether he is bound to me by either debt or oath. I'll claim a friend, though."

"Then your friend I shall ever be."

With a great laugh, Draven clapped the bard on his back, nearly knocking him over. "Come, let us leave this place, my friend."

Callum took the blade and stood. "Where will we go?"

"Wherever adventure may lead us," Draven said, then smiled wide.

"Then I hope it leads us to a tavern with cold ale and pretty wenches," Callum said.

Draven laughed. He lifted the great axe to his shoulder and headed toward the exit. "I'm sure there will be many adventures beginning or finishing within the depths of a dram of ale."

END

We hope that you enjoyed this title and look forward to many more to come. Please, leave us a review! Reviews matter to all of our authors.

Take a look at some of our other award-winning series at
https://threeravenspublishing.com/series-universes/

Visit us at https://www.threeravenspublishing.com and sign up for our newsletter for the latest and greatest news on upcoming titles and events.

Other series and titles you might enjoy.

THE RAVEN
AND
THE CROW
MICHAEL K. FALCIANI
FIND ME
ON AMAZON

William Joseph Roberts Presents:
Misfits of Magic
Opening by
Piers Anthony
Edited by
William Joseph Roberts
& Kristina Barnes
Stories by:
Michael K. Falciani - N.V. Haskell - Michael Morton
Kristina Barnes - Jennifer Brinn - Megan Higgins
Jon Michael Kelley - Benjamin Tyler Smith - Wayland Smith
William Joseph Roberts

You can also keep up to date with our latest release announcements on Scifi.radio and get some of the best fandom programing on the planet.

Scifi for your Wifi

And don't forget to check out our other Sponsors and Affiliates

A southern Appalachian jewel for craft beer lovers, Buck Bald Brewing offers something for everyone.

To discover more visit us at buckbaldbrewing.com

Revolution X is a testament to the power of collaboration, blending four unique styles into a cohesive, revolutionary sound. When these four individuals unite, the result is nothing short of musical Revolution!

Would you like to learn how to write and market your own titles? The following affiliates links might be helpful.

Don't forget to check out the latest edition of Car Warriors: Autoduel Chronicle fiction series.

https://threeravenspublishing.com/car-warriors-autoduel-chronicles/

…or the latest in the *Car Wars* game series

http://www.sjgames.com/car-wars/

Or the other amazing titles from

Steve Jackson Games

http://www.sjgames.com

Comprised of active or retired servicemen and civilian volunteers, Shepherd's Men enthusiastically raises awareness and funds for the SHARE Military Initiative (SHARE) at Shepherd Center in Atlanta, GA.

This nationally renowned program focuses on assessment and treatment for American military veterans who have sustained mild to moderate Traumatic Brain Injury (TBI) and Post-Traumatic Stress Disorder (PTSD) during post-9/11 service.

Find out more at: https://www.shepherdsmen.com/

www.ingramcontent.com/pod-product-compliance
Lightning Source LLC
Chambersburg PA
CBHW030130010826
48973CB00002B/501